Sign up for our newsletter to hear
about new and upcoming releases.

www.ylva-publishing.com

Other Books by A.L. Brooks

The Club

DARK HORSE

A. L. BROOKS

Ylva

Acknowledgements

I owe a huge debt of gratitude to Sharine and Arti, possibly the two best research assistants in the entire world. Thank you, guys, and to Cat too, for answering my endless—and, let's face it, sometimes bizarre—questions about daily life in Ballarat. If there are any mistakes in this context, they are purely mine. Sharine and Arti are also the actual owners of the Bike Rack Cafe—yes, it's a real place, but it's in Ballarat, not Manly. I used literary license to transpose its location for this story. But if you're ever in Ballarat, pop in to their place for one of the best coffees you're ever likely to be served. And don't get me started on the cakes…

As ever, massive thanks to the awesome team at Ylva—Astrid, Daniela, Gill, and CK.

Thank you to my two awesome beta readers, Emma and Katja, for their priceless guidance and encouragement.

And heartfelt gratitude and love to my Lesvos Crew, whose almost daily support and nurturing kept me sane and encouraged when my doubts threatened to take over. You rock, guys.

Dedication

For Jane

CHAPTER 1

"Me and Tash are moving in together."

Nicole's face shone with excitement.

Sadie was stunned. Out of nowhere, a blanket of hurt and misery swamped her. She knew it was childish, but once her old insecurities reared their ugly heads, she couldn't shake them off.

"W-when?" Sadie's heartbeat pounded in her ears; her hands shook, and she didn't know if it was from anxiety or anger.

Nicole tilted her head.

"Whenever we can find a place we both like." Nicole's voice grew quieter. "Tash will sell her place, and I'll give notice on the house-share. Then we'll put our savings together and get a great big, fucking, grown-up mortgage." She grinned, but it faded quickly at the lack of response from Sadie.

Somewhere, deep in the recesses of her mind, Sadie knew she should be pleased for Nicole and Tash. They were her friends. They had been seeing each other for nearly three years, and this was it. The real deal. And that meant living together. It made perfect sense. But somehow, Nicole's excited words unleashed a torrent of repressed memories and old anger. The thudding in her ears got louder, and her stomach twisted in knots.

Nicole was leaving her.

Nicole was going off to find a life for herself. A life that didn't include her. It was irrational, and not too far from the surface of her brain Sadie knew that, but she couldn't stop herself from overreacting. She shuffled in her seat, fighting the urge to run.

"Sades?" Nicole reached out a hand and tried to touch Sadie's arm, but she flinched away. "Sades, this doesn't change anything, you know that, right?"

Sadie stared at her, willing her mouth to open and the right words to come out, but they wouldn't appear. Of course it changed things; it changed everything. Nicole was her best friend, her rock. How could she just leave?

"Babe, I know what is going through your mind right now, but I swear to you, *nothing* changes. We'll still be hanging out together just as much as we always have. I will still be ragging on you via text message night and day. You don't get rid of me that easily, remember?" Nicole's tone was earnest and pleading, but Sadie's mind had gone into free fall and she couldn't—or didn't want to—stop it.

Tears formed, stinging her tired eyes. Nicole reached across the short distance between their chairs, but Sadie brushed her off and stood up.

"Sadie, this doesn't change a thing." Nicole stood too and planted herself squarely in front of her, hands on her hips. "Not a fucking thing, you hear me? Tash knows how important you are to me, yeah? Christ, the three of us have been hanging out ever since I started seeing her, so just because I'm moving in with her doesn't mean that stops, right?"

She grabbed Sadie's chin before Sadie could move out of the way, and pulled her round to look her straight in the eyes. "I love you, you stupid lump—always! Never forget that. Never." Her eyes blazed, and Sadie wanted so badly to believe her. And yet…

Whatever it was Sadie's mind couldn't get past, it squelched all rational thought. She pulled sharply away, waving a derisive hand between them as if swatting a fly. Without a word, not trusting herself to speak with so much fear and anger eating her up, she stomped away.

"Sadie, *please*." She heard Nicole's plea but refused to turn back.

It was a lonely walk home in the balmy evening air. When she quietly let herself into her home, she had no recollection of which route she'd walked or any idea what time it was. She went straight to her room and threw herself onto the bed, acutely embarrassed at her immature response to Nicole's news. But, simmering under the surface, there was still the anger. The fear. Nicole had been there for Sadie through the best and the worst, and Sadie couldn't imagine life without her.

She tried to sleep but it was fitful. She tossed and turned in and out of dreams until, eventually, as the sun began to rise and a gentle light seeped under the blinds at her window, she gave up. Staring at the ceiling, she sighed. Thinking time was required, and that could only mean one thing.

She pulled on her clothes and reached for the keys to her Harley. Picking up her phone, she saw that Nicole had texted her about twenty times, each message saying essentially the same thing: nothing changes, I still love you, you're still my bestie.

The ride out to Turimetta Beach helped—time on her beloved Harley always did. At first she rode too fast, as her anger and embarrassment about her actions the night before had her gripping the bike's controls way too tightly. Gradually, the empty roads, the breeze flowing over her body, and the rising sun lighting her way eased her mood. The thrum of the bike beneath her as it ate up the road gave her a satisfying buzz, despite the gloom that still pervaded her mind.

The beach was small but beautiful, enclosed by two headlands that broke the incoming waves. She found a spot on one of the vegetated hummocks at the back of the sand and watched the waves smash against the rocks. They didn't boom like big surf, but somehow whatever noise they did generate always helped ease her mood. The rhythmic flow and the shush of the water as it scurried back down the beach was almost hypnotic in its effect.

Sadie had never seen the ocean until she was seventeen and first arrived in Manly. It was love at first sight—something about the endless power of it had touched her deep inside and never let go. When she needed to think, the ocean always called her.

She sat for a while with an empty mind and let the rapidly warming sun and the gentle ocean breeze soothe her. Only then did she let her thoughts run and force herself to face up to what had brought her there in the first place. Nicole's news shouldn't have sent her over the edge like that. She had such a good life, and she made herself mentally tick off all that she had in that life to be thankful for. A fantastic friend in Nicole, and, by extension, Tash. An amazing home that she shared with her equally amazing grandmother. A great job that she loved and was good at. Why would she think for one minute that Nicole wanting to move in with Tash threatened any of that?

Stretching out her legs in front of her, she shifted her ass on the sandy hummock. She knew where her insecurity came from, but she also knew that, where Nicole was concerned, it wasn't justified. She cringed with embarrassment at how...pathetic she'd been the night before. She was more than this. Stronger than this.

The overwhelming need to make things right had her reaching for her phone. She tapped out the message quickly, her brain already formulating the plan for what to do next.

Sorry. I'm an idiot. Will see you soon. Luv u xx

She stood up and brushed the sand off her jeans. She knew what she needed to do—go to Nicole's place and apologise. Wholeheartedly. For all the times that Nicole had been there for her in the last twelve years, this was a shitty way to repay her. Sadie should be hugging her, congratulating her, and being excited for her. Nicole was the first of her friends to make this big move, the first of them to find *the one* and attempt the settling-down thing. Not that Sadie ever thought there was much hope of that for herself. She could see what Nicole and Tash had and, deep down, she knew she wanted it. She just had no idea how to get it, no idea how to let someone get that close.

As she climbed back up the steep steps from the beach to the road, she smiled. While an apology was definitely due, she knew Nicole would not let her grovel. There might be some arm slapping and maybe a bit of shouting, but they'd be right. They always were.

The ride back was almost as pleasant as the ride up, just slightly busier, because the morning had really started. Rather than heading straight to Nicole's house, she decided to detour home first to shower and check in with her grandmother. Eating would be good too, she thought, as her stomach loudly reminded her that she'd skipped brekkie again.

The bike slid to a gentle stop on the small paved yard in front of the weatherboard house she shared with her seventy-four-year-old grandmother, Elsie Thomson. Tucked in behind Pittwater Road, in Smith Street, the location was perfect for being near to everything Manly had to offer.

Taking a seventeen-year-old granddaughter in at the age of sixty-two had never been in Elsie's plans, but when the circumstances arose, she gamely agreed, and Sadie moved into the spare room. Elsie let Sadie decorate it and the adjoining bathroom however she wanted—and made Sadie do all the work herself. *Character building*, her gran called it. One of her favourite phrases, Sadie was quick to discover.

Over their years of living together, they'd settled into a very easy rhythm that worked for them. The idea of moving out once she was old enough had never crossed Sadie's mind.

She dumped her helmet in her room and went in search of food before her shower. She strolled down the long hallway that ran the entire length of the house from the front door to the kitchen. Both her and Elsie's rooms, with their en suite bathrooms, were off that hallway, and the door at the end of it led into the open-plan kitchen/diner at the back. The generous space opened out via sliding doors to the small yard at the back, which had a paved area surrounded by planted beds. The doors were open most days, allowing them to pass freely from inside to out, and the paved area tended to be their lounge room.

As she passed through the door into the back of the house, Elsie was coming through it from the other side. Before Sadie could greet her, her grandmother whipped out a bony arm and slapped her hard in the bicep.

"Idiot," she muttered as she pushed past, ignoring Sadie's stunned face.

"Wh—?" Sadie began, then she heard Nicole's throaty chuckle from inside the kitchen, and she knew. She turned to say something, anything, to her gran, only to be met by her retreating back as she trotted determinedly up the hallway towards her own room. Sadie took a deep breath. *Okay, so that's the way it's going to be today. Right.*

Inhaling another deep breath, she stepped into the room. She came face-to-face with Nicole, who was standing in the middle of the kitchen with her hands on her hips, trying very hard to keep a stern expression on her face. Somewhere in Sadie's mind, a giggle formed—Nicole looked adorable attempting the fierce stance. Her black hair, its natural curls cascading down over her shoulders, framed a face that was quietly beautiful. Her petite frame was stretched to its full height, pushing her not insubstantial breasts fully out from her slender body. Nicole wore the usual multitude of thin bracelets on her left wrist, and they jangled softly like wind chimes each time she moved her arm.

Sadie had never been attracted to Nicole, thankfully—she wasn't sure they'd ever have become such good friends if she had been—but she could appreciate her friend's sexy gorgeousness in that moment. She knew remarking on that right then was not the way to go, and instead focused her attention on the scowl that Nicole was attempting to maintain. But Nicole's eyes gave her away. Her deep-blue eyes, such a contrast to the bright green of Sadie's own, were sparkling with humour, and Sadie grinned, albeit sheepishly.

"Sorry," she mumbled, her chin somewhere down in her chest while her gaze flitted up to Nicole's and back down again.

"Elsie's right," Nicole snapped, but not without warmth. "You are an idiot. A great big, fucking idiot, actually."

Sadie exhaled and looked up properly this time. "I know. I…" Words wouldn't come, not past the big lump that had suddenly formed in her throat. She'd let Nicole down, after everything Nicole had done for her.

Nicole's entire demeanour changed in an instant, her face relaxing and a gentle smile parting her lips. She took three quick strides across the room to wrap her arms around the much taller Sadie, pulling her head down onto her shoulder.

"I know what you are afraid of," she whispered against Sadie's ear, "but I'm not them. Remember that, yeah?"

Sadie nodded, tightened the hug for a moment, then pulled herself clear. She swallowed and took a couple of deep breaths. Finally, she let her gaze meet Nicole's.

"I am so happy for you and Tash. That's what I should have said last night. Instead, I ruined it with my stupid insecurities. But, really, I am so pleased for you."

"Thanks." Nicole blushed and nudged Sadie gently with her shoulder. Then she threw her head back in a loud laugh. "It's a bit fucking scary, yeah? It's like this big grown-up thing to be doing. Fuck knows if I can handle it, but I won't know unless I try, will I?"

Sadie chuckled. "That's why Tash is so good for you—she'll stop you from screwing it all up too badly."

Nic didn't join in with Sadie's laughter. Instead, her face creased into a frown and her eyes widened.

Sadie took Nicole's hand in hers. "You're really scared, aren't you?"

"Fucking terrified," Nicole whispered.

"Hey, Nic, come on." She squeezed Nicole's fingers. "This is you and Tash. The mighty duo! You two have been so bloody right for each other since the minute you met. I'm amazed you haven't moved in together before now, actually. What is it that scares you so much?"

"I don't know, really. I guess I'm scared I'll let her down somehow, once she sees me all day, every day. Or that I'll find there's something about her that annoys the fuck out of me. Or that—"

Sadie cut her off with a sharp pull on her hand. "Firstly, there's no way you could let her down. She's seen you, in all your glorious and not-so-glorious moments. Remember your birthday last year?"

Nicole blushed. "Jeez, don't remind me!" She grimaced.

"And second of all," Sadie ploughed on, "you are an amazing person, and Tash knows this. And she's an amazing person too. I'd find it hard to believe there'd be anything about you or her that would annoy each of you so much that you couldn't just talk it out, right?"

Nicole sighed, and nodded. "You're right. I know you're right. Why do I keep doing this?" She groaned and dropped her head.

"Because you care," Sadie said without hesitation, "and that's a good thing. Just don't let it get in the way of actually…being." She envied Nicole and Tash, and what they had. It seemed odd to be giving out relationship advice when she'd never really had one of her own. But seeing what they had together, she didn't want Nic to run the risk of messing it all up.

Nicole raised her head and stared at her intently. "You are a fucking great friend, you know that?"

"Hey," Sadie said softly, swallowing hard against the ball of emotion that was swelling in her chest. "I was taught by the best, remember?"

Nicole grinned, and pulled Sadie into a rough hug. "Yeah, and don't you fucking forget it," she whispered.

Sadie smiled into Nic's hair. "Had brekkie?"

"No, and I'm starving! What've you got?"

And just like that, they were okay again. As always.

For the next few minutes Sadie busied herself creating a mountain of fruit toast and brewing them up a large pot of coffee. They took the food and their mugs out to the yard, and munched contentedly in an easy silence borne of twelve years good, solid friendship.

Nicole left about an hour later when Tash called. They were off to view a couple of apartments.

"Tell me how you get on," Sadie said as she gave Nicole a quick hug goodbye.

"I will. Wish me luck!"

Sadie shut the front door behind Nicole and turned to find Elsie leaving her room. Sadie wasn't sure what sort of reception she'd get this time. Elsie's face held the hint of a smile, and it widened as she took a few steps towards her. Sadie smiled in return, relief washing through her.

"Come here, you silly bugger," Elsie said, opening her arms.

Sadie fell gratefully into them. Her gran was only a few centimetres shorter than Sadie's 175, and although a thin rake of a woman, she still had some considerable strength. Her hug was tight around Sadie's body.

"Glad you got that all sorted?"

Sadie nodded and pulled away to look her grandmother in the face. "I'm sorry if you were worried about all that." She waved vaguely down the hallway towards the kitchen.

Elsie chuckled. "No, I wasn't. Never going to worry where you two are concerned. Been joined at the bloody hip ever since you met, and nothing's going to change that."

"I guess you're right, Gran." Sadie smiled. "Shame I couldn't remember that last night."

"Shit happens," Elsie threw out, turning to walk back down the hallway to the kitchen.

"Gran!" Sadie said in shock. "Language!"

"Whatever." Her gran wafted a hand in the air somewhere over her left ear. Sadie laughed, and followed her to the back of the house.

They spent the rest of the beautifully sunny day in the yard, finishing off painting the new raised beds they'd been installing over the last couple of weeks. They chatted intermittently—about the weather, about the ride Sadie took that morning, about work at the cafe. Mostly they just worked alongside each other, Elsie giving instructions and directions with Sadie doing the harder graft.

Finally, they sat back on the outdoor rattan chairs and admired their work, Sadie with a very cold stubbie in her hand, and Elsie with a glass of wine. They'd only taken a few sips each when the doorbell rang. Sadie opened the front door and was grabbed into a full-body hug by Tash. She let out a very girly squeak. Nicole stood behind Tash, laughing her face off. Sadie flipped her the finger behind Tash's back.

"I would never take her away from you!" Tash exclaimed in Sadie's ear. "Never! I can't believe you would even think that."

"Oh," Sadie muttered, mortified. "She told you, then."

"Yes!" Tash pulled back to glare at Sadie. "What the fuck?"

Tash rarely swore, unlike Nicole, so this just made Sadie giggle.

"Sorry," Tash said, blushing. "But, really!"

Sadie held her hands up in surrender. "I know, I know. I'm sorry. Please, let's just never speak of it again."

Tash nodded. "Absolutely fine by me. Now, can we come in?"

Sadie laughed and stepped aside, making sure to pinch Nicole's arm as she walked by.

"Ouch! No fair." Nicole's tone carried amused annoyance.

"Whatever," Sadie murmured, grinning as Nicole reached up on her toes and gave her a quick peck on the cheek.

Beers in hand, Nicole and Tash joined Elsie out in the yard.

Sadie watched as Nicole took Tash's hand and smiled at her lovingly. Tash's pale blonde hair was a shade lighter than Sadie's golden crop, and shone in the late afternoon sun. Tash was slightly taller than Nicole, and slightly more solid in build. She looked good in a singlet over long denim shorts, so different from her daywear of full business suit with her hair normally pinned back.

Tash lifted Nicole's hand to her lips and kissed her knuckles softly.

"Are you two going to get all gooey again?" Elsie rasped, but there was mirth in her eyes.

Sadie laughed as Tash blushed. Despite the number of times Tash had interacted with Elsie since she and Nicole had hooked up, Tash still was never totally sure when Elsie was joking or not. Elsie knew that and teased her mercilessly.

"Leave them alone, Gran," Sadie chided. "They can't help it. It's pathetic, actually."

"Gee, thanks, buddy!" Nicole reached across Elsie to slap Sadie's bare knee.

"So, are you staying for dinner?" Elsie asked over the laughter. "I've some chicken breasts we could grill."

"Aw, thanks Elsie, that's really sweet. But we've got other plans," Tash replied. "I'm taking this one out for a little one-on-one time. I've got a crazy week at work lined up and won't be home until late most evenings."

Elsie smiled widely. "Ah, bless you," she said softly.

Tash blushed again, this time clearly from emotion rather than embarrassment.

Sadie smiled to herself. Sometimes her gran made her so proud it was like a physical sensation in her chest. Elsie hadn't batted an eyelid when the newly out Sadie had been dumped on her doorstep, and had refused to see her granddaughter's sexuality as anything other than just one more aspect of her personality, certainly nothing worth making a huge song and dance over.

Nicole noisily cleared her throat, and Sadie knew, without looking, that the emotion of the moment had affected her too.

"Right, well, I guess we'd better get going." Nicole stood, placing her empty beer bottle onto the table. "Don't get up, you two, we'll let ourselves out. You've earned a rest."

Sadie smiled at her friend and stood anyway to pull her into a quick hug. She turned to Tash and repeated the gesture, then watched fondly as they both bent down to give Elsie a kiss on the cheek before walking back into the house.

"They're good girls, those two," Elsie said, looking straight into Sadie's eyes. "Good girls."

Sadie beamed. "Yep, Gran. They are."

CHAPTER 2

Sadie groaned when her alarm chirped at six the next morning. Although she should be used to getting up at this time, some days were just harder than others. Especially Mondays after the kind of weekend she'd just had. Sadie had—uncharacteristically for her—sunk four beers over the course of Sunday evening, and she was regretting that. The headache was one of those low-grade but persistent ones, just above her left eyebrow. She slapped the alarm clock into silence and pushed the sheets off her body. Stumbling into the bathroom, she stepped into the shower and sighed in gratitude as the warm water worked its magic.

She made herself walk at a sharp pace to the cafe, swinging her arms to get the blood flowing, rolling her head on her shoulders a few times to loosen up. After work she'd go for a run, really shake it all off. But first, she had to get through the day. With a sigh, she remembered the other reason she hadn't been looking forward to this particular Monday. She had to seriously wear her manager hat and give Nathan a final warning about his timekeeping and general attitude. She prided herself on remaining calm in most situations—Saturday night with Nicole being a very rare exception—but Nathan had pushed all the wrong buttons lately. She knew she'd have to work hard to keep her annoyance in check.

Trixie had just opened up the cafe by the time Sadie strode in through the front door, and there was already a short line of customers queuing for their early morning caffeine fix. The Bike Rack Cafe was in Darley Road, just where it flattened out at the bottom of the hill that led up to the Sydney Harbour National Park. Sadie had started working there just after finishing high school. Within a couple of years, Bill and Marie had taken Sadie to one side and offered her the chance to train up to manage the place. They wanted to open a second cafe over in Mosman, and they needed someone they could trust to take over in Manly.

To her surprise, she'd discovered she was good at managing a cafe. She had a very organised brain, and she revelled in the decisions over shift patterns, orders with the wholesalers, and organising small events hosted at the cafe. She had a good team now—Nathan's issues aside—and the atmosphere was usually pretty happy.

She waved at Trixie as she walked through to the back of the building where her small office was located. It was nothing more than a converted cupboard. However, it did have a small window, and she popped it open the moment she reached her desk. The cafe backed onto someone's yard, and her window faced a line of gum trees. On just the right kind of day, with enough heat and breeze in the air, the scent of the gums wafting into her small room was heavenly.

She quickly changed out of her tee shirt into the plain white, cotton, short-sleeved shirt she liked all the staff to wear for work. Grabbing an apron and tying it around her waist, she left the office and headed behind the counter to help with the busy early shift.

The first two hours of the day sped by, as time usually did when serving a steady stream of commuters. When Nathan appeared at nine to start his shift, Sadie beckoned him into her office. She braced herself; better to get this over with.

"Hey, boss," he said with his usual swagger. Nathan was a good-looking young man, and Sadie didn't doubt that his appearance paid dividends for him in lots of situations. It just wasn't going to cut any ice with her.

"Nathan," she said, aware that her heart rate was already picking up. She breathed deeply to stave off her annoyance at his too-casual attitude. "Have a seat." She gestured to the chair. She herself stood by the desk, not intending to intimidate by standing over him, but not being able to help it in the confined space.

He flopped into the chair, his long legs sticking out in front of him. "What's up?" he said, and then he met her gaze. Suddenly, a little of the swagger was gone.

"On Friday you called in sick, yes?" Her voice was sharp.

He nodded warily.

"Right. So please explain to me how you were too sick to work but well enough to surf down at Bondi only two hours later?" She kept her tone firm but didn't raise her voice.

"Who told you that?" He smirked, and Sadie's hands clenched tight into fists against her thighs.

"Don't even go there," she snapped. "You were seen. By Bill. You know, the owner of this cafe?" She inhaled slowly, willing herself to keep it under control.

"Oh." His eyes widened as he sat up straighter in his chair. He swallowed. "Look, I—"

"Don't," she said curtly, crossing her arms as the sudden urge to shake him almost overwhelmed her. "You know I'm pretty fair with everyone around here, yes?"

He nodded, his face a few shades paler than when he'd first walked in the room.

"So, hopefully, you can understand that I don't really like it when someone abuses that, yes?"

He nodded again. Sadie noted the slight sheen of sweat on his forehead. He was blinking rapidly.

"Good. So, this is your last warning. You want this job, you need to respect it and me *and* the rest of the team. No slacking off, understand? There's plenty more kids out there would love a job like this. You told me yourself you want to save up for that big trip next year, so don't do anything to jeopardise that, okay?"

He nodded vigorously, and some of the colour came back to his cheeks. "I will, I promise. I really do want to work here. I-I'm sorry," he croaked. "It won't happen again."

"It better not. Now go help clear up after the morning rush."

He scrambled out of the chair, and she could hear his steps beating out a rapid tattoo down the short hallway to the front of the cafe. She let out a deep breath and allowed a smile to spread across her face. That hadn't gone too badly. At least she hadn't strangled him. And in dealing with him, she'd given herself yet another reminder of just how…grown-up…she herself had become. She was only twenty-nine, but the responsibility of running this place sat well on her shoulders.

She liked it.

The air was still warm from the day, but Sadie didn't mind a little perspiration. Her feet pounded the footpath in an easy, regular rhythm. She was just finishing up her five-kilometre run, a run that had, as usual, given her the time she needed to decompress from her day.

Slowing her pace, she turned the last corner onto her street and stopped to stretch against the side of the house. Once her breathing had evened out, she headed inside for a shower. Cleaned up and dressed in her favourite cut-off sweatpants and a sleeveless tee shirt, she went in search of Elsie.

She found her out in the backyard reading a magazine in the sunshine, and she paused for a moment to admire the older woman. Elsie still had her looks. Her hair, whilst a dark, platinum grey, was still quite lustrous, and her face retained its strong beauty, despite the ever-increasing creases and wrinkles.

"Hey, Gran." Sadie stepped out onto the warm slabs. Elsie looked up, smiling warmly as Sadie bent to kiss her on the cheek. "How's your day been?"

"Hello, love. It's been very pleasant, thank you. I went shopping with Diane and then had lunch with the Wilsons. I've been out here since I got back. Beautiful day again."

"Sure is. Just had a really good run." Sadie turned back to the kitchen. "I'm getting some juice. Do you want anything?"

"No, I'm fine. Thank you."

Sadie poured herself a tall glass of orange juice from the carton in the fridge and gulped down half of it in one go.

"So, Gran, what are your plans for tea? I'm meeting Nicole at that nice pub near her place, if you want to join us."

Elsie often ate with *her girls*, as she called Sadie and Nicole. Other people may have found it odd, but Sadie couldn't care less about that. Her quick-witted grandmother was great company, and as Nicole had spent a significant portion of her life hanging out with Sadie at Elsie's house, she was considered an adopted granddaughter to Elsie too.

"Thanks, love, but no. I think these old bones need to stay home for the evening."

Sadie smiled. "Cool. I'm just gonna watch some TV in my room before I head out to meet Nic."

"Okay, I'll see you later." Elsie smiled affectionately at her before returning to her magazine.

For a Monday night, the Park Hotel was busy, but Sadie and Nic arrived early enough to snag one of the small tables in the quietest corner. They ate well and were feeling very mellow in the sultry, warm evening air when they moved out to the garden with their second beers.

"So, how did apartment hunting go yesterday?"

Nicole sighed. "You know, apartment hunting is *hard*. I mean, never mind the prices, which are pretty fucking terrifying, let me tell you. And the condition of some places was just gross. I mean, seriously, don't people get that they're supposed to be tempting us through the door? I swear, one place, I couldn't even get beyond the lounge room. There was no way I was going to even look in the bathroom."

Sadie laughed. "Ew! I am so glad I am at Elsie's and never have to worry about that."

"Honey, you are *so* lucky it's not funny. I kind of got a bit disheartened by it all, you know? Tash tried to talk me down from the ledge, because even after one day, I'd pretty much had enough. Patience isn't exactly my fucking strong point, you know?"

Sadie patted Nicole's hand across the table. "I know you, remember?"

Nicole gave her the finger.

"Hey, it will just take time, and at least you're doing it together. Tash will see you right."

"True," Nicole murmured. "But…we did kind of come up with another idea too."

Sadie raised her eyebrows.

"Yeah, well." Nicole paused, then cleared her throat. "Given that I'm still having fits over the whole let's-be-grown-ups-and-live-together thing, we wondered if maybe the easiest solution in the first place was for me to move into hers. Kind of take it a bit slower than buying somewhere together straight away, yeah?"

"Yeah, that could work. Try-before-you-buy kind of thing."

Nicole nodded vigorously. "Might be better for both of us. I'm freaking her out with my freaking out."

Sadie laughed. "I'll bet you are."

They called it a night after two beers and hugged goodbye on the front steps of the bar.

"Catch up later in the week, yeah?" Nicole called as she walked away.

"Any time."

The house was quiet when Sadie opened the front door a little after nine.

She walked through to the kitchen to get herself some water, and found her grandmother sitting out in the low-lit yard, seemingly staring at nothing. The house phone was on the table beside her, along with a glass of wine that looked like it hadn't been touched.

"Gran," Sadie said softly, stepping out of the open doorway. "Everything okay?"

Elsie turned to her then, and even in the semidarkness, Sadie could see such pain etched across her face it made her breath catch.

"Sit down, love." Elsie's voice was quiet and tremulous.

Sadie quickly did as she was told, her heart thumping. "What is it, Gran? You're scaring me."

Elsie cleared her throat, but her voice still croaked as it came out. "It's not good news. Your sister called about a half hour ago. It's…it's your mum. Christine is…"

Sadie felt her heart and stomach clutch in unison. She was estranged from her entire family, had been since that awful day twelve years ago. But that didn't mean somewhere, deep down, she didn't still care what happened to them.

"Tell me." She shakily reached for Elsie's hand.

Elsie stared at her. "Christine's dying," she managed to gasp out before huge sobs racked her chest, and Sadie gathered her up into her arms.

CHAPTER 3

Sadie took Elsie's hand and led her into the house.

"Sit down, Gran. I'm going to make you some tea, okay?"

Elsie nodded and didn't resist as Sadie gently pushed her into a chair at the kitchen table.

Sadie moved quickly to the other side of the room and filled the kettle.

"Tell me what Izzy said. Please, Gran." Sadie's hands were clenched tight as she sat down next to her grandmother. "If it's not too hard for you."

Elsie shook her head slowly from side to side. "Izzy didn't have too many details. It's…it's a brain tumour. They've found it late because her symptoms didn't show for ages." She dragged in a ragged breath. "And where it is and how big it is and how quickly it's growing, it's…it's just too late for it to be operated on." She stopped, her chest heaving.

"Stop, Gran. That's enough. I'll find out the rest later." Sadie was deeply concerned for her grandmother's own health right now—her breathing was too short, and her hands were shaking where she'd placed them on the table.

"No." Elsie waved one trembling hand. "I want you to know." She looked deep into Sadie's eyes. "The doctors have apparently said she could last up to six months, but really, they're looking at much less than that." At that her voice deserted her and sobs took its place.

Sadie wrapped her grandmother in her arms and held her tightly, rocking her gently as she would a child. She didn't know what made her feel worse—the news about her mum or the impact it was having on Elsie.

After some minutes, Elsie's sobs subsided, and she eased herself out of Sadie's arms.

"Thank you, love," she said quietly. "I don't know what I would have done if you hadn't come home when you did."

Sadie squeezed her fingers. "I'm glad I was here. Let me make that tea."

She quickly boiled the kettle and made them each a mug of tea.

"So," she said when she'd sat back down alongside Elsie at the table, "I assume we need to get you out there?"

Elsie nodded and carefully sipped her tea. "Yes. Can you help me with that? I'll need to get a flight booked and—"

"Don't worry, Gran, I'll take care of it." She left the room and jogged down the hallway to her room. She grabbed her laptop from her desk and her wallet from her jacket pocket.

Back in the kitchen, she opened the Qantas website. "So, as soon as possible, yes?"

It took over half an hour, but they finally got Elsie booked on a Jetstar flight that left for Melbourne around eight the next morning. Sadie didn't stop to question how frantic this all was; this was no time for dwelling on any memories the stunning news dredged up. Elsie needed her, and she would be there for her. As she finished paying for the flight, plans of her own began to form in the back of her mind.

Because if her mum didn't have that long to live, Sadie didn't have long to try to understand all that had happened back then.

"It's already past ten now, Gran. We should get you sorting clothes and stuff now, so that we can just throw them in your case first thing."

Elsie nodded and slowly stood. She was still shaking, and Sadie hated seeing her so…vulnerable. Her gran had always been the strong one, never letting anything get her down.

Sadie escorted a trembling Elsie to her room, where her gran slowly directed her to all the clothes she'd want packed for her trip.

"It might not be the best time to talk about this," Elsie said as Sadie rummaged in the back of Elsie's walk-in wardrobe, hunting for her suitcases under piles of blankets and spare doonas. "But you ought to give some thought as to whether you will come visit too."

Sadie snapped her head up, only just catching herself from thumping her head on the rail above her.

"Do you think so?" She didn't want to let on just yet that she'd been pondering the same idea. Elsie had always held strong views on what had been done to Sadie all those years ago.

Elsie stared at her through the doorway. "I do. She's dying. You will never get another chance to talk to her. To see if...well, to see if things can be mended."

Sadie was stunned. Elsie had supported her wholeheartedly in her resolution to have nothing more to do with her family. She wouldn't have imagined her gran feeling so strongly that she should return home.

"I'll admit, the thought has crossed my mind, ever since you told me the news. But do you think it would really achieve anything, Gran?"

Elsie shrugged. "You won't know unless you try."

"Call me when you get there, okay?" Sadie told her gran firmly as she handed the taxi driver her grandmother's two small cases for stowing in the boot.

Elsie nodded, and eased herself carefully into the back seat of the taxi. "I will. And please, think about what I said. I think it's time. If not now, then when?" Her stare was piercing, and Sadie trembled slightly under its power.

"I've pretty much made up my mind to go, Gran. But let me know if she's totally against it. I don't want to make things worse."

"I know. I'll talk to her."

Sadie leaned into the car and kissed her on the cheek. "Travel safe, Gran."

Elsie smiled wanly and busied herself with fastening her seat belt. Then she was gone, whisked off to catch her flight. Sadie's sister, Isobel—Izzy—was meeting Elsie to drive her back to the family home in Ballarat.

Sadie wandered back into the house. It was still early, not even five thirty yet. On any other day, she'd be getting ready for work but had texted Trixie late the night before to briefly explain events and ask her to handle the morning without her. She yawned. In spite of the circumstances, she thought she might be able to sleep some more.

She wandered back to her room, slid into bed and wrapped her doona over her, completely covering her head. She closed her eyes, but sleep wouldn't immediately come. Her mind was in turmoil. What was happening to her mum was awful, but could Sadie actually go back and see her? She knew what her grandmother had said was valid. *If I don't go now, I might never have the chance.* But going back had the potential to cause even more pain than she'd already suffered. What if her mother didn't want to see her? Just because her gran thought it was a good idea didn't necessarily mean her mother would. And what about Izzy? And him?

She woke about three hours later, amazed that she'd managed to sleep given how much her thoughts had been whirling when she first lay down. She texted Nicole to say she was awake, and walked into the kitchen to make some coffee. Nicole would arrive soon, and she'd need her caffeine fix.

There was a message from Elsie on her phone. She'd landed and Izzy had met her as planned. There were a few more details about her mother's diagnosis, but she couldn't take them in. Despite the extra rest, Sadie was operating on autopilot. A numbness was slowing her movements, her thoughts, as if her brain knew it was too much for her to deal with and had painted a haze over it all to dull the confusion. When the doorbell rang, she found herself standing before the front door with no recollection of having walked down the hallway.

"Hey," Nicole said quietly as Sadie swung the door open. "I'm here all day, if you need me. I told Lynn she'd just have to cope without me for the day. I gave her the short version of why, and she was cool with it." Nicole worked as the receptionist for a medical centre. She'd worked there for over seven years, and Sadie knew she was one of their most reliable employees. If Nicole had said she needed a compassionate day, Lynn would have known it wasn't an excuse for something else.

"Thanks."

Nicole gave her a quick hug. "Come on, let's get some much-needed coffee inside me."

Sadie managed a weak smile at that and followed Nicole back to the kitchen. A few moments later, they were each flopped on a couch with hot mugs clutched in their hands.

"So, tell me the rest now. Obviously, you only had time to give me the short version in your text last night, but how much do you know?"

"To be honest, not much more than the short version. They call it a grade four malignant tumour. A high…some name that begins with *a* that I can't pronounce. She'd been having headaches and getting really tired, but apparently, she's been working really hard on some of her charity projects, so everyone just thought she was overworked from that. By the time the headaches got bad enough that my…father—" she stumbled over the word "—made her go to the doctor, it was too late."

"Jesus," Nicole breathed. She reached out a hand across the armrests of the two small couches that sat at right angles to each other, wrapping her fingers in Sadie's and holding tightly. "High-grade astrocytoma, yeah?"

Sadie glanced at her, realising suddenly that of course Nicole would know the correct term, given her job. "Yes, that's it."

"Shit," Nicole muttered, "prognosis for those is never good."

"That's what the doctors told her. Izzy was in floods telling Gran, apparently. She and Mum have got really close…since I left, she said. So it's hitting her hard."

"How was Elsie?"

"Oh, God, Nic. I've never seen her like that." Sadie's voice broke slightly as she remembered her gran's pain. "She just…crumpled in front of me. She's… I've always thought of her as so strong, you know? But this has just completely knocked her. I know she hasn't seen much of…Mum over the years either—it's not like she ever really forgave them for kicking me out—but she's still her daughter, and you're not supposed to outlive your kids, are you?"

Sadie took a shuddering breath, fighting back tears; the memory of holding her gran while she sobbed was still very raw. Nicole rose from her couch and moved to sit close to Sadie, pulling her into her arms. Sadie sank into the embrace, needing the comfort Nicole was offering and not being shy about accepting it.

"And how do you feel about all this?" Nicole's words were quiet, but they packed an emotional punch.

Sadie's voice cracked, and she didn't recognise how it sounded as she spoke next. "I have no idea." She paused. The numbness that had protected her earlier had worn off, and raw emotions were searing her brain. It was a crazy and confusing mix of sadness, fear, anger, and concern. "Ah, that's not true. I'm torn. Gran wants me to head back to Ballarat too, visit with Mum before…before she goes. And I'm thinking that's probably a good idea. But I don't know, Nic." She huffed out a shaky breath. "They made it perfectly clear they never wanted to see me again. You know what happened back then. And how the hell am I supposed to deal with *him* in the middle of all this?" Fear crept over her, and suddenly, thoughts of going home seemed like a step too far. "What would I even say to Mum? It just seems like too much time has passed. What's the point in going back now?" Insecurity pushed back all the resolutions she thought she'd made about making the trip.

Nicole pulled away slightly. She gently cupped Sadie's chin, rubbing her thumb along one cheekbone.

"So that you don't always ask 'what if'." Nicole's voice was gentle yet insistent. "So that you can maybe see if your mum has any regrets about what she did back then. To see if you can reconnect with Izzy. There are lots of reasons to go, Sades. You have to decide if any of them are strong enough to make you do it."

Sadie looked away briefly, pondering the words. They stirred up the emotions that were swirling through her. She clutched at the sides of her head as if somehow physical action could temper the maelstrom inside. After a few moments, she looked back at Nicole. "I told Gran I probably would go, but I asked her to talk to Mum, to see if she was against me visiting. I definitely don't want to just march in there and maybe make things worse if she's not interested. I can't even think about what his reaction would be, but if Mum definitely wanted me there, I'd feel it was the right decision."

Nicole squeezed her. "See, that sounds like to me that there's a big part of you that *does* want to go. That does want to see her."

Sadie looked at Nicole for a long moment. Did she? Did she want to open up that box again and see what was inside? The lid had been kept locked tight for so long, and yet…

"You're right," she admitted, more to herself than to Nicole. "There is. It's awful to have to do it in these circumstances, but…yeah, I do want to see her." As she said it, she knew it was fundamentally true. If she set aside all the memories and the baggage, then deep down, this chance to understand what had happened twelve years ago was just too tempting. "Even after all this time, there's definitely a part of me that refuses to believe she doesn't have any love for me. Maybe that's wishful thinking." She shrugged. "With him, it was always clearer. He'd really struggled with who I was for so long that it didn't come as a huge surprise when he did what he did. But with her…with her, I always thought she would stand up to him, when it came down to it. And she never did." Her voice was rising. "And, fuck, that hurt, you know? I guess I just want to ask her—did she ever regret that? Did she ever look back and think, 'You know what? I should have stood by my daughter. I should have loved her no matter what.'?"

Nicole nodded slowly. "Then, I think your decision is pretty obvious, yeah? If you want to ask those questions, unfortunately you've now only got a limited amount of time to ask them in. So if not now, then when?" Nicole's gaze was penetrating.

Sadie stared, as Nicole had unknowingly repeated Elsie's words from earlier that morning. She exhaled slowly. She had no idea how she'd feel about facing…him, or Izzy for that matter, but she knew that not going to talk to her mum would end up being the biggest regret of her life. She pulled out of Nicole's arms and sat back. She pushed her hands through the tight tufts of her hair.

"I need to make some calls," she said, pushing up off the couch and heading for her room.

Elsie rang at midday. When she'd arrived at the family home, she had briefly seen her daughter before Christine went to sleep. She sounded drained, emotionally as well as physically. The normal spark in her voice was gone; sentences trailed off as if she didn't have the energy to finish them.

"Gran, I definitely want to visit."

"Oh, Sadie." Elsie's voice quavered. "I'm so glad. I know it won't be easy, but I think it's for the best. When can you come?"

"End of the week—I'm going to ride there on the Harley. It'll mean an overnight halfway there, but I need…I need the freedom the bike gives me. Can you understand that?"

Elsie sighed. "I can. I won't question it, love. I'm just happy you're going to make the journey. However you make it."

"Okay, so I'm going to aim to leave here Thursday, get to Ballarat Friday afternoon. Please let me know before then if…if she says she doesn't want me there, okay? Otherwise I'll call you when I get to town. I'm going to book a hotel room—I don't think it would be smart to stay in the house."

"Okay, love. I understand. And yes, I will let you know if she has any problem with you visiting. But I honestly don't think she will. Please, come. She seems… different. Something…" Elsie's voice trailed off again, but Sadie didn't push her to finish her thought. She guessed facing death much earlier than you anticipated would change a person. It really didn't need a lot of explanation. They ended their call, and Sadie leaned back against the kitchen counter.

"Elsie get there okay?" Nicole asked as she stepped back into the house from the yard.

"Yeah. She said Mum's really tired. And, you know, changed."

Nicole nodded. "I can imagine. Want some lunch?"

Sadie smiled at her friend, overwhelmed with love for this woman who had been there for her through everything during the last twelve years.

"You know," she said, walking across the room to pull a surprised Nicole into her arms. "For me, *this* is what family means."

"What do you mean?" Nicole's arms wrapped around her waist.

"It's not the bloodline you happen to be born into. For me, it's the people who stand by you, no matter what. The people who love you for who you are, not who they want you to be. It's why you will always be my real family. Not them. No matter what happens when I go back to Ballarat."

"Aw, Sades." Nicole sniffed, and Sadie could feel her friend's tears dampening her neck.

The next day, Sadie went into work but only to hand over the reins to Trixie.

"I've decided to visit my mother. I spoke to Bill and Marie, and we all agree that you should take over here while I'm gone. Are you okay with that?"

Trixie nodded enthusiastically, a wide smile on her face—and then stopped herself. "Sorry, I don't mean to be insensitive—"

"Don't worry," Sadie interrupted, managing a small smile herself. "I know you're keen to take on more responsibility. It doesn't matter that it's because of what's happened now."

"Cool."

"So, let's get the rush hour out of the way, then when Nathan comes in, you and I can come back here and I'll hand over as much as I can, okay?"

"Sure. Sadie, I am really sorry about your news. But, if I can say this, I'm really pleased you all think I can do this."

Sadie smiled again. She knew she was leaving the cafe in capable hands.

By late afternoon, she had finished going over the Harley and packing for the trip. There wasn't much of anything edible left in the house, so she locked up and walked down to a noodle bar on Pittwater Road she used to visit quite regularly. She'd just finished her last bite when Elsie called.

"Hey, Gran, give me a second. Just need to pay for my tea, and then I'll call you right back, okay?"

"That's fine, love. I'm settled in for the evening now, so whenever is good for you." Elsie's voice still had that same distant quality to it.

Sadie rang off, her nerves jangling. Had Elsie called to say that her mum didn't want to see her? Just when she was all set to go? Would she go anyway, regardless of her mother's wishes? Her mind went into a whirlwind again, and she pushed herself out of her chair. She needed to get moving to work off the nervous energy that was buzzing through her.

She paid for her food and strode out of the restaurant. Once she turned off the main street and into the quieter residential blocks that led back to their home, she pulled out her phone.

"Hey, Gran."

"Hello, love. How was your tea?"

"Good, thanks. I went back to that noodle bar I used to like so much."

"That's nice," Elsie replied, but Sadie had the distinct impression she hadn't really heard her response.

"So, Gran, how's it going?" Sadie tried to sound calm, but wasn't sure she succeeded; her heart rate was picking up again with the anxiety.

Elsie let out a big breath. "Oh, Sadie, it's so hard to see her like this." Sadie's heart clutched as her gran emitted a little sob.

"I'm here, Gran," she whispered, wishing she could reach down the phone and wrap her grandmother in her arms again. Sadie waited while she cried, and then heard her noisily clear her throat.

"Sorry, love," Elsie said quietly, after a few moments.

"No worries, Gran. Really."

"Look, I spoke to Christine this afternoon. She's glad you're coming."

Sadie shut her eyes and came to a stop in the middle of the footpath, her body flushing with relief. She hadn't realised how tightly she'd wound herself, waiting to hear that. If her mum was willing, then maybe…maybe she could get some answers, finally. At least she wouldn't have to worry about regrets.

"Good. I'm all packed up, ready to leave first thing."

"Izzy wants to see you too. She's…well, she's changed too. Not the stuck-up little girl she used to be."

Sadie chuckled—her gran's bluntness in some things still had the power to shock. The fact that Izzy *had* been totally stuck up when she was younger was not news. Elsie's refusal to be the blindly doting grandmother, and to see her grandchildren exactly as they were, without the benefit of rose-tinted glasses, pleased Sadie no end.

She inhaled deeply before asking the next question.

"What about…him?"

"That…bastard," Elsie spat. Sadie could hear her breathing rate increase slightly.

"Okay, Gran, calm down."

"Well, really! He hasn't changed one little bit, let me tell you. Not one." Sadie heard her snort again. "That's probably all you need to know, isn't it?"

Sadie breathed out slowly. "Yep, I guess it is. But thanks for the warning. Now, at least I know what I'll be up against."

"Remember, love, you're an adult now. Yes, technically, you're still his daughter, but he has no control over you now, okay? You have every right to come back here and visit. Every right." Her voice was suddenly strong again, the normal voice Sadie was used to. It made her smile with love and pride.

"Gotcha, Gran."

The hotel room in Albury-Wodonga was a welcome sight for a sore body. Sadie threw the panniers onto one of the beds and her body down onto the other. She let out a groan of relief as her bones melted into the soft mattress. The room even had a full bath, which she planned to take complete advantage of just as soon as she could get vertical again. Trouble was, the bed just felt *so* good…

She snapped her eyes open, aware that she had started to drift off. No, no time for sleep just yet. Her aching muscles needed easing in a hot bath, and food would definitely be in order after that.

She stepped into the full tub and let out sounds she normally reserved for very good sex, as she eased her body into the hot water. Oh, God, that felt *so* good. She closed her eyes in blissful appreciation. As much as she loved her bike, six hours on its albeit comfy seat took its toll.

Still, if there was one good thing that had come from the ride, it was the time to think. As the distance to her destination—the town of her birth she never thought she'd see again—had diminished, hour by hour, so it seemed the distance to her past diminished also. The memories had become more defined, rather than the hazy blur they usually took when she didn't want to focus on all that past pain. She found she didn't want to fight them this time, though. Somehow the journey itself made it seem the perfect time to step into them again, to look at them with older but fresher eyes, to examine them from different angles. She'd lost herself easily in remembering, and had been pleasantly surprised at how the pain, whilst still there, seemed more manageable. Perhaps because she *was* going back and was going to be able to face at least some of it head-on. And deal with it, once and for all.

She kept her eyes closed as she replayed all that she had remembered during the journey.

CHAPTER 4

Ballarat, twelve years ago

"I just don't understand why you think Ryan isn't a suitable choice for a date." Her mother's condescending tone irked Sadie, and she gripped the table hard with both hands.

"Because he's just not my type."

"But he comes from such a good family, your father and his are great friends—"

"What is this?" Sadie scowled. "The royal family? We don't have to date people just because it makes good sense for you."

Across the table, her younger sister, Izzy, snorted but quickly fell silent at the admonishing glance their mother sent her way.

"That isn't quite what I meant," her mother said, returning her focus to Sadie. "I just think he's the right sort of boy for you to be seeing."

Her father stayed out of the conversation, but she could feel his gaze on her. She didn't meet it—she and her father did best when they were ignoring each other.

Sadie sighed. "I don't want to date Ryan. Can't we just leave it at that?"

"Well, who do you want to date, then? There's always the Gordons' son—"

"Oh, will you just stop?" Her irritation was transforming into outright anger. "I don't want to date him. I don't want to date any of them. I like girls, not boys."

It was out before she could stop it, and it fell into the room like a lead weight. Her mother's fork clattered to her plate. Izzy gasped and then giggled.

Her father took only a moment before pushing his chair back and standing so that he loomed over her.

"What did you just say?"

She dared to look up at him. His face was reddening, and his nostrils were flared. She flicked a glance down to his hands, which were clenched into tight fists. Swallowing hard, she wondered how to respond, or even if she should. His voice cutting through the silence saved her from having to make a decision.

"No daughter of mine is going to be one of those...*perverts*." He ground the word out. "Are you deliberately trying to ruin everything we have? Is it not enough that you keep getting into trouble with the police? Now you want to make me the laughing stock of this entire town!"

Even though she was newly out to herself and to Mrs Duncan, her high school counsellor, Sadie knew being openly gay in Ballarat was not the easiest thing to do. There were strong country values still held by a large portion of the population. She'd heard stories at school of the few brave students who'd come out before her in recent times, and the abuse they faced from their peers and families.

"Dad, it's not like it's something I have a choice over," she began and then stopped when he strode around the table. She scrambled to get out of her chair and away from the terrible anger that pervaded his entire demeanour.

"Of course you have a choice, you stupid little—"

He raised his fist, and Sadie flinched, preparing for the blow, but her mother suddenly pulled at his arm. She spoke softly to him, promising to "talk some sense into her." Amazingly, he stepped back and the moment was defused. Sadie fled to her room.

As she munched on toast the next morning, her mother walked into the kitchen. It was just the two of them, and Sadie braced herself as her mum moved to stand in front of her, her hands worrying at the hem of her shirt.

"I need to talk to you," her mum said, her voice croaky. "About that...what you said at dinner."

"Mum, I'm—"

Her mother held up her hand. "I don't want it repeated. You will never say anything about that again, do you understand?"

"But—"

"No!" Her mum's face flushed red. "It's completely unacceptable. That's the end of it."

Sadie stared at her, anger clashing with almost hysterical amusement inside. Her parents were…ridiculous.

"Fine," she snapped, and pushed back from the table. "Whatever you want, Mum." Her voice dripped with sarcasm. "But it doesn't change who I am, whether you like it or not."

Without waiting for a response, she marched out of the room.

"Meet me tonight?" Chloe's whisper set Sadie's heart thudding, half from arousal, half shock.

She hadn't heard Chloe approach and quickly looked around to see if anyone was within earshot.

Chloe smirked. "Don't worry, there's only us."

She was right; for some reason the homewares department was miraculously empty. Thursday evenings were usually a little busier than this. Sadie blushed, which happened a lot when Chloe was around.

Chloe Turner—twenty-four, insanely pretty and sexy, and for the last few weeks, Sadie's lover. Even the word made Sadie blush. *Lover.* It sounded so grown-up. And Chloe *was* a grown-up—a full-time employee at the Myer department store in Sturt Street, assistant head of the children's department, with a house in the suburbs. The whole works.

Including a husband.

When Chloe had first made a play for Sadie, she'd refused. She wasn't going to get involved with a straight, married woman, no matter how gorgeously tempting she was. Newly cognisant of her sexuality, Sadie was keen to explore—but she wasn't completely stupid. Visions of Kyle, Chloe's husband, coming after her with some kind of weapon had filled her brain and sent her scurrying from Chloe's attentions.

Until one Saturday in September, when Chloe had insisted on giving Sadie a ride home on a cold night. About halfway home, Chloe pulled off the main road and into a quiet back road. Killing the lights, she turned to Sadie, a sly grin on her face.

"You can't keep saying no to me, Sadie," she purred. Her enticingly manicured fingers lay on Sadie's denim-clad thigh. Sadie trembled, in spite of her resolve. When the fingers squeezed, flexing against her thigh muscle, she swallowed audibly, and Chloe's laugh was triumphant. The next thing Sadie knew, Chloe's mouth was on hers, her tongue demanding entry, and Sadie's resistance folded like damp paper. It was exhilarating, scary, and just plain sexy as hell. They kissed—and more—for about half an hour, before Chloe finally pulled back, straightening her shirt where Sadie's hands had been only moments before.

"Yum." Chloe was smiling. Sadie simply stared at her in an arousal-induced fog. "We need to find somewhere a bit more private next time, I think. Let me work that out and let you know." With that, she took Sadie home, thoroughly kissed her goodnight, and drove quickly away.

Sadie stood on the footpath in front of her family's home for a few minutes, calming her breathing and letting the passing time dull the crimson flush on her face.

In the cold light of day, she'd resolved not to respond to any further advances from Chloe. While it had been exciting, of course—her first full-on pash with a woman—it was crazy to think about anything more. Chloe was *married.* That had to mean she was off limits. Never mind the fact that they worked at the same store.

But only a week later Chloe cornered her in one of the stock rooms. Pushing the door closed behind her and leaning against it, she beckoned Sadie over. Sadie tried hard to resist, but Chloe had some sort of magnetic pull that just sucked her in. The next thing she knew, she was standing in front of Chloe, her chest heaving with anticipation, her gaze glued to Chloe's plump, pink lips.

"Mm, you look ready to pounce," Chloe murmured, and Sadie nodded shyly. "Good. Keep that thought in mind. Come over to mine tonight—Kyle's gone down to Geelong with his mates. He won't be back until at least midnight."

Sadie garnered some courage and shook her head. "I can't—" she began, only for Chloe to plant a forefinger on her lips and stop her.

"Yes, you can," Chloe said firmly. "You know you want to. And God knows I want to," she breathed. "Any time after seven. I'll be waiting."

She slipped out the door, leaving Sadie panting with an uncomfortable mixture of desire and fear.

Determined not to give in, Sadie retreated to her room that evening. An hour later, in spite of all her resolve, the memories invaded her mind. How sweet Chloe's mouth tasted. How soft her breasts felt under her hands, and how her breath hitched every time Sadie pinched her nipples.

Twenty minutes later, she was on Chloe's doorstep, ringing the bell. Twenty minutes after that, she lost her virginity to Chloe Turner, sprawled on her leather couch with their breathy cries echoing around the quiet stillness of the house.

Since then, they had met at least once or twice a week, sometimes at Chloe's house, sometimes snatching moments in Chloe's car. They talked and laughed, but mostly they kissed or touched or—if they were at Chloe's house—fully made love. Sometimes, Chloe stopped being the teasing, wickedly taunting woman who had first seduced Sadie, and she softened, quietened, and held Sadie close in her arms. In those moments, Sadie lost herself completely, and never wanted to find her way back again.

She was going to tell Chloe how she felt and hope that Chloe would open up too. Then, they could see what they could do about it. She was going to be brave and get it all out there. Sadie was young, but she'd done a lot of growing up in the last year, and she knew what she wanted.

"So, can you? Meet me tonight?" Chloe repeated. Her eyes sparkled, and her tongue darted out to lick her lips.

Sadie met her eyes. "Yes."

They were parked in Chloe's car behind a primary school, the road quiet and dark. It wasn't ideal, having this talk in a car in some backstreet, but Sadie was overwhelmed with what she was feeling. Waiting for somewhere more romantic wasn't an option. Chloe looked irresistible. Her tight, black skirt displayed her lovely, long legs. Her red shirt was tight across her breasts, with the hardness of her nipples tantalising Sadie through the fabric. Sadie's blood surged through her veins, her senses sparking from both desire and a total adoring love for the woman who had turned her world upside down.

They were in the back seat, holding each other close, kissing deeply. Chloe had a way of swirling her tongue in Sadie's mouth that literally had her coming undone. She moaned deep in her throat and clutched Chloe even closer, running her hands up inside the back of Chloe's shirt across her hot skin. Chloe pulled back slightly, her teeth nipping gently at Sadie's lower lip, before she lifted her mouth away completely.

"Mm," she murmured, gazing at Sadie, her eyes so dark Sadie couldn't read them. "You are so…God, I don't even know what the word is. Tonight, you're different somehow." She smiled warmly, and Sadie knew it was time. The words were bubbling up, and Chloe was so near and so delicious. Sadie wanted nothing more in that moment than to tell her.

"I love you," she whispered, smiling widely at the joy she felt in saying those words. "I love you so much. I want us to—"

Chloe wrenched herself out of Sadie's arms, causing Sadie to pitch forward slightly. She stopped herself from landing in Chloe's lap and sat upright, staring at Chloe.

"What—?" she began, but Chloe cut her off.

"Why did you say that? Why did you have to spoil it?" Her words snapped into the space between them like pellets from an air gun.

Sadie blinked, her heart pounding.

"I… It's true. I said it because it's true. What do you mean, *spoil it*?" But she knew before asking. She knew, instantly, that she had got this all wrong. She watched Chloe close down in front of her, watched the warmth drain out of her face, and she knew how stupid she had been to believe they could be anything more than just a fumble in the dark.

"This…we…it was just *fun*. Nothing serious. Just a nice way for each of us to get what we needed. There's no love involved here, Sades. Jesus, did you really think we were more than just a quick fuck here and there?"

Chloe's tone was patronising and hurtful, and Sadie suddenly couldn't bear to be breathing the same air as she was. She turned, reaching for the handle, and opened the door to the cool night air. She was half turned away from Chloe, before she felt Chloe's hand on her arm.

"Sadie, where are you going?"

Sadie turned back to face her, annoyed at the tears that were wetting her face but unable to do anything about stopping them.

"You don't have to go." Chloe's face was a picture of puzzlement. "We can still, you know, meet each other. Just don't say that stuff again. I mean, we're good together, aren't we? So we can carry on doing this, if you want."

Sadie stared at her, one leg out of the car, her body twisted uncomfortably around to be able to meet Chloe's eyes. She wiped at her tears, aware that Chloe hadn't even acknowledged that Sadie was crying. What did that tell her about how Chloe felt? God, what an idiot she'd been. What a total, fucking idiot.

She gently prised her arm out of Chloe's grip. "No, we can't carry on," she said quietly, her throat aching with the effort not to sob. "I don't even know how you can think that."

She turned away and pushed herself out of the car. Zipping up her jacket, she strode off down the street, wiping away the rest of her tears.

"Well, it's your loss!" She heard Chloe's bitter voice behind her, but didn't look back. "And don't you even think about telling anyone about this!"

Without turning, she flipped Chloe the finger and carried on walking. When she reached the corner, she picked up her pace to a slow jog, suddenly eager to put as much distance between herself and Chloe as possible. Head down, all she could focus on was how completely stupid she felt. How could she have let herself think they had something more than just sex? How had she not seen it? She'd let herself be seduced by someone who just wanted her as a quick fuck here and there, and she'd mistaken what they'd shared as a prelude to love. The embarrassment swamped her. Oh God, so *stupid*!

She cried out as she ran smack into someone. The other person let out a pained grunt and they stumbled back from each other.

"Sades?" The voice sounded shocked.

Sadie glanced up into the face of her sister, Izzy. Then her line of sight widened to take in the four other people behind Izzy, all of them shuffling on the spot and looking in all directions.

"Come on, Iz, we have to go," said one of them impatiently, a boy Sadie didn't recognise. He looked a little older than Izzy's fifteen years and had a hardness about him that instantly put Sadie on alert.

Izzy grinned, gave a quick glance back to her friends. "Yeah, okay. See ya later, dyke!" She smirked before she laughed outright, as all of her friends guffawed behind her. They were gone, running up the street that Sadie had just left, their laughter and jeers carrying back to her on the breeze.

She stared after them for a moment. Izzy ran with a gang? Izzy, the straight-A student who was the apple of her parents' eyes? What the hell was going on? Shaking her head, she turned away from their retreating forms and returned to her route. She had enough problems without thinking about what her little sister was up to.

She became aware of the smell of smoke in the air a few moments later. As she neared the gate that led into the school grounds, she could see bright flames flicking up the side of a small building. The gate's lock was busted, the gate itself partly open. Taking in those facts, her stomach sank. She knew what Izzy and her gang were running from. She also knew she needed to get out of there. Fast.

Quickening her strides, she shot across the road, away from the gate, and cut up a side street. She could hear sirens approaching as she zigzagged her way back to the main road to jump a bus for home. Getting home was her number one priority. There had been too much crap, and all she wanted was to crawl into her bed and shut it all out.

Sadie slept badly. Her day at school on Friday passed by in a blur. She tried hard not to think about Chloe but continually failed. Images of her and Chloe together haunted her. She missed her deeply but at the same time knew there was no future there. Chloe had made it perfectly clear how little Sadie meant to her, and Sadie wasn't that stupid to go back. As much as it hurt, she had to stay away.

By the end of the day, she was just angry. All cried out and hardening her heart against what had happened, she was resolved to just get on with her studies. Having scraped by most of her school life, she was working hard to make amends. Even if her parents didn't quite believe her. She knew, from all her sessions with Mrs Duncan, that getting a qualification was the surest way to get her out of that house the fastest.

She arrived home after four, stunned to find both her parents sitting at the kitchen table. They should have been at work; they never came home before six. She stopped just outside the doorway to the room. Her heart started to hammer as she took in the scene. Her mother's eyes were puffy and red, and she was clutching a tissue tightly in one hand. Her normally perfectly coiffured blonde hair was a mess, and her make-up had run from her tears. Her father sported the red blotches on his cheeks that usually signalled intense anger, and his body was rigid in his chair.

She shifted on her feet, not sure whether to enter the room or run away. The noise of her shuffling caught her father's attention. He looked up.

"She's here," he said roughly.

"Wh-what's going on?" Sadie stammered as her mother finally looked up. She looked…vacant, like she was beyond caring about anything. Sadie swallowed nervously. "Mum, what is it? Are you okay?"

"No, she's not okay!" her father yelled, his voice stunningly loud in the small room. He stood, and Sadie involuntarily took a step backwards. His entire demeanour threatened violence, just like the night she came out. There were veins bulging in his neck as his chest heaved and his hands clenched and unclenched. She was suddenly, gut-wrenchingly, terrified.

"Peter…" her mother said softly, and he paused on his way round the table to look down at his wife.

It seemed to take all of his effort to rein himself in, but he managed, exhaling loudly as he took two steps back.

Sadie could feel tears welling up; she had no idea what was going on, and she was the most scared she'd ever been in her life.

"Please," she whispered, "I don't understand."

Her parents looked at each other. Her father spoke, his voice clipped, as if it was an effort not to shout each word. "The police were here this morning, just after you left for school. Someone set fire to some outbuildings down at St John's Primary School last night. There is one witness who thinks it might have been you." He glared at her, as if daring her to speak. She kept quiet. "Luckily for you," he spat, "the police have deemed the witness unreliable."

Sadie started to speak, but he sharply held up a hand. "No! Don't say a bloody word." He breathed in deeply. "So, your mother and I have decided. This is the final straw."

Her mother made a slight whimpering sound.

"You've been a bloody menace for years now," her father continued, his voice rising again, "and we can't take any more. I've phoned your gran—you're going to live with her."

Sadie stared at him. They were kicking her out? *What the—?*

"But—" She flinched as he roared at her.

"Enough! I have fucking had *enough*!" He pointed a stubby finger at Sadie, his arm shaking slightly, his face even redder. "You have made our lives a misery for far too long now, and it's got to stop. It's either this or someone will find some real evidence against you and you'll end up in prison. Trust me, you'll prefer being in Sydney with your grandmother. Maybe being somewhere new will wake you up to the mess you've made of your life so far."

He stepped towards her, and she tensed.

"And believe me, if you weren't underage I'd just bloody kick you out on the street. But I can't do that, so the only option is your gran. She said she'll take you, and you can transfer your schooling over and finish it there. And once you've done that, you can do whatever the hell you like, as long as it doesn't involve coming back here. You're never setting foot in this house again. Do you hear me?"

Shock ran through her body like ice water. In its wake, anger at the injustice of his words set her hands trembling and her heart thumping. She looked at her mum, hoping for some kind of support, some sort of reaction against the rage of her father, but she was met with the same blank look she'd been wearing since Sadie came home. She wasn't even sure her mum knew she was there.

"But, Dad, it wasn't even me!" She tried to defend herself, tried to get the words out to explain how unfair this all was, but even as she did so, the crushing weight of her situation bore down on her. She realised how trapped she was by circumstance. Her alibi—a married woman who would deny everything Sadie said. The real culprit—more than likely the perfect little Izzy, who'd never put a foot wrong in anyone's eyes. Her own reputation was working against her. No matter what she'd done the previous three months to get herself back on track, it was the previous four years of trouble that everyone was focused on.

"Enough with the lying! Go to your room and pack your suitcase. Anything you can't pack we'll box up and ship to your gran's next week. You're booked on a late flight tonight. You've got about an hour to get ready, then a car will be here to take you down to Melbourne."

She stared at him, her body tumbling into shock so fast it was making her head spin. *Tonight? They're making me leave tonight?* But what about her friends and her school and all her plans? What about Christmas, only a few weeks away?

"Well, what are you waiting for?" Her father's voice was hoarse. She glanced up at him, tentatively wondering if what he was doing to her was causing him discomfort, but one look at his face belied that. She'd never seen him so angry. Livid, in fact. She knew there would be no reasoning with him. With either of them. Her mother was practically catatonic, with her eyes glazed, her face slack.

As if on autopilot, Sadie's legs turned her round and carried her slowly along the short hallway to her bedroom. Some forty minutes later, she had a full suitcase and her small daypack containing her phone, a paperback she'd started reading only the day before, and her jewellery and wallet. Looking round the room, she felt nothing. It was as if all emotions had shut down, as if her mind couldn't take it on. She should be screaming, she thought dimly. She should be screaming and shouting and fighting, defending herself. But her position was hopeless, and she knew it.

She hauled the case down the hallway and left it by the front door, dropping her daypack alongside it. She walked back into the kitchen and ignored her parents as she drank a glass of water. The front door slammed. Moments later, Izzy strolled into the room. She stared at Sadie standing by the sink. Her gaze drifted to their parents, who were sitting in silence at the table.

"What's going on?" Izzy's voice was harsh, an undercurrent of fear evident in the tremble it carried.

"Isobel—" their father refused to shorten either of their names, "—your sister is going to live with your gran. She's leaving tonight."

Sadie dried her hands on a towel, watching her sister's reaction.

Izzy snorted. "What is this, some kind of joke?" She looked at Sadie. "What's he talking about?"

Sadie felt a tingle of satisfaction somewhere deep inside. Izzy actually looked as if she cared. But the sarcastic response shot out before she could stop it.

"Well, apparently, I set fire to St John's Primary School last night, so before I cause any more trouble, I'm being shipped off to Gran's."

Guilt and fear paralysed Izzy's face for a spilt second before she regained control. In that brief instance, Sadie had her confirmation; Izzy and her gang *were* the ones who'd set the fire.

Sadie was taking the blame for her little sister, and Izzy knew it. Sadie clenched her jaw. Izzy would never speak up and defend Sadie. Not when she had so much to lose herself if she did so. Sadie supposed she couldn't blame her—it wasn't likely their parents would believe Izzy, even if she did suddenly confess all.

Before anyone could say any more, the doorbell rang. Sadie's stomach clenched, and tears filled her eyes again. Her father stood without a word and walked to the front door, pushing past Izzy, who stumbled back against one of the kitchen cupboards, her mouth wide in an O of shock.

Sadie looked at her mum, willing her to lift her head, to meet Sadie's gaze. Willing her to say something. Anything.

Nothing.

"Mum?" she said, her voice trembling as rage at her mother's silent acquiescence coursed through her veins.

Nothing.

"Jesus," Izzy breathed, staring at Sadie. "Sades, I—" She looked distraught. Sadie shook her head, silencing her. Izzy swallowed hard. She threw her hands to her face as tears flowed down her cheeks.

"It'll be okay," Sadie murmured, looking at Izzy. "Just…look after yourself, okay?"

Izzy sobbed and nodded. Suddenly, she was across the kitchen and hugging Sadie tightly, something they hadn't done since Sadie was about ten. Sadie gave her a quick hug in response and then pulled away.

When she walked into the hallway, her father had already taken her suitcase to the car. He stood at the end of the driveway talking to the driver like he didn't have a care in the world. Sadie was nauseous watching him. She picked up her daypack and glanced back at a wide-eyed Izzy watching her from the kitchen doorway. There was no sign of her mother. Sadie conjured up a weak smile for her sister, then turned and walked down the driveway.

When she reached the car, she let herself in. She didn't look back at her father, didn't say a word. Just climbed into the back seat and shut the door.

She stared straight ahead as she fixed her seat belt in place. The driver started the engine and pulled them away from the curb.

CHAPTER 5

Present Day

Sadie stepped out of the bath and slowly towelled off, the memories lingering but already dissipating in power. After dressing quickly, she went out for a pizza at the cafe next door. She called both her gran and Nicole after her tea.

Nicole was not surprised that Sadie had gone back down memory lane on her journey.

"Totally makes sense that would happen," she said. "But how did it make you feel?"

Sadie pondered that question for a moment.

"Well, it obviously stirred up all the hurt from that day, the unfairness of it all. But at the same time, it almost felt like it happened to another person. I'm not that young girl any more. I've built a great life for myself since then, and in a way, I'm kind of thankful that I did get to move to Manly. I'm not sure what my life would have been like if I'd stayed back in Ballarat."

"Yeah, I know, and that's great. Obviously, I'm delighted you came to live here." Sadie could hear the smile in Nicole's voice. "But," Nicole continued, "what about going back there now to see them all, after all this time? Aren't you just itching to get into it with them? If it was me, I'd at least want to confront Izzy, and oh, seriously tell my father just what I fucking thought of him. Not sure about your mum, though—maybe given what she's going through, I'd go a bit easier on her." She paused. "I guess if it was me, I'd still be so angry I couldn't hold it back. What they did to you was *so* wrong, in so many ways."

Sadie sighed and tried to tamp down the agitation that Nicole's words stirred in her. It was feeding the buried anger, and she didn't need that fire stoked. She had real fears of how she might react if all that repressed anger came out. Especially if faced with her father.

"I know, and I guess there is a little part of me that feels that same depth of anger as you do about it." She flinched at the white lie. "Maybe I should want to finally say what I couldn't say back then. But, Nic, it wouldn't change anything. I can't turn back the clock and make things go differently. As the saying goes, it is what it is." She sighed. "Look, don't get me wrong, it's not like I'm going to walk into that house and pretend that nothing's happened. Or that I'm not worried about going back there. But for me, the only reason I'm going back is to see Mum. And yes, I do have some questions for her, and yes, I do want to get into it a bit with her, as you put it. But the other two? Them I am happy to just ignore." She paused, then ploughed on as her fears came to the fore. "I'm scared of seeing him—he's not changed, so I won't get anywhere with him—but I am dreading what he'll say, how he'll act. And how I'll react. I can't lie about that." She exhaled slowly as the anxiety about meeting her father again hit her in a series of uncomfortably hot waves through her chest. "Izzy has apparently changed a lot. If she wants to talk, that's okay, but I won't initiate it. This trip is not about her. Anything that happens there will just be a bonus."

"And what about Chloe?"

Sadie snorted. "Nic, I haven't given her a second's thought in about ten years. She is not important at all in this. Anyway, the chances of seeing her are pretty remote."

"You know what?" Nicole giggled before continuing. "I bet she's like fucking *huge* now, with four ugly, snotty brats in tow. She dresses like shit, and her husband has an enormous beer gut."

Sadie laughed out loud at the image of the impeccable Chloe turned slob, and they chuckled together. Once again, Nic had known just how to take the edge off things. They chatted on about Nicole's day and her plans with Tash for the weekend, before hanging up with a promise to speak as soon as Sadie was settled in back in Ballarat.

The ride the next day from Albury-Wodonga to Ballarat wasn't as long a stretch as the day before, about four and half hours including a refuelling stop. As she left the Hume Freeway and headed across country to Ballarat, her nerves started to tingle. Less than two hundred kilometres from what used to be her home, thoughts and memories crowded in. The what-ifs started parading through her mind, making her feel uneasy and not liking it. She concentrated harder on the road, trying to keep the fears away.

At the first road sign pointing the way for Ballarat she winced a little. Definitely too late to turn back. She took a deep breath and rode on.

The hotel was just off Victoria Street, near Bakery Hill. Not near the family home, but it was the only hotel she could afford with a week's vacancy at such short notice, and only then because they'd had a cancellation.

As she cruised down Victoria Street towards the centre of town, she took a few looks around. It was strange, being back. Especially, because nothing really looked any different. Yes, some businesses had clearly come and gone, but generally, this way into town didn't look that much changed in twelve years. She made sure to keep to all the speed limits through town, no point attracting the attention of any police officer who may remember the name Sadie Williams.

The hotel was a converted colonial building, set back off a side street. It looked well maintained. The owners had clearly gone to a lot of effort in making the small hotel look inviting. Tubs of bright flowers flanked the front door, and the brass door handles gleamed in the mid-afternoon sun. It was just after three when Sadie swung the bike into a small space in the almost-full car park. She eased her body off the bike and immediately undid her leather jacket to let in some air. The weather in Ballarat was a couple of degrees cooler than what she had left behind in Albury-Wodonga earlier that day, but the sun had shone down on her for the whole of the ride. Her body temperature had steadily climbed, and she could feel the dampness of perspiration across her back and shoulders.

She stretched for a few minutes, easing out the small of her back in particular. After hoisting her daypack onto her back, she locked the bike, lifted the panniers, and headed for the front door.

The lobby she stepped into was surprisingly classy. The floor was formed from what looked like polished jarrah that continued up to adorn the front desk and the half panelling along each of the walls.

Behind the reception desk stood a young woman so gorgeous Sadie found herself staring in unabashed appreciation. The woman smiled warmly, pushing her stylishly thick-rimmed glasses up onto her hair in a move that was so unconsciously sexy it stole Sadie's breath away. Sadie smiled back at the woman, blinking rapidly in an attempt to pull herself from the spell she seemed to be under.

"Hi," said the woman. "Welcome to the Queen Victoria Hotel. My name is Holly. How can I help you?" Her hair was a deep chocolate colour and fell straight to just brush her shoulders. She was dressed in a smart black jacket over a white shirt, the top two buttons undone and showing off a pleasing V of tanned skin. Her face still held a hint of the softness of her youth—Sadie had her at about twenty-one, maybe twenty-two. Subtle make-up highlighted full lips and big brown eyes that gazed expectantly at Sadie, who still hadn't found a way to form words. The faintest of blushes stole across Holly's cheeks as Sadie continued to stare. It was only when Holly cleared her throat slightly that Sadie finally came back to herself.

"Sorry," she spluttered, shifting the panniers in her hand. "Just had a long journey." Hopefully, that covered her well, she thought, because God knows what the woman thought of her at that precise moment.

She stepped closer to the desk.

"Hi," she said, her face flushing as her voice came out croaky. She cleared her throat. "Sadie Williams, I have a reservation."

Holly smiled and turned her gaze to the computer screen just to her left. Sadie forced herself not to look at Holly's fingers tapping the keyboard. She was having such an intense reaction to this woman, she didn't need to put any more dangerous thoughts in her head.

"Okay, I've got it." Holly looked up after a moment, smiling warmly. "For one week?"

Sadie nodded. "Through to next Saturday, at the moment, although I might stay longer. It's not decided yet."

"Oh." Holly used one of her slim hands to push her hair back behind her ears, the move as mesmerising in its subtle sexiness as the push of the glasses had been only moments before. Sadie tried very hard not to stare again. "Well, just let us know your plans and we'll see if we can extend your stay. We are pretty busy at the moment, though, just so you know."

"Yeah, I know—I only got this room because you had a cancellation. I'll see how it goes."

Holly nodded and prepared the check-in form and key card. Sadie found herself watching the slim hands again and shook herself in disgust. The woman in front of her was too young, and more than likely too straight, for Sadie to be getting distracted by. And besides, that was definitely not what this trip was about.

Holly passed Sadie the form to complete and sign, then handed her the key card.

"So, you're in room twelve. It's in the modern annexe at the rear of the hotel, on this level. Just through those doors there and along the hall." She pointed to a set of double doors behind her right shoulder. "You've got a small kitchenette in your room, so let me know if you need any extra packets of coffee or sugar, et cetera. Breakfast is served in the restaurant from six thirty until ten, but obviously you've got facilities to make your own if you prefer." She smiled widely, and Sadie's stomach gave a pleasant little jump at the sight. "Anything else you need, just ask—dial nine on the room phone to get through to reception, okay?"

Sadie nodded dumbly. What was it about this woman that rendered her so bloody speechless?

"Great. Well, I hope you get settled in okay." Holly's voice sounded just a little uncertain, and Sadie realised she was probably freaking her out with her silence.

She smiled ruefully. "Sorry, I am normally much better at speaking than this. I'm just really tired." She hoped it sounded convincing, given that it was a complete lie.

Holly's smile was dazzling again. "No problem, I understand."

Sadie decided it was definitely time to put them both out of her misery, and grabbed her belongings. She gave Holly a quick grin and strode off to the double doors. She found the room a minute later, towards the end of the hallway. She let herself in and was pleasantly surprised at the light, airy space she found. It looked very new and well fitted out. She dropped her baggage on the floor at the foot of the bed and looked around. Crisp, white walls; a small kitchen area with a kettle, toaster, microwave, and small fridge; bright blue linens on the bed; and what looked like a spotless shower room through a door on the opposite side of the room.

Home for the week, or possibly more, and she already knew she would be very comfortable here. It would be good knowing she had this to come back to each day—God knows she might need the escape it would offer.

CHAPTER 6

Holly watched Sadie Williams push her way through the doors that led to the annexe, and exhaled slowly.

Oh. My. God.

She'd heard about people who said that all it took sometimes was just one look or glance, one meeting, to know you'd found someone who was going to turn your life upside down. She'd never believed it; she was far too pragmatic for that kind of...silliness. But oh my, just one look at Sadie Williams and everything that had happened to Holly up to that point in her life literally faded away to nothing. Sadie was...magnificent. There was no other word for it. Kind of like some Amazonian goddess who'd just stepped off the pages of a ridiculously trashy novel.

She rolled her eyes at herself. Amazonian goddess? *Seriously?*

Still... Slightly taller than Holly, Sadie had short, messy, blonde hair that curled cutely behind her ears and just to the nape of her neck. A sort of solid build, not slim at all, but from what Holly could tell, it was mostly muscle and conjured up an image of soft strength. That sounded contradictory in her head, but the description perfectly fitted the body that had walked through the hotel door minutes before. Her stunning eyes were a shade of green that reminded Holly of the sea on a bright, sunny day, and were framed by long, pale eyelashes. The way she'd stared at Holly...she experienced goosebumps just thinking about the effect that look had on her. She had no idea how she'd managed to keep herself from oozing into a puddle on the floor.

Holly O'Brien was twenty-two and had spent the last two years slowly coming to terms with how fluid her sexuality appeared to be. Since her first boyfriend at sixteen, she'd had two more relationships with men, but also two with women. She didn't do labels. She was just Holly, a woman who found both sexes attractive.

And Sadie Williams, in all her glory, was stunningly attractive.

Holly sat down with a thump into the chair behind the desk. God, she'd never had such a reaction to someone in her life, male or female. She didn't know it was possible. She ran her hands through her hair, coming across her glasses in the process, which she had completely forgotten she'd pushed up there earlier. To be honest, she couldn't even remember her own name, never mind where her glasses were.

Shit. This sort of thing just didn't happen to her. Just her luck, it was with someone who was only visiting Ballarat. She nearly growled in frustration. So unfair.

"Holly, is everything okay?"

Her mum's voice broke into her thoughts, and she jumped in her seat.

"Yes, sorry, I'm fine," she muttered as she quickly stood and turned to face her mum, who had appeared with a sheaf of paperwork in her hand.

"Good." Her mum walked behind the desk, giving her daughter a quick squeeze of a hug with one arm. "Has it been busy?"

"Only with check-ins. A few phone inquiries but all wanting something over the next few days, and obviously we're fully booked."

Her mum peered over Holly's shoulder at the computer screen.

"It's not looking too bad, though, is it?" Her finger tracked across the screen.

Holly pulled her glasses off her head and quickly popped them on her nose as she inched nearer to her mother's side to look at the screen with her.

"No, not too bad at all, really. A few gaps over a couple of weekends next month. Maybe I could put together a quick e-mail campaign to people who've booked weekends before. Offer them a small discount for a last-minute booking."

She looked at her mother cautiously, still not sure if her parents fully trusted the skills she'd recently acquired through attaining her marketing degree. But her mum was smiling, and her expression was one of pride.

"I think that sounds like a great idea! Do it. I'll tell your father."

Holly beamed. "Cool! Thanks, Mum, I'll get right on it."

She smiled to herself as she heard her mother walk away. She had been working for her parents on the reception desk since university, taking odd shifts around her classes and homework. Graduated and with her degree in hand, she was working full-time for them while she figured out what to do longer term. It was supposed to have been a temporary fix to give her thinking time, but it had been six months, and the thinking really hadn't led anywhere.

Her whole life she'd been so focused, so driven. She always knew what she was aiming for and how to get it. She'd sailed through university, keeping her head down, not partying it up like some of her fellow students. And yet, the minute she gained her degree, it was as if something switched off inside her. Something she couldn't quite switch back on.

With the e-mail campaign, she had a project. That was good. Distraction from her worries over the future, and from her extraordinary reaction to the woman in room twelve, was very welcome.

Sadie smiled as she arched her back under the shower spray. She was still amused at her pitiful performance in front of that gorgeous receptionist. It had been some months since her last physical connection with someone. Somehow, she just hadn't been remotely interested in anyone else since then. Sure, she missed sex, but she'd never found enough energy or willingness to go out looking for it. She'd helped herself on that score whenever the urge arose, and it had been…sufficient. But Holly stirred up feelings that had been dormant for a while, and her libido was sitting up and saying hello. She shook her head. How was that possible in the midst of what she was going through?

She towelled off quickly and dressed in her jeans and a fresh tee shirt. She'd call her gran in a while and see about arranging to go to see her mum. She knew going right then might risk bumping into her father—he would more than likely be home for the evening, and she wanted to avoid him as much as she could.

She remembered the white lie she'd told Nicole on the phone the day before. There was more than a little part of her that still carried that depth of anger about it all and about him specifically. She was so resentful of him, at the memories of what he'd done, that sometimes she shook with it. She would feel it wash over her, catching her out with its power, when she was tired or run-down. She would fight it with everything she had, because the things it made her want to do, under its influence, terrified her.

She took a deep breath and picked up the phone. Elsie answered after only a couple of rings.

"Hey, Gran, I'm here."

"Oh, good, I'm glad you made it. How was the ride today?"

"It was okay, not as long as yesterday, but no real heavy traffic to deal with. Hotel's nice."

"Good. I…" Her gran paused.

"Say it, Gran, whatever it is."

"Well, love, I was just going to say it's probably just as well you're in a hotel. Christine told him last night that you were going to visit and, well, he wasn't happy, as I'm sure you can imagine."

Sadie sighed. "Yeah, I can imagine. Shit."

"I know, love." Elsie inhaled sharply. "Look, we always knew this was likely, didn't we? But I was proud of Christine for standing up to him last night. He started in on a big argument, and she just cut him off. I didn't know she had it in her, to be honest."

Sadie laughed, softly. "Wow, that doesn't sound like my mother at all."

"Yes, well, I suspect that knowing you're going to die soon puts a few things into perspective, doesn't it?" Sadie heard the mix of emotions in her gran's voice.

"Good on her," Sadie murmured, and heard Elsie's small sound of agreement. "So," Sadie continued, after a moment. "When shall I come over? I'm pretty nervous, Gran, I have to admit. But now I'm here, I do want to do this. To see her."

"Come over tomorrow, after about ten in the morning. Even though it's Saturday, he's off on some business trip all day, something to do with the council—as usual, bloody politics comes first. Anyway, by ten she's usually properly awake and ready to talk. I'll tell her you're coming."

"Oh, that's…that's great, Gran. I knew I'd left it too late today. That's really good that I can come tomorrow." Her voice trembled; the realisation that she would see her mother tomorrow was surreal. "Cool. So, I'll see you then. Take care, Gran."

"You too, love. Don't be nervous, okay? She does want to see you. I know it won't be easy for you, but I'll be here too." She paused. "I'm looking forward to seeing you, Sadie. I've…I've missed you." Her gran's voice caught, and Sadie's throat tightened.

"I've missed you too, Gran," she whispered. "I'll see you in the morning."

She hung up and flopped backwards onto the bed. Her gran had been everything to her for the last twelve years, and she loved her so much for it. She'd never really told her, though—they didn't do emotions very well, either of them. Elsie always put a stoic face on everything, and Sadie was always too scared to let anyone know how she felt about them, in case they left her. Just like her family had, and just like Chloe had. But her gran's words had hit home hard, perhaps more so because they didn't ever say things like that to each other. If nothing else came of her time here, she resolved to tell her grandmother just how much she meant to her, and how grateful she was for all she'd done for her.

Holly saved the final draft of the marketing e-mail she'd been working on and sent it to her parents for approval.

Sitting back in her chair, she gazed out of the front door. The sun was still shining brightly, as it had been all day. She'd go for a run after she finished at five, a little under an hour away. An ex-girlfriend had introduced her to the joys of running, and she'd carried on even though the girlfriend was long gone. She smiled in memory. Sam had been her first. God, what a bundle of energy that one had been. She laughed to herself. And God, she herself had been insatiable…rampant. Sam had been almost wide-eyed at what she'd unleashed.

She shook her head as a dizzying collage of erotic images flashed through her mind's eye. She still had an hour's work to do, and dreaming of sex—hot, achingly delicious sex—wasn't going to help. She fanned herself and stood up. Filing needed doing. Yes, filing, that would help.

A couple of minutes later, she turned out of habit as she heard the doors to the annexe open. Instantly, images of hot, achingly delicious sex invaded her brain again as Sadie Williams stood in front of her at the desk.

Oh, God.

"Hi," Holly managed to squeak out. "Need something?"

"Hi," Sadie said. "Where's the nearest place to get groceries? I think there used to be an IGA around here, didn't there?"

Holly smiled. "Yeah, but it's changed a bit since then—it's a Coles now, quite a big one. Just head out of here, turn left, then left again. Then it's about, oh, a hundred metres down. You can't miss it."

"Great, thanks." Sadie hesitated, and Holly raised a questioning eyebrow. Inside, she was delighted Sadie wasn't immediately heading out the door; she could look at her all day.

"Holly," came her mum's voice from behind her. "I love the e-mail—" Her voice stopped as she arrived in reception and saw Sadie standing there. Holly watched in shock as her mother's face went from open to openly hostile in the blink of an eye.

"Oh, I'm sorry, I didn't realise anyone else was here," her mother said, her tone sharp and bordering on rude.

Holly, her mind whirling at the strange behaviour her mother was exhibiting, cleared her throat before Sadie could speak. "Mum, this is one of our guests, Sadie Williams. She just checked in today."

"Yes, I know who you are," she said, glaring at Sadie with undisguised contempt. "Will you be here long?" The unspoken message was *how quickly will you be leaving?* Holly was astonished; she'd never seen her mum like this.

Sadie didn't seem perturbed by the behaviour, which confused Holly even more. Instead, she pulled herself a little straighter, her expression bland.

"About a week, maybe longer. Depends on how things go. I take it you know my parents?"

Holly's mum nodded abruptly.

"Well, then I guess you know what's going on. I'm here to visit my mum before…before she passes." She moved her focus to Holly. "Thanks for the directions," she said, smiling faintly before turning sharply and pushing open the main door to the street.

Holly waited until the door had closed behind her before turning to her mother. "Mum, what the hell was that about? You were unbelievably rude to her!"

Her mum exhaled, slowly. "Yes, I'm sorry. I-I was just so shocked to find her here. I'll…I'll apologise to her later. Although, I'm not happy she's staying here, I'll be honest."

"Why?" Holly demanded. "What has she ever done to you? And what was all that about her mum?"

Her mother sighed and leaned against the desk, finally meeting Holly's gaze. "It's a long story from the past. Sadie was a real wild child, always getting into trouble at school and with the police. She set some outbuildings on fire at a school back when she was, oh, seventeen I guess. Peter and Christine, friends of ours from back then, had had enough. They packed her off to live with her grandmother in Sydney, I believe. Good riddance; she caused so much trouble." She paused, her eyes drifting out of focus. "Her mother is dying—we found out just yesterday. I guess, maybe, I was feeling a bit raw from hearing that and that's why I lashed out at Sadie. Christine has a brain tumour, only has a short while to live. I suppose Sadie found out and thought she would visit her before she dies."

"God, how could parents do that to a child? What on earth—?"

Her mum rounded on her, eyes blazing. "You don't know anything about it!" she snapped. "That child was a nightmare. We all knew about her, knew all the stupid and dangerous things she did. She made her parents' lives hell."

"Right, so instead of helping her, trying to understand why she was doing what she was doing, they threw her out?" Holly was incensed. She wasn't really sure why she felt the need to defend Sadie, but everything she was hearing about this story made her blood boil.

"You don't understand." Her mum's tone was resigned. "She was just so much trouble. No one could reach her. And now she's back, to cause God-knows-what trouble."

"Oh, right, so because she was a wild child, she can't possibly be a good person now? I thought she was really nice from what I saw of her. I think you're being very unfair assuming she's out to cause trouble again. You don't know anything about the person she is now."

Her mum took a step back and smiled wanly at her. "Yes, I suppose you're right." She took a couple of deep breaths. "How did you get to be so much smarter than me all of a sudden?"

Holly smiled in relief. "I was brought up right, I guess."

Her mum's eyes sparkled. "Yes, you were," she murmured. She straightened up. "God, I am being grossly unfair to her, aren't I?"

Holly nodded and pulled her mum in for a quick hug. "You always told me never to prejudge anyone until you'd got to know them."

"All right, missy, point taken." She pulled out of Holly's arms. "I'll be sure to apologise to her later, I promise."

"Thanks, Mum."

Sadie marched up the street, her mind reeling. That woman—great, Holly's *mother*—had looked at her with such…contempt. And Sadie didn't even know her. What the hell had people been told about her? God knows what shit her father had spread to justify his actions in kicking her out. Was she going to meet that kind of venom everywhere she went this trip? Maybe she should just pack up and go. Maybe it had been a stupid idea to come back here.

But then she thought of telling her gran that, and her mind calmed. Elsie would be so disappointed in Sadie, and she couldn't bear to do that to her. *No, I'm here now, and I'll see it through.* But clearly she needed to harden up a little in anticipation of the reaction of other people to her presence. She hadn't known that was how it was going to be. It would take a lot out of her, but better that than let her gran down.

She needed a run; after she picked up her groceries, she'd get out and work out a nice five-kilometre circuit round the local streets to soothe her soul. And then a call with Nicole, who would be outraged at how that woman had talked to her but would make her laugh about it in some way, Sadie was sure.

The supermarket had all she needed—bread for toast, a small tub of butter, peanut butter, and a bottle of orange juice. She noted the bottle shop next door; she'd come back later to get some beers to keep chilled in the fridge.

She walked back to the hotel in a calmer frame of mind than when she left it, taking her time to make sure she had hardened her armour in readiness for returning through the brass-handled doors of the hotel. If Holly's mum was still at reception when she returned, she had to brace herself for the possibility of yet more vitriol.

Pushing through the doors with some trepidation, she was careful not to bash the glass with her groceries. She didn't need to give that woman any more fuel to hate her. She flinched when she saw Holly's mum walking across the reception area towards her, but then she took in the apologetic smile on the woman's face and paused her steps.

"Sadie, I want to apologise for the way I spoke to you earlier. It was very wrong of me to make any kind of assumption about you based on the past. I think it's admirable that you are back here to visit with Christine, given what did happen in the past."

Sadie blinked. God, she hadn't seen that coming. She swallowed and noticed Holly hovering behind the desk, listening in.

"Um, thanks. I really appreciate that," she said quietly, pleasantly surprised at this turn of events.

"We didn't even properly meet." Holly's mum extended her hand, smiling and blushing slightly at the same time. "Judy O'Brien, owner of the hotel."

Sadie quickly put down the bag she'd been carrying and shook Judy's hand. Their handshake was firm, and Judy held her gaze the entire time.

"Nice to meet you, Judy," Sadie said, still stunned at this change in atmosphere.

"Holly tells me you only arrived this afternoon. Are you settling in okay, have everything you need?" Her smile was considerably warmer than half an hour ago, and Sadie relaxed in this new ambience between them. She nodded and gestured to the bag of groceries.

"Just got all stocked up for brekkie, so yeah, I'm good, thanks."

"Well, you must be tired, so I won't keep you. But again, I'm very sorry for earlier and if there's anything we can do, just let us know."

"Thanks, Judy."

She watched Judy turn and walk off towards an office area at the back of reception. Sadie met Holly's eyes across the reception desk. She noticed Holly's held the same level of relief she was sure her own were carrying. Holly smiled then, and Sadie couldn't help the broad grin that spread across her face.

"Sorry about that," Holly said quietly. "And I'm really sorry to hear about your mum. Mum told me a little about…everything, while you were out shopping."

Sadie's back stiffened, and her armour came crashing into place. The idea that Holly knew anything about her past was uncomfortable, to say the least. "Oh, right," she said, picking up the grocery bag and walking towards the doors that led to the annexe. "Thanks, I'll see you later."

"Wait!" Holly called, darting out from behind the desk. Sadie gazed expectantly at her. "Sorry, I didn't mean anything by that. Please don't be offended."

"Okay," Sadie replied, knowing her tone was a little less than friendly but not caring enough to do anything about it. She really didn't need to know what Holly knew about her. The fact that she knew anything about Sadie's past would presumably have already tainted her in Holly's eyes, and she suddenly couldn't bear that.

"Look," Holly continued. "I get that we don't really know each other. But would you like to go for a drink tonight? I'm going for a run after my shift finishes at five, but I could meet you back here around six thirty, and we could go to a great pub I know not too far from here. It's got a nice garden we could sit in. You know, if you wanted to talk about anything."

Sadie cocked her head in astonishment. The last thing she thought she'd get out of the drama of the last half hour or so was an invite out for a drink from the gorgeous Holly. Judging from the rapid blinking of Holly's eyes, it wasn't quite what Holly had anticipated either.

"Oh," Holly murmured when Sadie didn't immediately reply. "Sorry, I guess I should have known you probably have plans for tonight, don't you? Sorry," she said, her face flushing. She started to turn back towards reception.

"No, wait." Sadie finally found her voice. "You said something about a run?"

Holly turned back to stare at her, wide-eyed. "Yes?"

"Well, I run too. I was thinking I needed one today, to loosen me up after the long ride. Would you mind if I joined you? You could maybe map me out a route around here?"

Holly's smile lit up the hallway they were standing in and sparked a small warm spot somewhere in the centre of Sadie's chest. She wanted to make Holly smile like that again. And again, and again.

"That would be great—I haven't had a running partner in a while. I normally do about six kilometres on the streets around here. Does that sound okay?"

A little longer than she normally ran each day, but something told her she'd cope if she was running it alongside this beautiful woman.

"Sounds great," Sadie replied, and grinned. "I'll meet you back in reception at what, about five fifteen?"

Holly nodded. "Perfect. See you then." Her smile then was a little shy, and Sadie felt her insides do a flop.

Oh, God, what was she getting into here?

CHAPTER 7

Holly shuffled papers around the desk and rearranged the placement of the stapler for the fifth time. She gripped the desk edge and forced herself to stand still. She was nervous about seeing Sadie later, true. But there was no need to get this worked up about it, was there? Sure, it had been a tad unlike her to be so bold and ask Sadie out. But it wasn't a date. Not really. Oh God, what if Sadie thought that's what she meant?

Her mum appeared moments later to take over the desk, and her presence interrupted Holly's panicked musings. She exhaled slowly as she headed off to change, willing her whole body to calm down. As she slipped out of her suit, she sighed. Why, oh why, had she agreed to going running together? God help her if Sadie wore anything skintight to run in. Holly wouldn't know where to look if that body was revealed in all its muscular glory. She herself ran in a loose tee shirt and shorts, and she prayed, desperately, that Sadie did the same.

At five fifteen, she found her prayers had been answered and mentally sent a word of thanks skyward. Sadie appeared in a sleeveless but loose tee shirt, shorts that didn't cling and finished mid-thigh, and a pair of well-worn Nike running shoes. Holly was using the reception desk as a stretching bar. Her mum was behind the desk and smiled at Sadie as she appeared from the annexe.

"Holly told me you two were running together. It'll be nice for Holly to share it with someone. I don't like her out running on her own," Judy said, dropping a concerned look Holly's way.

"It's broad daylight, Mum." Holly groaned, rolling her eyes. "I'd be fine on my own."

"Hey, if you'd rather—" Sadie began.

"No!" Holly interjected, sharper than she meant to. "I mean," she continued, softening her tone, "it's okay, I really want to go running with you. I'm just saying that normally I'd go on my own in broad daylight and be absolutely fine about it, safety wise." God, she needed to get a hold of herself—her reactions were way over the top at the moment.

"Oh, okay. Cool." There was an awkward pause between the three of them, which Sadie eventually broke. "So, shall we?" She motioned to the door, and Holly gave her an embarrassed grin.

"Yep, let's do it."

"Have fun!" her mum called as they exited the hotel.

They stood outside in the late afternoon sun. The day was still pleasant but not overly warm.

"So," Holly said, looking at Sadie and trying hard to keep her gaze focused somewhere on Sadie's face and not let it drift down her body. "What kind of pace do you run?"

"Oh, I'm a really easy pace, about thirty-five minutes for a five kilometre. What about you?"

"A little bit faster, but not much. You set the pace, then, and that'll be fine for me. I'm not training for a race or anything. I just love to be outdoors running at the end of my day."

Sadie smiled, and it was the first freely open smile Holly had seen her generate since they'd met earlier that day. It gave Holly a gentle glow all over.

"You sound just like me," Sadie said. "I love my run at the end of the day. Totally works off everything that's happened and takes me to a different place that's just about me." She ducked her head shyly at those last words, and Holly tingled at how adorable it made her look.

Holly dared to poke Sadie in the bicep. Wow. Solid muscle. Inwardly, she tamped down the quiver that started somewhere deep in her belly. "Well, we won't achieve that kind of time unless we actually start moving, will we?" She hoped Sadie would read the cheekiness in her tone.

"Lead on then, smart-ass." Sadie smirked, and Holly giggled as she took off.

They didn't talk too much on the run, keeping their verbal interactions limited to Holly pointing out the route so that if Sadie wanted to run it again on her own, she'd know where she was going. Their non-verbal interactions, however, were constant. Holly found herself flicking glances to her left with alarming regularity, only to be secretly pleased each time she did to find Sadie looking right back at her. They smiled often, and Holly found her imagination leaping away from her, thinking ahead to their drink after. Maybe they'd then go for tea, a walk in the late evening air, and then…

She pulled herself up, mentally, as they turned the last corner before home. What was she doing, getting carried away with this fantasy? Sadie was only in town for a week, and then she'd go back to her life. For all Holly knew, Sadie was straight or she already had a partner waiting for her back home. Why was she torturing herself with ideas about something that had next to no chance of happening?

A few minutes later, they slowed in front of the hotel, and both stood with their hands on their hips, panting.

"Good circuit," Sadie said between breaths. "And pretty easy to remember, I think."

Holly inhaled deeply, then exhaled slowly. "Well, if you want someone to run with while you're here, I finish work at five and run nearly every day. Well, except one day at weekends. I usually only work either Saturday or Sunday, not both. But then, I guess you'll be with your family all weekend, won't you?" To Holly's ears it suddenly sounded as if she was rambling so she quickly shut up.

Sadie appeared to notice her discomfort and smiled encouragingly. "I'm going there tomorrow, but I doubt I'll be there all day. Are you working tomorrow?"

"Yes, then off on Sunday."

"Okay, so how about we run again tomorrow when you finish?"

Holly grinned. "I'd like that. A lot."

They used the wall bordering the car park to stretch.

"So," Sadie said, after a moment. "You still want to get that drink tonight?"

"Oh. We really don't have to, if you have plans."

Sadie looked at her, her head cocked slightly to the side. "Okay, if you've changed your mind, then—"

"No! Sorry, that's not what I meant. I'd… Well, I'd really like to go for a drink. I just don't want to impose."

Sadie smiled. "You're not imposing. About all I would do tonight is sit in front of the TV, maybe make a couple of phone calls." She paused, and looked around. "I don't really remember this area from when I lived here, so I wouldn't know where to go to eat. And it's been a long time since I've been…home…so I don't know anyone else in town except my family, really." She turned back to look at Holly. "So, if you are free, I really would like the company."

Holly silently admonished herself for the happy thrill that buzzed through her at that moment. "Okay, so it's decided, then. I need to go home and clean up, but we only live about five minutes from here." She glanced down at her watch. Six o'clock. "How about I meet you back here in about forty-five minutes. Does that give you enough time to get ready?"

"Well," Sadie drawled, with a grin. "I mean, I'll have to set my hair and all, but I guess I could make an effort to be ready by then."

Holly laughed, and playfully slapped Sadie on the arm. "Okay, now who's the smart-ass?"

Sadie stood in front of the meagre collection of clothes she had hanging in the wardrobe. What to wear? It wasn't exactly a date, but even so, she wanted to make an effort. Holly was…lovely, and Sadie wanted to get to know her, wanted to spend time with her. Yeah, and what else?

Stop being stupid. She's probably straight, so just take it for what it is—an excuse not to spend the evening on your own.

For some reason, that had been what grabbed her the most about the offer of a drink—the chance to avoid being on her own for the evening. That had been a daunting prospect and she knew exactly why. All the fears would resurface, and she worried she would get very little sleep as a result. So spending some of the evening with Holly, talking about other things, might be just what she needed to avoid delving into her own thoughts too much.

She finally decided on an outfit and headed out to meet Holly.

The reception area was full of a group of elderly couples checking in, keeping Judy busy while Sadie waited for Holly. Judy did catch her eye at one point. She smiled, but there was a small frown hidden behind that smile. It deepened slightly when Holly arrived and greeted Sadie warmly. Sadie tried not to stare. She'd thought Holly looked gorgeous in her suit when they first met, then sexy in her running gear, and standing right there, she looked simply stunning in her casual clothes. Tight-fitting, skinny, cropped jeans, a green V-neck tee shirt that clung to her torso in all the right places, and a black leather jacket slung casually over one shoulder. Her hair was brushed until it shone, and she'd touched up her make-up again. The musky scent of her skin sent all sorts of tantalising signals to Sadie's brain.

Sadie avoided looking at Judy as she and Holly left, not entirely sure what the frown was about but willing to hazard a guess.

Holly led them to what she called the best pub in the area. The place was buzzing on a Friday night, but they managed to find a table for two out in the garden.

"So," Holly said, as they sipped their drinks. "How are you feeling after the run?"

Sadie smiled. "Yeah, pretty good. I think I really needed that one." It was true—although she'd rushed through her clean-up afterwards, her body had been humming with endorphins.

Holly seemed to hesitate, and Sadie knew she was wondering how much to ask. Strangely, it didn't make Sadie uncomfortable to think about sharing with her. She nudged Holly's leg with her knee.

"Go ahead, I know you have questions."

Holly looked startled at the physical contact, and pulled her leg away slightly.

Shit, that clearly overstepped a mark. Note to self—no more touching.

But when she looked up, Holly's eyes said something different, and the first dawning of awareness sent an unexpected tingle down Sadie's spine.

"Well," Holly said into the awkward silence between them. "It's none of my business, so please tell me if I'm being too nosey."

"Don't worry, I will," Sadie replied, smiling as warmly as she could in reassurance.

Holly cleared her throat. "Your mum?"

Sadie swallowed. "Yeah, dying of a brain tumour. Only diagnosed at the beginning of this week but too late to do anything about it." She stopped, surprised at the strength of emotion that blunt statement engendered.

"Sorry," Holly whispered, her face openly displaying her regret at touching such a sensitive topic so soon.

"No worries," Sadie whispered back. She sat back in her chair and exhaled slowly. "It's why I'm here, after all. There'd be no other reason for me to come back here. I can't pretend it's easy, but at the end of the day, she is my mum."

They sipped their drinks quietly for a few moments.

"So," Sadie said eventually, her own curiosity coming to the fore. "What exactly did your mum tell you about me?"

Holly blushed. "Shit, I'm so sorry about that."

Sadie shrugged.

"Well, she said that you had been...well, a bit wild. Always in trouble. She kind of assumed that hadn't changed."

Sadie laughed, but it sounded empty even to her own ears. "Yeah, I reckon there'll be a lot of people who will remember who I was and assume that nothing's changed. I don't really care what other people think, though. I know I'm better than the person I was then. My gran and Nicole, my best mate, know too. That's all I need, really." She struggled to keep the defensive tone out of her voice.

Holly reached across and gently touched her arm. Sadie stared at the warm fingers on her skin for a moment, then looked up into Holly's eyes.

"Why are we here?" she asked. The question came unbidden, and she flinched slightly as Holly blinked rapidly. She instantly regretted putting the other woman on the spot, but before she could apologise, Holly spoke.

"I guess I thought you looked like you could do with someone to talk to." She exhaled and swallowed. "Here on your own, having to deal with...stuff. Somehow, I just didn't want you to have to do that alone." She looked away from Sadie, her blush very apparent even in the fading evening light. Sadie knew that answer wasn't the whole of it, but she also knew it wasn't the time to press. There was clearly something happening between them, and she had no idea if she wanted to pursue it or not, so she wouldn't push. A romantic, or even just physical, entanglement was not something she'd be looking for on this trip.

Of course, sometimes things appeared even when you weren't looking for them.

"So," she said quietly, after a few moments, catching Holly's attention again. "What's your story? How long have you worked at the hotel?"

Holly shot her a grateful look at the sudden shift in direction of their conversation.

"Well, technically I've worked there since I was about sixteen, which is when my parents took over the hotel. I'd help out in the office, stock up the breakfast room, stuff like that. When I graduated, I didn't really know what to do with myself. Mum suggested I work full-time with them until I did know. Their receptionist had just left to have a baby, so it all kind of fit."

"Do you like it?"

"Um…it's okay. Just not really what I pictured myself doing when I was at uni, you know?" She sighed, and took a few more gulps of her beer.

"So, what do you want to do?"

Holly smiled ruefully. "Yeah, that's the problem. I still don't really know." She paused and then let out a sharp breath. "It's like, my whole life I've been working really hard to get a good degree, get myself set up for a proper career—didn't want to end up doing a nothing job—and now, suddenly, here I am with a degree in my pocket, and I have no idea any more what I want. It's so not like me, and I'm… Well, I'm having a hard time trying to figure out why, actually."

"I fell into my job," Sadie mused. "Wasn't exactly a top student at school here or in Manly, which is where I live now. Just about finished high school, although it was hard after all the upheaval of transferring. Then just drifted around doing pizza delivery and stuff for a few months, until Nicole saw an ad for a job in a cafe about twenty minutes walk from where I live. Now, I manage the place. I love it, and I wouldn't want any other job."

Holly smiled. "Lucky you." Her voice was wistful.

"I guess what I'm saying is that sometimes you don't really need it all mapped out. Sometimes it all just kind of happens."

Holly nodded, her gaze unfocused while she finished her beer.

"Another?" Sadie asked, motioning to Holly's empty bottle.

"Sure." Holly brought her gaze round to fix on Sadie's, and their eyes locked for a moment. Sadie blinked once, astonished at the heat that passed between them in that one look. She stood quickly, breaking the spell, reaching for the wallet she'd tucked into the back pocket of her jeans. No matter what sparks were flying between them, she wasn't going to go there. She needed to just get through this week—visit with her mum, maybe see how things were with Izzy, avoid her father. If she could manage all that, it would be a week well spent. Anything else would simply get in the way. No matter how tempting a guise it wore in the face and body of Holly O'Brien.

They drank their second beers as they made small talk about Ballarat and its changes over the years. They decided to eat at the pub, neither of them interested in losing their comfy spot in the garden. They ordered burgers with a shared order of fries, laughing as they split the portion into two distinct halves so that Holly could smother hers in ketchup, and Sadie's with mayo.

When they'd finished, the conversation somehow returned to Holly's predicament over her career.

"I just don't know what's going on with me," she said, exhaling in obvious exasperation.

"Did you get pressure from your parents to push for this degree? I mean, you haven't mentioned any brothers or sisters, so are you an only child? Did they pin all their ambitions on you?"

"No, nothing like that. And no, I don't have siblings. Mum…she almost didn't survive my birth, so they decided then and there that one child was all they would have. And yes, they've smothered me with love and attention my whole life but not in an overwhelming way." She smiled. "More like they're just grateful they got me, and they wanted me to always know that. But no pressure on school or a career. I was just naturally bright and loved learning, so it totally came from me to push myself to do as well as I could." The statement didn't come across as arrogant, and somehow Sadie knew that wasn't in Holly's nature. "And I mean, of course they were pleased, because they're both pretty smart and well educated too. But I always knew that even if I didn't turn out to be that academically minded, they'd have supported me just as much."

"So, maybe that's it. Maybe you achieved what you set out to, academically, so now your brain is like, *okay, what the hell is next?*"

"Yeah, maybe." Holly grinned. "Perhaps I should go off and do an MBA or something, just keep studying until I get some kind of inspiration about a job."

Sadie chuckled. "Assuming you live at home with your parents, do you think they'd be willing to support you for another few years?"

Holly laughed out loud. "I doubt it! They love me, but I'm thinking they probably wouldn't want to bankroll me forever."

"What about taking a year off to travel—loads of young people do it. I've got a kid working for me at the moment who's planning to do that next year."

Holly pursed her lips, looking thoughtful. "You know, someone else suggested that. But I don't really have anyone in a similar position who could go with me, and I definitely would be too scared to do it on my own. The farthest I've ever been from home is Melbourne." She looked embarrassed. "Mum and Dad were always way too busy for us to have exotic holidays. Any time away we spent as a family was down on the Great Ocean Road, camping."

"I've never been," Sadie admitted and laughed at Holly's shocked expression.

"Seriously? It's like, just down the road, and you've never been?"

"I know." Sadie ran her hands through her hair and puffed out a breath of frustration at the memories that suddenly crowded her brain. Her parents "discussing" holiday plans—which meant her father dictating his ideas and her mother capitulating.

"My father has always been big on local politics. He's on the council, has been for years. He'd love to make mayor one day. It's his biggest ambition in life. So our holidays were always short breaks, nothing too far away from home, so that he was always available for all the 'important'—" she used her fingers to make air quotes around that word, "—stuff he had to do. And he *hates* the beach, with a passion." She snorted in derision. "I never saw the ocean until I moved to Manly."

Holly's eyes widened comically. "No way! You mean you never even did the hop to Geelong or Torquay?"

Sadie shook her head. "Crazy, huh?"

"Unbelievable," Holly breathed.

"So," Sadie said, after a moment. "No boyfriend to go travelling with?"

And the award for biggest fishing attempt goes to…

Holly looked at her, her expression for once unfathomable, and then looked away. "No." She paused. "And…no girlfriend either," she said eventually, her voice quiet and yet strangely loud in the space between them. When she dared to look back, Sadie couldn't help but smile.

"Okay. Me neither," she replied, and then wondered why she'd felt the need to give away that little nugget of information.

Holly smiled. The silence settled between them again. Only it wasn't uncomfortable. It was a natural pause in the evening, and they sat with it, watching people, observing interactions, hearing laughter and snippets of shared stories. Sadie let her mind gently focus on Holly's subtle revealing of her sexuality. Just as gently, she set it aside. For the moment.

Holly cleared her throat. "What time are you seeing your family tomorrow?"

Sadie sighed. In the last few minutes, she had almost forgotten the reason why she was back here. "Gran said any time after ten. My father's out for the day, thankfully. He and I need to avoid each other. We have...history." She didn't feel the need to elaborate on that. "So it'll just be me, Mum, and Gran. Should make things easier. I hope."

"Are you nervous about seeing your mum?"

Sadie shrugged, trying to portray an indifference she knew she didn't actually feel. "Yeah, I guess. Twelve years is a long time." She glanced up at the night sky. "I should probably get back to my room now," she said, standing. She didn't want the evening to end, but the day was catching up with her, and she was stifling a yawn. "I'm pretty tired."

"Of course." Holly rose and pulled on her jacket. "Sorry, I completely forgot how long a day you'd had. It's just... Well, it's been so good talking with you, sharing this evening with you." She looked up at Sadie, a shy smile on her face, her eyes honest and earnest.

"Yes, it has. Thank you. I don't think I would have liked to spend this evening on my own." Without thinking, she reached out and brushed Holly's fingers with her own. She saw, rather than heard, the brief intake of breath, saw the slight widening of her eyes, and inwardly cursed herself again. *Back off. Don't make this more than it should be.* She pulled her hand back quickly.

They walked back mostly in silence. As they neared the turn-off for the street where the hotel was located, Holly slowed her steps.

"I'm going straight home," she said, not meeting Sadie's eyes, and pointing vaguely farther forward in the direction they were walking. "Our house is about five minutes' walk that way."

"Shall I walk you home?" Sadie asked quietly. She wasn't comfortable letting her walk home alone at this hour, especially given what Judy had said earlier about her worries for Holly being out on her own.

Holly hesitated.

"Come on," Sadie said, assertively. "Let me." She wanted just five more minutes together, and quelled the voice in her head that told her she was giving Holly mixed signals.

Holly smiled, and motioned them down the street. "Okay, I accept." She grinned, and Sadie glowed at the pleasure written all over Holly's face.

After the brisk walk to Holly's home, they lingered a little awkwardly at the end of the pathway that led to the front door of the impressive two-storey house.

"Listen, about the run tomorrow," Holly said, after a few moments. "I will totally understand if you're not up for it after seeing your mum, okay? Just leave me a message at reception if that's the case."

Sadie was grateful for Holly's astuteness, her awareness that tomorrow was a huge deal for her.

She nodded. "Thanks, that's good to know. I'll see how I go."

Holly smiled.

"Well," Sadie said, shuffling her feet. "I'll hopefully see you tomorrow."

"Bye." Holly gave her a final, shy smile and then walked up the path.

Sadie waited until she was safely in the house, then quickly made her way back to the hotel.

Back in her room, she undressed and slid under the cool sheets. She texted Nic, telling her she was too tired to talk, and received an immediate answer.

Totally understand. Good luck for tomorrow, I'll be thinking of you. Call me after xx

Part of Sadie was itching to tell Nic all about her evening with Holly, and yet she was reluctant to verbalise it. She knew an element of that was denial—if she didn't talk about it, it wouldn't sound that big a deal. But partly it was because she didn't understand, herself, how she and Holly had connected so easily, so quickly, and she was scared to admit it out loud. Scared of what it might mean.

A few blocks away, sleep was the last thing Holly was capable of. She tossed and turned, twisting the doona until eventually she pushed it off her naked body in sheer frustration. She couldn't help replaying key moments from the evening through her mind's eye. Sadie's smile, their obvious comfort with each other, the spark that had lit a fire deep in Holly's belly at that briefest of touches as they stood up to leave the pub. If she wasn't careful, she was going to be in big trouble here.

Shit, who was she kidding? She already *was* in big trouble.

CHAPTER 8

The rain-soaked streets were busy with Saturday shoppers, and Sadie kept the bike at an even pace within the speed limit as she skirted the city centre and rode up Doveton Street North, heading for the golf course. Her family home was in a quiet street in Invermay Park, behind the course. As she pulled into the street, she slowed and eventually stopped some fifty metres from the driveway to the house.

To say she was nervous was an understatement of epic proportions. Her stomach was churning. Her hands were trembling, and her heart was pounding against the inside of her leather jacket. Underlying all of that was the sour taste of old anger coming to the fore. She was trying very hard to keep that down, but it was proving stronger than she'd anticipated.

There was sweat trickling down the back of her neck, but it wasn't that warm a day. She pulled off her gloves and looked at her fluttering fingers. A wave of nausea swept through her, and she swallowed hard. Looking at the driveway, she was instantly right back there. Saying goodbye to Izzy, getting in the car, ignoring her father. Wondering how her mother could have just sat there and said nothing. Done nothing. Suddenly, she was seventeen again and terrified. Angry. Numb. She pulled the helmet off her head and raised her face upwards, letting the soft rain cool her face, which was hot with the remembered shame and rage.

After a few minutes, she came back to herself, because her face was noticeably wet and cold. She reached into her jacket pocket for the soft cloth she kept there for wiping the helmet visor, using it to wipe her face instead. From the other pocket, she pulled out her phone.

Nicole answered on the third ring, sounding sleepy.

"Hey," she mumbled. "What's up?"

"Sorry, didn't mean to wake you," Sadie said quietly.

"S'okay."

Sadie heard her yawn, then her voice, stronger, was back in Sadie's ear.

"What's going on?"

"Shit, I don't know. I'm parked just down the road from the house, and I can't seem to get myself to go the last fifty metres to the front door." She huffed out a frustrated breath. "I thought I could do this, but now that I'm here, I really don't know."

"What is it that's holding you back? Can you name it?"

Sadie waited a moment, knowing if she admitted it, Nicole would know she had been bluffing all this time.

"Anger," she said eventually.

"Ah" was all Nicole said.

"What? That's it?"

"Mm."

"Jesus, Nic, I need more than that!"

Nicole chuckled. "I'm not trying to be difficult, okay? It's just, well, I'm glad."

"Glad? About what?"

"Glad that you're finally facing up to your anger. I've watched you bury it for years, and now it's coming out and that's a fucking good thing."

"How can it be a good thing? I'm… God, I'm ready to walk in there and just scream at her. How can that be good?" Sadie's frustration climbed. She didn't want to feel like this. Didn't want to be this angry person, ready to lash out at her dying mother. How could that be right or fair?

"Because it's good for *you*. Because you are the one who was treated like shit all those years ago and who has never let out all that she felt about it. God knows I've tried to get you to go and talk to someone over the years, but you've always fought me on it. You seemed to think that burying it all was the best way forward. But, in my humble opinion, it just made it a whole lot fucking worse. That's why I was on at you the other night on the phone about how if it was me, I'd let them have it. Both barrels, full-on. You need to do this, Sades."

"But, I can't. She's *dying*. How can I march in there and rip her head off? What would that make me?"

"Well, maybe you don't have to do it that way. Yes, she's dying. But this is the woman who stood by and let her husband kick you out of the house. She fucking abandoned you. What mother is supposed to do that? So what if she's dying? Your feelings are still here, aren't they? You still have to live with what she did to you. Why not get it out? Why not just tell her how you feel? And if you end up shouting a bit, so what? I mean really, so fucking what? Doesn't she deserve to know what she did to you?"

Sadie breathed out slowly and swallowed hard.

"Thank you," she said, after a few moments of silence, and then snorted softly. "You should have been a therapist."

Nicole chuckled. "Nah, somehow I only have the patience for your troubles. And you're welcome, by the way. Any time." She paused. "You gonna be okay?"

"Yeah," Sadie murmured. "I think so."

"Give my love to Elsie when you see her. I went by the house last night and watered the yard. Everything's okay there."

"Thanks, I'll tell her. Say hi to Tash for me. I'll call you later, yeah?"

"You better. I'm gonna need to hear how it all went."

"Sure." Sadie smiled, glad she *could* smile. "Later."

After sitting in the rain for a few more minutes, she finally hooked the helmet over her left arm and coasted the bike the short distance to the driveway. She pulled it up behind a shiny Mercedes C-Class and climbed off. She hesitated only momentarily before pressing on the doorbell. Her heart was still thumping away beneath her ribs, but she knew nothing would calm that down in the near future.

The door opened, and her gran smiled warmly at her. Sadie was overcome with emotion at the sight of her and stepped forward to pull her into a hug. Elsie returned it, her thin yet strong arms gripping on to Sadie's shoulders, despite the wet jacket.

"Hey, Gran," Sadie whispered. "I missed you."

Elsie patted Sadie's back and pulled away.

"I missed you too, love," she said, smiling again. She cocked her head, staring at Sadie. "Everything okay?"

"Oh. Yeah. I…wobbled a bit out there. I had a quick call with Nic to kind of calm down."

Elsie nodded. "Well, let me get you a towel, and you can take your jacket and boots off here. When we've got that sorted, we'll go through, okay?"

Sadie nodded, her gaze drifting around as Elsie wandered down the hallway. From what she could see so far, the house hadn't changed much since she'd last been there. The walls were a deeper shade of cream than she remembered, and the hallway table was new. But the layout looked the same, and, strangely, the house still smelled the same as she remembered. She wouldn't have known she'd remember something as innocuous as that until she stood there breathing it in.

Elsie soon reappeared with a dark blue towel, and Sadie wiped roughly at her face, hands, and hair.

"Ready?" The question jarred something in her stomach, but she quelled it and nodded.

Elsie turned and walked off towards the lounge room. Sadie followed, breathing deeply against the rising tide of emotions that were bubbling to the surface. Elsie pushed open the door to the lounge room. Sadie's gaze was quickly drawn to the woman sitting in a reclining armchair, a blanket over her legs, a magazine abandoned in her lap.

Christine Williams looked at least twenty years older than her age of fifty-three. Her blonde hair was thin and cut short, and her eyes were dull and lifeless. The skin across her cheekbones was drawn, and her once beautiful face looked sallow and…sad. She had lost weight, but that actually sat well on her.

They stared at each other in silent appraisal for a minute. Finally, Christine smiled weakly.

"Sadie," she said, her voice tremulous. "I'm so glad you came."

Sadie couldn't speak. Her pulse was racing, throbbing somewhere at the back of her head. She nodded and swallowed.

"Sit down, love," Elsie said from behind her, and she felt her grandmother's hand gentle in the small of her back. She took a couple of steps farther into the room and sat on the nearest couch, diagonally opposite her mother. This was…surreal.

"Would you like a coffee?" Elsie asked.

Sadie tore her gaze away from her mother to look up at her gran. "Coffee would be great," she said gratefully. "Do you need a hand?"

"No, I can do it." Elsie's glare pinned Sadie in place. "Christine, anything for you?"

Christine shook her head, still staring at Sadie.

"Okay, be right back," Elsie said brightly.

Sadie tensed as Elsie left the room. She stared at her mother, feeling more uncomfortable by the second and willing her grandmother to reappear. Inwardly, she chastised herself for her cowardice. *What is the point of coming here if I don't say what needs to be said?* Bracing herself, she opened her mouth to speak, but her mother beat her to it.

"You are so beautiful, Sadie," Christine said. Sadie's heart lurched. "My God, so beautiful." Christine's eyes watered over, and she raised a hand to wipe away the tears that fell.

Her mother's words stunned her; it was the last thing she was expecting to hear. At the same time, those words fired up the anger that was already lurking deep inside her gut. Did her mum think that was enough? That a simple compliment would suddenly make it all okay? Twelve years of pain and agony and heartbreak, and all her mum could think of was a meaningless statement about Sadie's looks?

Before she could rationalise it, temper it, or control it, she was standing again. There was a foul taste in her mouth; acid was burning her stomach, and a cold sweat broke out down the length of her spine.

"I honestly don't know what you expect me to say to that," she said sharply. "Is that supposed to make it all okay? You think some stupid bit of flattery magically makes it all go away?"

"No—"

"No, it doesn't!" Sadie's voice, its volume reflecting the years of pent-up anger, was overly loud in the small room. She raised her gaze to the ceiling momentarily, trying to get the rage under control and only just managing it.

Elsie walked into the room, carrying a tray. She quickly put it down on the coffee table and stood beside Sadie.

"Sadie," she warned gently, her thin hand clutching at Sadie's forearm.

Sadie shook her off and took one step closer to her mother, whose eyes were wide, her bottom lip trembling.

"I… You have every right to be angry," Christine said, her tone mollifying but her voice quivering nonetheless. "But please, can we just talk? There's so much to say."

"Sadie, please," Elsie said quietly from behind her.

Clenching her hands tight into fists against her thighs, Sadie sucked in a couple of deep breaths. For a moment, she'd wanted to run, get away from the intensity of this meeting. But if she did that, she knew she'd never come back. And then she'd never know.

"Okay," she said from between her gritted teeth. Forcing her jaw to relax, she stepped back. "Okay. I want to do this."

Relief flooded her mother's face. Sadie stumbled backwards to the couch and sat down again.

Elsie handed them each a cup of the coffee, and they sat back. Sadie took a couple of fortifying sips of the hot drink.

"I can see what I just said has upset you." Christine's voice sounded as tired as she looked. "I didn't mean to do that. I think I was just overwhelmed by you being here, by the realisation that I have a beautiful, grown-up daughter whose life I have missed out on for all these years." She paused, and Sadie saw her swallow hard. "I'm so glad you're here now."

Sadie exhaled slowly. "I am too." She hesitated before saying, "I-I'm sorry I lost my temper. Shouting at you isn't going to help."

Christine smiled wanly. "Like I said, you have every right to be angry. It's okay."

Shaking her head, Sadie shuffled to sit on the edge of the sofa, her hands gripping the mug they held. This had to be a two-way street. If they were going to talk, they had to *really* talk. Sadie couldn't shy away from the part she'd played in their history. "Maybe. But shouting is what he did to me all those years, and being like him is the last thing I want. And…" She paused, swallowing hard before she said the next words. "I gave you both a lot of heartache when I was younger, and probably a lot of your anger at me was deserved too."

"We could have tried harder. To understand. But…oh, there's so much to explain."

Sadie shrugged. "I'm here all week. We don't have to say it all today."

Elsie made a small sound of affirmation next to her, and she glanced around quickly to find her gran smiling warmly at her. She returned the smile, feeling some of her tension easing away.

When she turned back, Christine was staring at them both.

"It looks like you and your gran have a wonderful relationship," she said, the wistfulness obvious in her tone.

Sadie nodded. "We do." She caught herself before her tone became more scathing than would be helpful. "Gran's always been good to me."

Christine nodded, and Sadie saw a few more tears leak down her mother's face.

"She's always been a pleasure to live with," Elsie said, without malice, and Sadie's chest swelled with pride and love.

"You probably wouldn't think that, I guess," Sadie said quietly, looking at her mum. "But for some reason you couldn't see how much I'd changed by the time you…that night." She forced herself to speak calmly in spite of the conflicting emotions running through her. It would be too easy to just blame it all on her parents, no matter how bad their final decision had been. "I was really working hard to turn myself around. I did some bloody stupid things when I was younger. I appreciate now, as an adult, how much trouble that was for you. But it did really hurt me when you couldn't see the changes in me. I was trying, Mum, trying so hard to be a better person. To get an education. To keep myself out of trouble." She stopped as the anger threatened to swamp her again.

Christine shook her head. "I was blind to it. I can't even explain it now. I became so used to expecting the worst from you, I…I couldn't see anything else."

"I know, Mum, it's—"

"I know it's twelve years too late," Christine interjected. "But, I'm sorry." Her voice broke. "I'm so sorry for everything that day and for everything that led up to it. For everything I didn't say as I let him throw you out. Everything I should have done and didn't."

Christine's tears fell freely, and she made no effort to stop them. Sadie sat absolutely still on the couch, shocked at what she was hearing.

"I wanted that to be the one thing I said to you, if you visited. If nothing else, I wanted you to know that." Christine's voice was firm on that last statement, her fingers gripping the armrests of her chair.

To see this much emotion from her mother, this much regret, tore at Sadie. Why couldn't they have talked like this back then?

"I'm sorry, too, Mum." The apology hadn't been planned, but as the words left her mouth, the rightness of them lifted something in Sadie. Only by both acknowledging all that had led up to that fateful night could they hope to have a chance at redemption and reconciliation. "I'm sorry for causing you so much trouble. I never meant to. I think I just wanted to try and get your attention. I…I was jealous of Izzy, and how perfect she seemed to be in your eyes. So I lashed out and did the stupidest things possible to make you notice me. Only it backfired, because you just thought less of me instead." She could feel a sob threatening and hurriedly reached for her coffee to take a big gulp.

"Oh, Sadie," Christine said hoarsely. "I…I don't—" She broke off, her hands flying up to cover her face. Her body shook with her sobs, and before Sadie knew what she was doing, she'd pushed herself off the couch and was across the room. She knelt on the floor beside her mum's legs, wrapping her arms around her weakened body. She heard Elsie sob quietly behind them, but all she could focus on was how hard her mum was hugging her back and how good it felt. Their tears mingled on the blanket beneath them as they cried, and cried, for twelve lost years and a relationship they could never have.

After a few minutes, Christine gently pushed her away so that she could reach for the box of tissues alongside her chair. They pulled one each from the box and wiped their faces.

"Finish your coffee," Christine said gently. "And let me try and explain everything that went wrong back then."

Sadie stood and walked back to sit down on the couch. Picking up her mug in shaky hands, she took a few sips. It was difficult to swallow around the lump in her throat.

"Remember, you don't have to do it all today, Mum," she said quietly. "You look pretty tired."

Christine waved her hand. "No, I need to. You deserve to know it all." She wiped at her eyes again, then settled herself back against her chair. "I was obsessed with my place in our local society," she said, frowning. "I look back now, and I don't recognise myself. I'd always been a bit full of airs and graces, but somehow I'd just got completely carried away with it when he got elected to council. Up myself, I think Izzy called it."

Sadie chuckled, surprising herself at how natural that reaction was, despite what she was being told.

Christine sighed. "Is that true, what you said about being jealous of Izzy and how we treated you in comparison to her?"

Sadie nodded slowly. "Yeah. Izzy could do no wrong, because she was always smarter than me. When I didn't bring home glowing reports and grades, neither of you seemed that interested. Not even disappointed, actually, just not interested." She shook her head. "And you were both so busy with everything that meant something to you. Anything else I wanted to achieve, like basketball, you wouldn't give any energy to." The resentment in Sadie's tone was palpable.

Her mum flinched at the harsh words, but Sadie pressed on. Since they were having this exchange, it all had to be said.

"It's why I stopped playing—you were never around or willing to drive me to games, or practices. And he barely even knew I was alive." Sadie was amazed she could say all this without spilling over into a screaming rage again. But this version of her mother was so receptive to what she was saying, *wanted* to hear it, that Sadie's rage didn't need to come into it. Anger, yes—she couldn't shy away from that. But the deep rage she'd feared she'd express, like the one that had overtaken her earlier, had seeped away with her mother's openness, her simple yet powerful acknowledgement of all that she had done wrong.

"But I know, now, that all that bad behaviour did was just push you two further away from me, give you more ammunition to see me as the troublemaker. My school counsellor, Mrs Duncan, helped me see how self-destructive all that gang stuff was. I guess the problem was I never took the time to sit down and talk to you about what she was teaching me and what I was learning from it."

Christine shook her head. "I had no idea. But then, equally, I didn't pay enough attention to notice all the changes in you." She paused, pulling haphazardly at threads in the blanket with her fingertips. "Knowing what's happening to me now seems to have opened something up in my mind during the past week." She turned to gaze out of the window. "It's as if I've stepped outside myself, somehow, and I'm looking at me as if I am an observer, a reviewer of the life I've lived. And, God, I am not proud of some of the things

I've done." She turned back and stared at Sadie. "And the worst I've done is let him talk me into kicking you out. Abandoning you."

Sadie trembled, and heat flashed through her body. The word *abandoned* was her worst trigger. Suddenly she was back there in the kitchen, watching his red-faced tirade, her mum immobile and silent beside him. She stood as sharp anger knifed through her. Uncontrollable.

"You just sat there, Mum!" The words spilled out of her, her voice cracking with the effort not to shout. "You didn't say a word. Not one *fucking* word." She'd never sworn at home as a kid, and the word somehow amplified in the air between them. "You...you made me feel like I was *nothing* to you." Her voice cracked completely, and she struggled to continue talking. But she had to finish. "He stood there accusing me of s-something I didn't do, and t-telling me you'd both decided I had to go, and y-you said nothing! How c-could you do that, Mum? How could you—"

She stopped, her anger dissipating like a spent wave. Christine beckoned her over and Sadie went, her steps stumbling, her eyes unseeing. She was pulled into an intense hold, her mother's arms around her neck, pressing Sadie's face into her chest. Sadie's tears dampened the V of skin that was revealed by the opening of her mother's shirt. She was vaguely aware of her mum saying the words "I'm sorry," over and over again.

How long they stayed like that, with her mum rocking her, Sadie didn't know.

Eventually, pulling herself away from her mother's embrace, she excused herself to visit the bathroom. She washed her hands and splashed cold water on her face. Her emotions were all over the place, and she was exhausted.

When she walked back into the lounge room, there was fresh coffee on the table, and Elsie looked as if she'd spent some time composing herself too.

"Thanks for the coffee, Gran."

Elsie smiled and patted her arm.

The three women sipped their coffees in silence, until Christine broke it with a question Sadie least expected.

"So, do you have a boyfriend?"

Sadie stared at her mother. *What the—?*

She glanced at Elsie, who looked as bemused as Sadie felt.

She turned back to her mother. "Mum, I'm a lesbian. I told you that years ago."

Her mother's eyes widened, and she raised a trembling hand to her mouth. "But…but I thought…?" She shook her head.

"Thought what? That I only said it to piss you off?" Just when they were making such good progress, she thought wryly. She hadn't anticipated having to deal with this on top of everything else.

"Well… Yes." Christine's voice was tight. "And you were so young. How could you have known something like that at that age? And is that really how you want to live your life?"

Sadie snorted. "Mum, I knew when I was fourteen. And yes, it is exactly how I want to live my life." Oh great, her mother may yet turn out to be a homophobe. Perfect.

Christine's eyes widened further. "Fourteen?" she whispered.

"Yes." Sadie slumped back into the couch and shook her head. "So you never even believed me on that, either?"

Her mother had the grace to look embarrassed. "No. That element of you, your announcement about liking…girls, didn't play that big a part in his…our decision to move you to your gran's." She winced as Sadie let out a quiet snort. "Throw you out," she amended, breathing deeply. "We just assumed… Well, we assumed you'd said it because you knew we wouldn't like it. We didn't take it seriously. It was all your trouble with the police that made up our minds. He was just so driven in his goal to be mayor, he didn't want anything standing in the way of that. And I was so driven to be the perfect mayor's wife that I didn't argue with him."

Sadie shook her head. "And yet, twelve years later, he's still not mayor, is he?" She didn't keep the sarcasm out of her tone.

Her mum blinked rapidly a few times and cleared her throat before speaking. "Well, no. He's not." She shifted in her seat.

A light flipped on in Sadie's brain. "Oh, wait a minute. He blames *me* for that?"

Christine flushed slightly. "Well, let's be fair, Sadie. Your troublemaking really didn't help his reputation, did it?"

"I know I acknowledged my part in things, but are you sticking up for him? Even now?" Sadie was incredulous, half rising out of her seat in disgust.

"No! Don't be ridiculous." Christine sighed. "Sit down." She waited until Sadie did as she was told. "Sadie, I'm not defending him. He's... I've come to realise what an idiot your father is. I won't defend him. Not now. But really, the things you did..." She put a hand to her forehead and closed her eyes for a moment. "You caused us so much trouble."

"You know, half the things you thought I did were actually done by other kids," Sadie said, pushing her hands through her hair as frustration threatened to get the better of her again. "I just happened to be there." She held up a hand as her mother attempted to interrupt. "Yes, I know. Being there was bad enough. But the fact that you found it so easy to think that of me, every time. That hurt the most. No matter what I actually did or didn't do, you always thought the worst of me. I don't think you have any idea how that made me feel."

She did stand and paced across the room, trying to let out some of the angry energy that had built up again over the last few minutes. She shook her hands out, like a boxer preparing to go into the ring, breathing slow and deep to bring her heart rate under control.

"So," she said, turning back to face her mother. "You say you've realised what an idiot he is. Congratulations. Then why are you still married to him?"

Christine looked upwards briefly, flinching slightly at whatever she saw in Sadie's expression. "Life is funny, isn't it? Or cruel." She sighed. "I woke up at the start of this year thinking this was the year I'd do it. Divorce him." She met Sadie's gaze. "I spoke with a lawyer a couple of weeks ago, to talk preliminaries, then I had that follow-up at the hospital, to see what they'd found out about the headaches." She shook her head slowly from side to side. "And now, I'm...dying, and there really doesn't seem much point in wasting money, time, or energy on a divorce now, does there?"

Sadie stared at her, such sadness washing over her in that moment it took her breath away. She flopped back down on the couch.

"And, even more ironic, I was also determined to reach out to you." Her mum leaned forward in her seat, her expression fiercely earnest. "I'd been tempted so many times, but I always feared he'd find out. God knows what he would have done then. And so, along with a resolution to get divorced, I'd started composing a letter to you, to open up communication, see if I could convince you to let me come and visit. I wanted you back in my life, Sadie. I wanted my daughter back." Her voice broke. "I just wanted you back."

Sadie's body caved in on itself, releasing the tension she'd been holding in throughout the day. A good part of it leeched out by the words they had shared, the cleansing of so much that had gone before. It wasn't all fixed, not by a long shot, but it was a start. The sexuality issue they could deal with later. Right then, some of the most important words Sadie had needed to hear had been said.

The woman sitting across from her bore only a physical resemblance to the mother she remembered. Her personality, her demeanour, were so different from the woman Sadie had last seen twelve years previously. She knew people changed over the years, but she also knew that the shock of the diagnosis, how significantly it was changing the path her mother had set out for herself this year, had played a huge role in this transformation. Despite the circumstances, it was pretty good to meet this new Christine Williams. She was a woman Sadie hoped she could talk to, be honest with. She was a woman Sadie wanted to know more about.

And yet, they had so little time.

CHAPTER 9

When she saw Sadie pushing through the front door, Holly couldn't help herself standing just a little taller. She pushed her hair back off her face and beamed widely at the tired-looking woman who stood in front of her.

Their eyes met, and Holly saw the redness that rimmed Sadie's.

"Okay?" Holly whispered as Sadie continued to gaze at her.

Sadie nodded. "I…I'm tired. It was…hard, but it was worth it." Her gaze drifted away slightly and then back again. "I'm sorry, but I'm too tired for our run, I—"

"No, it's okay, me too. I'm really beat today. If I hadn't seen you now, I was going to leave you a note saying I couldn't make it."

Sadie smiled, a small smile, yet it tugged at something in Holly's chest.

"Okay, great. I don't feel so bad now."

They stared at each other. Holly saw something in Sadie's eyes she couldn't quite identify. All she knew was, it made her heart flutter.

"Do you have plans tonight?" she asked suddenly, into the silence.

Sadie shook her head. "I'd like to get a nana nap right now, but other than that, no. What did you have in mind? I have to be honest, as much as I would like your company, I don't know that I want to go anywhere with lots of people. Could we just maybe get pizza in my room or something?"

Holly smiled widely, unashamedly delighted that Sadie wanted to spend time with her again. "I can do a little better than that, if you like? My parents are out tonight, so I have the house to myself. I make a mean spaghetti carbonara, if you're interested?"

Sadie grinned. "That sounds like heaven. If you're sure it's not too much trouble?"

Holly shook her head, desperately trying to downplay her excitement at having Sadie all to herself. Alone. She immediately chastised herself—Sadie'd had a really long, emotional day. The last thing she'd need would be Holly getting carried away with her attraction for her. Mentally, she slapped herself. Outwardly, she rearranged her features into a friendly smile.

"It's no trouble. Do you remember where the house is?"

Sadie nodded.

"Okay, so how about seven thirty? Gives us both time to nap—God knows I need one too."

Sadie grinned again. "Sounds like a plan." She turned and started to walk towards the annexe, then stopped and looked back with concern written all over her face. "You sure your parents won't mind me coming over? I mean, your mum…"

Holly shrugged. "I don't see why they'd have a problem. I have friends over there all the time." Her eyes widened at the assumption inherent in that last statement, but she was immediately comforted by the pleased look that crossed Sadie's face.

"All right, then," Sadie said. "I'll see you a bit later."

Sadie's head jerked as her alarm went off. She'd been in a deeper sleep than she would have imagined. Although the day had taken its toll, her mind had still been spinning when she'd climbed into bed earlier.

She flicked off the alarm and leaned up on her elbows. The room was not quite dark; it was six thirty and the evening was starting to draw in. She lifted one hand to rub at her tired eyes. They felt sore, and she imagined they wouldn't look crash hot. She puffed out a breath. Oh well, it wasn't like she was hitting the town—the only person who had to look at her was Holly, and maybe it wouldn't be a bad thing if Sadie didn't look her best.

She knew the attraction between them was strong, and she'd finally realised this afternoon that it was totally reciprocated—Holly may have thought she was hiding it well, but she wasn't. Sadie chuckled softly to herself. No, Holly wasn't very good at hiding it at all. It was flattering, and it gave Sadie a warm glow to think that someone as gorgeous as Holly was interested her. But, Holly was too young, too seemingly innocent, and the whole situation was too… temporary. Sadie just couldn't bring herself to pursue it. Having someone to talk to this week, to just hang out with, seemed far more satisfying, somehow. It was also, she admitted to herself, safer.

She reached for her phone and saw the text message from Nicole she'd yet to reply to. She had thought about calling Nic when she'd left her mum's place. She'd ridden up to Mt Buninyong, but the peace and quiet she'd found up at the top—there were surprisingly few people around—had resulted in her just enjoying the solitude and time with her thoughts. She still had a *lot* of processing to do of everything she had shared with her mother.

She swiped through to Nic's number.

"Hey!" Nicole's tone carried a mixture of relief and pleasure at hearing Sadie's voice. "How's it going?"

"It's okay. There's… Well, I've got a bit to tell you, if you have time?"

"Go for it," Nic said, and Sadie could hear her whisper to someone, presumably Tash, and then the sound of a door closing. "I'm all yours, as long as you need."

"Thanks." She hesitated, not sure where to start.

"So, you made it inside the house, I take it. And you talked. Was it difficult?"

Nicole's peppering of questions made her smile. She exhaled as she composed what she wanted to say. "Yeah, it was, but kind of not, at the same time. It was good, mostly. She's changed so much. The diagnosis has changed her, she admitted that herself, but it seems like she's been waking up to a lot of stuff the last couple of years anyway."

She filled Nic in on the details of the emotional morning.

"And then she flat-out apologised for *everything*."

"Holy shit," Nic breathed. "I'd hoped that's what would happen, but I never really imagined it."

"Nor me. It… God, it really threw me. I'd gone there expecting to have to get into a big fight. And, I mean, there *were* harsh words, from both of us, but it was all right. They were things that needed to be said. I apologised to her, too. For being such an idiot all those years. It felt…right, you know? Good to admit that I could have done better too. Then we—" her voice broke as the remembered emotions flooded through her again, "—just ended up hugging and crying and talking so much."

Sadie heard a small sound and realised Nic was crying softly on the other end of the line.

"Oh, hey. Don't cry. Please."

There was a loud sniff. "Shit, I'm sorry. But God, I'm just so glad! So glad you have the chance to reconcile with her, but even more, so fucking glad she's accepted how wrongly she treated you. It's eaten me up all these years, how your own mother could do that to you. Did she explain why?"

"Yeah, kind of. I'll be honest, as much as it's good she's apologised, and I'm glad about that too, the explanation of it all still hurts. She says she was all wrapped up in trying to be the kind of wife a mayor would have, rather than being a mother. That still cuts deep, even though she says she's not that person now."

"Yeah, well, it would, wouldn't it? But, if she's willing to talk about it and get some kind of relationship and understanding with you now, before she dies, that's a good thing, yeah?"

"It is." Sadie paused, sifting through her emotions. "I guess I'm still raw from it. It isn't all fixed in one day. She seems to have a bit of a problem with me being gay. But, yeah, it does help that she clearly wants to have something more like a real mother-daughter relationship with me before she…goes. Hopefully we'll work through stuff. Hopefully she doesn't turn out to be a raging homophobe."

Nic sighed. "Let's hope. So what else have you done with yourself since you've been there?" Nic diverted the conversation in a way that made Sadie realise her friend knew she didn't want to talk about her mum anymore.

Sadie blushed and inwardly groaned. She couldn't *not* tell Nicole about Holly, but she braced herself for the comebacks.

"Well, I've kind of made a new friend."

"Friend?" Nicole's voice was laced with sarcasm. "I'm guessing this *friend* is female and gorgeous. Shit, you don't waste any time, do you?"

"Oh, ha. Look, it's not like that." Sadie laughed as Nicole snorted. "Okay, maybe a little bit like that." At this, Nicole laughed out loud. "Okay, shut up! Look, her name's Holly. She works on reception here—her parents own the hotel in fact. We just…connected, really quickly. We went for a run together after I arrived yesterday, then had tea and a couple of beers. And tonight she's cooking for me."

Nicole was giggling. "And how soon before you get into her pants?"

"No! Listen, it's not like that. Yes, she's gorgeous, and yes we are obviously both attracted to each other. But Nic, she's only twenty-two, I'm guessing fresh out of the closet. I'm not sure she's even been with a woman before, and I just…I just can't face adding any more stress to the week."

"Who says it would be stressful?" Nicole asked. "Can't you just enjoy being with her? When's the last time you had sex anyway—months now, isn't it?"

"Yeah, it is, but it's not like I can't live without it. What do you think I am?" Sadie couldn't hide the hurt in her voice.

"Hey, hey, I didn't mean it to sound like I thought you were some sex-starved loser! Or that that was all you needed to make you happy. I just thought, I don't know, that maybe something like that would help this week—switch your brain off, switch your emotions off, and just, you know, be physical."

Sadie knew the idea had some appeal, but somehow, thinking of Holly as just something physical didn't sit right.

"Yeah, I know what you mean. But not with this girl."

"Oh," Nicole said. And then, after a moment, "*Ohhh.* Okay, I get it."

"What does that mean?"

"You like her, don't you?"

Sadie felt herself blush again. "Yeah, I do. So I'm not going there, not when I'm only here temporarily."

"Okay, I get it. Sorry I pushed."

"No, it's okay. My fault, I should have maybe explained a bit more."

"Okay. But don't go getting your heart into any trouble now."

"I won't. That's why I'm keeping it just friendly. I can't risk anything else."

Sadie still felt a little jaded when she rang the doorbell to the O'Brien home just before seven thirty. The end of her conversation with Nicole was still ringing in her ears. Surely the sensible thing would have been to cancel this evening? If she was serious about keeping Holly at arms' length, keeping it only friendly, then having dinner alone with her at her house was probably the stupidest thing Sadie could be doing. Especially when her emotional defences were so weakened from the events of the day. But, at the same time, the last thing she wanted was to be on her own with her thoughts.

Holly smiled warmly when she opened the door, and Sadie felt it all the way down to her toes. *Friends*, she reminded herself, *just friends*.

She stepped into the house at Holly's invitation and let herself be led on a quick tour, not really taking in anything that she was seeing. Her senses were overwhelmed by the sensual perfume Holly wore, and the snug-fitting jeans that showed off a deliciously curvy ass and firm thighs. Holly had her glasses pushed up into her hair again, a look that Sadie found mystifyingly sexy. The short-sleeved top she wore skimmed her shoulders, and that collarbone looked so open to being kissed… Sadie mentally pulled herself up.

Stop. Now.

They ended up in the spacious kitchen, where a pan of pasta was simmering on the back of the stove, and an enticing aroma drifted from a smaller pan at the front.

"Smells fantastic!" Sadie enthused, taking position on a stool Holly gestured to at the breakfast bar.

"Thanks." A hint of a blush pinked Holly's cheeks. She pulled her glasses down onto her nose and turned to stir the sauce, asking over her shoulder, "So, do you feel rested from your nap?"

Sadie shrugged. "Some, I guess. Sometimes sleeping in the day makes it worse. I wake feeling all fuzzy in my head, you know?"

Holly giggled, an adorable sound. "Yeah, I know what you mean. Mine was good, though, I feel pretty awake now."

Sadie grunted. "Not sure I can say the same."

"Well, you don't have to stay long tonight, if you don't want to. I'll understand." Holly had turned around to face her, and her expression was sincere.

Sadie nodded. "Thanks. Let's see how I feel after eating. It's been a long few days, and I'm not sure I'll be that good company tonight anyway."

"I'll be the judge of that," Holly said quietly. She was staring intently at Sadie over the top of her glasses, her eyebrows pulled together in a small frown that seemed to dare Sadie to contradict her.

Sadie gazed at her, wondering again why she was putting this temptation in her path. Holly was so…lovely. Just all-round loveliness. Without a doubt, the most put-together woman Sadie had spent any time with in a very long while.

The urge to reach over and pull Holly into her arms, to experience what that body would feel like next to hers, was almost overwhelming.

"What?" Holly's confusion was obvious, her eyebrows scrunched together.

Sadie realised her face must have shown something of what she was feeling, and she blushed at being caught. "Sorry, ignore me. Just tired, and I keep drifting."

Holly stared at her for a moment longer, then shrugged slightly. "Perhaps I'd better feed you, then," she said, smirking. It broke the tension between them, and Sadie laughed, gratefully.

"Yep, come on, woman. I'm starving." She winked, and she felt her mood lighten as Holly's laughter rang around the kitchen.

Sadie woke as her head nodded down into her chest.

"Wha—?" she mumbled as her eyes popped open and she took in where she was. The heat of mortification scorched through her body. She was slumped on Holly's couch, her arms folded in front of her, a line of drool easing its way down the left side of her chin. Holly sat slightly farther along the couch. A movie played on the TV in front of them.

Holly turned to look at her and giggled. "I'm guessing you just nodded off."

Sadie pulled herself upright. *Okay, now I remember.* They'd eaten—fantastic pasta—and then, because Sadie was feeling jaded, Holly had suggested a DVD. Clearly they hadn't progressed that far into it before Sadie had drifted away. Jesus, how rude.

How embarrassing.

"Shit, sorry," she muttered, roughly rubbing her hands through her hair to try to wake her head up.

Holly waved off her apology. "No worries." She paused. "Look, maybe you should get back. You're obviously really tired."

Sadie stared at her. She could hear the hint of disappointment, but she knew she couldn't do anything to help that. She *was* tired. And staying would be a mistake, because her willpower was fading fast with Holly looking at her like she wanted to pull Sadie into her arms and kiss all her cares away…

"Yeah, I think I should." She stood, and stretched. "I'll just get my jacket." She walked out of the room before Holly could respond. As she slipped her jacket on, she was aware of Holly standing behind her in the doorway. She eventually turned to face her and saw Holly quickly mask the desire that her eyes had briefly held.

Yeah, staying would definitely be a mistake.

"What will you do tomorrow?" Holly asked hesitantly.

Sadie shrugged. "Not sure. I'm not going to the house again until Monday." At Holly's questioning look, she shook her head. "Long story."

"Oh. Okay." Holly's face fell.

"You're not at work tomorrow, are you?" Why had she asked that?

Holly shook her head.

"Well, how about you give me your number? Maybe we could meet up, do something." That little voice, the sensible one, was firmly chastising her in the corner of her mind, but she was just as firmly ignoring it.

"Sure," Holly replied. She sounded calm, but Sadie could see her hands trembling. "Sounds good."

They swapped numbers into each other's phones, and Sadie let herself out of the house with a last thank-you for the meal.

Holly shut the door behind Sadie and slumped against it. Shit, this was so hard. There was a sensible voice in her head telling her to just let this go. There was no point in wasting energy pursuing it. Sadie was only in town for a week or two. She had a whole life elsewhere, and Holly would only be a temporary interlude for her. But Holly couldn't help wanting to be that, if that's all she could have. Her attraction for Sadie was consuming her; she'd never felt like this, and she didn't want to stop. She wanted to act on it, to grab Sadie and kiss her. To feel those muscular arms around her, that body pressed up close to her own. She burned with it, and she wanted to know how it would feel to let that feeling loose. But a part of her feared it would leave lasting damage if she did.

Something told her Sadie would be a very hard act to follow.

CHAPTER 10

"What do you mean, you had Sadie Williams here for dinner last night?"

They were in the kitchen, the breakfast things cleared away. Her mum had been telling Holly about their meal out the night before, and Holly had casually responded with a comment on how she'd spent her evening.

Holly stepped back in shock. Her mum's face blazed with anger.

"What's so bad about that?"

Judy sucked in a breath. "Look, I know you told me not to judge her on her past behaviour, but she has, you know, got a bit of reputation. I'm just not comfortable knowing she's been in our house."

"What, you think she was going to steal the family silver?" Holly was beyond outraged, and her voice shook with her passion. "That is just the most ridiculous thing I've ever heard!"

Judy sighed and leaned back against the breakfast bar. "Look, it's hard to talk rationally with you about this. You've got rose-tinted glasses where she is concerned." She held up her hand when Holly made to protest. "Okay, I understand. You say she is different now. Fine. I just want you to exercise some…caution around her. You don't know anything about her and her life since she left here. I only know what she was like back then, and as much as I want to believe she's not that person any more, I would just be happier if you weren't spending so much time with her."

Holly cocked her head and folded her arms across her body. "Because she has a bad reputation? Or because she is obviously a lesbian?"

Her mother blinked rapidly and shifted slightly from one foot to the other. Holly knew she'd hit the target. Since coming out to her parents a few months back about her sexuality, she knew neither of them had yet to grow comfortable with it. She hadn't wanted to label herself but had settled on bisexual so they had something to name it by. Something they could roll their minds around.

They hadn't totally rejected her, but she knew they both couldn't help holding out for a Mr Right to come sweeping Holly off her feet.

"I know you're still struggling with this, Mum," Holly said, softening her voice. "But I'm an adult now. I can make my own choices, and yes, my own mistakes. You've brought me up to be able to make good judgements about things, and all I'm asking is that you respect me to do just that. Both about my own feelings and about other people." She met and held her mum's worried gaze. "Sadie Williams is not the girl you remember. She's a really caring, down-to-earth woman with a great job and a great outlook on life, from what I can see."

Judy sighed and held both hands up in submission. "Okay, you win. But I can't help how I feel. Since you told us about…well, about liking girls as well as boys, it's been…difficult. I want you to be happy, I do. I just…" She trailed off, then breathed out slowly, meeting Holly's eyes. Holly could see she was making a real effort to be understanding. "As long as you're careful, please?"

Holly nodded. "I always am. Please just give me a little credit on that, okay?"

Sadie woke slowly and immediately knew she'd slept better than she had in days. She lazily rolled over and grabbed her phone to check the time. It was eight o'clock, which would normally seem too early to rise on a Sunday when she had no plans. Considering she'd been in bed asleep by ten the night before, she was absolutely fine about the hour. Ten wonderful hours of uninterrupted sleep, and her body—and mind—felt heaps better for it.

She watched the local TV news while she munched her toast, and caught a weather forecast at the end. Yesterday's clouds and almost constant drizzle had cleared the area overnight. They were predicting a beautiful day, twenty-eight degrees and sunshine all the way. As she looked at the weather map on the TV screen, she suddenly had an idea. It grabbed hold of her and wouldn't let go, even though that quiet voice in the back of her mind urged caution.

Before she could let that voice talk her out of it, she reached for her phone and found Holly's number.

"Hey," Holly said, a little breathlessly.

"You okay?"

Holly giggled. "Yes, I just had to run from the kitchen to grab this before it went to voicemail. Seems like I really sprinted."

Sadie chuckled. "Am I interrupting your brekkie?"

"No, not at all. Just having a coffee and flicking through the paper. How are you?"

"I'm really good, thanks. Slept for ten hours!"

"Oh my God, that's so good! You so needed that."

"Yeah, tell me about it." Sadie paused, wondering if she should ask what she'd been planning to ask. She plunged on anyway. "So, I kinda had this idea. If you're not interested that's okay, but I was wondering if you'd be up for a road trip today?"

"Road trip?" Holly's voice came out a little squeaky, which Sadie hoped was from excitement, and not fear. "You mean, on your bike?"

Sadie chuckled. "Yeah, on my bike. You know how I said I'd never been down to the Great Ocean Road?"

Holly squealed in her ear. "Oh my God, are you *serious*? I would love to do that! Wow, that would be *so* cool!"

Sadie laughed in delight; Holly's enthusiasm was infectious. And completely adorable.

"Well, we have to cover off two problems first," she cautioned. "One, I don't have a spare helmet. And two, no idea where to go."

Holly laughed loudly. "Okay, neither helmet nor destination are a problem. My friend Kirsty is dating a guy who has a bike. I'll call her and see if I can borrow her helmet. If I can't, she's bound to know someone else who can lend me one. As for location… Well, if you're open to suggestions, my favourite spot is Lorne. It's not the biggest town down there, but Apollo Bay's got a bit busy the last few years, whereas Lorne has stayed a bit quieter. The drive down goes through part of the Otway Ranges, all forest and waterfalls. It's lovely. How does that sound?"

Sadie could visualise just how lovely that would be, and her soul yearned for something simple and beautiful from the day. "It sounds *perfect*. How long does it take to get down there?"

"Oh, probably about two hours. Is that too long?"

"Not at all, I love cruising on my bike. You ever been on one before?"

"Only once—Kirsty's boyfriend took me out for about twenty minutes. I loved it, though," Holly finished, quietly.

"Cool, then let's do it. When can you be ready?"

Holly revelled in the feeling of blissful contentment that permeated her every cell as she held on to the firmness of Sadie's body in front of her. Riding on the back of Sadie's bike, with this gorgeous woman so close, the warm wind caressing the exposed skin of her legs, the sun shining down on her back—all of it felt so perfect she didn't want their journey to end.

The small coastal town of Lorne was, however, only a few minutes away.

They cruised slowly into town and dropped down to the coast road.

"Your first bit of the Great Ocean Road," Holly called above the throaty purr of the engine. She felt, rather than heard, Sadie laugh.

Sadie pulled them into a parking spot at the visitor centre, and kicked the stand down as she killed the engine. After she'd locked the bike, they strolled the short distance into the centre of Lorne and into one of the bakeries. They smiled often at each other as they walked, and Holly was delighted to see Sadie so relaxed. Such a contrast to the exhausted woman she'd spent a short evening with the night before. They'd agreed to pick up a picnic and eat it on a reserve that Holly knew of just out of town. Set up on a rise, it had a great view back across the bay and town, and Holly had fond memories of lazy days there with friends from uni. She wanted to give Sadie just such a day.

After loading up with deeply filled chicken salad rolls, chips, and some water, they headed back to the bike.

"You okay to go straight to the reserve, or do you want to wander down to the beach first?" Holly asked, as they reached the bike. "Sorry, I probably should have asked that before we bought the food."

Sadie smiled. "No, this is great. I'm getting hungry, so lunch first overlooking the bay sounds great. Then maybe later we could come down to the beach."

"I'd like that," Holly said distractedly, marvelling again at the colour of Sadie's eyes, especially in the bright sunshine. The green was almost translucent in the sharp light.

Ten minutes later they were spreading their picnic out on a table in the reserve, a welcome arc of shade draped over them from the tree canopy above. They each gulped from their water, then shed their jackets before sitting down to eat. Holly took a moment to clip her hair back and to sneak a glance or two at her companion. Sadie was probably unaware of the impact her tight, sleeveless top had on Holly's libido, and Holly made every effort to keep it that way. But, oh God, those tanned arms, all toned muscle, were doing a serious number on her heart rate. The top sat snugly across Sadie's breasts, which looked firm and perfectly sized to fit in Holly's cupped hands. She deliberately kept her gaze away from Sadie's long legs in the low-slung jeans she wore. There was just something so unbelievably sexy about the whole look, it left Holly aching.

They ate in silence, but it wasn't awkward. Down on the beach, they could see surfers lounging around in-between taking turns in the waves, and families picnicking along the length of the sand.

Sadie scrunched up the paper her roll had been wrapped in.

"That was good," she said with a contented sigh. "Hey, maybe later we could get an ice cream."

Holly laughed at Sadie's childlike expression. "Sure, why not? It's your day out, after all—you get to call the shots."

Sadie smiled, and hesitantly reached across the table to briefly touch Holly's hand. "Thanks," she whispered. "I really needed this."

"You're welcome," Holly replied, equally quietly. They stared at each other for a moment, and Holly didn't know how Sadie couldn't hear her heart thudding in the space between them. Sadie's face was completely open, and for the first time, Holly truly believed the attraction between them wasn't one-sided. She'd thought Sadie had maybe looked at her that way over the last couple of days, but she hadn't been one hundred percent sure. Suddenly, it was abundantly clear. Sadie's eyes had darkened a little, and her mouth held a hint of a smile that warmed Holly from the inside out.

But, saying or doing anything about the attraction was a different matter. Holly knew that, despite her infatuation threatening to get the better of her. So she took a deep breath, squeezed Sadie fingers gently, and then let go. *Later.*

Sadie's smile widened, and she turned to face the ocean. Holly watched her breathe in deeply.

"Would you…would you tell me a little of what's going on?" Holly asked tentatively. "It's okay if you don't want to talk, but I guess… Well, I guess I don't really understand how you've been away from home this long. Or what you meant about not going to see your family today."

She saw Sadie's shoulders tense, just slightly, and then relax again before she turned back to face Holly.

"I don't really mind telling you, it's just… I'm not proud of the person I used to be, and I don't…" She looked up to meet Holly's eyes. "It's important to me that you not think bad of me." She blushed but held Holly's gaze.

Holly swallowed, blown away by the implication of that statement. Without thinking, she reached for Sadie's hand and, this time, held on to it.

"I doubt I would think that. Everyone has a past. It's who you are now that I like, who I want to spend time with."

Sadie nodded slowly, and a breathtaking smile formed across her features.

"Thank you." She exhaled audibly. "Okay, I'll give you the story, then."

Holly listened, entranced, as Sadie opened up to her about her teenage years, her trouble with the police and school, and her dreadful relationship with her parents once she'd reached a certain age.

"I think my father had almost convinced himself he'd got the son he wanted, when I was such a tomboy at ten or eleven. I'd do everything with him—helping him in the yard, washing the cars, fixing things." She frowned. "Then I hit puberty. Suddenly, I was so obviously *not* a boy, it's like something just switched off inside him. It was almost overnight too. One day he was my best mate, the next he wouldn't have anything to do with me."

Holly nodded sympathetically, still holding Sadie's warm hand, the fingers of which had curled neatly around her own without either of them realising.

"So how bad did it get—for you, I mean? Were you ever arrested?"

"Never quite that far. For all his bluffing about what a big man he was politically, he really did have some influence in town. He knew all the local cops, and they'd all look out for him as much as they could. They'd usually give me a bit of a talking to at the scene of whatever petty shit I'd got up to and then drag me home to face him."

"And what about your mum in all this? What did she do?"

Sadie winced and closed her eyes for a moment. "Completely ignored me," she murmured, and opened her eyes again. "Gave all her attention to my sister, Little Miss Perfect." Her voice dripped with sarcasm on those last three words.

"I don't think I realised you have a sister."

"Yeah, Izzy—Isobel. Two years younger and a total princess when we were teenagers. The joke of it is—and I have no idea if my parents know this, even now—Izzy and her mates actually set the fire that got me kicked out of home."

"No!" Holly clapped her free hand to her mouth. The injustice of what had happened to Sadie was eating at her, and she was in danger of commenting on things that were not her place to speak about.

"Yeah, crazy huh? I was out with…someone who couldn't alibi me." She hesitated, then blurted out, "A married woman." She looked up at Holly, perhaps fearing she'd see judgement, or disgust. Holly felt neither and sent a warm smile in her direction. Sadie visibly relaxed. "That night, someone saw me running from the fire and told the police. The next day, they told my dad, and when I got home from school, all hell broke loose. The next thing I know, I'm on a plane to Sydney to live with Gran."

"God," Holly breathed, squeezing Sadie's hand. "And now," she continued, "your mum is dying, and what, she asked you to come home and visit? I'm guessing you've had next to no contact with them since they kicked you out, from what little you've said about it so far."

"Yeah, you guessed right. No contact at all. They literally shut me out, completely. Gran has had some contact with them, but even though Mum is her daughter, Gran's really struggled to talk to her. Obviously, she thinks what they did was totally wrong. Not that she doesn't like me living with her—we get on great. It was just so wrong that they threw me out at that age."

Holly felt Sadie's fingers tense under her own.

"You're allowed to be angry," she whispered.

Sadie smiled weakly. "Yeah, I know. And I still am, despite how okay things went yesterday when I saw Mum."

Briefly she filled Holly in on the time she'd spent with her mother, and Holly's eyes welled up at the recounting.

"So, now I get why you won't go there today. He'll be home, won't he?"

"Yep. And he's the last person I want to see while I'm here. I'm going to avoid him completely if I can. Apart from letting rip about what he did to me, I don't have anything to say to him. And yelling at him isn't going to change him one bit, so I'd just be wasting my energy."

Holly nodded in agreement. "Yeah, I think you're probably right. What about your sister, though? Do you want to see her?"

"Hm, that's a difficult one." Sadie shrugged. "Part of me resents her for getting me into that mess, but I know she couldn't have foreseen that. Plus, being younger than me, it would have taken a lot for her to stand up to him. He was so intimidating. I mean, I was terrified of him sometimes, so there was no way she'd have been confident taking him on to try and defend me." Her face creased into a frown. "And, you know, regardless of what happened that day and whether she could have helped me, we weren't actually that close during our teenage years. So, I guess I don't know. What would we talk about?"

They sat in comfortable silence for a few minutes after that. Holly could see that Sadie was tired again, at least emotionally. She sat slightly slumped on the bench, and her eyes looked unfocused. Although Holly's curiosity burned, she didn't want to push. There'd be other opportunities, either later in the day or through the week. That they'd be spending more time together wasn't in doubt; the fact that they were still holding hands told her that much.

"It's really beautiful here," Sadie murmured. "Thank for you for suggesting this. Obviously, I don't know Apollo Bay, but I do love how relatively quiet Lorne is. Just what I needed."

Holly smiled, a satisfying warmth invading her chest. "Totally my pleasure, believe me."

Sadie laughed, suddenly. "Can we get ice cream now? Please?" She jigged up and down in her seat, and Holly couldn't help the loud guffaw of laughter that burst from her lips.

"Oh my God, what a big kid! Yes, all right, come on. Back the way we came, and we'll park up on the main road, if we can."

Sadie grinned and pulled Holly to her feet. To Holly's astonishment, and surging physical pleasure, she wrapped Holly into a hug. Stunned, all Holly could do was wind her arms around Sadie's waist and hold on, soaking up the exquisite feeling of being enveloped by this amazing woman's body.

"Thanks," Sadie mumbled against her hair, and a delicious shiver ran over every inch of Holly's skin.

Sadie sighed happily as she licked the last of her chocolate ice cream off her fingers. It always had to be chocolate; there just wasn't an alternative as far as she was concerned. She glanced round to see Holly watching her, her eyes wide and dark, her face slightly flushed. The temptation was to smirk, or comment, but she decided better of it. *Not here, not now. Maybe later...*

They were down on the beach, using their jackets as beach blankets. Sadie tried hard not to look at the tanned, bare skin of Holly's legs alongside her. Holly's cut-off denims showed off her shapely legs perfectly; the tight tee shirt she wore, in army green, showed off all her other curves equally well. It was a casual outfit, nothing spectacular, and yet she wore it like a second skin, oozing sex appeal. Holly had unpinned her hair, and it wafted around her face in the gentle sea breeze. As strands tumbled around her eyes, she would flick them casually away. Sadie watched each action with an intense craving she couldn't begin to identify. They were sitting close but not quite touching. The proximity of Holly's warm skin to her own was making goosebumps flash up and down her arms.

Being with Holly was so easy. Nothing had ever felt this easy. But the temporary nature of her visit to Ballarat was weighing heavily on her thoughts. As much as she was attracted to Holly, she needed to protect herself from more hurt. She'd been very good at that all these years, never letting anyone get too close, keeping her secrets. Only Nicole had been allowed to know the real Sadie. Even that had taken a while. The ease with which Holly had disabled Sadie's self-protection in two short days shocked her. A big part of her didn't want to let her in any closer as a result. The rest of her wanted to bury her face again in that rich, chocolate-brown hair, pull that body close to hers, and lose herself in what looked like the softest lips imaginable. Sadie would never have described herself as overly romantic prior to meeting Holly. She knew if Nicole could read her thoughts she'd be laughing up a storm at her best mate. But the woman sitting next to Sadie was bringing out some seriously gushy notions that she couldn't seem to curtail.

"So," Holly said suddenly, clearing her throat in a way that spoke volumes about how she'd been affected by the visual of Sadie's tongue licking her own fingers. "What shall we do now?"

"What are the options?" Sadie knew her own voice sounded croaky too and hoped her face wouldn't colour with her combination of arousal and embarrassment.

Holly blushed a little, her mind clearly taking her places elsewhere with Sadie's question. Again, Sadie resisted the urge to throw out a flirtatious comment. All it would take was one flippant remark to fan the fire that was smouldering between them, and for some reason, that scared her. Maybe, because she so badly *wanted* to set off that spark.

"Well, we could obviously sit here a bit longer. Or we could have a drink somewhere. Or, if you like, we could ride up to Erskine Falls, which is just out of town. It's very pretty up there. It means more time on the bike, though."

"Actually, that sounds nice," Sadie replied, thinking that at least if they were looking at gorgeous scenery, her mind would leave her in peace about how completely besotted she was becoming with Holly.

The ride up to the falls didn't take too long. Sadie enjoyed, a little guiltily, the feel of Holly pressed against her again. Holly's thighs tucked up so snuggly against her own was causing all sorts of fantasies to skitter through her brain. She was trying supremely hard to push them away and just focus on the road, which curved and climbed steadily higher up into the hills.

They parked and took the path that led to the upper lookout, winding their way through the ferns and trees. The air was lush and a little damp, as moisture from yesterday's rain evaporated off the vegetation and forest floor.

"Wow, it's like something out of *Lord of the Rings*," Sadie whispered, gazing at the scenery around her. Raising her voice any louder would intrude on the ethereal atmosphere.

"It's great, isn't it? We came here heaps when I was a kid. Apparently, I just fell in love with this the first time my parents brought me here. Every time we came down here for a holiday, I insisted on being brought back again."

"What age were you the first time?"

Holly paused for a moment, her eyes narrowing in concentration. "I guess about six?"

Sadie chuckled. "Yeah, somehow I'm not struggling to imagine you as a feisty little kid who knew what she wanted and wasn't going to take no for an answer!"

Holly stared at her. A slow smile formed on her lips. She nodded imperceptibly, and her gaze flicked to Sadie's mouth and back again to her eyes.

"Yeah, that's me," she said quietly, but in a tone that hinted strongly at the heat that had been simmering between them all day.

Sadie swallowed, suddenly feeling like she was way out of her depth in a game she didn't know the rules for. Holly might be young and inexperienced, but oh God, could she play the seductress when she wanted.

Holly smiled again and focused on the path ahead of them. Sadie fell back into step beside her, trembling. Jesus, she was so close to grabbing this woman and just—

"So," Holly said, breaking into her thoughts. "This is the upper lookout." She threw her arm out like a TV game show hostess, and Sadie grinned.

The view was blocked a little by the trees, but she could still see the ribbon of water that cascaded some thirty metres down to its pool below. It wasn't a huge flow, which wasn't surprising given the time of year, but it was still very pretty. She could see why Holly loved it here. Birds sang and trilled nearby, and the sound of the falling water was a soothing background to the view across the lush forest around them.

"Nice," she breathed. "Thanks."

Holly hooked her hand through Sadie's arm, the intimate contact shooting Sadie's temperature up by a few degrees. She was suddenly tinglingly aware that, for the moment, they had this lookout area to themselves.

"You're very welcome," Holly murmured. Suddenly, she was in front of Sadie, placing her other hand on Sadie's waist, just inside her open jacket. The heat from her fingers burned through the cotton of Sadie's tee shirt to her skin below. She was having difficulty breathing and didn't dare look at Holly. When she did, because her eyes just wouldn't obey her instructions not to, the fire in Holly's eyes left her completely breathless.

"I don't want to wonder anymore," Holly whispered, moving ever closer, her thighs touching Sadie's.

"W-wonder what?" Sadie wondered where her normal composure had gone.

"What this would feel like." Holly closed the last few centimetres between them and touched Sadie's lips with her own.

For the briefest of moments, that was all she did, just touch. And then she moved her lips tantalisingly slowly across Sadie's, and Sadie's hands moved of their own accord, up into Holly's hair, grasping soft handfuls as she pulled Holly in. Holly groaned as Sadie brushed her tongue against Holly's bottom lip. In the next moment, Holly opened her mouth and let her in, their tongues colliding delicately in a hot, wet tangle that turned Sadie's knees to jelly. She sank into it, her hunger increasing exponentially with every minute they kissed. Holly moaned quietly every few moments, and it was quite possibly the sexiest sound Sadie had ever heard.

Like a cold bucket of water being dumped on them, noisy voices drifted from the pathway behind them, and they rapidly pulled apart. They stared at each other, their chests heaving, both of their faces flushed. Holly's eyes were hooded, and Sadie suspected they matched her own exactly.

Holly stepped back just as the loud family group appeared, but left her arm linked through Sadie's. Sadie wondered if she needed it for balance, because if Holly's knees were shaking even half as much as Sadie's, she would understand the need for an anchor.

They stood for a few moments, ignoring the other people, neither of them looking at each other. When the family moved off a couple of minutes later, Sadie carefully extricated herself from Holly's gentle grip.

"I…that…" She trailed off, not entirely sure what it was she wanted to say. A myriad of thoughts swirled through her brain.

Holly's intuition seemed to kick in instantly, and she stepped back slightly, giving Sadie some room.

"I'm not sorry," Holly said quietly. "But equally, I'm not going to push if it's not something you're ready for. I can tell you're…conflicted."

Sadie nodded, looking away. "I think…it's obvious I'm attracted to you. I just…" She waved one hand vaguely in the air between them. She didn't know what to do with this, whatever it was, between them. Especially if Holly was only just coming into her sexuality. "Can I ask you something?"

Holly nodded.

"Have you ever been with a woman?"

Holly smiled, and chuckled softly. "Yes. More than one." She made to reach out a hand and then stopped, still respecting Sadie's need to maintain a physical distance. "You are not my experiment. That's not what this is about."

Sadie exhaled. "Good. Because this is…complicated…enough, for me, without that in the mix." She smiled wryly.

"I know." Holly's voice was a soft caress.

Sadie met her gaze and saw that understanding had replaced the desire from minutes earlier.

"But just for the record," Holly continued, "I want to see what we can make of this. If you're interested. So, just keep that in mind, okay?"

Sadie could see it took some effort on Holly's part to sound so casual about it, and on the one hand that made her feel better. She definitely wasn't alone in this. On the other, she worried about just how far in she was likely to get, and how quickly. And how painful it would be to walk away from that at the end of the week. Because she would *definitely* be in danger of falling into something that would be difficult to walk away from. Holly was just too much of a temptation, both physically and emotionally, for that not to happen.

CHAPTER 11

Sadie pulled the bike up onto the driveway alongside the Mercedes. It was just before eleven, later than she'd planned to be at the house, but she had overslept. It had taken her quite some time to get to sleep the night before—memories of the day with Holly, especially the kiss, had left her tossing and turning before sleep finally claimed her.

Her mum greeted her at the door, which was a surprise.

"Hello, darling," she said, smiling widely.

"Hey," Sadie responded slowly, not sure how to handle the term of endearment. She wasn't sure her mother had ever called her darling when she was younger. "You're okay to be up and about?"

"Yes, I am. I've rested a lot this weekend. And," she motioned for Sadie to follow her into the house, "after seeing you on Saturday, it seems as if I feel a little…lighter." She turned to gaze at Sadie warmly. "You did me good, I think."

Sadie swallowed down the emotion that suddenly threatened to engulf her again. She nodded in acknowledgement of the words, and saw her mother smile in recognition of the moment and its effect on Sadie.

"Coffee?" Elsie's voice came from down the hallway, and Sadie looked past her mum to see her grandmother smiling at her from the kitchen.

"Thanks, Gran, that'd be good."

They all settled in the kitchen with mugs of coffee on the table in front of them.

Sadie looked at her mother and noted the brightness in her eyes, the improved colour in her cheeks. She looked good, amazingly better than on Saturday.

"So what did you get up to yesterday?" Christine asked.

Sadie cursed the blush that shot across her cheeks at her mother's innocent question. She cursed even harder when she heard Elsie snort.

"Got something to tell us?" Elsie's face was radiant with her pleasure at catching Sadie out. And she was clearly enjoying stirring things up, as Christine shuffled in her chair, looking distinctly uncomfortable.

Sadie sighed and glared at her grandmother. "I went for a long ride on the bike." Her tone was shorter than she felt comfortable with, and she winced as Elsie frowned.

Sadie exhaled. "It's just...complicated." Talking in front of her mum about her potential involvement with Holly was a prospect that filled her with nerves. She'd need more time to feel comfortable around her mother before she could divulge that level of detail about her private life. Especially when she wasn't sure how easily her mum could accept her sexuality.

Elsie thankfully turned the conversation onto a new subject without further comment.

"We met that new boyfriend of Izzy's yesterday," she said, and Sadie giggled as her gran's nose crinkled in disgust.

"Oh, yes." Christine made an indelicate sound. "That was an experience."

"In what way?"

Christine sighed. "Your sister has always had a...questionable taste in men, but this one was something else." She paused. "He's...well, he has some rather interesting views on a lot of topics."

"That's one way of putting it!" Elsie exclaimed. "Don't know what she sees in him."

Sadie smiled. "How serious is it?"

"Oh, it's really new, only about a month," Christine said. "I...well, I shouldn't really say this, but I have high hopes it won't last too much longer. Even Izzy seemed to be embarrassed by some of the things he said. I don't see it working out."

Elsie had occasionally filled Sadie in on news of Izzy, but she realised she knew next to nothing about her sister's life.

"What about you, Sadie?" Christine said after a moment. "Anyone special?"

Sadie could tell it took a lot for her mum to ask, and she appreciated the effort, even if she wasn't ready to share that much just yet.

"No one, really. I never... I wouldn't have made a good partner for anyone. I've had a lot of fun with my friends, and I've had the occasional girlfriend."

She noted the slight wince from her mother at the word. "But…stuff from the past has made…well, it's made it hard for me to let anyone close, you know?" The honest response was not something she'd planned to reveal, but it felt right to put it out there.

Christine nodded, tears in her eyes. "Can that change for you, do you think?" she asked quietly. Sadie stared at her. The question seemed to have been delivered with genuine concern. And without any implication that Sadie's sexuality was the cause of any problem Sadie had with relationships. Maybe there was hope yet.

The corners of Sadie's mouth lifted as thoughts of Holly flashed into her mind's eye.

"Yeah, maybe," she said.

They had lunch at the Lake View Hotel, sitting out on the covered deck with an oblique view of Lake Wendouree across the road. Sadie had driven the three of them down there in Christine's Mercedes, admiring the luxury and performance of the vehicle as she drove. Her mum had surprised her with her response to Sadie's compliments about it.

"Not my choice!" she snorted. "Your father bought it for me last year. Thought I needed something more 'appropriate' for the wife of a politician. I wanted a cute little hatchback, just for running around town, and he suddenly appeared with this. Complete waste of money."

Sadie smiled and caught Elsie's eye in the rear-view mirror, smiling even wider at her gran's disdainful expression.

They ate a slow lunch, talking about Ballarat in general and how much it had changed since both Sadie and Elsie were last there. Twice, they were interrupted by people Christine knew, all offering their sympathies for her diagnosis. One couple cast a sidelong glance at Sadie, their faces indicating recognition. A quick glare from Sadie had them backing away without comment. Christine accepted each person's words gracefully, even as her hands shook.

"You okay, Mum?" Sadie gently wrapped her fingers over her mum's forearm after the second group of people had finally walked away.

"I'm fine, darling. But, thank you."

They sat like that for a few moments, looking at each other, warm smiles on both their faces. Sadie's emotions were still a confused jumble, but moments like this they were sharing were helping to bring some order to that jumble. The calm was a balm to her fractured soul.

When their plates had been cleared away and coffees ordered, Christine turned back to her and reached for her hand.

"Now, I'm not trying to nag," she began. "But I was wondering if you had given any more thought to seeing your sister while you are here?"

Sadie looked away for a few moments. It was still a difficult concept to get her head around, given how things had been left between them. They'd had no contact since she left. She had thought that maybe Izzy would reach out with a call or an e-mail, but nothing had been forthcoming. Stubbornness meant that there was no way Sadie was going to make the first move, so they hadn't communicated in any way for twelve years.

"Would she want to see me?" Sadie turned it around, finally looking back at her mum. "I admit I haven't made any attempt to contact her over the years, which I realise now was probably pretty stupid. But equally, she hasn't reached out to me in all this time, so I'm not really sure she'd be that interested."

Christine sighed and sipped at her coffee for a few moments. "She has changed, especially in the last couple of years. She never really spoke about you, after you…left, but she did kind of withdraw for a few months straight after." She sat back in her chair, her hands twisting in her lap. "Shock, I suppose. But in the last year or so, she has asked about you, asked if I know how you are doing. She's seen things change between me and your father. She's aware of how unhappy I've been, even though we haven't exactly sat down and talked about it outright." She smiled weakly. "And, you know, she's led her own life. She's had her ups and downs, so she's much more mature and aware of other people's lives and problems. Much more so than when she was younger."

"Mm, that much I noticed too," Elsie chipped in. "Nowhere near the princess she used to be."

Christine looked shocked, and a giggle burst out from her lips. "Yes, well, we didn't do a good job of getting on top of that when she was young enough for it to make a difference." A deep frown creased her brow. "Another mistake we made in our selfish pursuit of his political career."

She met Sadie's gaze with regret written all over her face.

Sadie lifted one shoulder. "You can't change the past, Mum. At least you're making moves now to make up for it."

"Bless you," Christine whispered.

"So, in answer to your original question," Sadie continued, "I guess my answer would be, if Izzy wants to meet me this week, then yeah, okay, I'll give it a go." It would feel strange, she imagined, but she was there to make sure she had no regrets going forward. She may as well tick her sister off that list if she could.

After their lazy lunch, Sadie drove them back to the house and said her goodbyes for the day to ensure she was out of the house long before her father came home.

Christine hugged her close at the door. "It is so lovely to be sharing this time with you," she said. "Thank you, again, for coming back to Ballarat to see me."

"You're welcome." Sadie smiled, her heart full of a new kind of joy at what was happening between them. "It's really good to be here. I'll come back tomorrow, yeah?"

"Please do, he'll be out all day again."

She rode back into town with her thoughts rapidly transitioning from the time she'd just spent with her mum to the time she was going to spend with Holly. She'd managed to relegate Holly to the back of her mind during lunch, but images of her were starting to bombard Sadie from all angles. They already had their arrangement to go for a run, and Sadie was happy to do that, but she wasn't sure she could handle any more. As much as she'd enjoyed their day yesterday, she needed some time to herself. She tried to tell herself she wasn't really running away from what Holly was so obviously offering.

Holly heard Sadie's bike pull up in the car park outside. She tried to stop the fluttering that instantly invaded her chest and laughed at herself. Oh God, she was in such a mess over this woman, and she'd only known her three days. Crazy.

Sadie strolled through the front door, and a big smile spread across Holly's face at the sight. Sadie returned the smile, but at the same time Holly could see an uncertainty in her eyes.

"Hey," Holly greeted her, keeping her voice as neutral as possible. "How was your day?"

Sadie nodded. "Good, thanks. Mum was up and about—we went to the Lake View for lunch. It was…good. We talked some more."

"Nice." Holly paused, unsure how to proceed.

Sadie saved her. "Still up for a run when you finish?"

Holly's smile was wide again, but she tamped down the excitement that flared. "Definitely. Happy to do the same route?"

"Yep, no problem. I'll come back here at just after five, yeah?"

"Perfect."

She watched Sadie walk off to her room, and took a deep, calming breath. So, they'd at least be running. She wondered how hard she'd have to work to get Sadie to agree to a drink or even tea as well. Something told her it would be a battle, and although she thought Sadie was worth the fight—and God knows she wanted to pick up where they left off with that kiss the day before—maybe pushing Sadie too hard too soon would only backfire on her.

She worked out the rest of her shift and rushed off to get changed into her running gear as soon as Matthew appeared to take over for the evening. She was stretching at the outside wall when Sadie appeared, looking more relaxed than when she'd returned to the hotel earlier. Sadie said a quick hello, then started her own stretches. Holly noted how far she kept herself away from Holly as she did so.

Yeah, maybe there would only be the run.

After a few minutes of silent stretching—and stretched silence—Sadie caught her eye.

"Ready?"

Holly nodded, not trusting her voice to come out without revealing her own uncertainty about where they were. She headed up the street at a gentle jogging pace, and waited for Sadie to fall in beside her before upping her speed.

They ran in total silence, and it wasn't comfortable. The farther along the route they travelled, the worse Holly felt. Eventually, about a kilometre from the end, she couldn't stand it any longer.

"Are you okay?" she asked.

Sadie glanced at her, then away again, not breaking stride.

"I'm fine."

The words came out clipped, and although Holly suspected—hoped—that whatever frustration lurked behind them wasn't directed at her specifically, it still hurt. She ran on for a couple more minutes, and then her own frustration and confusion boiled over.

"Look, I'm not going to apologise, you know."

Sadie whipped her head round to stare at Holly, almost losing her balance in the process.

"What do you mean?"

"For yesterday. The kiss. I'm not going to say sorry."

"I-I wouldn't want you to," Sadie replied, sounding genuinely confused.

"Right, so this cold shoulder you're giving me is nothing to do with that, then?"

Sadie slowed, then stopped. Holly pulled up beside her, hands on her hips, her breath expelling in angry chops. They stared at each other for a moment.

Sadie broke the deadlock.

"It's not about that. Well, not totally. I just… I've had a very emotional time since I got here. I just really need some time to myself. Maybe I shouldn't have agreed to the run. I'm sorry."

Holly exhaled, shutting her eyes for a moment in an effort to will away the annoyance she had felt only moments before. She was being irrational and unfair, and she hated it.

"No, I'm sorry," she said, shaking her head. "I should be more understanding, less…selfish. I guess I'm scared that I've blown it, that I pushed too hard with the kiss yesterday."

Sadie blinked rapidly a few times and seemed to be struggling with how to respond.

"Don't," Holly said, after a tortured moment, holding up a hand. "You don't have to say anything. Let's just get back to the hotel."

Embarrassment was consuming her. She'd clearly overestimated the impact of the kiss on Sadie. It had obviously not affected her quite as much as it had herself, and she was in danger of making a huge fool of herself. She turned and took off again, not really caring if Sadie followed or not.

In a few long strides, Sadie was beside her. To Holly's surprise, Sadie reached out a hand to grab her forearm, pulling her to a sudden stop.

"Holly," she said, and the ache in her voice sent a shockwave through Holly's body. She stared at Sadie, meeting her eyes and almost flinching at the depth of hurt she saw there. "Please, believe me, it's not about you, about what happened between us yesterday. I just have so much to think about at the moment. I really do just need some space. I didn't mean to hurt you."

"Are you sorry I kissed you yesterday?" Somehow she couldn't let that go. She had to know they felt the same about this.

Sadie shook her head. Her fingers, still wrapped around Holly's arm, stroked her skin softly, generating a level of heat in Holly's body out of all proportion to the actual contact between them.

"No, I'm not." Sadie's eyes darkened for just a moment, and Holly wondered if she too was remembering how incredible their mouths felt when merged together. "I just don't have space to think about it right now. Please, just give me some time."

Holly swallowed and reached out a tentative hand to stroke the side of Sadie's face. Sadie's eyes closed. Holly felt her tremble, and she understood, right there, that the kiss *had* impacted Sadie just as much, that she too wanted more. Her heart leapt.

"Of course," she whispered. "Take all the time you need. I'm here, whenever you want to talk, or run, or...whatever."

Sadie leaned in, ever so briefly, to Holly's touch, then backed away. "Thanks," she said. Without another word, they resumed their run.

"Home for tea?" Judy asked, as Holly wandered into the kitchen.

Holly nodded and helped herself to a piece of raw carrot off the chopping board. Her mum playfully slapped her wrist.

"Don't steal the ingredients!"

Holly giggled, and Judy smiled.

"You seem...better than you were earlier. You okay?"

Holly smiled and found herself blushing a little. "Yeah, sorry about earlier, I was in a bit of grump. And yeah, I'm feeling much better now, thanks."

"Anything you want to share?"

Holly pondered that for a moment. Her mum sounded casual, but the tense set of her shoulders said something else entirely. Presumably, she'd guessed it had something to do with Sadie, given that she knew they'd shared a day out together yesterday. Was Holly really ready to talk to her about Sadie and what seemed to be happening between them? What if it did just turn out to be nothing, or just a one-night stand? That wasn't what Holly wanted, but she had to acknowledge it might be all that Sadie could offer. Was it worth getting into a difficult conversation with her mum if that's all it became?

"Nothing special," she replied. "Guess I just got out of bed on the wrong side." She left the kitchen before her mum could respond.

"Dinner in twenty minutes," Judy called after her.

She walked back to her room and flopped onto her bed, puffing out a big breath. She thought back to the morning and the bad mood her mum had made reference to. Holly had woken up anxious. Fearing she'd pushed Sadie too hard by kissing her, despite how…enthusiastically Sadie had responded to her ambush, Holly's mood had got bleaker by the minute.

Now, yes, her mood had improved, based on that exchange she and Sadie had shared towards the end of their run. Sadie was all she could think about. That dilemma about her job, her career, her future, had all been pushed so far back in her mind, she'd forgotten what she was worrying about in the first place.

The pragmatic part of her was frowning at her almost adolescent obsession with the woman. She was more than this, she knew that. She'd always scoffed at those people who ended up so wide-eyed over their romances that everything else paled into insignificance. Yet, there she was, travelling that road far easier than she would ever have imagined.

It kind of annoyed her. She'd prided herself on her maturity, her level-headedness, for years. But she was coming apart at the seams over some… woman.

Crazy.

CHAPTER 12

"I never liked the way you just let Peter take over," Elsie said. Her voice was hesitant, as if she felt she had no right to say what was on her mind. "But you were so sure he was what you wanted."

They were drinking tea in the Convent Gallery in Daylesford, an afternoon trip that had opened up memories of the past to the time when Christine had first started dating the man who would become her husband.

"You never said anything." Christine looked shocked.

"Didn't think it was my place," Elsie muttered.

Sadie watched the interaction between them with interest.

Christine held her mother's hand. "Well, perhaps you'd have saved us all a lot of heartache if you had said something," she chided gently. "You just let me get on with it."

"You say that now, love, but you wouldn't have listened." Elsie snorted, but there was humour in her eyes. "You can't blame me now."

Christine smiled and nodded. "I know. And I don't mean this to sound like I'm deflecting my share of responsibility in all this, but after Dad died, Peter was what I needed. Strong. Dependable. Knew where he was going. I literally hung on every word he spoke." She shook her head. "That all seems so long ago now."

"Well," Elsie said, "to give him his due, he was very handsome, and he was on the up. And he was totally smitten with you, that much was obvious to all of us." She patted her daughter's arm. "Don't torture yourself with regrets. Not now. Use your energy for other things. More positive things." She glanced at Sadie.

Christine followed her gaze, and smiled warmly at Sadie, who blushed under their joint attention.

Sadie spoke to Nicole after leaving her mum's house later that day, finally opening up about how things had progressed with Holly and her dilemma over whether to pursue them or not.

"Try and explain to me what's holding you back," Nic prompted. "Is it because you're only there temporarily? Because, you know, I don't think she's proposing marriage just yet."

Sadie smiled, in spite of herself. "Yeah, okay, I know that." She closed her eyes and took a deep breath. "She gets me. She doesn't care about my past. She really likes who I am, I think. I've never had that, and I want that—God, I really do. But how can I have it with her when we live so far away from each other? If I give in, if I open myself up to her… Nic, I could really fall for this woman. Then what? Then we have to manage some long-distance thing that has so much stacked against it."

"But you don't know that! You may not fall for her. You may have a quick fling and that's enough. Or you may fall for her and the distance thing doesn't make that much difference. Or it does and you have to make some changes to make it work. Do you see what I'm saying? If you spend your whole life not getting involved with amazing women because of what might or might not happen in the future, all you're gonna have is just a whole lot of lonely time. And I don't want to see you go through that, Sades."

When she returned to the hotel, Holly was on the front desk. Judy hovered just over her shoulder as they discussed something on the screen in front of them.

Holly glanced up as Sadie pushed through the door, and her smile lit up the room. She laughed as Sadie shook herself off like a wet dog onto the doormat beneath her feet.

"Get a little wet, did you?" she asked, and then a hint of a blush stole across her cheeks.

Sadie couldn't help but smirk. "Very," she said, lowering her voice a touch and winking. Okay, so she was outright flirting with Holly. *When did this start?*

Holly cleared her throat, casting a quick glance at her mother, who seemed oblivious to the interaction.

"I'm guessing we won't be running tonight?"

Sadie shook her head. "No, it's way too wet for that. I don't mind running in a light rain, but it's pouring down out there." As if to emphasise the point, she brushed copious liquid off the sleeves of her jacket onto the doormat.

Holly shrugged. "Oh, well. We've done pretty good this week, so one missed day isn't so bad."

Sadie nodded and headed to her room—Judy was giving her the evil eye, and she didn't need to deal with that while she was standing there soaking wet.

She had just finished drying off her hair when her phone buzzed on the bedside table. Picking it up, she trembled slightly when she saw a message from Holly.

How about a drink tonight?

She stared at those five words for a few moments. Holly was pushing, ever so slightly, and Sadie couldn't blame her. The flirting would have sent a very new signal Holly's way, and she had—bravely, Sadie acknowledged—picked that up and run with it.

Actually, Holly had been brave all along. Unlike Sadie. All Sadie had done was run, except for that weak moment by the waterfall. But actually, that wasn't weakness. It was what she'd wanted. Still wanted. Yet she was trying—and failing—to come up with reasons why she shouldn't pursue what it was she really wanted.

It was time for a leap, to take a chance on something that had the potential to bring her a lot of happiness. Or a lot of pain and disappointment, but for once she was going to try to live for the moment, not second-guess the future.

Sounds good. What time? she messaged back, and a grin split her face.

Hop Temple was packed. Happy drinkers of all ages squeezed around the tables of the warehouse bar dedicated to all things beer. The lights were low, the noise level high.

"Jesus, I didn't think it would be this crazy in here!" Holly raised her voice and it enabled Sadie to hear her over the background thrum. "Although, I just heard someone say the food trucks are out back, so that might explain it."

"Food trucks?" Sadie wriggled a space for herself at the bar as she queried Holly.

"Yeah, once a week all these cool food trucks pull up somewhere in town, doing gourmet burgers, tacos, stuff like that. They create like a mini food court, and people hang out around them, eating and drinking. So, apparently, they're out the back of here. I'm guessing lots of people are eating out there and drinking in here."

"What can I get you?" The barman leaned forward to hear their order.

"Two stubbies of One Fifty Lashes," Holly said, before Sadie could respond. She turned to smile at Sadie. "Trust me, it's good."

Sadie smiled back and nudged Holly's arm. "Don't worry, I do trust you."

Holly stared at her, her gaze intense, and Sadie calmly returned the gaze, before nodding slowly. *Yes, I trust you.*

Holly smiled then—a deep, sexy smile that Sadie felt all the way to the ends of her fingers.

She fidgeted and searched for a conversation starter to break the intensity of the moment.

"I can't get over how much Ballarat has changed since I left," she said. "I mean, for things like this—bars, cafes, food trucks."

She gazed around at the bar, all exposed brick, mismatched sofas around the open fireplace, and industrial fittings on the ceiling.

"Yeah, it's really taken off in the last few years. Ballarat's a real commuter town for Melbourne now, so the night-time entertainment has picked up off the back of that. There are so many good places to eat and drink now."

They grabbed the cold bottles handed to them and wandered away from the bar to find a place to sit. Finally locating a small table tucked into a relatively quieter corner, they shrugged out of their slightly damp jackets and placed them on the backs of their chairs. The worst of the rain had eased off by the time they'd left the hotel, but they'd still been dampened by the light drizzle that lingered.

Sadie took a moment to admire, somewhat surreptitiously, the incredibly sexy outfit Holly had on for their date. Because it was a date, there was no question of that. Sadie had met Holly outside the hotel at seven; she and Holly had simply stared at each other for a moment, standing in the light rain, then both smiled shyly before heading into the city centre.

Something indefinable had passed between them, and Sadie felt as if a weight had been lifted from her shoulders. She had walked to the bar alongside Holly with a determination that grew with every step. *Tonight, I am going to take that leap and tell Holly that I'm ready to pursue this.* Briefly, flashbacks to another night—twelve years ago, when she'd last laid her feelings on the line—threatened to derail her, but she forced them away.

Now, studying Holly in front of her, she had no doubts about committing them to the path she had in mind. The black jeans clung to Holly's slim legs and curvy hips. The off-white top had skintight, lacy sleeves that led up to a lace panel that crossed her chest. There was a teasing hint of cleavage, and the tightness of the top emphasised, albeit subtly, the fullness of Holly's breasts. Small, gold earrings completed the look, and there was a delicious hint of perfume reaching Sadie's nostrils. The whole package left her just slightly breathless.

They clinked bottles, and each took a deep gulp.

"So, things still going good with your mum?" Holly asked as they both placed their bottles down on the table.

"Good beer," Sadie said first, and Holly nodded, smiling. "Yeah, it's all good," Sadie continued. "I still can't believe it, actually. She's really had a long, hard look at her life and hasn't liked what she's seen. We've...we've shared a lot, and it's been emotional, but I'm so glad I'm here. And what's also nice is that she and Gran have reconciled too. Not that they ever broke off contact altogether, but they didn't have a brilliant relationship since my parents sent me to live with her."

"So definitely worth the trip?"

Sadie nodded and leaned forward on her forearms, bringing her face closer to Holly's. She didn't want to talk about her family anymore. All she wanted to focus on was them and what they might have.

"Definitely," she murmured, boldly taking a long, obvious, and slow perusal of the beautiful woman sat opposite her. She saw Holly take in a shuddering breath, and when their eyes met, Sadie smiled.

"You...you're a hard one to read," Holly said after a moment, her fingers fiddling with the label of her beer bottle.

Sadie raised a shoulder apologetically. "I don't mean to be. I haven't meant to give you such mixed signals, it's just been—"

"I know," Holly said quietly, reaching out a hand to lightly grasp Sadie's wrist. "You don't have to explain, I get it."

Sadie smiled. "Yeah, you do, don't you?"

Holly cocked her head to one side, a small frown etched across her forehead.

"I mean you really seem to get what's going on for me. And you're not judging. You're ignoring who I used to be, and you're just accepting me for who I am now. I like that. A lot."

Holly smiled, and blushed a little.

"Well, I happen to like you. A lot," she whispered.

Sadie's breathing hitched as she placed her free hand over Holly's and let their fingers entwine. Flutters skittered all over her body as Holly's fingertips softly stroked against her hand, and she in turn stroked Holly's palm.

"Is it okay to do this?" Sadie asked, in a voice not much above a whisper, flicking a quick look round the other tables nearby. "Not inappropriate, or likely to lead to us getting bashed?"

Holly shook her head, her gaze never leaving Sadie's. "Ballarat's all grown-up now, don't worry. Some people might stare, but they're unlikely to do or say anything. Besides, I like it, so don't stop. Please."

That last word came out in a breathy exhalation that sent a jolt of heat straight between Sadie's legs. How long they sat like that, gently playing with each other's fingers, eyes alternating between locking in a heated gaze and roving over each other's faces, Sadie couldn't say. But, eventually, a loud rumble from her stomach pulled them apart, sending them both into giggles.

"Food?" Holly smirked.

"Sounds like it's time, doesn't it? What have they got?"

They glanced over the simple menu and both ordered pizzas. Although a little irritated that her hunger had interrupted that beautiful moment they were sharing, Sadie took it as a chance to check in with herself, to make sure she still wanted to do this. Listening to Holly as she told Sadie a little about her day, watching how she used her hands to animate her stories, only served to confirm that Holly was a woman she wanted in her life as more than a friend. She was mesmerising, and Sadie didn't want to come out from under her spell.

Once their pizzas were delivered, they ate slowly, around sporadic conversation that touched on a few generic topics, but always with their eyes drinking each other in. Sadie knew any resistance she'd had to this was long gone. Whatever this was going to be, for however long it could last, she wanted it with a hunger that was startling in its intensity. But it didn't scare her anymore, and that felt really good.

"You okay?" Holly asked.

Sadie realised she had drifted off and was staring into space. She chuckled and met Holly's gaze, letting her desire shine through in the way she took in Holly's features, lingering on her lips. Those lips parted as a small sound escaped Holly's throat.

"Want to get out of here?" Sadie voiced the question quietly, but filled it with the heat she was feeling all over her body.

Holly merely nodded; it seemed words had escaped her. Her eyes were wide, her cheeks touched with a hint of pink. She pushed her hair back behind her ears and took a deep breath. Sadie drank in the sight of her, astonished by the need she had for this woman who had so easily broken down her barriers.

After a long moment, Sadie reached for Holly's hand to pull her gently from her chair, and they each hung their jackets over their free arms until they'd left the bar. The night was cool, after the rain. As they exited the laneway where Hop Temple was tucked back off the main street, they parted hands momentarily to slip into the warmth of their outer clothing. Then, blindly but easily, they instantly found each other's hands again.

They walked back towards the hotel in a silence heavy with sensual anticipation. Sadie kept her gaze forward, not daring to look at Holly. She knew if she did she'd be overwhelmed by the need to pull Holly into her arms, to kiss her, to touch her. As much as Ballarat had grown up, she didn't think Sturt Street was ready to witness *that* just yet. They walked briskly in the cool air, up to Bakery Hill, then zigzagged their way to the quiet street that housed the hotel. Sadie had assumed Holly was coming back with her, and was therefore surprised when Holly pulled them gently to a stop as they reached the street corner.

"Wait," Holly said, her gaze flicking between Sadie and the lights of the hotel fifty metres away.

"You okay?" Sadie rubbed Holly's hand gently with her thumb.

Holly nodded and swallowed, her deep brown eyes coming to rest on Sadie's. "This is…tricky. I'm pretty sure I know where we're heading right now, with us, and trust me, I want that. God, do I…" She shivered slightly, and Sadie knew it wasn't from the cold. "But I would have a hard time explaining to Matthew why I'm back at the hotel at this time of night. We lock the back door at seven, and I don't have my keys with me, so we can't go in that way. If we walk through the front, he sees me, and it'll get back to my mum." She exhaled a loud sigh. "Sorry, I don't know why this didn't occur to me before."

Sadie smiled and squeezed her hand. "Don't worry, we'll figure something out. It doesn't have to be tonight. Maybe it was enough tonight just to acknowledge this."

"Yeah," Holly expelled. "But I can't help it—I want to kiss you so badly right now it's killing me." Holly's face was a sad picture of disappointment, and Sadie laughed softly in empathy.

"Yeah, me too." She paused, then grinned wickedly. "So how about I walk you home. I seem to remember it was a dark and quiet route. I'm pretty sure we can find a private little spot on the way where we could, you know, fulfil that need of yours." She delighted in the small gasp that Holly emitted, and tugged her a little closer until their faces were only centimetres apart. "Yes?"

"Oh, yes," Holly breathed, and she leaned forward suddenly to graze her lips over the side of Sadie's neck, totally turning the tables and spinning Sadie into a maelstrom of heated desire and need. She closed her eyes briefly, and gripped Holly's hand tighter. Holly's lips were sending extraordinary levels of stimulation throughout Sadie's body, and that stimulation seemed to concentrate rapidly in one very specific spot. Her heart raced. Holly smiled against her neck, and then raised her head and winked. That sent a blistering spike of want straight to Sadie's clit, and she nearly moaned aloud.

"Come on, then, walk me home," Holly said huskily.

They were kissing. Which was a complete understatement of the activity they were currently engaged in. Holly could barely stand; only Sadie's strong arms around her were holding her up. That and Sadie's firm body pressed up against hers, their breasts moulded against each other's. Holly knew her heart was beating faster and louder than it ever had, and she was well aware of the loud, gasping breaths she kept having to break their kisses for. The only thing that helped her from sinking into embarrassment over the obliterating effect the kisses were having on her was the fact that Sadie was clearly suffering the same response.

They couldn't get enough of each other. They were pushed up against a fence at the back of an abandoned property, a block away from her home. They had laughed at the ridiculousness of two adult women sneaking around like teenagers, but the hunger between them sent propriety out the window. Clearly, if the hotel was off limits, then so too was Holly's home. This dark and impromptu venue was the best they could come up with.

Holly couldn't care less; at this precise moment, Sadie's warm lips were gently nibbling their way along her jawline, down her neck, and back up to her earlobe. That was all she was focused on. The sensations just those simple kisses were engendering everywhere in her body were all she could think about. She'd never been so turned on in her life. Sadie's hands moved under Holly's top, caressing the skin of her abdomen, then upwards until her fingertips rested just under Holly's bra. Correction: *now I've never been so turned on in my life.*

She almost couldn't believe they were here, finally acting on the heat that had been building between them over the last few days. Sadie's sudden switch into outright seduction mode this evening had confused Holly, initially. It had taken her a while to gather herself, and—strangely—to feel ready to engage with the new tone Sadie was bringing to their fledgling relationship. Once she did, and Sadie made it clear that whatever had been holding her back was no longer an issue, Holly had found it remarkably easy to bring her own seductiveness to the fore. It was a new feeling, and she revelled in it. Seeing and hearing what she could do to Sadie made her feel incredibly powerful. It was addictive. She only hoped Sadie wouldn't shut down on her again. They'd come so far.

She moaned, loudly, as Sadie's hands moved the last few centimetres to push under the cups of her bra, and both her warm hands cupped Holly's breasts, gently and reverently. Sadie groaned, and her hot mouth moved back to Holly's, just as her fingertips pinched both of Holly's hard nipples. Holly gasped into Sadie's mouth and pushed herself farther into her hands. Holly's underwear was soaked; she was aching, and desperate for this to go further, but at the same time, she was not comfortable with their first time being a secretive quickie up against a fence.

Slowly, and reluctantly, she pulled away from the sexy warmth of Sadie's embrace, her chest heaving as she tried to pull more oxygen into her lungs.

"Sorry, did I—?" Sadie looked alarmed.

"No," Holly said quickly, still panting. "I just… God, I want you so much, but not like this. Not here."

Sadie looked into her eyes and nodded in understanding, a small smile on her swollen lips. *God, that mouth.*

"Yeah, me too." Sadie carefully removed her hands from under Holly's bra, grazing her fingertips sensuously down Holly's body as she pulled them slowly away. "There must be a way to sneak you into my hotel room. Please?"

Her voice expressed how tortured she was by their circumstances, and it made Holly glow.

"Probably," she murmured, still in a heated haze in the aftermath of the kisses they'd shared.

"Tomorrow? After our run? Hell, forget the run," Sadie said, growling, and Holly smiled. Sadie rubbed her thumb across Holly's bottom lip. "I'm not going to be able to sleep at all tonight, thinking about you."

Holly shuddered in excitement at the words. God, when Sadie finally opened up, she didn't hold anything back. It was beyond arousing.

"I want you. *God…*"

Sadie lunged against Holly's mouth again, searing her with a kiss that left her reeling. She clutched at the waistband of Sadie's jeans, anchoring herself against the onslaught of pleasure that Sadie's kisses unleashed. Had anyone ever kissed her so thoroughly? Sending heat all the way down to her toes and back again?

Sadie pulled her mouth away after a few moments, but Holly held her close, pressing her face into the warmth of Sadie's neck.

"Yes, tomorrow," she murmured against Sadie's skin, breathing in the scent of her. Perfume, soap, and just…Sadie. "I'll figure out how to get to your room without anyone knowing. Make sure you tell me when you're back from visiting your mum, if I don't see you come in."

"I will," Sadie replied. She gently kissed Holly's forehead. "I guess you should get home now."

Holly nodded and squeezed Sadie tightly before releasing her. They stepped back and stared at each other, smiling a little sheepishly, almost bashfully. After a moment, Sadie reached for Holly's hand and led her back onto the street.

CHAPTER 13

Just to warn you, Izzy bringing the boyfriend too

The ping of the text from her gran woke Sadie from an extremely pleasant dream that had left her more than a little turned on. That the dream had featured Holly was no surprise. Trying to get to sleep after their lust-filled walk home and subsequent passionate interlude against that fence had been impossible. All she could remember was how incredible Holly's body felt up against hers, how wonderfully soft and warm her lips were, and how equally they'd matched each other's hunger. They fit so well together, and she knew that wasn't just physically. She wouldn't let her brain jump forward through the forthcoming day to their plan to meet that evening. The plan that only contained one thing—their rendezvous in her room. In this very bed. If she let herself dwell on what was to come in just over nine hours, she'd never get out of bed in the first place.

But Elsie's text reminded her that first, Izzy and she would attempt to reconnect. She'd asked her mum to invite Izzy over for lunch, a small chunk of time that was easy to escape from if things blew up between them. She hoped they wouldn't—she wanted to meet the grown-up version of her sister, especially one who wasn't such a princess anymore. She wanted a chance to talk to Izzy about that night, understand just what Izzy had been doing back then. And see if Izzy felt any remorse for how her actions had unwittingly changed Sadie's life so dramatically.

She still took her time showering and eating her plate of toast for brekkie, easing herself into the day. She also took joy in texting with Holly, who she knew was sitting only metres away on the reception desk around the corner.

Good morning, gorgeous. How are you?

Holly's response was quick.

Tired. Didn't sleep. Couldn't stop thinking about you...

Sadie smiled to herself as she decided to ramp it up a little. She couldn't be the only one sitting there feeling crazily horny at nine thirty in the morning.

I remember how wonderful your breasts felt in my hands. Can't wait to do that again

Holly's reply this time took a couple of minutes to come back. For a while, Sadie wondered if she'd gone too far. But when she read the response, she just grinned.

Oh God, you can't say stuff like that when I'm working! I nearly slid off my chair into a (very) wet puddle. Go do whatever you need to do for the day and let me know when you're back. I'll be thinking of you xx

Sadie texted a couple of kisses back in response, a wide smile on her face as she did so. She'd never had this kind of interaction with a woman. She'd always shied away from it, always wondering what the other woman was after, what was her angle, could she be trusted. With Holly that just wasn't a factor, and being in this situation felt good. Really good.

"They're here," Elsie said, unnecessarily, as they all heard the car pull up on the driveway. There was a tension in the room; it had been building slowly for the last thirty minutes or so. Izzy had said she and Luke would be there by one. It was nearly twenty past. Sadie tried not to read too much into their tardiness—perhaps they'd had trouble getting away from work. She knew Izzy worked as an advisor in a bank out at Wendouree, but she had no idea what Luke did.

Sadie braced herself as she heard the front door open.

"Mum!" Izzy's voice rang down the hallway. "We're here."

"In the lounge room," Christine replied, standing up. Sadie and Elsie also stood, and Sadie rubbed her damp palms down her jeans. She turned to the door just as Izzy walked in.

"Oh," Izzy said quietly, coming to an abrupt halt. She slowly met Sadie's gaze after looking briefly at their mother. "Hi, Sadie," she said, her croaky voice revealing her nerves.

"Hey, Izzy. How's it going?" She had promised herself earlier that she'd be calm and pleasant to give them the best chance of opening up.

"Good, thanks. You?"

"Oh, yeah, not so bad."

They stared at each other for a moment.

"Shit, it's cold out there today, huh?" Luke's gravelly voice invaded the quietness and broke the spell.

Izzy turned to him, smiling weakly. "Luke, this is my sister, Sadie." She motioned towards Sadie, who had not moved from her spot in the centre of the room.

"G'day," he said, barely giving her a look. He was tall and broad, and from the looks of the less-than-clean blue overalls he was wearing, she guessed he was a mechanic of some sort. He was good-looking, in a rough kind of way—thick, cropped, dark hair, a strong chin, half the makings of a beard across his jaw. He towered above Izzy, who—Sadie had to admit—had matured into a beautiful woman. She'd grown her blonde hair longer, and it hung straight down her back. Her eyes, just as green as Sadie's, were highlighted with subtle make-up, and she wore a skirt suit that fitted perfectly on her slim body.

Sadie decided instantly, from Luke's nonresponse towards her and the possessive way he draped his arm over Izzy's shoulders, that she didn't like him. She switched all her attention to her sister and attempted a smile.

"Lunch break?" she asked.

Izzy nodded and hesitantly returned her smile. "Yeah. Sorry we're a bit later than I said. Luke…had a little trouble getting away."

Somehow Sadie knew what she meant was that Luke didn't want to be there and had delayed them as a result. She wondered why Izzy had brought him. As some kind of buffer? If so, against what? Or who?

"No worries," Elsie chimed in, and Sadie was grateful for the break in the tension. "Want some lunch? We made chicken and avo sandwiches."

"That'd be great, Gran," Izzy said.

Christine stepped forward to give Izzy a brief hug, then led her towards the kitchen. Luke followed, but not before giving Sadie a less-than-subtle once-over, which set her hackles rising. Ugh, what a sleaze.

They made uncomfortable small talk about the weather, their work—Luke was indeed a mechanic—and the trip to Daylesford. Their father wasn't mentioned at all, which suited Sadie just fine. She and Izzy slowly and organically shut everyone else out of their quiet conversation until they had their heads close together at one end of the kitchen table, oblivious to everyone else in the room.

"I'm sorry I never wrote to you, or anything," Izzy said, out of the blue, wiping her hands on her napkin after she finished her sandwich.

Sadie watched her, waiting to see where this would go.

"I just…it was such a shock. And I knew you were covering for me," Izzy whispered, flicking her eyes to their mother to make sure she couldn't hear what was being said. "I can't believe you did that, actually."

Sadie snorted softly. "Like they would have believed me if I'd said it was you," she said, but there was no malice behind her words. It was just…what it was. Izzy reached across to lay one hand gently on Sadie's forearm. The touch stunned Sadie.

"Well, I want to say thanks now. You don't know this, but that night changed everything for me too. I left my stupid little gang soon after that. I got so scared about what had happened to you. I realised what an idiot I was being. I kind of pulled myself up at school, too, and made sure I did as best I could."

"You didn't really have to try at that, though, did you? You were always way smarter than me."

"Yeah, I guess, but I could have blown it all if I'd carried on doing all that stupid shit." She paused and smiled, squeezing Sadie's arm a little more firmly. "So, anyway. Thanks."

Before Sadie could respond, Luke's voice boomed across the table.

"Better not get too close, Iz," he said. "It might rub off on you!" He laughed at his own comment and failed to notice that none of the four women joined in.

"What the fuck?" Sadie said quietly, turning to stare at Izzy for explanation. Had her sister's boyfriend really just gone *there*? In front of their mother and grandmother?

"Luke," Izzy admonished, but it was half-hearted at best. He grinned inanely and stuffed the rest of his sandwich in his mouth.

"Come on," he said, around the mouthful of food. "I need to get back." He stood and glared at Izzy when she didn't instantly move.

Sadie was still staring at Izzy, waiting for...well, what was she waiting for? An apology? Maybe some kind of acknowledgement that what Luke had said was crass, if nothing else? Izzy stared back for a moment. She looked away, her discomfort apparent in the way she was fidgeting in her seat.

"Thanks, sis," Sadie whispered, lacing her words with sarcasm.

Izzy flinched but stood without looking at Sadie and followed the already departing Luke towards the front door. Sadie couldn't let it slide. Never mind what he'd said to her, he'd not even bothered to thank her mum for the lunch in his haste to get out of the house.

"Aren't you forgetting something?" she asked, marching after her sister and her boyfriend. They both turned, he wearing a look of confusion, she embarrassment. Sadie gritted her teeth. "It's polite to thank someone who just fed you lunch."

Just as Izzy started to apologise, Luke cut her off. "I don't need no dyke telling me how to behave," he snarled, and he took a step towards her. She heard both Elsie and Christine gasp behind her, but before she could respond, Izzy grabbed hold of Luke's arm with both her slim hands.

"Luke!" she said sharply. "Enough." She looked past Sadie to their mother. "Sorry, Mum," she mumbled. "Thanks for lunch, I'll...I'll call you later." Then she pulled at Luke, who was busy sneering at Sadie. "Come *on*, we're going."

With one last smirk in Sadie's direction, he turned to follow Izzy from the house. Christine made to go after them, her pale face drawn into a deep, angry frown, but Sadie caught her arm and halted her momentum.

"Don't, Mum," she said softly. "Leave it."

"How dare he?" Christine's voice was full of disgust, and she turned to face Sadie. "How dare he talk to you like that? And how dare she let him?"

Sadie felt a warm glow start to melt the ice that had taken a grip on her insides in the previous few minutes. Her mum was outraged at how she'd been spoken to, and that felt really, *really* good.

"Whilst I'm not saying it didn't piss me off, I've…well, I've had worse. Tell me," she said, exhaling a slow breath. "Does my sister share his opinions?" Memories of the night of the school fire, of Izzy calling out *See you later, dyke*, rushed into Sadie's mind.

Her mum shook her head. She looked dazed. "I didn't think so before today. But, given what she just did—or rather, *didn't* do—I… Well, I have no idea." Her gaze darted away and back again. She pressed a hand to her forehead and winced slightly. "I think I'd like to have a lie-down now, if you don't mind. Sorry, darling." She patted Sadie on the shoulder.

"No problem, Mum. Please, do what you need to do. Maybe I'll see you if I'm still here when you wake later?"

"That would be nice, but don't risk staying too long and your father coming home. I'd say that's the last thing you need today after that little episode." Her smile was feeble, but the love in it was clear.

Sadie returned the smile and stepped forward to give her a careful hug. "Have a good rest. If I don't see you later, I'll definitely be back tomorrow."

Christine nodded distractedly and gave Sadie a quick peck on her cheek before heading down the hall to the master bedroom.

"Was he like that when you saw him on Sunday?"

Sadie and Elsie were in the kitchen, talking quietly over large mugs of coffee. They'd cleared away the lunch things and tidied up the kitchen. It was still too cold to sit outside, even though Sadie thought some fresh air might do her good. She was still angry at how lunch had disintegrated. Until Luke had opened his big mouth, she'd thought she and Izzy were getting somewhere. *Now, I don't know where we are.*

"Not about homosexuality," Elsie replied. It always made Sadie smile how she used the more formal term for lesbian or gay. "But something came on the news about those poor Syrian refugees, and he had a *lot* to say about that. None of it good, or pleasant." She tsked into her coffee mug.

"And did Izzy let him, like today?"

Elsie sighed and looked up at Sadie over the rim of her mug. "I'm sorry to say, yes." She put her mug down. "I just don't understand her. When I first arrived here last week, she was an angel. Picking me up from the airport, taking me shopping so I could cook for your mother, calling me every evening she couldn't be here just to see how I was." She sighed. "But when I saw her on Sunday, with him, it was like she was another person entirely. Just like today." She shook her head. "I just don't understand," she repeated, and her sorrowful confusion wrenched at Sadie's heart.

"Well, I didn't like him," Sadie declared firmly, "and that was pretty much before he opened his mouth. He…he checked me out, when they arrived, when he thought no one was looking."

"You mean he—?" Elsie's face displayed her shock.

Sadie nodded.

"Disgusting," her gran muttered.

"Gran," Sadie said, after a few more sips of coffee. "Can I ask you something?"

Elsie cocked her head. "What?"

"Is… What's all this stuff about Mum not realising I'm gay?"

Elsie huffed. "Don't ask me, love. I've never made a secret of it with her, because I knew you'd told them."

Sadie shook her head. "I can't believe she didn't believe me. That she thought I'd just make up something like that."

Elsie patted her hand. "That was then. This is now. I'm guessing his little display today has got her thinking. She certainly seemed riled up about it, didn't she?"

Sadie grinned. "Yeah, she did. That felt kinda good."

"She'll come round, I think. Don't worry too much about that." Elsie's smile was warm, and Sadie leaned into her for a quick hug.

"You're the best, Gran."

Elsie beamed.

CHAPTER 14

"Not that I don't appreciate the sparkly new reception area, sweetheart, but we do have a cleaner to do that, you know?"

Judy gazed around the spotless and gleaming room. In an attempt to distract herself from what might happen that night, Holly had gone a tad overboard on tidying her workspace.

"Are you okay?" Judy stared pointedly at her daughter, who tried very, *very* hard not to blush.

"I'm fine, Mum. Just, I don't know, full of energy today for some reason. Maybe because I haven't run in a couple of days."

"Hm." Her mother sounded unconvinced. "Well, you're planning to let off some of that energy tonight, aren't you?"

What? Oh shit, had she guessed? How did she know? And why was she being so blasé about it? Holly's heart attempted to slam against her ribs, and she feared it would stop entirely at any moment.

Judy tilted her head slightly when Holly failed to answer. "You are going running with Sadie tonight, aren't you? Isn't that what you told me over breakfast?"

Holly let out a long, relieved breath and nodded vigorously. "Oh. Yes. Running. Of course." Oh, great—now she was babbling.

Judy shook her head and walked back to her office, clearly thinking her only child had completely lost her mind.

Holly slumped against the desk, one hand on her chest, trying to get her heart and breathing back to their normal rates of operation. Hiding this, whatever it was between her and Sadie, was going to kill her. She knew if it developed into even half of what it promised, then she would neither want to, nor be able to hide it. From anyone.

Thanking all the travel gods known to man, Holly found the next two hours blurring by in a steady sequence of check-ins and information requests that left her no more time to dwell on Sadie's return. When her phone buzzed discreetly just before five, she absent-mindedly picked it up to read the incoming message and shivered at the wave of excitement that rippled through her when she saw who it was from.

I just got back, came in the back door so I wouldn't distract you :-) Please, let me know if you have changed your mind. If not, then whenever you can get free, I'd love to see you x

Steadying her breathing, and taking a quick look round to ensure her mother was nowhere in sight, Holly quickly typed her response.

Just waiting for Matthew to arrive to take over. And no, I haven't changed my mind. Far from it...

Sadie paced nervously. She wasn't even sure why she was nervous. But pacing was helping. A little.

She knew part of the problem was that she was still on edge from her encounter with Izzy earlier. Or rather, with that idiot boyfriend of hers. She had mostly shaken it off, taking a slow ride around the entire circuit of the lake to help calm things down after she'd left her mother's place. She hadn't seen her mum again that afternoon; she had still been sleeping when Sadie felt it was prudent to leave the house. Elsie had promised to text her later to tell her how she was. That was another thing that had made her so mad about what Luke and Izzy had done—her mum was dealing with enough without them giving her more to worry about, and who the hell did they think they were treating her house like that?

She blew out a breath. She was letting it get to her again, and she really didn't want that to interfere with what she hoped was going to happen this evening. In a way, this all seemed a bit odd—planning for Holly to come to her room specifically so that they could have sex. She could honestly say she'd never really done that before. Sure, she'd set up dates where both she and her potential partner knew where the evening would probably end. But this almost seemed a bit…clinical in its execution. She smiled to herself; thoughts of how they'd felt together the night before, how unbelievably arousing it had been to kiss and touch Holly, meant that she was feeling anything but clinical while she awaited Holly's arrival.

When the gentle knock came it startled her. She grinned ruefully.

Yep, still nervous.

She gave herself one last look in the bathroom mirror, pushing a few stray strands of hair down on the back of her neck. She exhaled very slowly.

She opened the door, and Holly, smiling shyly, quickly stepped in. Sadie knew her speed probably didn't have too much to do with eagerness but more to do with making sure Judy didn't spot what was going on. But that was okay, she understood Holly's predicament.

When Holly stepped up to her moments later, her hands snaking slowly around Sadie's waist, she didn't worry anymore about how invested Holly was in whatever this was between them. They smiled at each other—slow, warm smiles that said so much more than words could. One of them moved, Sadie didn't know who, and their mouths met and opened instantly. Sadie moaned into the kiss, wrapping her arms tightly around Holly, pulling her closer, increasing the pressure of the kiss. Her tongue brushed Holly's, and she heard her groan softly. It sent tremors cascading down her spine.

After a few more moments of intense kissing, with Holly pushing her fingers through Sadie's hair—which only served to increase the tremors of arousal in Sadie's body—Holly pulled back, panting.

"Hello," she whispered, grinning at Sadie, who chuckled in response. "I have wanted to do that all day long," Holly murmured, briefly kissing Sadie again.

Sadie nodded, unable to form words through the warm, erotic haze that seemed to have swept over her entire body in the last two minutes. She reached to pull Holly closer again and was surprised when she stepped back out of her arms.

"I need a shower," Holly said. "I honestly can't go any further until I clean up. It's been hectic, and I just, well, you know…"

Sadie smiled and leaned forward to kiss the tip of Holly's nose. "I get it, it's okay. Go ahead."

Holly smiled and stepped towards the bathroom, then turned abruptly. "Wait. God, I'm so selfish—how did your day go?"

A shadow involuntarily passed through Sadie's mind. She waved vaguely in the air between them. "Later," she said quietly. "For now, I just want to focus on us. This. You."

She saw Holly swallow hard and wondered who had turned up the heating, because suddenly the room was extraordinarily warm. Holly nodded and turned back to the bathroom.

She had been in there only five minutes, when Sadie metaphorically slapped herself in the head. *What the hell am I doing out here when Holly is getting naked in there?*

Holly jumped when she heard the bathroom door open. She had just removed her bra, and was wearing nothing but skimpy lace undies when Sadie walked into the room. Okay, so apparently Sadie couldn't wait. She could live with that.

With uncharacteristic boldness—it seemed to be a recurring theme these days—instead of moving to cover herself up, she pulled herself up straighter and turned to meet Sadie's heated gaze. She had stopped just inside the door, arms hanging loosely by her sides, and she shifted her gaze to roam slowly over every inch of Holly's exposed skin. Holly's nipples hardened in response; with the intensity of that gaze, it was almost as if Sadie was caressing her skin from more than two metres away.

"God, you're beautiful," Sadie breathed, and Holly felt the moan form in her throat moments before the sound made it out into the room.

"I still need that shower," Holly whispered.

Sadie lifted her singlet up and over her head. "I'll join you," she said quietly, reaching for the button on her jeans.

Holly watched, breathless, as Sadie slowly stripped in front of her. Her breasts, dark nipples already hard, tumbled out of her black satin bra, and Holly had to send urgent messages to her lungs to keep her breathing. Sadie's body was…magnificent. There was that word again. But, oh God, she was glorious. Strong, muscled, solid. Just…glorious.

When they each stood there in nothing but undies, Sadie motioned with her head to the shower, and Holly reluctantly pulled her gaze away from the vision that was Sadie in all her naked glory. She fumbled with the shower controls until she managed to get a steady stream of warm water flowing into the tray. She reached for the waistband of her G-string, but Sadie held up a hand and slowly stepped towards her.

"Let me," she murmured. And then she was there, only centimetres away, and Holly could feel the heat of her skin scorching the air between them. Sadie's fingertips eased into the G-string, sensual against the skin at the base of Holly's spine, sending tingles up and down the length of her body. Sadie gently, tortuously, pulled the fabric down over Holly's hips.

"In," Sadie murmured, her eyes never leaving Holly's as she gave her shoulder the softest of nudges. Holly did as she was told, but turned her head for a moment to watch as Sadie divested herself of her bikini briefs. Reluctantly, she pulled her gaze away to move under the water, sighing in contented bliss as she pushed her hands through her wet hair. She felt Sadie step in alongside her. Somewhere, her brain thanked her parents for building slightly larger walk-in showers in the new rooms in the annexe. So much more room to manoeuvre…

In the next moment, she stopped thinking altogether as Sadie stepped in front of her, not touching her with her body, but giving her a spectacular view of it as rivulets of water ran down between her breasts, over her flat stomach, and down to…oh *God*. She raised her eyes to meet Sadie's gently teasing ones, and smirked in response.

"You cannot blame me for looking. Not when this—" she waved in the general vicinity of Sadie's body— "is what you are displaying to me."

Sadie smiled and reached behind Holly for the small tube of body wash on the shelf. Holly swallowed. She knew what Sadie intended, and she wasn't sure she'd survive it. She watched, chest heaving, as Sadie squirted a generous amount of body wash into her hands. Holly feared her legs would actually give way as those hands reached out and gently started washing her. Sadie's left hand moved over Holly's shoulders and chest, but steered clear of touching her breasts. Her right hand moved across Holly's abdomen and over her hips. She used both hands to wash Holly's back, reaching around so that she was almost hugging Holly, their breasts not quite touching. When she pulled back, she bent to run her hands down each of Holly's legs and back up again. She kept her fingers away from the now-throbbing zone between Holly's legs and stood, reaching for the tube of shampoo.

"Turn around," she whispered. Holly obeyed, her body moving sluggishly in its aroused state. Then she moaned—loudly—as Sadie's strong fingers worked the shampoo into Holly's scalp and hair, massaging firmly, easing away the last of the day's tension. Sadie gently nudged Holly round to face her again, and tipped her head back to carefully rinse all traces of the shampoo from her hair. The whole experience was an intoxicating mix of eroticism and tenderness that made Holly's heart perform a strange little fluttering in her ribcage.

When Sadie had finished rinsing out the shampoo, she reached for the body wash again. Holly met her eyes, curious as to what she planned next. And hoping it would happen quickly, because her need for release was becoming more urgent by the second. Sadie's cheeks were slightly flushed, and her breathing was coming out in small pants. Knowing she was affecting Sadie this way made her ache even more.

"Hold out your hand," Sadie said.

Holly did so, and Sadie squeezed another good dollop of the citrus-scented liquid into her cupped palm.

"Now," Sadie said, stepping back slightly, her voice sounding strained with what Holly could only assume—and hope—was arousal. "I deliberately left two areas unwashed." Sadie swallowed before continuing. "I want to watch you wash them."

Holly's breathing stopped and then juddered into action again. *Jesus…*

As seductively as she could manage, given that her hands were shaking so badly, she gently cupped each of her breasts and washed them, moving in slow circles over and around the heft of them, letting her aching nipples pass between her slippery fingers. Sadie, she could tell, was mesmerised and only just holding herself together. Holly could see her fingers flexing as if fighting herself against joining in with Holly's ministrations. Holly could only admire her restraint. If the tables were turned, she was sure she'd have lunged in.

Slowly, even though her body was screaming for her to move much faster, Holly let her soapy hands wander downwards. She shifted her feet so that she could part her thighs, then ran her fingers between her own legs. Careful not to rub directly on her clit, she skimmed her fingers through the unsurprising—and abundant—slipperiness she found there. She held Sadie's gaze and, in doing so, realised that Sadie wasn't looking at what her hands were doing. Despite her request to watch Holly, she had remained staring into Holly's eyes. Holly sucked in a breath at how incredibly intimate the moment seemed to be. She turned her body slightly under the spray to rinse off every last residue of soap. Sadie waited, not moving, and Holly's mind spun at the thought that soon, their bodies would finally know each other.

Sadie gently tugged Holly into the bedroom. She had enjoyed every activity in the bathroom, but her body was crying out for more. Holly was, quite simply, the sexiest woman Sadie had ever laid eyes on. She could barely wait to show her just what effect she was having. After the erotic interlude in the shower, they had towelled off quickly, Holly insisting she didn't need to blow-dry her hair, for which Sadie was grateful. She wasn't sure she could have coped with yet more delay. The need she had for Holly was threatening to devour her from the inside out.

They both climbed slowly onto the bed and knelt, facing each other. The late afternoon light cast a golden glow across the room and across the skin of Holly's body. Her eyes were hooded, dark with desire, and Sadie's breath caught at the sight. She let her gaze wander over the delicious body in front of her. Holly was a work of art; everything was perfectly proportioned. She had a stunning hourglass figure, with a curve to her hips that took Sadie's breath away. Her breasts were temptation personified—looking as if they would be a little more than a handful, with deep pink nipples that were already hardened to stiff peaks.

Sadie slowly inched closer, aware of her own body's response to the sight before her. A flush formed on her chest as her arousal pulsed through her. She carefully placed her knees either side of one of Holly's, and then, as if a switch had been thrown, they suddenly came together. Lips, teeth, and tongues clashed; their hands were everywhere all at once, their breasts and bellies pressed against each other. Holly pulled her in tight by wrapping her arms around Sadie's shoulders, and Sadie responded by grabbing Holly's ass to bring her even closer.

"God," Holly breathed in-between kisses, and Sadie simply nodded. Gradually their kisses slowed and gentled, and so did their hands. Sadie took control—as much as parts of her wanted to surrender to Holly's delicious touches, her own desire to touch and taste won out. Knowing she wanted to reach and touch all of Holly at once, she sidled carefully round behind her. She pushed Holly's legs apart with her knees until Holly could sit back slightly on Sadie's thighs. Holly turned her head to look at her, and Sadie leaned in to kiss her again, her hands roaming over Holly's thighs, up over her belly, cupping her breasts. Holly's chest was heaving, and her fingers twitched where she'd wrapped her arms behind her to grasp Sadie's hips.

"Please," she breathed, and Sadie felt her clit jolt in response. Holly's breathy gasps filled the room as Sadie swept her hands over every piece of exposed skin she could reach. She lingered on Holly's breasts for what seemed like hours, revelling in the hard texture of her nipples as they rolled between her fingers. Holly responded in ways that only ramped up Sadie's excitement, squirming and whimpering at every touch.

By the time Sadie moved her fingers down to Holly's thighs, she was more turned on than she could ever remember. The ache between her own legs was intense, and she fought to keep it under control while she focused her attentions on Holly. She slowly moved her fingers inwards, grazing against the curly hair between Holly's legs, and then dipping down into the abundant wetness that awaited her.

She used the fingers of one hand to gently rub at Holly's clit, and circled her entrance with the fingertips of the other, but didn't push inside. Not yet.

Holly arched her back, her head thrown back on Sadie's shoulder. Sadie kissed her neck, and Holly turned towards her, mouth open slightly, the warmth of her breath tickling Sadie's face.

"Yes?" Sadie murmured, her fingers still circling, Holly's hips bucking to meet those questing fingers.

Holly's gaze was barely focused on Sadie, her eyelids half shut. "Yes," she whispered, fingers squeezing Sadie's hips in reflex. "God, yes."

Sadie plunged into her, and Holly cried out. With one hand gently working on Holly's clit, she fucked her slowly with a single finger of the other hand. She set an even rhythm, diving as deep as she could, then pulling almost all the way out before pushing back inside. Holly felt incredible—so tight around her finger, so responsive to her touches, her clit swelling with each stroke. Holly's ass ground against Sadie's thighs with each one of Sadie's thrusts, and the soft roundness of those cheeks on her skin sent ripples of desire snaking all the way to her clit. Holly's head arched back again as she moved, and Sadie licked and kissed at the exposed neck in front of her.

When Holly wrenched out the words, "Faster, *please*," Sadie had to clench her thighs together to still her own impending orgasm. She'd never come just from making love to someone before; this level of intensity was new and unbelievably exciting. She ramped up the speed of her arm, two fingers filling Holly at a frantic pace, her finger on Holly's clit also moving faster. In the next moment, Holly lunged upwards as her orgasm claimed her.

"Je-sus!" Holly's strangled exclamation sent a deep pulse of something beyond sexual through Sadie's body. Sadie groaned and kept her fingers buried deep inside her beautiful lover as Holly rode them, eliciting every last drop of pleasure she could from Sadie's hand. This was pleasure like she'd never known—want and satisfaction and a deep, undeniable emotional connection to the woman slumped back against her. Sadie continued to gently stroke Holly as she came down from her high until Holly let her know, with a gentle last squeeze of Sadie's hip, that she could stop. Sadie withdrew her trembling fingers and sat back. Her legs ached from kneeling for so long, but she was beyond caring.

Holly slowly turned her head, and they stared at each other for a few moments, smiling. Then, with a speed that astonished Sadie, Holly sat up, turned, and before Sadie could say a word, pushed her down onto her back and lay out on top of her. She kissed Sadie with a fierce intensity. Sadie moaned into the kiss, pouring into it everything she was feeling right at that moment, and Holly responded in kind. When Holly moved a hand between them and slid her fingers through Sadie's wetness, they both gasped at the contact. Holly stroked slowly, agonisingly slowly, and Sadie thrust her hips upwards, desperate for more contact, more pressure, just…more. Holly obliged, kissing her deeply at the same time. When Sadie's orgasm hit, sparks ricocheted off the back of her brain and exploded like fireworks across her closed eyelids.

"Oh, babe," Holly whispered, and somehow, that innocuous term of endearment did it for Sadie. Tears leaked from her eyes, and she pulled Holly to her, turning her head on the pillow slightly so that Holly's face was snuggled against her neck.

"You okay?" Holly's voice was soft, tentative, and she raised a hand to brush delicately at the tears on Sadie's face. "What's wrong? Did I do—?"

"It's not you," Sadie said softly. "I just..." She trailed off, unsure how to finish her sentence. What did she want to say? *I think I'm falling for you? Hell, I think I might already be there?* They'd known each other a week; how could she spring that on Holly now? She turned her head to look at her. Holly's hair, still damp from the shower, was splayed erratically over the pillow. Her eyes shone; her lips were sensually swollen, and her skin glowed.

"It's fine," Sadie said, smiling as encouragingly as she could. "This was just pretty special. And you made me feel so good, it just overwhelmed me a little."

Holly smiled, a little shyly, which was very cute. "Well, I'm glad to hear that I made you feel good. It kind of felt good from where I was too." She winked, and Sadie laughed out loud.

"Mm," Sadie said, making a concerted effort to throw off her serious thoughts from a few moments ago. "Perhaps there are some more things we could try in the 'making each other feel good' department, huh?" She waggled her eyebrows. Holly snorted in derision, and then squealed as Sadie suddenly flipped her onto her back. "I've got a few ideas right now."

Sadie dipped her head to Holly's left breast, and sucked—hard—on her pink nipple. Holly's long, drawn-out moan made her smile against the warm skin beneath her lips.

"Oh, yeah," she murmured, and then turned her attention to the other breast.

Sadie rolled over in the bed, half awake and not sure what it was that had roused her. She reached out for Holly's warm body but met only the cool sheet that covered the mattress. Snapping wide awake, she raised her head off the pillow to look around and confirm that, yes, she was alone in the bed.

Confused, she sat up and flipped on the bedside light. No Holly. She glanced at her phone to see the time.

Four a.m.

Where the fuck was Holly? Quickly, she replayed their last conversation through her head, the one they'd mumbled their way through after completely sating their bodies from hours of lovemaking and before falling into a wonderfully deep sleep, wrapped up in each other's bodies. She didn't think she'd said anything to push Holly away, so why had she gone?

A moment later it hit her, like ice-cold water. Holly had taken what she wanted. She'd made no pretence of her desire for Sadie all through the week. Once that desire was satisfied, she had gone. Just like before, when Sadie was ready to give her heart to someone, they used her for what they wanted and then just left her behind.

She thought she'd done it right this time. She'd thought Holly was different. She'd thought it was mutual.

She slumped back onto the pillow, her arms crossed against her forehead. She gazed up at the darkened ceiling, the anger burning deep in her belly.

How could she have got it so wrong? Misread it so badly?

CHAPTER 15

"What do you mean, she left? When? Why?" Nicole's voice carried the exact same bafflement Sadie had felt at four that morning. And was still feeling.

Sadie sighed and gazed, unseeing, at the lake before her. She'd got up way too early, her sleep from four onwards plagued with unsettling and disturbing dreams. Giving up at six, she'd taken herself out for an early run to try and clear the upsetting thoughts that filled her brain, but it hadn't worked. After showering, she'd slipped out of the hotel's back door, not in any hurry to confront Holly about her baffling departure during the night. She'd ridden out to the lake again and was slumped on a bench overlooking the water, the calmness of the morning only occasionally broken by a morning jogger.

"And what, no note, no text message to explain?"

"What is there to explain?" Sadie snapped, her anger and frustration spilling over. "She got what she wanted, didn't she? And me, idiot that I am, thought there was more to it than just a one-night stand. God, I am so stupid," she groaned and hung her head.

Nicole huffed out a breath. "But, that's the thing, Sades. From everything you told me about how this week has gone with you two, this just makes no fucking sense at all. She was really into you. *Really.* So there has to be another explanation as to why she left. Maybe she was ill?"

"If that was the case, why didn't she just wake me, huh? No, I know what this is. It's happened before, so I know what it feels like. This is me reading it all wrong again and putting my heart at risk when I didn't need to. This is the universe telling me I don't get to do this. I don't get to find that *one*, like you've found Tash."

"Shit, get off the fucking pity bus, will you?" Nicole's sharp words sliced into Sadie, causing her breath to catch in her throat. "Sorry, maybe that was a bit harsh," Nicole continued quietly, after a moment. "But, honestly, I think there's something more to this. I really, really don't think this is her using you and then throwing you away. Please, promise me you'll talk to her. Don't just walk away from this. Find out what happened last night before you write this off. Please?"

Sadie sighed and rubbed her free hand through her hair. *Maybe* Nic was right. Maybe there was an outside chance it wasn't as bad as she feared. She tried hard not to build up her hopes, given it was gone eight o'clock and she'd still heard nothing from Holly, despite knowing she'd been at work for nearly an hour. But she'd promised herself these past couple of days that she would stop running from situations she couldn't handle. She just had to grit her teeth and get on with it.

"Okay, I'll talk to her. I promise."

Nicole's relieved exhalation hissed down the line. "Cool. And when you know what's going on, let me know too, okay? I'm there whenever you need me, remember?"

"I know." She swallowed down the emotions that threatened to spill over. "Thanks, Nic."

"Any time, sweetheart. Any time."

Holly was beyond irritated at how her morning had panned out. She'd overslept, having to be practically hauled out of bed by her mum when she slept through her alarm. Focused entirely on getting through her shower, dressing, and eating breakfast as fast as was possible in the twenty minutes she had before she needed to be behind the desk at reception, she had given no thought to her plan to text Sadie. When she'd been at work for about half an hour and had a quiet moment in which to send the message, she'd discovered that in her haste to leave the house, she'd left behind her phone. It was annoying, but it didn't overly concern her, because she knew she could just ring Sadie's room. Only she'd tried that a few times, and there was no answer. Clearly, Sadie had already left the hotel, and without coming to greet Holly.

She hadn't yet memorised Sadie's phone number, so had no chance of contacting her while she was out. She was really worried about what was going on. How could Sadie just leave without even saying good morning? She thought the night they'd shared was incredible. She'd thought that feeling was mutual, but with Sadie's silence, she was deeply worried she'd got it all wrong. Her stomach roiled at the thought.

"Are you okay, sweetheart?" Her mum's voice was quiet, yet still had the power to shock her out of her musings. Such was the depth with which she'd immersed herself in them.

She glanced up quickly to meet her mum's concerned gaze. "Yes, sorry. I guess oversleeping has just, you know, frazzled me a bit."

"Well, I'm worried you're coming down with something. It's just not like you to sleep through like that."

Holly shrugged. "I'm fine, honestly." She turned back to the screen in front of her and made a big show of opening up an inquiry e-mail, hoping her mum would get the hint and leave her alone.

How on earth could she explain what was gnawing away at her insides when to do so would involve confessing everything that had happened over the last few days? She and her mum had always been close. For a long time, Holly had felt she could share almost anything with her. But, over the last couple of years, coming to the realisation about her sexuality and seeing how much her mum had struggled with that, even that relationship had cooled. A distance had grown between them, Holly knew. Her mum was the last person she would consider telling about Sadie and how she felt about her, what she feared was going wrong between them. Because being rejected by Sadie, if that's what this was, was just about the most painful thing Holly had ever experienced. Somehow, she knew her mum just wouldn't give her the level of comfort and support she needed for that. And that knowledge pained her almost as much as Sadie pushing her away.

"Come in, love," Elsie said warmly, as she pulled open the door. Sadie stepped through into the house and gave her grandmother a quick hug. Elsie held her at arm's length as they pulled apart, tilting her head slightly, a small frown appearing between her brows.

"Everything all right?" she asked.

Sadie nodded, trying to glance away from her penetrating gaze. "Fine. How's Mum?"

Elsie glared at her for a moment, then sighed. "Okay, if that's the way you want to play it," she said, with a hint of sarcasm. "Your mother is fine. She wants to go out again today, if that's okay? Needs a change of scenery."

"Sure," Sadie replied, pointedly ignoring her gran's first comment and walking away from her down the hallway. She could hear her following and could also hear the slight tutting sound she made as she did so.

"Hey, Mum." She walked into the kitchen to find her mother sitting at the table, sipping at a glass of juice.

"Hello, darling," Christine said, and then paused. She cocked her head as she stared at Sadie, a perturbed look on her face. "What's wrong?"

"Nothing," Sadie expelled, with a frustrated sigh. Frustrated at herself for obviously not being able to hide the discomfort she was feeling with the Holly situation. Frustrated that Holly still hadn't contacted her, even though Sadie had finally plucked up the courage to send her a short text asking if she was okay.

Christine held her hands up in supplication. "Okay, sorry. You just seem… upset, that's all."

Sadie closed her eyes briefly, then opened them to cast a quick glance at both of the older women before her.

"I-I can't really talk about it, not yet. Maybe later," she offered and was relieved when they both nodded gently.

"Can we go for a drive today?" Christine asked, breaking the uneasy silence.

"Of course," Sadie said, grateful for the shift in focus. "How about somewhere like Buninyong? Either for coffee or lunch, or even for a drive up the hill and back. I went to the lookout last week, and it was still as beautiful up there as I remembered. I know you won't be able to do the climb, but the drive up is pretty scenic anyway."

"Well, that sounds lovely. I haven't been out that way for quite a while. Let me just go and get ready."

After the drive, they parked up in front of the The Old Bluestone Cafe. Inside, they found an unoccupied table and settled in with hot coffees and a slice of cake each from the mouthwatering selection on offer at the front counter.

"Your grandmother has some news, by the way," Christine said as they all tucked in to their cakes.

Elsie chuckled, and Sadie looked up from her decadently dense chocolate cake, intrigued. "What have you been up to, Gran?" She smiled when her grandmother actually blushed.

"Oh, Mother, don't be embarrassed. It was a good thing you did. Even if she didn't think so." Christine's voice sounded amused.

Sadie placed her fork on her plate, her cake forgotten for the moment. "Okay, now you really do have to tell me."

"Well," Elsie began, clearing her throat. "I decided after that incident with that boyfriend of Izzy's, and that chat we had about how your mum thought I should have said something about Peter before they got too serious… Well, I decided that I wouldn't let Izzy make that kind of mistake. So I called her."

"You did not!" Sadie laughed loudly. "Did you tell her off?"

Elsie grinned, and Christine smirked. "There might have been a telling off in there, yes." Her grandmother's eyes sparkled with mirth. "You know me, I don't like to beat around the bush."

Sadie couldn't stop giggling. The idea of her gran telling Izzy off was just too perfect. *Payback's a bitch, sis.*

"I'm guessing she didn't take it so well, though, from what Mum said."

Elsie laughed. "Well, you could tell she was trying to be polite—I am her grandmother after all. But no, she clearly wasn't happy about being told off by this old bird." She huffed. "Tough, she needed to hear it. That waste of space she's seeing is nowhere near good enough for her. I told her she needed to take a long, hard look at herself and what she wanted before she spent any more time with the likes of him."

Sadie guffawed, drawing amused gazes from the other patrons in the room. "Oh God, I would love to hear a recording of that call!"

The three of them laughed together, and Elsie sat a little taller in her chair. "I don't regret a word of it," she declared. "She needed to hear it. Just hope part of her listens to it."

Sadie leaned into her grandmother to give her a quick hug. "Gran, you are a legend. I love you." She was surprised at the small gasp of emotion that escaped her grandmother's throat, and felt her squeeze Sadie just that little bit tighter. Their eyes locked, and Elsie smiled.

"Bless you," she said quietly. "Bless you."

By the time they left the cafe, after a second round of coffees, the sun had broken through the thin cloud and the temperature had risen to a very pleasant level. Christine requested a visit to the lake on the way back, and Sadie found herself inexplicably drawn to the same bench she'd sat on much earlier that morning.

Christine, sandwiched between Sadie and Elsie, and wrapped up in a coat and scarf, breathed in the fresh air coming off the water.

"This is lovely," she said, gazing at the water whilst absently patting Sadie's knee. Sadie smiled and realised that, apart from the memories stirred by this bench, her time with her mother and grandmother had successfully held thoughts of Holly at bay. But as soon as she thought that, she couldn't help but want to check her phone again. She slipped it out from her jacket pocket and tapped in her passcode. No messages. She swallowed hard and shoved the phone back in her pocket.

"Ready to tell us yet?" Elsie asked quietly, and Sadie shifted as both women casually turned to look at her. She exhaled slowly and nodded. This was as good a time as any. Whether her mother was ready or not.

Slowly, with many pauses while she struggled to articulate feelings that were, for her, so new and so unexplored, she gradually told them of how events had unfolded over the past week with Holly. Although she touched on the intimacy they'd shared, she respectfully glossed over any details, choosing instead to focus on the emotions that had surfaced, especially the pain of the overnight rejection. It was hard to talk so openly about how she felt. But, to their credit, especially her mum's, both women simply listened, occasionally interrupting with a question, but neither of them showing any hint of a struggle to be anything other than what Sadie needed right then; supportive.

"I'm with Nic on this one, love," Elsie said, when she'd finished. "I think something came up that is nothing to do with what you two just shared."

"I agree," Christine said slowly. She was blushing, but Sadie was immensely grateful that her mother was pushing past her own discomfort to be there for Sadie. "I'm obviously no expert on all of this, and I don't pretend to fully understand it." She paused and touched Sadie's hand. "But I can see that you do care for this girl. That she means a great deal to you already." Her blush deepened. "So, I think you should get back to the hotel and find out what's going on. Right now."

"But what if—?"

"No," Christine said firmly, raising a hand. "No more what-ifs, Sadie." She turned fully to her and took a hand between both of hers. "I know you're scared. And after…everything, I don't blame you at all. But if there's any chance this girl can make you happy, you have to take it, don't you?" Sadie stared at her in shock. This was way beyond where she thought they'd be with this. "And if you run away, you might lose that chance. Better to be strong and face up to whatever it is now than always wonder what might have been."

Sadie's mouth was dry, and her heart was beating double time. There was a part of her brain struggling to understand how she could be sitting on a park bench getting relationship advice from her mother. About a woman. It was surreal.

"Holly sounds like a wonderful young woman. And it does sound like she cares for you, despite what you think might have happened earlier this morning. Please, don't walk away from her until you've heard her story. Promise me? I just want you to be happy." Christine's voice caught. "That's all I want for you now, just to be happy."

"That's all I want too," Sadie replied, her voice husky, and she shivered slightly at the realisation of just how strongly she *did* want that.

"Then try, my darling. Just try."

Holly was clock-watching again. She seemed to have done an awful lot of that this week. Her lunch break was at one, fifteen minutes away, and she planned to be sprinting out of the hotel doors at precisely that time so that she could get home and retrieve her phone. She was nearly in a panic about what Sadie must think, and not being able to do anything about it had been torturous. Sure, she had admin tasks to perform, but they didn't distract her enough. The one thing she had managed to achieve was juggling rooms around for the afternoon check-ins so that Sadie could stay on in room twelve. Sadie hadn't said when she wanted to leave yet, but they'd had two cancellations for the following week, so Holly had been able to book her through to the following weekend. Another thing she needed to tell her, and no means of doing so.

She twitched in her chair as she heard the front door open. Her breath caught in her throat when she saw Sadie walk hesitantly into the lobby. She looked hurt and confused, and it nearly broke Holly's heart.

Glancing quickly round to ensure her mother wasn't within earshot, Holly stood and leaned forward slightly towards the approaching Sadie.

"I'm so sorry," she whispered, when Sadie was close enough to hear. "I left my phone at home after I overslept this morning. I haven't had any way to reach you all day."

Sadie blinked, and tilted her head slightly. "I… What about last night?" she asked, and her voice sounded strained, as if she was keeping a tight lid on something. And then Holly saw her eyes, and saw the anger Sadie was trying to contain. *Oh shit.*

"Wh-what about last night?"

"Sweetheart, I don't think this last invoice—" Her mum rounded the corner from the office and came to a swift halt. "Oh, my apologies, I didn't realise anyone was here," she said coolly.

"That's okay, Mrs O'Brien," Sadie said pleasantly. Holly was amazed at her poise. "We were just catching up. I'll see you later," she said towards Holly and, without waiting for a response, she strode off through the doors that led to her room.

Holly closed her eyes and willed her stomach not to heave its contents all over the polished wood of the reception desk. Oh God, this was such a mess. Sadie was obviously really angry about how things had developed, and Holly knew, with absolute clarity, she was only going to have one shot at fixing all this. To make matters worse, her mum clearly knew something was going on, if the frown on her face was any indication.

"Everything okay?" Judy's voice carried an edge of distaste that only churned Holly's stomach more.

"Fine," Holly said shortly, her frustration at the situation threatening to boil over. "I'm just getting ready for my break. Are you okay to take over here?"

Judy stared at her, and Holly used all of her remaining strength to unflinchingly hold her mother's gaze. Eventually, Judy broke the deadlock, and Holly breathed out a surreptitious sigh of relief.

"Yes, just give me two minutes."

Holly watched her mum walk back towards the office, and looked down to find her hands gripping the edge of the desk, her knuckles white. Slowly, she unclenched her fingers and stepped back, repeatedly pushing her hair back behind her ears in an action she had long ago recognised as her stress response. How could everything suddenly be getting so messed up, and so quickly? A week ago her life was the same as it had been for about the previous two or three years. Everything was changing, and she didn't seem to have the brain capacity to keep up.

The next two minutes seemed to crawl and gave her enough time to formulate a very simple plan. She would go to Sadie's room and see if she would talk with her. Beyond that, she had no idea how to dig herself out of the extraordinarily deep hole she found herself in.

When her mother finally returned, they barely spoke as Holly handed over the desk to her. She walked quickly out of the front door. When she saw her mother turn away, she shot across the car park and down the driveway at the side of the hotel that led round to the back door. Moments later, she was standing outside Sadie's room, her fist raised to knock on the door. She hesitated only slightly, pulling her thoughts together, before knocking firmly.

CHAPTER 16

Sadie was mortified. She slumped back against her hotel room's door. Why couldn't she just act rationally? Why couldn't she just talk things through with Holly? Ask the questions she wanted answers for without doing her disappearing act? Sure, Judy had turned up just as they started talking, but Sadie could easily have hung around until she'd gone. Instead, she'd done her usual—run. Furious at herself, she decided to get back out there, when a rap at the door reverberated through her, making her jump.

She wrenched the door open and was relieved to see Holly standing in the corridor.

"Come in," Sadie said, her voice quivering slightly. She noted, with some shame, Holly's fearful expression.

They moved to the middle of the room, standing a metre or so apart.

"Sadie, I'm sor—"

Sadie held up her hand. "Don't, it's okay." She tried to tamp down her anxiety. She needed one question answered before they went any further. "Please, tell me why I woke up alone at four this morning."

She stared at Holly, noting that she still looked scared. But at the same time, she definitely didn't look like someone who didn't want anything more to do with Sadie. Her eyes still held the longing in them that they'd displayed all of last night.

"I panicked," Holly said, her face flushing. "I can't stay here, overnight, with a guest. My parents would have a fit. When I realised I'd fallen asleep with you, all I could think about was getting home before they figured it out. It wasn't until just now that I realised how that might have seemed to you. And when I left my bloody phone at home… Oh God, that just made it ten times worse."

Sadie huffed out a breath, feeling more than a little disappointed with herself. What an idiot she'd been. Of course there was a perfectly reasonable explanation for Holly to need to leave earlier, and to not contact her during the day. And Holly's reaction, her obvious distress at causing Sadie such confusion, left no doubt in Sadie's mind that she was telling the truth.

"God, I'm sorry," Sadie said earnestly, wishing she could wipe that awful look from Holly's face with one magic word. "Just when I think I'm learning to control my old fears, I overreact and think the worst." The heat of her embarrassment at her childish response flushed through her. She pushed her free hand through the back of her hair.

Holly was gazing at her in confusion.

"You were so angry, Sadie. Out there." Holly gestured in the direction of the reception area. "I…I had no idea how to deal with that."

Sadie tentatively reached out for her, and relief flooded through her when Holly moved into her arms.

"I'm so sorry," she said against Holly's hair. "I should never have started that conversation the way I did." She pulled back slightly so that she could see Holly's face, glad to see that it was relaxing somewhat. "I have this thing about being abandoned," she continued, knowing she owed Holly a full explanation for her side of the events between them. "When I woke up at four and you weren't there, my irrational brain decided you'd left me. That all you wanted was a one-night stand." She flinched as Holly's face fell. "It's like… I don't know, like common sense goes out the window and instead of carefully thinking it through, I go off the deep end. I did it to Nic recently too." She shook her head, and then relaxed a little as Holly's warm hand stroked the back of her neck.

"I get why you would have some issues over abandonment," Holly said. "After everything you've told me, I get it. But I honestly wasn't thinking things through either at whatever hour it was this morning. I can see how it would look like I was running out on you, and I'm sorry that's what you had to think for a while."

"Well, that's the thing that makes me even more embarrassed." Sadie sighed. "I didn't *have* to think that at all. I could have just calmly waited for you to explain instead of acting like a child."

Holly smiled and squeezed Sadie's hand. "If I could have texted or called, none of this would have happened."

"No." Sadie shook her head. "None of this would have happened if I'd just stopped for a moment."

Holly leaned forward and kissed her, slowly and gently. Sadie trembled at the sensations that simple kiss sparked throughout her body. Relief, arousal, and something…deeper. Something she didn't quite want to put a name to yet. Something that meant she had to work extra hard at dealing with her issues from the past so that they didn't ruin her future.

"I know you probably have trust issues from all your family history," Holly said, chuckling when Sadie snorted, "and God knows that's understandable. But you can trust me, you know? I'd like you to. Or, at least, you could promise to try?"

Sadie looked deep into Holly's eyes, hoping her face would reflect the sincerity she tried to imbue her next words with. "You haven't given me any reason not to trust you. It isn't easy for me, letting someone in, but I do want to try, with you."

Holly grinned and nuzzled Sadie's nose with hers. "Good. But talk to me, please. Tell me what you're feeling. I know some of what's happened to you in the past but obviously not all of it. I can't keep second-guessing."

"I know. It's all part of the same thing—me learning to let someone in. But I promise to try, okay?"

"That's all I can ask." Holly smiled. "I'm so glad we got this sorted. It's been a hell of a morning."

Sadie smiled, her heart and mind vastly lighter than they had been at the start of her day. "Do you need to get back to work?" she asked slyly.

Holly grinned and glanced at her watch. "Oh, look at that. I have at least twenty minutes of my break left."

"Well," Sadie said, pulling Holly to her again, feeling the softness and warmth of her body press close to her own in all the right places. "I'm sure there's something we can do to keep you occupied in that time."

Holly's response was to lunge in for a kiss that banished all the drama of the day far from Sadie's mind.

"You okay, babe?" Holly asked quietly, stilling her fingers just underneath Sadie's left breast. They had been in bed since Holly arrived back at the room at five, her shift over for the day and her intentions abundantly clear. Over the last four hours or so, Sadie had been astonished at how much they could give to each other and still come back for more.

Sadie blinked. "Yeah, sorry. Just thinking about how today has worked out. I can't quite believe it."

Holly smiled and kissed her softly. "Believe it. I'm here. It's real. All of it."

Sadie nodded and kissed Holly, more deeply this time, and there it was. Again. That deep need to have this woman, to feel her, taste her, all instantly switched on with just one kiss. She reached up and pushed Holly's shoulders firmly, tumbling her onto her back.

Holly giggled. "Hm, and just what do you have in mind now?" she asked, her eyes sparkling even as they darkened with her desire. She stretched seductively, arms above her head, back arched.

"I need to taste you." Sadie's voice was rough, strained, her need swallowing her up until she could barely breathe.

Holly moaned, and Sadie leaned forward, taking one of Holly's nipples into her mouth and nibbling it gently. Holly's breathing became ragged and erratic as Sadie moved swiftly down her body, kissing open-mouthed across her skin on her determined path to the apex of Holly's thighs. Pushing her lover's legs apart, using more force than before but thrilling in the excited sounds that Holly made as she did so, she briefly eyed the wet folds before her, then dipped her head. She couldn't wait a second longer.

Dragging her tongue slowly but firmly through Holly's sweet wetness, she grasped hold of Holly's hips and pulled her closer, wanting to lose herself completely in the taste and scent of the woman she was falling crazy in love with. She dipped her tongue inside her, thrusting as hard and as deep as she could, using her thumb to simultaneously rub slow circles on Holly's clit. When Holly came, her thighs closing despite Sadie's efforts to keep them open, Sadie gripped her, emotions rising to the surface in exciting yet scary waves. Moments later, she pulled herself up the landscape of Holly's body and kissed her deeply, wanting so much to tell Holly how she was feeling, but at the same time, terrified to do so. Instead, she kept her mouth occupied with kissing the beautiful woman beneath her until Holly had to pull away to take desperate lungfuls of air.

"God, babe, that was… *God.*" Holly laughed gently, shaking her head.

"I know," Sadie said, nibbling along her jawline. "I know."

Holly's arms pulled her tight against her, and they lay like that, simply listening to each other breathe, until it was time for Holly to head home.

CHAPTER 17

Sadie awoke slowly, pulled from a deeply satisfying slumber by thoughts of Holly, and she was smiling before she was even fully awake. She stretched, and her skin tingled with the pull of her muscles, which set off all sorts of chain reactions at the memories of those same muscles being used in other delightful ways only hours earlier. It was gone nine, which meant she'd slept for nearly nine hours. Bliss. Knowing also that she didn't have to get up to pack and move hotels, or even rooms, was a godsend, thanks to her girlfriend's nifty moves on the hotel's booking system. She really ought to think of a way to thank her for that, properly.

Feeling like a lovesick teenager, she reached for her phone to call Holly, only to find a text waiting from her already.

Good morning, gorgeous. I hope you slept as well as I did, although I missed your arms around me...

She grinned and quickly hit the call-back icon.

"Hey, you," came Holly's sultry voice as she answered. "You're awake at last."

"Uh-huh," Sadie murmured. "Didn't like waking up alone, though."

"I know," Holly whispered, "but you know why—"

"Yeah, it's okay," Sadie said. "I totally get that. I just wanted to be honest, that's all. You wrapped up against me is my new favourite thing. And I'm greedy, I want more of it."

She heard Holly chuckle. "Oh, don't worry, you're going to get plenty more of it."

Arousal shot through Sadie's body at the thought, and she clenched her thighs together in a vain attempt to still her throbbing clit.

"God," she breathed, "what you can do to me with just a few words."

Holly sucked in a quick breath. "I know," she said, and her voice ached with the same desire that was wrapping itself around every molecule in Sadie's body. Holly noisily cleared her throat. "So," she continued, "what time do you think you'll be coming back today? Are you guys going out somewhere?"

Sadie shook her head to clear her mind of all the libidinous thoughts that had taken up residence in the last few moments.

"Um, I'm not sure. Depends on how Mum is. The weather looks pretty nice, though, so maybe we'll head out. As for what time I get back, well, I guess around three. She said he was out at some meeting, then off for a round of golf that usually finishes about four. I've got into the habit of leaving at least an hour before he's due home, just to be sure of not bumping into him."

Holly sighed down the line. "It's such a crazy situation. I mean, don't get me wrong, I totally think this is right for you to avoid him, but really, how sad is that? Your own father is someone you have to avoid seeing because that's how bad things are between you."

"I know. But, it's for the best. I have no problem not attempting to reconcile with him. It's wonderful that I've been able to do that with Mum. I'd like to try for more with Izzy, but that may take a bit more time. But honestly, I'm totally fine with how much I've reconnected with Mum. That'll do for now."

"Good. I'm glad you've made peace with your mum too. You seem, I don't know, so much more relaxed than the person you were when you first arrived. Like you're not carrying such a heavy weight anymore."

Sadie smiled to herself. "Yeah, that's true, but I think you can take some responsibility for that too, you know. I've certainly felt a hell of a lot more relaxed these past few hours."

Holly snorted. "I'll bet you have," she said, laughing. "Okay, so I am going to let you start your day. I'm going out shopping to Wendouree with my mum today. Wish me luck, as I suspect there may be an interrogation somewhere along the way."

"Really? About me?"

"Oh yeah. She's not stupid; she knows something's been going on this week. She was acting all super cheerful this morning over breakfast, and I have a feeling that's because she's gearing herself up for a difficult conversation later."

"What will you tell her?" Sadie sat upright, leaning back against the headboard. What Holly was prepared to say about them to her mother suddenly took on an importance she wouldn't have imagined only days ago.

Holly paused. "I'll tell her the truth," she said quietly. "That you mean a huge amount to me, and that I want to be with you."

Sadie swallowed. "I told Mum and Gran about you. And Nicole too."

"You did? When?" Holly's voice contained a hint of excitement. She was clearly happy that Sadie had already shared the concept of "them" with the people she was closest to.

"Yesterday. When I thought… Well, you know, when I thought you had ditched me."

"Oh. Does that mean they hate me?" Her voice was so small, it made Sadie's stomach clench.

"No! God, no." She hated that she'd made Holly feel that way, even for just a moment. "In fact, you can thank Nicole. And Mum too. They both talked me into coming back to the hotel to ask you what was going on. And my mum doing that was freaky—she'd made it quite clear she was struggling with me being a lesbian, so for her to come out fighting for you was pretty special." She paused, blushing. "I was… I was all set to run away. Again." She hated admitting it. She felt so…immature.

"I understand why you would have," Holly said softly. "I didn't exactly give you a lot to go on, did I?"

"Maybe not, but I should have had the guts to face up to it."

"Yeah, but with your history…"

They were both silent for a moment.

"Anyway," Sadie said eventually. "All three of them think you sound really nice. And that you're good for me," she added quietly.

Holly's whisper breathed down the line. "And am I?"

"Oh, babe, *yes*. Definitely."

"Wow."

Sadie grinned, suddenly happier than she remembered ever feeling. "God, I wish you were here right now so that I could show you how happy you make me."

"Mm, later, babe. Later." The sultriness was back in Holly's voice, and it sent exquisite tremors cascading down Sadie's spine.

Holly mentally braced herself as she slipped into the car and clicked her seat belt into place.

"So," Judy said breezily as she slipped the car into gear and pulled them out of the driveway. "I need to start at Kmart. I know it's not your favourite shop in the world, but I need to stock up on napkins and those little vases for the breakfast room."

"No problem, Mum," Holly replied. "I'm just along for the ride. I need a new pair of jeans, but that's about it." She forced a casualness into her voice she didn't feel. She knew her mum was planning a "talk" and she'd rather she got it over with. The tense anticipation was killing her.

"Great, we can have a little wander through the mall and see what we can find."

They spent an hour or so in the shops, quickly finding what her mum needed, but having no such luck on the jeans for Holly.

"No worries, Mum," she said, after they'd tried the fifth clothing store. "I'll go into the city on my day off next week."

"How about a coffee, then?"

And here it comes. "Sure, sounds good." She fought down the urge to rub comforting circles on her churning stomach.

Cappuccinos in hand, they found a table in the small food court.

"So," her mum began, after a few sips. "I actually wanted to talk to you about something."

Holly smiled. "Yeah, I kind of guessed you did."

Her mother seemed flustered for a moment, then composed herself. "Oh, okay." She hesitated. "Anything you want to tell me?"

Although Holly couldn't understand exactly why, a sudden but perfect calmness swept over her.

"I've started dating Sadie." And there it was, out there.

Judy stared at her and blinked a couple of times. "I-I thought that's what was going on."

Holly exhaled, slowly. "Yeah, I know. We tried to keep it quiet to begin with, until we knew what was happening wasn't just, you know, a fling. But, it's definitely more than that." She watched her mother squirm slightly in her seat, but to her credit she didn't overreact in the way Holly had feared she might.

"And, um, you're sure that this is something you want?"

Holly suddenly felt really sorry for her mum. She was clearly struggling with the whole notion of her daughter not being straight, and yet was equally trying to do the right thing and understand her daughter. Holly leaned forward across their small table and gently took her hand in her own. Her mother's hand was cold and trembled slightly.

"Mum, I know this is hard for you." She watched her mum nod and take a deep breath. "Sadie is not my first girlfriend."

At that, Judy's eyebrows shot up into her hairline.

"I know, you thought me liking girls was just a concept, didn't you?"

Judy nodded, slowly.

"Well, no. It isn't. It is something I've already acted on."

She decided then and there that total honesty was what was required. If she wanted them to maintain the kind of close relationship they'd had all through her life, she needed her mum to know the real Holly.

"I've had five other relationships in my life, Mum. Three with men, then two with women. Sadie is the third woman I've been involved with."

Judy stared at her, her eyes glistening with tears yet to fall.

"I had no idea," she said quietly, and Holly saw her swallow down a sob. "I-I can't pretend this isn't difficult to hear."

"I know, Mum." She squeezed her mother's hand. "But I don't want to keep things from you anymore, or let you think I'm something I'm not."

"And this…thing with Sadie. It's serious? It's only been a week."

Holly smiled, gently. "Yes, it has only been a week, but it's very serious. We've spent a lot of time together, and we connect in so many ways. She means a lot to me, Mum."

Judy's tears fell then, silently, and she quickly reached into her bag for a tissue to dab them away. She glanced around, probably embarrassed to be coming apart like this in the middle of the shopping mall. When she'd blown her nose a couple of times, she looked back at Holly.

"It's just, it's not quite what I imagined for you, growing up."

"I know. But this makes me happy. *She* makes me happy. That's all I can say."

Judy blew her nose again and reached for a second tissue. She blotted her eyes and cheeks a few more times, then breathed out heavily.

"Just give me some time, please, sweetheart. To get used to the idea. Just… some time."

"This is just so fucking awesome!" Nicole was practically yelling at the FaceTime call screen. "I've wanted something like this for you for so long."

"I know." Sadie grinned. "Me too. Well, now I've got it, it seems. Holly's… well, she's just amazing. It's the only word I keep coming up with." It had been fun—and strangely thrilling—updating her friends on developments in her relationship with Holly. And it *was* a relationship, a real grown-up one, the first time in her life she'd experienced the concept. It gave her a buzz even just thinking about it.

Nicole gave her a cheesy double thumbs up. Tash sat beside her, rolling her eyes in mock horror.

"I'm really pleased for you," Tash said, in her more understated way. "We can't wait to meet her."

"Yeah, well, I'll see what I can do about that."

"Hey," Nicole said, "in all the drama of Holly having to leave the other night, you never told me how it went with Izzy."

Sadie groaned. "Probably because I was trying to forget it."

"That bad?"

"Oh, yeah. Actually, it annoyed the shit out of me." She filled them in on how the lunchtime meeting went and Luke's asinine behaviour. The bit that hurt her most—Izzy's seeming collusion—brought gasps of disbelief from Nic.

"Luke's a total fucking asshole!" Nic declared. Tash simply shook her head.

"Ah, forget him," Sadie said. "Something tells me he won't last long. But Izzy? What is she doing wasting herself on guys like him? She was always so smart, and that doesn't seem to have changed, so why be with him?"

"Yes, but there's brainy smart and there's life smart," Tash offered. "It sounds like Izzy has one without the other."

"She is so much better than that," Sadie said fiercely, and the knowledge that she wanted more for her sister came as a welcome surprise. "For a few moments there, she and I had the start of something. Something I thought could mean I'd get my sister back."

"You still might," Nic said quietly.

"Yes. But it will have to come from me, I think." She couldn't imagine Izzy reaching out. Or maybe she would, but Sadie didn't want to be the passive one in this. If there was a chance they could get something started again, she was prepared to do the work to make it happen.

"And is it easy avoiding your…dad in all this?" Tash asked the question hesitantly; both she and Nicole knew Sadie didn't like talking about him under any circumstances. But maybe that was something else that needed to change.

Sadie nodded. "It is, actually. He knows I'm in town, but I have no idea what Mum has told him about me visiting her so often. Probably very little, to give herself a quiet life. And no, before you ask, I don't want to see him. That would be a step too far." She shook her head. "It's more than enough to have managed what I have with Mum and the chance of what I could have with Izzy. That's way beyond what I thought would be possible even a month ago, before all this happened." She smiled at their faces in the small screen of her phone. "I think I'll quit while I'm ahead."

"Always a sound strategy," Nicole said, smirking.

Christine was sleeping when Sadie arrived at the house just after ten thirty. She followed Elsie to the kitchen. The house was quiet.

"Mum okay?"

Elsie sighed as she eased herself into one of the chairs at the table.

"She's just tired. Peter came home from work last night in some sort of mood, and they had a big argument. I didn't hear all of it, as I was in the lounge room and they were in here. It seemed it was something along the lines of him wanting them to take a big, romantic trip before she dies, and her telling him she wasn't well enough for something like that."

"That's crazy." Sadie shook her head. "He wants a holiday with her and yet he's not here looking after her when she's this ill? He's still going to work every day and leaving her here with you, so how much does he really care?"

"He's a hypocrite." Elsie snorted. "Acts like he's the best husband in the world but it's all for show, I'm sure."

Sadie grinned. "That's what I like about you, Gran. You never hold back on what you mean."

Her grandmother huffed out an indignant breath. "I don't see the point any more. Life's too short."

The phrase, and its implications, hung between them in the quiet room.

Christine appeared about an hour later. Sadie held back a gasp as she took in the haggard eyes and pale face.

"Mum," she said quietly, moving quickly out of her chair to pull her mother into a careful embrace. Christine's arms slid around her, one hand on her back, one laid gently on the back of her head.

"It's all right, love," she whispered against Sadie's hair. "Just one of those days."

They held each other for a few moments whilst Elsie busied herself warming some croissants and making them all a fresh pot of coffee.

"Gran said you had a bit of an argument with him last night?" Sadie asked as she carefully steered her into a chair.

Christine laughed softly. "Yes. Silly fool had this idea we could take off to Bali, or somewhere equally exotic, for a last romantic getaway." She grimaced. "We haven't had a romantic holiday since our honeymoon. Why on earth he thought I'd want one now, I have no idea." She nibbled at a piece of croissant, sending a grateful glance towards her mother as she did so. Elsie smiled and patted her hand.

Sadie pulled out a chair for herself, but had barely sat down before the sound of the front door opening snapped all three of their heads towards that part of the house.

"Christine?" her father's voice called. "What the hell's that bike doing on the driveway?"

Christine turned to face Sadie, her horror-struck expression mirroring Sadie's own.

Sadie's blood chilled in her veins.

God, no. I can't do this. I can't.

But she was paralysed in her chair, her limbs like lead. All three women sat as still as statues as time seemed to slow down, the seconds passing in infinitesimal steps as they awaited his arrival in the kitchen.

He appeared in the doorway, and Sadie stared at him, her emotions in turmoil, churning her stomach, making bile rise to her throat. He hadn't changed much, actually. He still looked in reasonable shape—no middle-aged paunch anyway. His hair was thinner, and only touched with grey at the temples. His eyes were still the same soft brown shade but just as hard as she remembered.

They hardened further as he took in the scene before him.

"Who the—?" He stopped as he stared at her, then let out a chopped sound that was half laugh, half snort. "Sadie?" He glanced quickly round at his wife and mother-in-law, a frown deepening on his forehead with every passing moment. Then his eyes came back to Sadie.

"What the fuck," he enunciated clearly and precisely, "are you doing in my house?" His face was reddening slightly, a sure sign that his temper was rapidly engaging. That hadn't changed either, Sadie noted, in a dim recess at the back of her mind.

She slowly pushed her chair back and got to her feet, in as unthreatening a manner as possible. The atmosphere in the kitchen crackled with the tension and anger emanating off her father, and she would do anything to ensure it didn't spill over into anything they'd all regret. Her mum reached out an arm and laid a gentle hand on Sadie's forearm.

"It's okay, Mum," Sadie said quietly, gazing down at her mother. "It's okay."

With a calmness she didn't know she could possess, given the circumstances, Sadie took two careful steps away from the table, giving herself room to manoeuvre. She was preparing, although for what she wasn't entirely sure. Some instinct was kicking in, something primal, that told her in no uncertain terms that she needed to be ready for anything in the next few minutes.

"I said—" began her father, his voice louder than before, but Christine cut him off.

"We all heard what you said, Peter," she snapped.

He turned to face her, his gaze boring into hers. She didn't flinch, and Sadie was inordinately proud of her mother at that moment.

Christine calmed her tone as she said, "Sadie is here, because I invited her."

Sadie could see he was struggling with his response to this. Not only was his wife defying him, but she was doing so in a way that clearly said she didn't care what he thought about it. His face reddened further, and his hands clenched and unclenched at his sides.

"No," he said, after a moment, but that single word was spoken with such venom it made Sadie's insides squirm with fear. "No," he repeated, taking one slow step forward, his eyes narrowing as he stared at Sadie. "I won't have this… person in my house. I won't have her visiting you. You need to leave. Now!" He shouted the last word, and Sadie took an involuntary step backwards at the sheer power of the rage contained in it.

"Peter!"

Christine's voice whipped across the room, but it had no effect on his momentum. In three quick strides he was across the room and grabbed hold of Sadie by her biceps. She heard Elsie and her mother gasp, heard their chairs being scraped back on the tiled floor. Peter Williams was a little taller than his daughter, and he used that to his advantage, leaning intimidatingly over her as he pushed her back across the room. She struggled in his arms, her chest heaving with panicked breaths, wondering just what he was going to do.

"Let me go!" she shouted, trying to pull her arms away.

He was strong, but so was Sadie. All the running and training she had done over the years had honed her muscles to a deceptive strength. She called on that strength, and with a deep breath, flipped both arms up and outwards, breaking his hold. She could feel her anger, her pain from all those years ago, forcing its way up through all the barriers she'd put in place over the years. She couldn't stop it, couldn't contain it. Not anymore.

When he made to grab her again she placed both hands on his chest and shoved, as hard as she could.

"Get your hands off me!" she cried, and took satisfaction in seeing him stumble backwards slightly. He roared and came at her again, but she dodged his approach.

"Peter!" Christine screamed. "Leave her alone!"

And suddenly her mum was there, between them, and Sadie watched in horror as her father, blinded by his feelings for Sadie, unthinkingly lashed out an arm towards her mother. Sadie didn't know what he intended, whether to simply push or—worse—hit, but instinct took over. She dived between her parents, and the arm that he had begun to swing towards his wife caught Sadie's shoulder, throwing her wildly off balance and spinning her into the fridge door. Her forehead hit the cool metal, not a blow serious enough to break the skin, but solid enough to cause her to pause for a moment, blinking back stars.

She turned, her body and mind utterly consumed with the anger that she had repressed all these years. Anger at this man she had to call father. Everything she'd bottled up over the years came crashing through, exacerbated by his thoughtless treatment of her mother just a moment ago. Eyes almost unseeing, she launched herself at him, reaching out with both hands to grab handfuls of his shirt, shoving him back hard against the countertop.

The anger was like a liquid heat, pouring through her veins, rupturing across her skin. She was shaking with it. The sounds of the room were drowned out by an incessant roaring that seemed to come from somewhere in the back of her head. Shifting slightly to grab hold of the collar of his shirt, she pulled him away from the cupboards behind him, and then slammed him back into them. His head hit one of the cupboard doors with a satisfying thud, and he grunted, his eyes blazing as he glared at Sadie.

"Sadie, no!" Her mother's voice was shrill and filled with fear. "Don't. *Please*, I beg you. He's not worth it."

Her father, his expression a mixture of anger and stunned surprise at the strength with which his daughter had slammed him against the cupboard, tried to bring his arms up to prise Sadie off his chest. She held firm, forearms locked across his torso and upper arms, adrenaline pumping through her veins and giving her a greater strength than she thought possible. She took a firmer grip on his shirt, ready to thump his head back again. There was no conscious thought working at the moment, simply pure emotion. As she made to pull at him again, her mother's voice came from close behind her.

"Sadie, *please*."

Sadie turned her head slowly to find her mother staring at her, her eyes watery.

"Please, he's really not worth it." Her voice was gentle, pleading, her gaze never straying from Sadie's. "He's just a mean old bully. He's not worth you getting into trouble over. Please, darling."

She felt her father flinch at her mother's words.

"Christine." His voice broke on that single word.

Her mum raised a hand. "Enough," she said, her voice as sharp as honed steel. "I've had enough. Of you. This marriage. Our pathetic little lives."

Sadie turned back to the man she had pinned against the countertop and watched his expression change, his eyes widening in shock and disbelief. She felt his body slump underneath her arms and the fight leak out of him. She released her hold, her chest heaving with deep, shuddering breaths, and she stepped back away from him. Her arms shook, and her knees suddenly seemed unable to keep her upright. She staggered back a few more steps.

"Thank you, darling," her mother whispered, and Sadie turned to look at her, seeing all the love and pride and support that she'd wanted to see twelve years ago. It was finally there, and it meant so much. She felt tears welling up, and didn't fight them. Christine reached out a tender hand to wipe them away, but more dropped to replace the ones she wiped off, and Sadie smiled weakly.

"Don't bother," she said softly, reaching out to take her mother's hand. "I'll probably be crying for a while yet."

Christine leaned in to kiss her softly on the cheek. "I should have done that twelve years ago," she said, her voice aching with regret, "and I'm so sorry I didn't."

Sadie gently pulled her mother into a hug. "It's okay, Mum. It's okay."

Sadie's whole body was shaking, and her mum held her tightly.

They pulled apart, and Sadie stepped back to reach for her grandmother, who was crying, and trembling. She held her close.

"It's all right, Gran. Everything's all right," she murmured against her hair.

Elsie clutched at her, and Sadie was alarmed to feel Elsie's heart beating erratically in her chest.

"Sit down, Gran, please. You need to stay calm, okay?" Elsie nodded, and allowed Sadie to guide her back to her chair.

"I think you need to go," Christine said as she turned to face her husband. He still stood where Sadie had left him, his hands clenched. "I don't want you here."

"But—" He looked shell-shocked and as if he'd aged another ten years in just ten minutes.

"No buts, Peter," she said tiredly, rubbing at her forehead. "You've caused enough damage for one day, don't you think? Come back tonight and we'll talk. But right now, please, just go."

They locked eyes with each other, and the silence stretched out. Sucking in a breath, he nodded slowly and pushed himself away from the counter. Without another word or a glance back at any of the three women in the room, he strode out of the kitchen. Moments later, they heard the front door slam, making them all jump.

Sadie moved then, reaching for her mother, pulling her close for a tender hug before urging her to sit down. She gazed at her mother and grandmother, and ran her still-shaking hands through her hair. Her stomach was churning again, but not from anger. She bolted from the room as the churning increased, vaguely aware of her mum's cry behind her, and only just made it to the bathroom before throwing up. After a few moments, she felt a cool cloth pressed against her forehead.

"Get it all out," Elsie said quietly. "It's okay."

"Oh, Gran," Sadie sobbed, the anguish tearing her apart. "What did I do?"

If this was how violent she could be, when really pushed, what did that say about her? It was all her worst fears coming true, and it terrified her.

"You reacted, that's all. He threatened you. Don't think what you did in return was wrong."

"But, I was s-so angry. It completely took me over. I-I don't want to be like that." She held the cloth to her face, hiding behind it.

"You're not," came her mother's voice from farther back in the room.

Sadie looked up. Christine was leaning on the doorframe, looking physically weak but mentally determined.

"You are not a violent person. Please, don't think that you are. That was an exceptional circumstance, and anyone would have done the same thing."

"I don't—"

"No," Christine interrupted gently. "There's nothing more to say. I understand you're upset, but don't you see? The fact that you are means that you aren't the person you're scared of being. If you weren't upset by what you just did, *then* I'd be worried." She smiled, and Sadie sighed.

"I guess so," she said slowly.

"Your mum's right," Elsie said, taking the cloth and wetting it again before tenderly wiping it across Sadie's forehead. "Come on, let's get up off this floor and go and have a cup of tea."

After they had made tea and all sat back down around the kitchen table, Elsie placed a gentle hand on Sadie's arm.

"Sadie, are you physically okay? Did he hurt you?"

Sadie smiled at her grandmother. "I'm fine, Gran," she replied. "Please, don't worry. Are you okay?"

Elsie nodded, slowly. "I am. It was a bit scary, I must admit. I-I worried what he would do to you."

Christine flinched at the words, and Sadie spoke up quickly to reassure her. "Mum, it's okay. It was more shock rather than actual hurt. I'm more worried about how violent I was, rather than the physical stuff he did to me." She held up a hand when her mother tried to interrupt. "It's okay, I get what you said about that. I'll need a bit of time to work through it, but yeah, I think you're right. I don't think I'm naturally that violent, not deep down." She paused and took a sip of her tea, aware of her hands still trembling as she lifted the cup to her lips. "As for the physical harm, maybe when the adrenaline dies down I might find I'm aching a bit. But, really, it's all okay. Please, don't worry."

Christine smiled, but not convincingly.

"Mum," Sadie said firmly, after a few moments, "I am so proud of you for standing up to him. And for supporting me. I can't tell you what that means to me."

Christine raised her mug and smiled warmly at her daughter. "It was the least I could do. And God, it felt good!"

CHAPTER 18

Well, totally out to my mum now! She took it pretty well, I think. How did your day go? Can't wait to see you, call/text me as soon as you can. God, I want to kiss you so badly…xx

Sadie sighed happily at the thought of more kisses. Holly's mouth on hers did the most extraordinary things to her body. She tingled with the anticipation of what was to come. After everything that had happened, her overriding desire when she'd returned to her hotel room was simply to be held. But given how her body was reacting to the thought of Holly's mouth on hers, making love could definitely be on the schedule too.

She grinned and texted back.

Back at the hotel. Bit of drama today. Want to grab food somewhere? Or just come here & we'll do pizza again?

The response was instant.

Pizza! Missed you too much to waste time going out. Will be there in 15 xx

Sadie jumped in the shower and took as long as she could, allowing the hot water to pummel her shoulders and back, where her muscles were complaining the most. Her skin was bright pink when she finally switched off the water and reached for a towel, but the heat had helped a little. She threw on a tee shirt and sweatpants just in time for Holly's quiet knock. The sight of the beautiful woman at the door soothed her in a way that reached deep into her soul. She gently pulled Holly into the room. Before she could speak, Sadie enveloped her in a close hug, wrapping her arms all the way around her, pressing Holly's body tight against her own. God, she felt good.

Burying her face in Holly's hair, she breathed in deeply. *This is what I needed.* Craved.

"You okay?" Holly whispered, her hands tightening on Sadie's shoulder blades.

"Crazy day," Sadie murmured into her hair. "I needed this. You."

Holly emitted a small sound of pleasure that sparked a deep-seated need in Sadie to stay... *Just like this, forever.*

"Missed you," Holly said, running her hands up and down the planes of Sadie's back.

"Mm" was all Sadie could manage—her brain and body were in a fog of desire so powerful it made her shiver. Holly's body in her arms, her soft breasts pressing into Sadie's, her firm thigh easing its way between Sadie's, all had her senses reeling and her mind strangely disorientated.

She pulled back slightly to be able to look at Holly and saw a flushed face with hooded eyes. She wasn't the only one affected by their greeting. Her gaze dropped to Holly's lips. She heard Holly's small growl, and it sent an aching throb through her clit. She crushed Holly's mouth to hers, kissing her as passionately as she could, meeting Holly's tongue with her own and groaning loudly from deep in her chest at the contact. Holly's hands drifted down to cup her ass and pull her closer yet. Their mouths were fused, their soft sounds of desire mingling in the quiet room. Holly pulled away first, gasping for air.

"Wow," she whispered, smiling.

Sadie nodded and grinned. "Oh, yeah."

"As much as I want to continue that," Holly said, tilting her head to one side as she looked at Sadie, "something important happened today, didn't it? I can see it in your eyes. Will you tell me?"

Sadie nodded. As much as she wanted Holly, she knew she would relax into their evening more easily if she got it all off her chest first. She motioned to the bed and sat on the end of it, waiting for Holly to throw her jacket on the chair and kick off her shoes before she joined her. Holly's hand instantly reached for Sadie's, and Sadie looked at their linked fingers for a few moments before she started talking.

"My dad showed up." She smiled as Holly's eyes went wide and her mouth opened in shock.

"Oh my God!"

"I know. It was... Well, it was a bit intense for a while."

She told Holly all about the events earlier that day. Holly's emotions ranged from anger to shock to compassion and sympathy. A few tears fell from Sadie's eyes, and Holly's too, but in retelling the story, Sadie realised the worst of her anger over it all had already dissipated, as well as her abiding fear that she had somehow unleashed a violent side to her personality she hadn't known about.

"I agree with your mum. You are not a violent person." Holly's voice was tender, as were her fingertips as they stroked soothingly across Sadie's brow. "You're one of the calmest, gentlest people I've ever met. It was just an extraordinary set of circumstances, and it was all about protecting your mother and grandmother. It was actually more an intense expression of love, really."

Sadie chuckled. "God, that sounds a bit weird, but yeah, I guess it was."

She shook her head, slowly, still reeling a little from all that had happened and all that she had witnessed.

"I think something may happen with Mum and him," she said quietly. "I know she said she couldn't be bothered divorcing him after her diagnosis, but there was something different about her when I left today. Like she'd made up her mind to make some changes. I wouldn't be surprised if one of them moved out of the house."

"Will she be okay? I mean, she's got her illness to deal with too, and that would be a big upheaval to deal with at the same time."

"True. But as much as I want to get involved now and help her, I reckon she needs to do this one on her own. This doesn't have anything to do with me. I'll offer, of course, but…"

"It's like it's something she feels she needs to wrap up before she dies," Holly said softly, unwittingly mirroring Sadie's thoughts.

"Yeah, I think so. Like she never stood up to him before and, somehow, she'll rest easier if she does it now." Her voice caught slightly. "Give her some peace, or something like that."

Holly wrapped her arms around Sadie and squeezed gently. "I love that you talk to me about this stuff. That we share."

"Me too," Sadie said, realising just how much she meant it as she said it.

"Shit, what a day." Holly exhaled loudly. "Are you sure you're okay? Physically I mean? You said you hit your head, and it sounds like it got very rough between you and him."

Sadie shrugged. "My arms and shoulders ache, I'll be honest. But my head's okay. It wasn't that much of a bump. I am pretty tired, though. I can't lie about that."

Holly shook her head. "I'm not surprised. Jesus. Are you sure you want me here? If you want to rest—"

"No," Sadie interrupted. "I really want you here. Need you here." She kissed Holly briefly. "I'm just not sure if…if I have the energy to make love. As much as I want to. And believe me, I really want to."

Holly grinned. "That's okay." Her smile made Sadie shiver, as it seemed to hold a promise of something more. "I can think of ways around that."

With that, she gently pushed Sadie back on the bed.

"First," Holly said, reaching for the waistband of Sadie's sweatpants, "let's get you out of these clothes."

Sadie stared. Holly's entire demeanour had moved from caring to seductive in the blink of an eye, and it was intoxicating. She was powerless to resist and lifted her hips quickly to allow Holly to move the soft pants down her hips and off her legs.

Holly raised her eyebrows as she discovered Sadie was not wearing any underwear.

"Well," she murmured, "that makes things easier."

She pushed Sadie's tee shirt up and motioned for her to raise her torso off the bed so that she could slip it quickly over her head. Sadie lay back, totally nude, and basked in the hot gaze that Holly passed over her from head to toe. Holly's tongue came out to slowly lick her lips, and Sadie groaned, aching to feel that tongue on her skin. She watched as Holly stood and slowly removed her own tee shirt and jeans, leaving her standing in just her underwear. The bra and G-string were a rich burgundy colour, edged with lace, and so beyond sexy it took Sadie's breath away.

"You are so gorgeous," she whispered, reaching out a hand towards her lover. She smiled at the faint blush that crept across Holly's face and neck. "You are," she insisted. "I don't know why you doubt that."

Holly shook her head. "It just means a lot to hear it from you. You make my heart stop with your beauty."

She leaned down to gently kiss Sadie's lips, her eyes, her neck.

"Roll over," Holly whispered as she lifted her head. "I want to massage your back, ease out some of what your father did to you."

Sadie's heart lurched, and she rolled over quickly before her emotions got the better of her. She heard Holly pad into the bathroom and return a minute later.

"It's only body lotion, rather than oil, but it'll work."

Holly planted herself astride Sadie's hips, her warm thighs tight against Sadie's cooling skin. Sadie could feel the heat at the apex of Holly's thighs on her ass, through the silk of her underwear, and her own centre became abundantly wet at the sensation.

Holly's massage began firmly, definitely therapeutic rather than sensuous, and her strong fingers worked into all the knots that Sadie hadn't realised she was carrying. Across her neck, her shoulders, and her upper arms, Holly's hands worked their magic, and it was blissful. Sadie groaned on a number of occasions, and she could hear Holly's answering chuckle each time.

"Feels so good," Sadie murmured for at least the fifth time, as Holly kneaded the hollows just above her ass.

"Mmhm" was Holly's only response, letting her fingers talk for her. Subtly and smoothly, over the next few minutes, she transitioned the massage into something much more like foreplay. Her touch gentled, and her strokes became languorous. Sadie's body hummed as Holly's hands brushed lightly over her ass and swept up her sides, skimming the edges of her breasts and drawing a long moan from her throat. Her body was on fire, and everywhere Holly touched simply stoked the heat higher.

"I want you," Holly whispered, near her ear. "But I want this to be all about you. Please, let me love you," she said as she pulled firmly at Sadie's hips to indicate she wanted her to turn over. "Lie back, and let me love you."

Sadie turned and studied Holly's face. It was intense, but with an underlying tenderness that made something tremble deep in Sadie's chest. Holly met Sadie's gaze, not moving until Sadie acquiesced.

Sadie lay back, her centre aching intensely, and gave in to Holly's ministrations. Holly gently pushed Sadie's arms above her head, and the submissive position thrilled her more than she would have imagined. She was normally the one to take charge, to lead, and to control. This was so different, and yet it felt so right to just give in. Holly's tongue went to work, and Sadie lost the power of thought and speech altogether.

It was exquisite. Tongue strokes and kisses trailed over every inch of her, lingering for long moments on her neck before descending to her breasts. Holly's hair draped gently on Sadie's skin as her lips wrapped around a nipple and sucked, sending pulsing throbs to Sadie's clit. She moaned, her breathing tortured with the anticipation of where Holly's mouth would go next.

The answer was down.

Down over her abdomen, over her belly, and onto her thighs. Licking softly at the tender skin on the inside of Sadie's thighs, Holly whispered one word, "Open," and Sadie thought she might come on the spot. She shamelessly spread her legs wide, giving Holly ample room to nestle between them, and then the erotic torture continued in earnest. Holly's mouth on her clit and her swollen lips was relentlessly teasing. Dragging the length of Sadie, Holly's soft tongue never lingered long enough in one spot to push her over the edge, yet all the while increased her arousal almost to breaking point.

"You taste so good," Holly gasped, breaking contact for a moment. "I want to do this to you for hours."

"Please…" Sadie replied, and she didn't know which she was asking for; release, or hours more of this delicious torment.

She felt Holly smile against her, then she cried out as Holly's tongue entered her. The slow, yet powerful thrusts sent Sadie careening towards orgasm. When Holly gripped her thighs and pushed even deeper, it was the spark that lit the touchpaper. Sadie rocked, her hips arching upwards, as wave after wave of her orgasm swept over and through her body. It seemed to start from everywhere all at once, inside and out, and a long, wrenching sound poured out of her throat as the sensations rippled through her. Holly held on to Sadie throughout, her tongue still buried deep inside her. She withdrew only when Sadie collapsed back down on the bed, panting for breath, her heartbeat pounding through her skin. She reached blindly for Holly, pulling her up the length of her body to lay her on top of her. She kissed Holly, tasting herself on her lover's lips, and that sent little aftershocks ricocheting through her clit.

Holly's kisses rapidly turned ardent, her tongue thrusting into Sadie's mouth in an action almost perfectly reminiscent of its motion between her legs moments before. Holly moved slightly to the side, so that she straddled one of Sadie's thighs, and Sadie grabbed her ass and pulled her close, knowing what Holly needed.

"Yes…yes… *Please.*" Holly's voice was husky as Sadie used her hands on Holly's silk-clad ass to grind her against her thigh, setting a rhythm that had them both gasping. She could feel Holly's hot slickness against her skin, her underwear drenched with her arousal. She could feel her tension as she worked herself against the firm muscles of Sadie's thigh. Holly's moans increased in volume as she increased the pace of her thrusts. The trembling started, first in Holly's thighs, spreading to her arms until, with a deep cry, she threw her head back as her climax hit. Her eyes were closed in pleasure, her mouth caught in an erotic grimace, and Sadie watched it play out on her face, entranced by the sight.

CHAPTER 19

"I promise I'll be discreet, Mum." Holly kept her voice low, not wanting to disturb the dozing Sadie next to her. She looked adorable—splayed out on her front, her arms thrown across her pillow above her head, the doona barely covering her delectable ass. Holly smiled as Sadie's nose twitched at something. Cradling her phone under her chin, she reached out a hand to rub a gentle pathway up and down Sadie's spine to soothe her.

"Okay." Her mother's voice was tinged with uncertainty.

"Trust me, Mum, ordinarily I would come home and not put you in this position. I swear. But she's had a really bad day, and I can't leave her." She paused. "I know that's hard for you to hear."

Judy sighed. "You seem so grown-up, all of a sudden."

Holly chuckled softly. "Sorry about that." She was pleased when her mum laughed gently in response. "No one will know I was here, I promise." She hesitated. She really wanted to ask, but feared the response. *Oh well, here's goes nothing.* "So, the other thing I wanted to run by you is the party tomorrow."

"Yes?" Her mother's puzzlement was obvious.

"Well, I was wondering if I could bring Sadie. As my date."

There was a long silence. "Would you introduce her to everyone as that?"

Holly shut her eyes briefly. She knew this was a big one for her mum. Maybe she should wait, give her more time. "I don't have to, if that would make you uncomfortable. I know this is very new for you."

"It is. I-I don't want to tell you what you can or can't do but…"

"It's okay, Mum. I understand. One day, though?"

"Of course, darling. I-I don't want you to think that I want you to hide this. It's just—"

"I get it, Mum, it's okay. You just need more time."

The sigh her mother exhaled was heavy. "I do. Please bring her to the party, but can she just be a friend, for now? I promise, this isn't me denying who you are."

Holly glowed at the words. "I can do that. And thanks, Mum, what you just said means an awful lot. I'll see you tomorrow."

"Bye, sweetheart." Her mum's voice was wavering with those last words, and Holly suspected there would be tears when she hung up. She was so proud of her for pushing through this. And so thankful that the relationship they'd always shared looked like it wasn't going to go astray.

"Everything okay?" Sadie mumbled, her mouth partly obscured by the pillow.

Holly giggled, and turned to place her phone on the bedside table. Wriggling down to wrap her body alongside Sadie's, she nuzzled at her lover's neck.

"Everything is just fine. Go to sleep, gorgeous."

"Mm. 'kay." Sadie snuggled up closer to Holly and threw an arm over her middle. Moments later, Holly heard the deep breathing that indicated Sadie had, indeed, fallen asleep, and she smiled, suffused with contentment. She kissed Sadie gently on the temple and closed her eyes.

"How do I look?" Sadie asked as she stared at herself in the mirror. Her nerves were getting the better of her; her hands were twitching, and she couldn't seem to stand still. They needed to leave for the party in about ten minutes, and she'd only just finished getting dressed. She'd tried on and discarded three outfits so far, and was trying very hard not to get rattled by the amusement this caused Holly.

"You look gorgeous," Holly replied, poking her in the ribs. She stepped past Sadie to check her own make-up. "Just as you did in the other three outfits you had on before this one."

Sadie growled. "I can't help it! This is a big deal, meeting a whole heap of your family. Even if they do think I'm just a friend. Later, when they all find out, I want them to remember me as—"

"As what?" Holly interrupted, her face splitting into a wide grin. "The best dressed at the party? That isn't what they'll remember, silly." She gave her another jab in the ribs. "They'll remember how charming you were, and what a delight it was to converse with you." Holly's voice had transformed into a terrible, upper-class English accent.

Sadie looked across the room at her smirking girlfriend. "Anyone ever tell you how annoying you can be sometimes?" She smiled as she delivered the words.

Holly laughed and turned to wrap her arms around her. After kissing Sadie soundly, she stepped back.

"Come on, hot stuff, we need to make moves."

Sadie raised her eyes heavenwards and sent a silent prayer. *Please don't let me fuck this up for her.*

The party was at the home of one of Holly's uncles. It was an annual event, combining the birthday celebrations of four family members, whose special days all fell within the same two-week period. There would be a barbecue, plenty of grog, and, apparently, guaranteed noisy mayhem. Across the extended family, there were ten children all aged under nine.

"It's usually bedlam," Holly warned as they walked out to Sadie's bike, helmets in hand. "I always try and find a quiet corner away from it all and chat to my older cousins. But the kids will usually try and pull us into their games. Last year it involved water guns." She shuddered. "God, that got messy."

Sadie grinned. "I'll protect you," she said, giving Holly a quick kiss before they each pulled on their helmets.

The ride out took only fifteen minutes, but Sadie loved it. Having Holly wrapped around her added a whole new, delicious dimension to time spent on her beloved Harley. Riding had, until recently, always been something she needed to keep for herself. On her bike she could escape whatever bothered her and just think. But the soft curves of Holly's body pressed up against her back, the surprisingly emotional satisfaction it gave her to feel her lover sharing the experience with her, utterly changed the concept. Of course, the awareness of Holly's centre against her ass also gave her a delicious thrill. By the time they pulled up outside the house, Sadie's body was humming nicely.

"What are you grinning at?" Holly asked, handing over her helmet for it to be locked to the bike.

Sadie laughed. "I'll tell you later."

She winked, and Holly slapped her playfully in the arm.

"Dirty thoughts, I'm guessing."

Sadie threw her head back and laughed loudly. "Shit, you're reading me too well already."

Holly chuckled. "You better believe it. Come on, dirty girl, come and meet my tribe."

Sadie moved to take Holly's hand, then stopped herself, remembering. Faking it was going to be extremely hard to maintain for the day. She'd got so used to touching Holly whenever she wanted these past few days.

Holly smiled sadly. "Sorry. I know it's asking a lot of you to pretend we're just friends."

"It's okay." Sadie shrugged. "I understand why we're doing it. I just need to remember not to grab you every opportunity I get."

Holly giggled. "Okay, tiger, I'll keep you in check."

They were met at the door by their host, Mark.

"Holly!" He grabbed her into a big hug, and Holly's breath left her in a big oomph as he did so. He was a bear of a man, over two metres tall and broad across the shoulders. When he finally put Holly down, she rearranged her now-rumpled clothes and stepped to the side to introduce Sadie.

"This is my friend, Sadie. I thought I'd show her the famous O'Brien hospitality."

"Good to meet you," Mark said, smiling warmly.

"And you," Sadie replied, responding to the genuine warmth of the man and smiling widely back in return.

"Well, come on in. Everyone's out in the yard, of course." He gestured them through the house, and they followed as he led them down the hallway.

The day was mild and bright, so it was inevitable that the main party was outside. Sadie took a moment to brace herself when she saw how many people were crammed into the space. For a big house, surprisingly, it didn't have that big a yard. The number of adults and children out there filled it easily. She saw kids of various young ages running around the adults. The hysterical screams of the children were already assaulting her ears, and she hadn't even stepped outside the door. She winced. This was going to take some effort. She plastered a smile on her face and followed Holly out.

Holly's parents stepped over quickly to greet their daughter and her "friend". They were pleasant enough, and Sadie was grateful for that.

"How are you, Mrs O'Brien?" Sadie asked politely.

Judy smiled tentatively, shifting from one foot to the other. "Please, call me Judy," she said, quietly. "And I'm…fine." She met Sadie's eyes only briefly before looking away.

Sadie swallowed. "Good. That's…good."

Holly rescued her. "So, want a drink?"

Exhaling a sigh of relief, she smiled at Holly and nodded. "Please, but just something soft. Juice will be fine."

"Cool. Back in a sec."

Realising that left her alone with Holly's parents, she tried to calm her breathing and find something to talk about. She was saved by Mark, who appeared by her side, greeting Judy and Patrick, and engaging them all in a conversation about the work he'd recently had done on the yard. As she listened to Mark talk, she looked around the yard at the gathering before her. There were at least five clusters of adults spaced around the paved area, all chatting animatedly and laughing in the sunshine. She frowned; she couldn't imagine belonging to such a huge family group.

She was just starting to wonder where Holly had got to when she heard a woman laugh, somewhere out in the yard. The sound made every drop of blood in her veins come to a standstill.

That laugh. She would know that laugh anywhere.

Frantically she swept her gaze around the yard, and then she saw her.

Chloe Turner.

Standing with a small group of women off to Sadie's left, she had turned slightly, in profile. She tossed her hair back, as she laughed again at something one of the other women had said. She was older, obviously, and her body had filled out a little over the years. But there was no doubt who she was.

Chloe.

No.

How the fuck was that possible? How, after twelve years, could they suddenly be standing in the same space as each other? At this birthday party, of all things?

Sadie's heart was pounding out a fearful rhythm. She took a step back, her palms sweating, her mind in free fall.

Oh, God.

She remembered Nicole raising the possibility of bumping into Chloe on this trip. If she'd thought about it at all, she'd assumed that, if it did happen, it would be somewhere innocuous—in a shop, or on the street. Not somewhere so inescapable.

Not somewhere where the exposure of their past could cause so much damage to others.

Footsteps sounded behind her, and instinct told her it was Holly even before she came into view. She tried to school her features into a semblance of calm, before she turned to face her.

"Here you go." Holly handed her a cold glass of orange juice. "Sorry it took so long, I got caught—" She stopped, staring at Sadie. "What's wrong?"

Sadie took a big gulp from the glass to buy herself more time. She wiped at her mouth with the back of her hand and sucked in a big breath. "Nothing, I'm fine. Just wondered where you'd got to." She was lying to Holly. She hated it, but what could she do?

"Oh, sorry. I didn't mean to abandon you." Holly looked so contrite, it tore at Sadie's conscience.

"No, no, it's okay. Please, it's fine." Guilt gnawed her insides. She risked a quick glance over Holly's shoulder to see if Chloe had spotted her. Thankfully, she still seemed engrossed in her conversation.

"Shall I introduce you around?"

Sadie shuddered inwardly. "Sure," she said, hoping she sounded way more pleased with the prospect than she actually was.

Holly looked at her quizzically, but said nothing. She turned, and Sadie followed her, her stomach lurching as she realised they were heading straight for Chloe and her group.

Oh, God.

Holly inserted herself into the group, and there were squeals of greeting from the five women. Quick hugs and kisses were shared.

Turning back to beckon Sadie over, Holly said, "And this is my friend Sadie."

Stepping up to the group, her legs feeling like lead, Sadie glanced quickly at each of them except Chloe.

"Sadie, these are my cousins." She motioned to the other four women. "Naomi, Jayne, Kym, and Ricki."

Sadie smiled at each of them. Her heart was threatening to pound its way out of her chest as Holly gestured towards Chloe.

"And this is my aunt, Chloe—hers is one of the birthdays we're celebrating today."

Her aunt? Shit, shit, shit.

Knowing she couldn't delay it any longer, Sadie allowed herself to look at Chloe, to meet the stare that Chloe was aiming her way. She was still beautiful, but it triggered nothing for Sadie. The glacial look in Chloe's eyes told her she had been recognised.

"Hi," Chloe said, and Sadie had to admire her ability to act as if nothing was wrong.

Sadie nodded, not trusting herself to speak.

"So," Holly broke in, seemingly oblivious to the tension between Sadie and Chloe, "what did Kyle get you for your birthday?"

Chloe looked relieved at the opportunity to turn away from Sadie, and launched into an overenthusiastic description of the spa day Kyle had surprised her with.

Sadie took a couple of surreptitious steps backwards, sipping at her juice, positioning herself just behind Holly so that she could bend to her ear.

"Be back in a minute. Bathroom," she whispered and turned without waiting for a response. Moving quickly into the house, she left her drink on a side table in the lounge room and floundered her away around the house until she found the main bathroom next to the laundry. Locking the door behind her, she closed the lid of the toilet and slumped down onto it, dropping her face into her hands.

Chloe was Holly's aunt.

CHAPTER 20

Oh God, how could this be happening? This was actually a nightmare, wasn't it? In a minute, she'd wake up, shake it off, and laugh at where her subconscious mind had taken her. She shook her head. No, this was reality and it sucked. And she had to get away from it. They couldn't go through the whole afternoon pretending they didn't know each other. Surely it would be easier all round if she just got out of there. She'd have to make some excuse to Holly, and then hope she didn't ask too many questions.

Fuck, what a mess.

The knock on the door startled her, and she snapped her head up.

"Sorry, won't be long," she called, hoping whoever it was would, maybe, go and find an alternative bathroom.

"I want to talk to you." The voice that hissed through the door was unmistakeable.

Chloe.

Sadie heaved in a huge breath. She stood. Opening the door, she stepped out into the hallway.

"What are you doing here?" Chloe's voice, though quiet, was venomous. Her eyes blazed with fury.

Sadie held her hands up.

"It's pure coincidence," Sadie said. She felt calm, and that surprised her. She was also relieved to realise that she felt nothing for Chloe. No attraction and no yearning for what used to be. The woman standing in front of her was a part of her past, yes, but that's where she was staying. The coldness about her that was so evident to the adult Sadie, the coldness she'd missed as an enamoured teenager, made her want to recoil. Such a contrast to the warmth of Holly.

"And how the hell do you know Holly?" Chloe stood with her hands on her hips. If she thought she looked threatening, or menacing, Sadie didn't have the heart to tell her it wasn't working.

She smiled, unable to help herself at the mention of her girlfriend's name. "We're…good friends," she said. Chloe was the last person who needed to know the truth.

"Does she know about us?" Chloe's tone was just as harsh, but Sadie could hear the fear underneath it.

"No one knows, Chloe. What happened in the past has stayed in the past. I never told anyone here about that."

Chloe's relief was evident as she exhaled loudly. The tightness in her facial expression relaxed somewhat.

"Told anyone about what?"

Holly's voice was tremulous, and the sound of it twisted Sadie's guts into a convoluted knot. She and Chloe both snapped round towards Holly in the same instant.

Sadie's breath stalled in her throat. Holly was standing about a metre away. Sadie had no idea how neither of them had heard her approaching. Holly's face was wide open in shock, her eyebrows high, her cheeks slightly flushed.

"Holly," Sadie breathed. Fear sent a trickle of sweat down her spine.

"What the fuck is going on here?" Holly's tone could have cut glass.

"Holly, it's nothing," Chloe said quickly, her tone sounding falsely cheery. "Just a misunderstanding. Come on, let's get back to the party."

She stepped forward, and put a hand on Holly's shoulder.

Holly shrugged it off, and said, in a voice laced with ice, "No, it's fine, you go on out. I'll be there in a minute." She didn't take her eyes off Sadie once.

Chloe stared at Holly for a moment, then flicked a quick glance at Sadie before walking away from them. In that glance, Sadie had seen Chloe's fear again, but she couldn't pander to that. If giving up Chloe's secret meant she had a chance to keep her relationship with Holly, then that was a price she had no trouble paying.

Holly waited until Chloe had disappeared out of earshot.

"Sadie?" Her whispered question ached across the space between them.

"Can we find somewhere a little more private? Or even leave this until after the party?" Sadie tried to keep her tone calm and tender, and hide from it the deep dread she was feeling.

Holly shut her eyes for a moment. When she reopened them, her expression was resolute, her mouth set in a thin line.

"As long as you promise you *will* tell me, then yes, we can wait until later. I guess I kind of have an idea. I'm not stupid. But I'd like to hear it from you."

Sadie nodded gratefully. "I swear, you will know everything. But please, trust me. It was in the past. It has nothing to do with you and me."

Holly turned, without another word, and left Sadie standing in the dim hallway on her own.

Sadie had never known time could pass so slowly. It was torture of the worst kind. Her face ached from forcing a smile onto it at every opportunity, and her heart ached watching Holly avoid her all afternoon. She was relieved when she discovered some of the guests had slipped indoors to watch a footy match, and she quietly joined them. It was better than having to make small talk with Holly's family, whilst at the same time avoiding Chloe, *and* sending reassuring smiles in Holly's direction on the rare occasion their eyes met across the yard.

She didn't know who won the game, or what the score was, but instantly jumped up from her seat when Holly suddenly appeared just after the final siren and asked if they could go.

"I'm a little tired," she said, her gaze darting around the room, falling anywhere but on Sadie's face.

"Sure, let's go." Sadie rushed to grab their jackets and accompanied Holly in finding Judy and Patrick. They said a polite goodbye, and Sadie watched Holly hug her mum more tightly than seemed normal. Swallowing hard, she led Holly out of the house and handed over her helmet. Holly gave her a half smile of thanks which lacked any real warmth, and slipped the helmet over her head, quickly pushing the visor down to mask her face.

It was hard to wrap her arms around Sadie, and hold her as close as she needed to on the bike, when her entire being was confused and hurt by what she'd overheard in the hallway earlier. She knew she needed to let Sadie explain about her and Chloe, but her mind kept stopping at the image of them…together. It was obvious that's what had happened, sometime in the past. Her own bloody aunt!

Oh God, it was *nauseating*.

Yes, Holly could accept that Chloe was attractive. But she was also a bitch and always had been. They all joked about it, in the family, and about how much she'd got Kyle twisted round her little finger. Holly didn't know if she was more pained that Sadie had had something with Chloe because she was Holly's aunt, or because she thought Sadie would have had better taste.

The ride back to the hotel was quick, and she hurried off the back of the bike once Sadie had rolled it into its parking spot. Slipping off the helmet, she turned to Sadie.

"Back door," she said, knowing her tone was abrupt but not able to stop herself. She was angry, and hurt, and…embarrassed.

Ugh, Sadie and Chloe. God, this is a nightmare.

She walked off without waiting to see if Sadie was following her, but felt her presence close behind as she pulled open the back door to the hotel. They walked in silence along the short hallway to Sadie's room. Holly stepped aside so that Sadie could unlock the door.

Once inside, Holly sat down in the armchair, knowing she needed to keep her distance, at least for a little while. Sitting on the bed where Sadie had perched really wouldn't help that.

"Do you want something to drink?" Sadie asked. Her voice quavered.

Holly shook her head. "Just tell me," she whispered, needing to know, but dreading what she was about to hear.

Sadie sighed and rubbed one hand through her short, tufty locks. Holly tried not to track the motion with her eyes, bombarded by memories of clenching her own hands in that hair in the throes of orgasm only the night before.

"Chloe and I worked together, at Myer, when I was in high school." Sadie stood and began pacing slowly across the room, her gaze fixed on the floor. "She… Well, she made a play for me. I'd only just accepted I was gay, but hadn't done anything about it at that point. She made it very obvious she was after me, and I-I couldn't resist. She was very persistent, and one night I gave in."

Holly swallowed, trying to tamp down the nausea Sadie's words had just triggered. "Just the one night?"

Sadie raised her head to look at Holly. "No." Sadie grimaced. "We started an affair. Every time Kyle was out for the evening, I'd go over to their house. Or sometimes, we'd just be in her car, parked up somewhere dark around town."

Holly didn't know what to say. She turned to gaze out of the window. It was so hard to hear this, to know that Sadie had been...intimate, with her *aunt*. She shook her head to try and clear the images that kept popping up of Sadie in Chloe's arms. And worse.

"I'm sorry," Sadie whispered, coming to a stop in front of her. "I know you don't like hearing this."

"No, I don't. But I asked you to tell me." Holly paused and then lifted her head and met Sadie's concerned look. "So, how long? And how did it end?"

Sadie exhaled and plopped back down on the bed. "Only a couple of months. And it ended when I told her I was in love with her. She was...furious. Told me I'd ruined everything, that we were just a bit of fun."

"Oh, Sadie." Despite her own heartache, she could feel for the young Sadie. She'd heard, over the years, various rumours of the string of men following Chloe around, leaving their broken hearts in her wake. It shouldn't come as much of a surprise that there were some female hearts in that trail of devastation.

"How did you deal with seeing her at work after that?"

Sadie's smile was strained. "I didn't have to. That night was the night of the fire at the school. The next day was when I got kicked out of home."

Holly stared at her, as her mind went into overdrive, and all the pieces of the puzzle slotted into place.

"Wait a minute. The married woman, who couldn't, or wouldn't, alibi you? That was her? Chloe?"

Sadie nodded and stood again. "Please understand. That is all in the past. I don't feel a thing for her now. Not a thing." She walked over to stand in front of Holly, and she looked so scared it made Holly's heart lurch. "It never occurred to me to tell you anything about her, because I would never have imagined even bumping into her, never mind finding out she's your aunt."

Holly raised her hands to silence Sadie. She needed time to think, time to sift through all the emotions that were washing through her in that moment. It was all too much. She stood, suddenly, and Sadie stumbled backwards away from her at the sharp movement.

"I need… I have to go. I just need some time to think about all this." Holly watched as Sadie's face crumpled. Although a part of her wanted to console her and hug her and tell her it would be okay, she just couldn't manage that. "Sorry, I just need to go. I'll call you later."

The door swung closed behind her, and she hurried down the hallway to the back door, heaving it open as the tears started falling.

"Nic, it's me. Please call me as soon as you get this message." Sadie hung up and flung the phone on the bed in frustration. Oh shit, this was all going so wrong, when it had all been going so right. The contrast between the incredible connection she and Holly had shared last night and the disaster zone she found herself inhabiting couldn't be greater.

It had been two hours since Holly left. Sadie had texted her twice in that time but had received no response to either message. She got the hint; Holly would contact her only when she was ready. Sadie just hoped that wouldn't be too far in the future.

The future. Holly was part of her future—or at least, Sadie hoped she would be. A big part of it. But Sadie's past had stormed in from behind her and slapped her, viciously, threatening to derail that future before it even got started.

She sat down on the bed. She couldn't imagine what Holly must be thinking. Disgust? Sadie wouldn't blame her. Knowing your current lover once had a sexual relationship with your aunt must be nauseating. It was a dreadful irony. Sadie came back to Ballarat to deal with her past, but would the price she had to pay for that be the loss of the most amazing thing that had ever happened to her?

Simply to have something to do, she slowly changed into her casual sweatpants and tee shirt, taking the time to carefully hang and fold the clothes she took off. Just to keep her occupied, to keep her mind on something other than what Holly was doing. She poured herself a juice and tried to sit down, but as soon as she perched in the chair, all she could remember was Holly sitting there a couple of hours ago, her face going almost white as Sadie told her all about Chloe.

Oh, God, what a mess.

Her phone rang, and she leapt up to retrieve it from where she'd thrown it earlier.

"Hey, what's wrong?" Nic got straight to the point.

"You are not going to believe this." Sadie told her everything that had unfolded during the afternoon.

"No. Fucking. Way." Nic's voice rose an octave. "She's her *aunt*?"

"Yeah, and still the class-A bitch she always was. Her only concern was that her dirty little secret didn't get out. I have no idea what I ever saw in her."

"Sades, you were young, she threw herself at you. You can't blame your past self for finding that exciting and attractive."

"Yeah, but look what it's ultimately led to. Holly doesn't deserve this." Sadie ran her free hand through her hair, pulling at the short tufts until her scalp ached.

"Can I ask you something?" Nicole's voice was quiet.

"What?"

"If…if Holly hadn't found you two talking, would you have told her who Chloe was?"

Sadie rocked back on her heels, as if the quiet words had been a physical force. "I… God, I don't know. I think so. I don't think I would have wanted to keep such a secret from her. I mean, when I thought there was no chance of seeing Chloe here, when she was just a nameless woman from my past, that was all Holly needed to know. She was okay with that. Same as I am about any of her exes." She exhaled slowly, searching her conscience. "But this… Yes, I'd like to think I would have told her when we got back here. I expect her reaction would have been the same, and I don't blame her. Can you imagine, Nic? It makes *me* sick thinking about it, so God knows what it's doing to her."

"I know. Let's be honest, it'd be a pretty gross thing to hear."

Sadie closed her eyes. "I hate that I've done this to her. I just wish she would contact me so we can talk about it, so that I can be there for her."

"She'll come round," Nic said firmly. "From everything you've told me about her this past week, she's pretty level-headed. She just needs some time to get her brain around it. I really can't believe this would be enough for her not to want to see you anymore."

"God, I hope you're right." Sadie hesitated, knowing her next words were, for her, monumental. "I'm falling for her, Nic."

Nic sighed heavily. "I know, babe, I know. It's been obvious for days now."

"You don't think it's too quick?"

"Nope." Nicole's response was definitive. "I knew Tash was the one for me within about ten days of meeting her. So, you got there with Holly in only seven. So what? The stuff you two have shared in just a week is more than some people share in months. It doesn't surprise me at all that you feel this much for her already. I truly believe, from everything you've told me, she feels the same way. I repeat, I don't think this latest, fucking *bizarre* revelation is going to stop her wanting to be with you. Just hang in there, babe, okay?"

CHAPTER 21

Sadie made herself some brekkie and sat sipping her coffee with the TV on in the background. She was tired; having not heard back from Holly before she'd gone to bed, her sleep had been fitful.

Her phone rang, and her heart leapt, hoping it was Holly. She saw her mother's name appear on the display and tamped down her disappointment.

"Morning, Mum, how are you?" She tried to keep her voice light. "How did things go yesterday?" Sadie had completely forgotten her mother's own potential drama on Sunday, having been so wrapped up in what had happened with her and Holly. Despite her own pain, she was itching to know how her mother had dealt with Sadie's father.

"Good morning, darling." Christine sounded cheerful, which was promising. "Don't worry, everything is fine. It was all quite sad, really. He claimed he had no idea how bad things were between us, but I could tell he didn't really believe that." She let out a sound of disgust. "His eyes gave it away. I think, all this time, he thought if he pretended everything was all right, and I didn't do anything to suggest otherwise, then we were fine. Hearing me spell it out so clearly has completely thrown him."

"But he wasn't violent, or aggressive in any way?"

"No, darling. I told you he wouldn't be. I'm not sure I really understand how or why he got so violent with you on Saturday. Although, I suppose, having me stand up to him and the realisation that all we had was not as he wanted it to be…"

"Hey, it's not your fault he lashed out at me. Well, maybe not directly. Look, it doesn't matter," Sadie said dismissively. "I'm okay, no lasting damage."

"And I'm very glad to hear that." Her mum cleared her throat. "Now, I also wanted to ask you something, before you left the hotel."

"Sure, fire away."

"Well, um, I would very much like to meet Holly. I was wondering if you two would like to come over here for dinner this evening?" Her mum sounded a little nervous, but at the same time determined. "It won't be anything special, just some roast chicken and vegetables."

Sadie didn't know whether to laugh or cry. Her mum was taking a huge step forward in her acceptance of Sadie's sexuality, right when Sadie had no idea if she and Holly were still together. Sadie wasn't remotely ready to tell her mum that, or explain why. It was bad enough Holly knew about Chloe; she had no intention of her mother ever having that knowledge.

"Mum, that's a lovely idea. The thing is, Holly might not be available because of work. I'll have to check with her and get back to you, is that okay?" The white lie didn't feel good, but she had no choice.

"Oh, of course. Yes, I didn't think of that. Well, you just let me know. Are you coming up this morning anyway?"

"Sure, Mum. I'll just finish my brekkie and then be on my way."

"Lovely."

Sadie hung up and stared, unseeing, at the room before her. What now? She glanced at her watch. If Holly was working, she'd be on the front desk. It wouldn't be ideal having the conversation there, but she didn't have a lot of options.

She pushed through the door from the annexe to the reception area. Holly was at the desk, her head bent as she wrote on a notepad. There was no one else around.

"Hey," Sadie said quietly.

Holly's head whipped up. She looked as tired as Sadie, her eyes slightly puffy, and her expression sad.

"Hi," Holly said, equally quietly.

"Are you okay?"

Holly shrugged. "So-so. I… I couldn't call you last night. I just…"

Sadie held up her hand. "No, it's okay. I get it. I would like us to be able to talk about it, that's all."

When Holly said nothing, Sadie took a deep breath. She didn't know where they were, but the fact that Holly hadn't immediately told her to get lost was a good sign, she hoped. "Look, my mum just called. She'd really like to meet you. She's invited us for dinner tonight. I'll totally understand if you don't want to, but… Well, I'd really like you to meet Mum, and my gran."

Holly's eyes had widened slightly at the invite, and she slowly sat back in her chair. "I could do that." She shrugged again. "It would be a bit rude not to, given her circumstances. And she does know my parents, so they'd probably like me to make the effort."

It wasn't the ringing endorsement Sadie had hoped for. It sounded more like Holly was doing it to be polite to Christine rather than to spend any time with Sadie. Ouch. Well, at this point she'd take what she could get and hope that would give them a chance to talk, really talk, later on in the evening.

"Okay. You can either ride out with me or meet me there."

"I think I'll meet you there." She passed a piece of paper and a pen over the desk. "Could you write down the address?"

Sadie swallowed. Holly's cool demeanour made her heart ache in a distinctly unpleasant way. But she'd do whatever it took to try to get them connecting again, to get past this, if they could. She carefully wrote out her mum's address, passed back the paper, and then waited until Holly met her gaze.

"About seven, okay?"

Holly nodded but averted her gaze almost immediately.

Swallowing down her hurt, Sadie smiled briefly, said a quiet goodbye, and left.

Holly ran her fingers through her hair one more time. The cab had just dropped her off; she was standing at the end of the driveway, battling her nerves over the evening ahead of her. She was early, and there was no sign of Sadie's bike on the driveway. There was no way she was going in on her own. Wrapping her scarf a little tighter around her neck, she shuffled on the spot to keep warm; it was a chilly night.

In the silence of the night around her, she sighed in exasperation at her circumstances and how her life had turned upside down this week. Especially in the last twenty-four hours. Since learning that Sadie had been…intimate with Chloe, she'd questioned everything about what she and Sadie had shared. Her feelings for Sadie had exponentially expanded through the week, and she'd fallen too deep, too quickly. It scared her. The revelation about Chloe only emphasised just how little she really knew about Sadie. Sadie could already have a partner, or make a habit of seducing women every time she was on the road on that damn bike.

And yet… Holly was standing outside Christine's house. So if Sadie was a player, and had a string of casual affairs behind her, or a partner waiting for her back home, how did a visit to her mum fit in? Of course the truth was, it didn't, and that was making Holly squirm. Being invited to meet her lover's family was a big deal, in anyone's book. Holly had never made it that far in any of her previous relationships. *Being here now is huge. And Sadie wants it.* So Sadie must be feeling all that Holly was too, right?

But Sadie had slept with Chloe, an awful image Holly was struggling to get out of her brain. What did that say about Sadie's choice of partners, for God's sake?

From behind her, she heard the purr of the Harley and stepped aside to allow Sadie to roll the bike onto the driveway. She watched, her pulse racing, as Sadie pulled off her helmet and ruffled her gloved hands through her hair. Holly inwardly cursed as her mouth went dry watching Sadie's denim-clad leg swing off the bike. Physically, her whole being yearned for this woman before her. Emotionally—well, that was proving a tad more difficult at the moment.

"You came," Sadie said. Even in those two words, her voice carried a depth of joy and pleasure that sent tingles down Holly's spine and a gentle admonition to that part of herself that was doubting what she meant to Sadie.

Not trusting her voice, she nodded.

"Thank you," Sadie said quietly. "Shall we?" She motioned towards the front door.

Holly walked up the driveway, until they both stood on the doorstep.

"Are you okay?" Sadie asked, staring at her.

"I… Yes. Nervous. Unsure." Holly let out a small chuckle—she didn't know how to describe what she was feeling, and Sadie's close proximity was only confusing things further. She wanted to touch her, hold her hand, kiss her. But…

Before Sadie could respond to Holly's garbled explanation, the door opened.

"Hello, lovebirds." The woman standing in the doorway was nearly as tall as Sadie, but thinner. Judging from the platinum-grey hair and aged skin, Holly guessed this was Sadie's grandmother, Elsie. She tried not to blush at Elsie's greeting or squirm under her intense stare.

"Gran," Sadie said, tugging gently on Holly's arm to bring her closer. "This is Holly. Holly, this is my grandmother, Elsie."

"Very pleased to meet you," Holly said, holding out her hand, which Elsie shook with a firmness that really didn't surprise Holly.

"Come on in." Elsie stepped back from the handshake and walked back into the house, leaving the two younger women to follow her.

"She's in the lounge room," Elsie called over her shoulder as she headed deeper into the house.

Barely registering her surroundings, Holly followed Sadie into a small but comfortably furnished room. As they entered the room, Sadie's mother pushed herself out of a recliner chair and stepped across to them.

"Hello," she said warmly, extending her hand. "You must be Holly. It's lovely to meet you." If she was nervous, she was doing an admirable job of not showing it. Holly was impressed.

She shook her hand, trying not to stare at the sallow skin or the dark circles under the woman's eyes. Trying not to remember that this woman was dying.

"It's really nice to meet you, too, Mrs Williams."

"Oh, please, call me Christine."

Holly smiled. "Okay, I will."

Christine smiled in return, and motioned for them to sit down.

Elsie reappeared. "Want something to drink?" she asked the room in general.

"Here, Gran, I'll help." Sadie leapt to her feet. "Is beer okay for you?" she asked Holly, and Holly could tell she was making a big effort not to sound anything but normal in front of her family.

"Sure. Thanks." Holly tried not to worry too much about being left on her own with Christine as Sadie followed her grandmother from the room.

"Don't worry," Christine said, from her position on the recliner. "I'm not going to interrogate you." Her face crinkled in a soft smile.

Holly chuckled. "Was I that obvious?"

Christine shook her head. "Not really, but I guessed you'd be a little nervous." She paused. "I am too, if I'm honest."

Holly cocked her head. "You? Why?"

"I've never met a…partner of Sadie's before. This is all very new to me. I'm worried I'll say the wrong thing, or—"

Inwardly flinching at the title Christine had bestowed on her, Holly interrupted. "Please, don't worry. Just you asking me here tonight, making that effort, that means so much to her." Her thoughts from earlier leapt into her mind. *Surely this shows how much I mean to Sadie too, for her to want me here?* The warmth that notion sent through her body almost left her breathless.

Christine nodded. "Well, it was long overdue. As was a lot of what we have shared this past week or so."

Her gaze lost focus, and Holly waited, knowing nothing needed to be said.

"Anyway," Christine said suddenly, shaking her head. "Enough of that. So, tell me all about yourself. You work at your parents' hotel, yes?"

Holly relaxed as she talked to Christine about her job and her parents. Elsie and Sadie came in with drinks, and, to Holly's relief, the four women chatted easily until the sound of the oven timer summoned them to the kitchen to eat.

They talked throughout the meal and found an easy camaraderie that had them all smiling warmly at each other. Holly was finding it increasingly difficult not to react to Sadie's smiles, her nearness. The hurt from yesterday was starting to ease, as were all of her doubts about Sadie's character, in seeing her so open and warm with her mother and grandmother.

"So," Christine said, partway through the meal. "I would like to talk about your father."

Holly saw Sadie flinch, and she only just resisted the urge to reach for her hand.

"If we must," Sadie said begrudgingly.

"We must," Christine replied firmly. She took a sip of her wine. "You need to know what's happening. He's moved out. Or, at least, he and his clothes have. He's gone to stay with his brother, and he'll be back this weekend to take the rest of his things."

Holly met Sadie's gaze, knowing that both of them were remembering their conversation about this only a couple of days ago.

"He doesn't like it," Christine continued, "but he does accept that these are my…final wishes. I've promised him that if he gives me this peace and quiet for my last however many days, weeks, or months, I won't try and divorce him. He'll therefore still inherit the house when I die, as is his right. But, I've also made it clear that I am changing my will. My car goes to Izzy. It's still worth a lot, so if nothing else, she can sell it. But all my other assets, or their net worth at least, which isn't a small sum, will now go to you."

Sadie gasped. "*What?*"

"I spoke to my lawyer this morning, and we'll have it all in place and signed off by the end of the week."

"I-I don't know what to say, Mum. That's… God, that is something I just don't know what to do with." Sadie slumped back in her chair, looking overwhelmed, and Holly's heart jumped in her chest. She knew Sadie would never have imagined something like this, to be welcomed back so comprehensively into the warmth of her family unit. God, everything that had happened to her, and she was still so self-effacing and so full of the potential for love. People like Chloe and Sadie's father had abused that, she could finally see. But it hadn't broken her—made her scared, yes. But it was all there, a huge heart capable of giving so much.

Christine patted Sadie's hand. "You don't have to do anything with it, other than to accept it. Please, it's truly what I want."

Sadie blinked rapidly. "Thank you, Mum. That means so much. So much." She turned to look at Holly, and Holly couldn't help the warm smile she gave her, so pleased to see Sadie understanding how much she meant to her mother. Sadie returned her smile, albeit tentatively.

They finished their food in silence; by unspoken agreement they all needed a little time to absorb the emotion of that exchange. The meal was simple but delicious, and Holly complimented Elsie on the cooking.

Elsie waved it off. "Can't go wrong with a roast chicken," she said, but her eyes sparkled nonetheless.

Once they'd finished eating, Holly insisted on clearing the table and washing the dishes. Sadie offered to help, and they banished the older women to the lounge room with cups of tea.

When they were alone in the kitchen, Sadie paused in her activity of stacking the dishwasher, and walked across to Holly, who smiled as she neared.

"You okay?" Sadie asked her.

Holly nodded. "I am. It's taken me a while, but I just needed to work my way through all…that," she said. "I'm sorry, I know that probably upset you."

Sadie shook her head. "Don't apologise. Of course you needed time to deal with what happened yesterday. I'm so sorry I hurt you with that. The last thing I would ever want to do is hurt you."

"I know. But I am sorry," Holly said softly, "because what I did with that knowledge was what other people have been doing to you ever since you got back here. I was judging you based on your past. My first reaction to learning about you and…her, was that it made you a bad person and a bad judge of character." She grimaced. "But even if that was true back then, that isn't who you are now. I did the same thing my mother did—held your past against you. And I really shouldn't have done that, me of all people, because I've seen who you are now."

Sadie's smile lit up her face. "That means so much, to hear that from you. I hated that element of my past catching up with me in the way that it did. I hoped you'd know how different I am now."

"I do," Holly said, and then there was nothing else she wanted to do than pull Sadie into her arms. She reached out, and Sadie moved instantly, holding her tight, sighing happily against Holly's hair.

Holly pulled back slightly, tilting her head up. Their lips met in a soft, chaste kiss, sealing the rift that the last day had rent between them.

"Oh my goodness!" Christine's voice hurriedly forced them apart.

Holly's cheeks were flaming, as were Sadie's.

"Sorry, Mum." Sadie looked mortified, and Holly squeezed her eyes shut in mutual embarrassment.

"Um, well, I-I just needed a bit more sugar for my tea."

Holly dared to look at Christine and could see her gaze flicking anywhere in the room except at the two of them.

"I'll bring it out, Mum," Sadie said, turning rapidly to the canisters that lined the back of the countertop.

Christine left the room quickly, and Holly hung her head in her hands.

"Oh, God," she groaned, "and it was all going so well."

Sadie chuckled beside her and gently cupped her chin to lift it up. "It's not the end of the world," she said, kissing the tip of Holly's nose.

"Yeah, but did you see her face? Oh, God, she's never going to speak to me again." Holly pulled away.

Sadie grinned. "She'll get over it, I'm sure. Look, I'll be back in a minute—" she gestured to the canister in her hand, "—and then we can get this clearing up finished, okay?"

"That's fine by me. I'll just stay here and hide until it's time to go home, okay?"

Sadie laughed and left the room.

Holly leaned back against the countertop, her cheeks still hot from blushing. Oh, God, of all the things for Christine to walk in on. Especially when it was one of the most special moments she and Sadie had shared yet.

She heard chuckling coming from the hallway and looked up just as a smirking Elsie walked into the kitchen.

"Well, that just raised my daughter's education on the homosexual lifestyle to a whole new level," she said, patting Holly on the arm. "Well done."

"Oh, God." Holly's head was back in her hands again, her face blazing. "This is just too embarrassing."

Elsie laughed loudly. "Oh, you're as bad as each other! Sadie's in there, her face a shade of red I've never seen on a person. And you're in here, almost as rosy. It was a kiss. Christine'll get over it."

Holly raised her head to stare at Elsie. "How are you so…cool about all this, Elsie?" She was genuinely curious. For her age, Elsie seemed extraordinarily laid-back.

Elsie met her gaze. "When your son-in-law conspires to kick his seventeen-year-old daughter out of home, and she pitches up on your doorstep with nowhere else in the world to go, you have a very quick, very simple decision to make. Support her, or not. There was no choice, obviously. And in supporting her, I support *her*. Who she is. What she is."

Tears pricked at Holly's eyes. For all her bluntness and her gruffness, Elsie had just demonstrated that she had an enormous heart full of love for her elder grandchild.

"You're amazing," Holly whispered.

Elsie huffed, obviously uncomfortable at Holly's words. "I just love my granddaughter." She paused and pierced Holly with her stare. "As do you, I think?"

Holly blushed. "I do." She hadn't told Sadie yet, but she knew it wouldn't be long before those words would be shared.

"Good. She needs someone like you. You're good for her, I can see that. You going to stick around?"

"If she'll have me." Holly shrugged. "As long as she wants."

Elsie smiled.

CHAPTER 22

Sadie woke slowly on Thursday morning, her body tingling with arousal before she'd even opened her eyes. She smiled as her awareness sharpened, and she realised that what had woken her was Holly's hot, wet tongue stroking determinedly up her inner thighs.

"You're insatiable," she murmured sleepily, her back arching as Holly dipped into her wetness, the flat of her tongue tracing a firm but lazy path over every fold and crevice.

"Uh-huh." Holly barely paused in her attentions, and Sadie gasped as the tongue strokes quickened. When Holly pulled Sadie's clit between her lips and began to gently suck, Sadie moaned, long and loud, into the quiet hotel room.

"Oh, God," she breathed, her hips writhing beneath Holly's hands, which clutched tightly at her as she moved.

The orgasm was rapid and pinpoint—exquisitely sharp and focused only on her clit. She grabbed handfuls of sheet as she rode it out, her breath leaving her lungs in a series of staccato huffs.

"Mm." Holly looked up at her from between her thighs. "I could wake you like that every day."

"And I would let you." Sadie laughed. "How long had you been down there before I woke?"

Holly giggled and moved her way up Sadie's body to lie carefully on top of her.

"Only a couple of minutes. I was curious to see how long it would take. I decided if you didn't wake when I licked your clit, I'd have to resort to stronger measures."

Sadie laughed. "Not sure I want to ask what those would have been." She wiggled her eyebrows, lifting up slightly to kiss her lover. Tasting herself on Holly's lips, she moaned and pulled Holly in for a deeper kiss.

"No." Holly groaned and pushed up on her elbows. "I've got to go. One of us has to go to work today."

Sadie pushed her bottom lip out in a pout. "Not fair."

Holly ran her fingers though Sadie's hair, her face softening.

"We'll be back together tonight. Promise." Her voice was husky, and Sadie cocked her head.

"Are you okay, babe?"

Holly nodded, but Sadie could see tears moistening her eyes.

"What is it?" Sadie stroked Holly's face tenderly with the back of her hand.

Holly shrugged, almost imperceptibly. "You're leaving in two days. I've known that all week, of course, but every now and then it hits me. And it hurts."

Sadie nodded, but couldn't find any words to make it all better.

Holly smiled wanly, kissed Sadie briefly, then hauled herself out of the bed. "Time for me to shower and get out of here." Her voice was cheery, but Sadie could hear the falseness in it.

Sadie flopped back on the bed and listened to the sounds of Holly going through her ablutions. Two days. That's all they had left together. *Tonight, we really needed to plan when and how to see each other again.* Sadie also needed to talk to her mum about how and when she could see her again too. She couldn't keep coming back to Ballarat for great lengths of time. Sure, Bill and Marie would probably be pretty understanding on that score, but they still had a business to run. Maybe in another couple of weeks' time she could take a four-day weekend, maybe fly this time. She had money saved up; that wasn't the issue. It was all about time. And time was something her mother didn't have a lot of.

Holly kissed her goodbye, taking her time, it seemed, and Sadie didn't begrudge her.

When she'd gone, Sadie showered and ate some breakfast. She could have tried to go back to sleep—it was still only just before seven—but her maudlin thoughts had her fully awake. She needed to ride. Whenever her head got full of...stuff, climbing onto her Harley usually sorted her out. She picked up her jacket and helmet, pushed her wallet into her pocket, and made sure to wander out via reception, just so she could gaze on her girlfriend once more. Holly was busy with a checkout but shot Sadie a wink when the departing guest wasn't looking. Sadie grinned and blew her a kiss before making her way out through the front doors.

After stopping to fill up the tank, she hit the road. She had only a vague route in mind; where she was going wasn't important. It was all about the ride.

"How was it?" Elsie asked as she stirred sugar into the tea she had made for her daughter.

"Good. I went out to Halls Gap, up to Boroka Lookout."

Elsie grinned. "That's not a short one."

Sadie laughed. "I know. I just needed to cut loose."

"Everything okay?"

"Yes. Mostly." Sadie shrugged. For all her happiness at how she had reconciled with her mother this week, and what she had found with Holly, her heart ached. Behind it all, lurking in dark corners, was the awareness that no matter how good their time was together, her mum would soon be gone. Each day this week had followed the same relaxing pattern—she'd ride up to her mum's house and spend all day with her and Elsie before meeting up with Holly later. They'd share their run, a light dinner somewhere, and then hours of talking, laughing, and lovemaking that brought them ever closer together. It had been blissful, but tinged with sadness.

"Are you two still coming for tea tonight?" Elsie's voice broke into her thoughts.

"Absolutely." Sadie pulled her mind back to the present, adding a levity to her voice she wasn't sure she felt. "And we promise to keep our hands off each other this time."

Sadie smiled as Elsie giggled. Sadie had been delighted when her mum had extended another invite for her and Holly to come over for dinner. A small part of her had been worried that the kiss incident, as she and Holly had taken to calling it, might have made her mum wary of seeing them together again. Christine had made it very clear her fears were groundless. Not that she'd mentioned the kiss, but she'd been adamant about wanting to see Holly again before the end of the week.

"What time shall we come?"

"Seven's fine. It's stir-fry tonight. Prawn—is that okay for you?"

"Sounds great! I'll cook. Give you a night off, Gran."

"I'm not going to argue with you." Elsie winked. "Now, come on through. Christine's got news of Izzy."

Sadie walked quickly through to the lounge room. Her mum was in her recliner again, and she looked tired. Actually more than tired—exhausted.

"Hey, Mum." Sadie stepped over and leaned down to give her a careful hug.

"Hello, darling." Even her voice sounded tired.

"You sure you're up for me visiting? You look really tired, Mum."

Christine smiled, wryly. "I am, I can't lie. Just stay a while, until I sleep. Please?"

"Sure, Mum, whatever you want. Just don't wear yourself out talking to me."

Christine waved a hand weakly. "Let me just tell you about my call with Izzy last night."

"Yes?"

"Very interesting. I hadn't heard from her since she was here with that boy. And as you know, your grandmother gave her a piece of her mind after that."

All three women giggled.

"Well, I couldn't leave it at that. Just because she'd been told a few home truths didn't mean she could ignore me. I'm dying, for goodness sakes," she muttered.

Sadie bit back a gasp at her mother's words.

"Anyway," Christine continued. "I called her last night. I was actually surprised she answered, but it seems she's been doing her own thinking too. The big news is that she has ditched that boy, thank God."

"Excellent!" Sadie couldn't resist the little fist pump, and Elsie snorted.

Christine laughed. "Yes, well, I told her I wasn't unhappy about that. So, we talked some more. She got a bit upset. She feels bad about what he said to you, and that she didn't stop him. At the same time, she does seem to be struggling with your sexuality. I don't know what that's about, and it might just take some time. I don't know."

"Is she staying away from you because of me?" Sadie's voice was quiet and tinged with her fear of the answer.

Christine shook her head. "Not directly. She's staying away, I think, because too much has come crashing down for her in the last couple of weeks, and she just needs some time to process it all. She'll come around, I'm sure of it. And soon, from the hints I got in talking to her." Christine fixed her with a sharp look. "Do not concern yourself with this, okay? Izzy and I will be just fine. I know we will."

Sadie sighed and threw her hands up. "If you say so, Mum. I don't like it, but you sound convinced it will be okay, so I'll trust you on this. God knows, you know her way better than I do." Sadie knew she could remedy that—*should* remedy it. She made a mental note to be sure to get Izzy's number from her mum before she returned to Manly.

"I do, darling. So yes, just trust me."

After getting Christine settled for a sleep in the master bedroom, Sadie took Elsie out in the car to stock up on groceries.

"We don't need much, but I'd like to get some fresh veggies and prawns for tea tonight."

"No problem, Gran."

They wandered around the supermarket slowly, chatting about Izzy.

"She was always more stubborn than you, if you can believe it." Elsie smiled at Sadie's raised eyebrows. "It's true. Your little temper tantrums barely lasted a minute, as I recall. But Izzy's could go on into the next day if she didn't get her way."

"So you think she really will come round and start visiting Mum again?"

Elsie nodded. "Yep. She just needs to take her own sweet time over it."

"You rode all the way out to Hall's Gap and back?" Holly was stunned—that trip wasn't just a little cruise around to clear the air.

Sadie laughed. "Yeah, I needed to cut loose for a while."

Holly cocked her head. "You need that sometimes, don't you? A good ride out to somewhere?"

"I do." Sadie nodded. "It's my therapy."

"Would you always want to be on your own for that?"

Sadie looked at her, a small frown forming on her features, and Holly squirmed a little. She hadn't meant it to sound so…whining. What was she doing acting so pathetically? All day, she'd been getting wound up by the smallest things. Discovering Sadie had taken off for half the day, with no word of where she was going, had really irritated her. More than it should, she realised. Sadie could do what she liked with her day. But Holly couldn't seem to do anything about her irrational response to it.

"What's wrong?" Sadie's voice was calm, but she crossed her arms over her chest in a defensive gesture.

Holly exhaled. "God, I'm sorry. I don't know what's the matter with me today."

She stepped over to Sadie, who was perched by the stove. Glancing quickly around to make doubly sure they were alone, she dropped a soft kiss on Sadie's lips.

"Ignore me." She smiled at Sadie. "When I figure out what's making me so cranky, I'll let you know. Until then, I shall just go and make small talk with Elsie and Christine. Unless you want my help in here?"

Sadie shook her head and relaxed her posture. She kissed Holly quickly, again, and turned back to opening the wine, the task that Holly had interrupted with her silly interrogation. Holly watched Sadie for a moment, watched her hands as she unscrewed the cap of the bottle and carefully poured out the golden liquid into four small glasses. Those hands mesmerised her, and she felt a flush along the full length of her body, remembering just what those hands could do to her. Would do to her later, if she could only shake off this crazy mood.

Abruptly, she turned away and headed to the lounge room. There was no sign of Christine. Plopping herself down heavily on the couch next to Elsie, she caught the raised eyebrow the older woman directed her way.

"Sorry, Elsie," she said sheepishly. "I'm in a bit of a funny mood."

"No worries, love." Elsie patted her on the leg. "You're allowed, if that's what you need."

Holly sighed and leaned her head back against the couch.

"Is…is everything okay with you and Sadie?" Elsie's voice was quiet and uncertain.

Holly turned her head to look at Elsie, and saw concern etched on her face. From everything Sadie had told her about her grandmother, she knew Elsie didn't often do deep and meaningful chats. For her to ask something like that outright showed how much she knew Holly meant to Sadie, and how much she wanted this relationship to work for her granddaughter.

"We're good, Elsie, please don't worry. It's just... Well, she leaves on Saturday, and I don't know when I'll see her again. I guess I'm really struggling, now that her going is so near."

Elsie nodded slowly.

"Plus," Holly hurried on, feeling the need to get it all out there, "I was already feeling unsettled with my life before she came along, and now it all just feels a whole lot worse."

Before Elsie could respond, Sadie appeared with a glass of wine for each of them. As she passed one to Holly, she ran a finger along Holly's arm, down to her wrist, where she stroked softly.

"You okay?" she asked gently.

Holly nodded, shivering from the delicate touch at her wrist. "I'm fine, baby. Don't worry."

She felt Elsie stiffen beside her. Yeah, so maybe she had just told a little white lie to Sadie. In front of Elsie.

Busted.

"Well," she amended quickly, before Sadie could walk away, "I've got stuff going through my brain that I need to think through. I'm not keeping secrets from you, I promise. I just need—"

"It's okay." Sadie smiled. "We'll talk later, okay?"

Holly squeezed her hand.

"Okay, I'm off to make the most amazing stir-fry you've ever had." Sadie's grin was wide, and both Holly and Elsie laughed.

"That's quite a boast," Elsie said, pointing a thin finger at Sadie. "It's a good job I know how good your stir-fries are."

"Have I ever let you down?" Sadie stood with her hands on her hips, looking proud, and Holly's heart thudded at the gorgeous vision in front of her.

Elsie chuckled. "Get back in the kitchen, missy."

"Ma'am, yes, ma'am." Sadie saluted and left the room at marching pace.

"What was all that about?" Christine walked in a moment later, gazing back over her shoulder, a glass of wine in her hand.

Elsie and Holly giggled.

Christine sat in her recliner and sipped her wine.

"How are you feeling?" Holly inquired. "Sadie said you weren't doing so good earlier."

"Much better now, thank you. I slept about three hours this afternoon, and that seems to have helped."

"So," Elsie said, putting a hand on Holly's forearm. "Back to what you were saying earlier."

Holly stared. Elsie wasn't letting this go, and suddenly Holly was embarrassed to be talking about her feelings in front of the two women who were most important to Sadie. Although, wasn't she important too, now? Elsie knew that, and despite the newness of their acquaintance, was clearly determined to let Holly talk it through.

Christine was looking at her quizzically.

Clearing her throat, Holly said, "Well, I was just telling Elsie earlier how I'm in a bit of a strange mood today. I think it's because it's so close to Sadie leaving, and it's unsettling me. I was already a bit lost as to what I was doing with my life before she came along, and now it's all even more confusing."

"I see. What was all the confusion about before you met Sadie?" Christine didn't seem rattled by the topic of discussion, and Holly was again amazed at how well Sadie's mother had adjusted to Holly's presence in her daughter's life.

"Career, I guess. My degree is in marketing, but I'm working as a hotel receptionist, because I don't know what to do with my degree. It sounds silly, because I could easily give Melbourne a go, try and get a job with one of the big companies down there. It's what all my friends from university are doing. But I just can't seem to get enthusiastic about that."

"You don't want to work in marketing now?" Christine sounded puzzled.

"No, that's just it. I really do want to use my degree. I loved what I studied and would love to put it into practice." She sighed. "I decided before I even finished uni that I didn't want to stay in Ballarat. I want to get out, go somewhere different. But Melbourne, the most obvious choice, just isn't grabbing me. I don't know why."

"How about Sydney?" Elsie's eyes sparkled as Holly turned to stare at her.

"What?" Was Elsie seriously suggesting that she move to Sydney?

Elsie shrugged and smirked. "Well, there's a woman who lives there that you want to spend more time with. There are lots of big companies in the city. It's still close enough to your family to visit quite often." She patted Holly's leg. "You might just want to think about it, is all I'm saying."

"I-I don't know. That seems like a big move to make, all in one go. I mean, God, I'd love to be near Sadie. But it's so early in our relationship, I-I don't know if that would be a good idea or not."

Why was she so frightened of this? Because she was, all of a sudden. Terrified, actually. Having someone spell out so succinctly an option that she hadn't even entertained, but which made perfect sense, was scaring her for all sorts of reasons. It seemed like a massive leap to take only ten days into what she and Sadie had. Moving that far away from her family was suddenly very daunting too. Never mind starting out on her own in a new city, a city she didn't know. Where would she live? Did she have enough money saved up to last while she job-hunted? Would Sadie even want her there? They hadn't talked about the future and what would happen when Sadie returned home. About what would happen to them. Her stomach clenched at the prospect.

She glanced at each of the two women and saw confusion written on their faces. Perhaps to them it seemed a hell of a lot easier than it did to her. Just because Elsie had upped and moved cities so easily all those years ago didn't mean Holly could do so just as smoothly. She realised they were waiting for a response from her.

"I-I guess I'll need to think about it." It was lame but all she could give them. Especially not knowing how Sadie felt.

Christine smiled, but it seemed to Holly it lacked her usual warmth.

"You've got plenty of time," Christine said. She looked away and drank from her wine.

Before Holly could say more, Sadie's voice called down the hallway from the kitchen.

"Tea's ready!"

Sadie pulled Holly to her, fitting her lover's soft curves against her own firmer body. They kissed languorously. Holly's mouth was exquisite. Like silk and whipped cream and soft, soft velvet.

"I love kissing you," Sadie whispered as she took a moment to breathe. "Love the feel of your mouth on mine, your tongue, your lips."

She'd never been so verbal with a lover. Never felt the need to try to express her desires other than through physical action. The obvious effect it had on Holly was something she wanted to generate again and again. Holly's breath quickened, her hips ground into Sadie's, and her hands tugged and twisted at Sadie's hair. She took Sadie's mouth in a searing kiss, her soft sounds as she did so setting Sadie's body on fire.

Later, when her heart had stopped threatening to thud its way out of her chest, and her body had stilled from the delicious onslaught of yet another toe-curling climax, she pulled Holly into the crook of her arm and smiled when Holly nestled in as tight as she could.

"Comfy?"

"Yep."

Sadie chuckled and squeezed Holly tight.

"So," Holly said, after a few moments. "We kind of haven't talked about what happens next, have we?" She sounded nervous.

Sadie shifted so that she could look down at her. "No. We haven't."

"Have you thought about it?"

"Yes and no. And that's not because I don't think it's important," she rushed on, seeing the beginnings of a frown appear on Holly's forehead. "It's just I've had so much else on my mind. I don't want you to think you're not important, because you are. Very. But, with Mum, and everything… I don't know. The future just seems so scary, at the moment."

Holly's face relaxed into an expression of tenderness.

"Of course. I understand. I'm not trying to be selfish and ignore everything else that you're dealing with. But, yeah—" she chuckled, "—I *am* a bit selfish. I want to know we have a future."

"God, Holly, we do! I promise. It's just, I don't know what, or when, that future is. Not right now."

Holly sighed and placed a gentle fingertip on Sadie's lips. "I get it. It's okay."

Sadie shivered as Holly ran her fingertip down Sadie's neck, across her collarbone, and then slowly down towards her breast. The intensity of Holly's gaze seared her; what they had together was beyond anything she'd known, or dared to dream about.

For only the second time in her life, she wanted to say the words, and for the first time in her life she knew she meant them with every cell of her being.

Stilling Holly's wandering fingers, she then cupped her face and leaned in to place the softest of kisses on Holly's lips. When she pulled back, Holly was staring at her.

Sadie smiled. "I love you, Holly." The words came so easily, and her blood sang with them. The song turned to a roar when Holly gasped and pulled her in for a long, deep kiss.

"I love you too," Holly said, breathlessly, when she finally let their mouths part. "In case that wasn't clear."

Sadie chuckled. "I was rather hoping that's what the kiss meant."

"Are you tired?" Holly smiled wider and pushed herself provocatively against Sadie's body. The movement ignited Sadie's lust in an instant.

"Not if you aren't."

"Good." Holly swiftly flipped her over onto her back, smoothly working her way down Sadie's body. "Because I'm not nearly done with you tonight."

Sadie groaned as Holly bent her head and began to taste.

CHAPTER 23

"I think you should have this evening with your mum and Elsie, without me being there." Holly spoke quietly, brushing her hair with fast, smooth strokes.

Sadie sat upright in the bed. In her sleepy state, she had simply enjoyed watching Holly get ready for work, but suddenly, she was wide awake.

"What do you mean?"

"Babe, it's your last night here. I think you should have that time for you. I saw them last night, and I'll… Well, I hope I'll see them again soon. But she's *your* mum, and Elsie's *your* gran, and I think I should stay away this evening. Besides," she said, grimacing, "my mum is making a lot of noise about hardly seeing me this week. I could do with being home for an evening too." She put down the brush and stood at the foot of the bed. "I'll still come back here, later, if you want."

"Yes! God, of course I want that. I have to see you tonight. Please, don't stay away the whole night." Sadie knew she was practically begging, but she didn't care. The idea of not spending her last night there wrapped up in Holly's arms was deeply upsetting. *How can Holly be so reticent about tonight? Is she having second thoughts about our future?*

"I won't." Holly was smiling, but it didn't quite reach her eyes. "Promise."

Sadie swallowed hard before daring to ask her next question. "Holly, are you having second thoughts about us?"

Holly vigorously shook her head. "No! Not at all."

"Then what is it? You seem…distant."

"I'm sorry. I'm okay, really. Just very aware you're leaving tomorrow. I'm going to miss you."

Sadie stared at her. Something told her that was only part of it, but they didn't have time for her to push it before work. Later.

"I'm going to miss you too. So you have to come back here tonight, okay?"

Holly grinned, and it was the most relaxed she'd looked since they'd woken. "Yes, of course. Just text me when you're leaving your mum's, and I'll meet you here as soon after that as I can, okay?"

Reassured by the warmth on Holly's face and in her tone, Sadie relaxed against the pillows. Not trusting herself to speak, she held out her arms and relaxed even further when Holly gladly threw herself onto the bed and into Sadie's embrace. They kissed for long moments, and Sadie could feel Holly's need for her in the ardency of her mouth. No, whatever was troubling Holly wasn't about her love for Sadie itself. Maybe it was just the uncertainty of where they were and where they were going. They needed to talk some more about that, and Sadie would make sure they did, no matter how tempting the idea of making love all night was.

Holly brought their kiss to an end and smiled ruefully. "Gotta go to work. I love you."

Sadie nodded and dropped one last soft kiss on Holly's now-swollen lips. "I love you too. I'll see you tonight."

"You will. Promise."

"Mum, can I ask you something?" Sadie was nervous about broaching this subject. It was uncharted territory, asking her mum for advice.

"Of course, darling. What is it?" Christine was pottering around the kitchen, wiping down surfaces and rearranging utensils. She was having one of her better days, and they were planning on lunch at the Lake View later.

"Did Holly talk to you at all last night? I mean, about me. Us."

Christine turned to face her. "She didn't talk to you about it last night?"

Sadie sighed. "A little. She was concerned that we hadn't talked about the future. She…she was worried I didn't want her to be part of it."

"And I hope you set her right on that?" Christine's eyes twinkled.

Sadie blushed. "I did. We… I love her, Mum." She braced herself for an awkward response but glowed with happiness when Christine simply smiled and pulled her in for a quick hug.

"That's lovely, Sadie. I'm very happy for you."

"Thanks, Mum. That means a lot, from you." Christine smiled. "It's just," Sadie continued, "this morning she seemed a little…withdrawn. I get the feeling there's something she's not telling me, but when I asked if she was okay, she said she was."

Christine sighed and motioned to the table. "Let's sit for a moment." She waited until they were settled before she continued. "I don't think it's for me to say what she talked to us about, but—" she raised her hand when she saw Sadie was about to interrupt, "—at the same time, you're my daughter and I don't want to see you upset."

She paused, obviously choosing her words. Sadie waited as patiently as she could, but one foot was tapping out a quiet rhythm on the tiled floor, and her hands twitched in her lap.

"I think she's a little lost in her life right now. She has some decisions to make, and I think she's trying very hard to work through them without burdening you."

"How could she think she'd be a burden to me?" Sadie slumped back against her chair, and her tapping foot came to a standstill. "Surely, if we're going to be a partnership we should talk to each other, share things like this?" She almost couldn't believe the words coming out of her own mouth. She used to be the one who shied away from talking about feelings, and yet she was complaining because her girlfriend was doing exactly the same thing. Nicole would be laughing her ass off if she could witness it.

Christine smiled. "Darling, she's doing it to protect you. She feels you have enough on your plate with… Well, with me and what happened with your dad and Izzy. She doesn't want you worrying about anything more than you already are."

Sadie sighed. Yes, that sounded like Holly. Although Holly had been quietly relentless in her pursuit of Sadie, recognising long before Sadie did that they had the potential for something wonderful, at the same time, she wasn't selfish. Of course she'd be aware of what Sadie was going through, and of course she'd want to protect Sadie from anything else that could upset her.

Elsie appeared, having been cleaning and tidying bedrooms, putting on a load of laundry, and putting fresh towels in both the bathrooms.

"I need a cup of tea after all that," she said, easing herself down into a chair alongside her daughter.

"I'll do that," Sadie said. After she made their drinks and returned to the table, she leaned forward and rested her chin on her hands.

"Okay, so what do I do?"

Christine chuckled. "Talk to her, sweetheart. Just talk to her."

Elsie looked at her. "Is this about Holly?"

Sadie nodded. "I was just a bit worried about how she was last night."

"She's a good one." Elsie smiled. "You keep hold of her, Sadie."

"I certainly plan to, Gran." Sadie winked, and Elsie smiled wider.

She was happier since she'd had that talk with her mum. Being able to be that open with her was more satisfying than she would have imagined.

Elsie stood up suddenly. "Can I borrow your phone, Sadie? I need to make a call and mine's charging."

"Sure, Gran." She pulled the phone from her pocket, entered the unlock code, and handed it over.

"Thanks, love. I won't be long."

"Sweetheart, are you okay?" Judy asked.

Holly blinked, bringing herself back to the room. She had no idea how long she'd been sitting there, just gazing into space. The conversation she'd had with Elsie earlier was whirring through her mind.

"Hi, sexy," she'd answered as Sadie's number came up in the display. Elsie's amused cackle had turned her cheeks scarlet. When she'd calmed down enough to speak to her girlfriend's grandmother, she'd done a lot of listening, but not a lot of talking.

"You don't have to make any decisions today, or even this week," Elsie said. "But I just wanted you to know that the offer is there. You probably need to talk to Sadie about it. But I'm serious. There is a home for you in Manly, if you want it." Elsie's voice was strong and determined. "I've never meddled in her life before, other than straightening her out a bit when she first arrived twelve years ago. I've tried to let her find her own way, even if I didn't agree with every choice she made. But I've… Well, I've never seen this side of her before. She loves you, and you're good for her." Elsie's voice took on a husky edge to it, and Holly had to fight back her own tears at the obvious emotion in the older woman's tone. "If I can do something to keep you in her life, I will. As long as that's what you want too."

"It is," she whispered. "Definitely."

"Good." Elsie cleared her throat. "So, just think about it, okay?"

"I will. Thank you, Elsie. Thank you so much." She'd held on to her phone for some moments after Elsie had ended the call.

Her parents were both staring at her. She noticed the fork in her hand, a mouthful of food speared on it.

"Sorry," she muttered and forced the food into her mouth. It was cold. She chewed quickly and washed it down with a sip of water.

Across the table, she saw her mother look at her father, who raised his eyebrows.

"Is there something you want to talk about?" Judy asked tentatively, as if afraid of the can of worms she might be opening up in her inquiry.

Holly stared at them, her mother first, then her father. For all that had happened since Sadie arrived at their hotel and into Holly's life, her father had said nothing to her about it. Had her mother told him about Sadie, about Holly's relationship with her? She'd always been closer to her mum, but her father wasn't completely aloof—he'd made a big effort to be there for her throughout her life, in his own way.

He cleared his throat and put down his wine glass. "You seem very preoccupied, Holly. I know you talk to your mother more than me, generally, but you know if there's anything you want to share, you can tell both of us."

Holly flicked a glance at her mother, raising an eyebrow in question. *Have you told him?* Her mother's almost imperceptible nod dealt with that obstacle, at least.

How to tell them? How to broach the biggest decision she'd had to make in her life thus far? The pull she felt towards Sadie was all-consuming. After only two weeks together, it shouldn't really be possible, her analytical brain told her. But her heart, and her body, completely disagreed. She and Sadie just… connected. It had been instant, and it had thrown her, but she couldn't fight it. She had a chance to follow her heart and let the rest of her life fall in behind, see where it took her. But in doing that, she had to take a bold step away from the family home she had known her whole life, from the parents who had loved and supported her through everything she'd ever tried to achieve. Would they feel the same level of support for this decision?

You won't know unless you ask. The thought came unbidden, but loud and clear. She realised the undeniable truth of it and exhaled a slow breath.

"Let's finish eating," she said, her voice calm even if her heart was pounding under her ribs. "Then we'll talk."

Sadie was torn. As much as she wanted to get back to the hotel and back to the beautiful body of her lover, she didn't want to say goodbye to her mother. Having spent a good part of nearly every day with her since she'd first arrived in Ballarat two weeks ago, leaving was harder than she'd imagined. Underlying it, she knew, was the fear that every time she said goodbye it was for the last time.

She held her mum close, careful not to squeeze the delicate woman too hard.

"I'll see you in the morning," Christine whispered.

"I know. It's just…"

"Yes, I know." Christine pulled back and held Sadie at arm's length. "You'll be back in a couple of weeks, won't you?"

They'd made that plan after eating. Sadie would fly back on a Friday morning, and stay for a weekend. Then she'd plan to do that as many weekends as she could, if Marie and Bill were willing, until her mother—

She cut that thought off as her stomach churned with premature grief.

Sadie smiled and tried to feel as positive as her mother.

"Now, come on. Go. I know you and Holly want to see each other tonight." Sadie watched her mother's face blush at the implications of her statement, and found her own face flaming in response.

She cleared her throat and turned to her grandmother.

"See you in the morning, old girl." She smirked as Elsie scowled.

"How many times have I told you not to call me that?" Elsie's tone was gruff, but her eyes betrayed her. She gazed at Sadie with warm affection and reached out her arms for a hug.

Holding her grandmother almost as carefully as she'd held her mother, Sadie wished her goodnight and then swept her bike keys up from the hall table.

"Okay, I'm going. See you tomorrow morning."

"All right, darling. Sleep well," Christine said.

Elsie giggled, and Sadie left before any sarcastic comments could come her way. Although she chuckled as she walked down the driveway to the bike parked at the end of it. She took a moment to text Holly to tell her she was on her way back, then fired up the Harley.

The hotel room was cold when she returned, and she turned on the heater to take the edge off. Although, hopefully, she and Holly would generate their own heat soon. She smiled to herself as she spent a few minutes tidying and preparing the room. With her belongings cleared away out of sight, the lights turned down low, and the bed covers turned back, she'd made the space as intimate as it could be.

They'd spent all their relationship in this room, it seemed. It would be odd to transfer it to her own home back in Manly. Odd, but exciting. The thought of having Holly come and visit her, possibly as soon as next weekend, had Sadie's heart aching with need. She couldn't wait to show Holly where she lived, have her meet Nicole and Tash, take her to their favourite pubs and restaurants. She could show her the Bike Rack Cafe, introduce her to Marie and Bill, and Trixie.

The more she thought about making Holly part of her life, the more she wanted it. They really should have that chat about the future again. With her mum's diagnosis, she knew things were still up in the air. But she also knew, with every beat of her heart, that she belonged with Holly, no matter what else life threw at her in the coming months. Although Holly hadn't pushed her on that, she thought she knew where Holly's desires lay. She resolved to have that conversation with Holly, lay the groundwork for a bigger commitment between them. It wasn't nearly as frightening a thought as she would have imagined.

Holly heard her phone ping the announcement of a new text message, and knew it was more than likely Sadie telling her she was back at the hotel. She willed herself to focus on her mum's voice, despite the almost desperate urge to stand, grab her bag, and get away from this conversation. It was going disastrously, and it had her reeling. Whilst she'd expected her parents to be surprised, possibly even shocked, at her thoughts about her future, she hadn't expected the level of anger they were displaying. Especially her mother, who was in full flow.

"I cannot believe you are seriously thinking of pinning your entire future on a silly little *fling* that isn't even two weeks old yet." She virtually spat the word *fling* into the room with a venom that had Holly wincing. Her mother's voice was rising in volume, and her strides around the room were becoming more forceful.

Holly thought "entire future" was probably the most ridiculous of the exaggerations her mother had thrown at her in the last twenty minutes or so. Although phrases like "threatening your career," "abandoning your family," and—her personal favourite—"devastating your father" had all been thrown in Holly's direction. Her father hadn't, to his credit, looked devastated at all. More confused, if anything. Holly wasn't entirely sure if his confusion was over what she had told them or her mother's reaction to it. He'd barely said a word, which left her to face the ranting of her mother.

"I knew that girl was trouble. She always was. And now look what she's done."

Holly blinked. Oh my God, her mother was going *there* again. She passed a hand over her face, trying to ease away the frown that was making her forehead ache. She couldn't take any more of this. She'd heard enough, more than enough, to bring back all of her doubts about doing something so radical, so very different from the behaviour that steady, sensible Holly normally displayed. She needed some air. And she needed Sadie's arms around her, helping her forget all of this…turmoil. At least for a little while.

She stood, abruptly, causing her mother's pacing to falter.

"I'm going out," Holly said quietly. "I probably won't be back tonight." Without waiting for a response, she grabbed her bag and walked out into the hallway. As she pulled on her coat, she could hear angry whispers coming from the room behind her. She yanked open the front door and tried very hard not to slam it behind her as she left. She nearly succeeded.

She took the long way to the hotel, which involved walking quite some ways in the opposite direction before taking a series of turns to bring her back on course. She needed the extra time to calm down, to try to rid her mind of her mother's voice. She realised she'd underestimated her mother's acceptance of her sexuality. It hadn't been mentioned since their shopping trip, and she'd naively assumed that meant her mum was going to be okay about it. Which, maybe she would be, given time. But broaching the concept of leaving home to move to Sydney to be near Sadie, only a week after telling her mum about them? Yeah, big mistake.

It was more than that, though. No matter how much it pained her to agree with anything her mum had thrown at her in the last half hour, she had to admit her own behaviour this week was so very much not like her. At all. To be seriously considering throwing herself into the idea of being with Sadie, transforming her life, her goals, and her direction overnight? Holly O'Brien didn't do that. She planned. Very methodically. She had done so her entire life, mapping out with almost clinical precision her academic pathway from the age of thirteen to achieve the exact degree she desired. But to her own mystification, ever since achieving the qualification, she'd lost her way. And none of that had anything to do with Sadie. Maybe Sadie was just a catalyst for a bigger decision about what she wanted from her life. Or maybe Sadie *was* everything, and all the other feelings around a lack of direction would just fall into place if Holly could only take that leap of faith.

She huffed out a breath as she rounded the corner and walked past the front of the hotel. She hadn't really shaken off much of her stress or concerns, but she couldn't wait any longer to see Sadie. To hold her and kiss her, and…other things. She knew she needed that, and she knew she needed to talk about this with Sadie. Everything was still so jumbled in her brain. While she didn't want to upset Sadie, she had to tell her what was going on. Sadie already knew, on some level, that there was something troubling Holly. It wouldn't be fair to shut her out, not when it was this important.

She let herself in the back door and paused to shake herself out a little before knocking quietly on the door to Sadie's room. It opened almost instantly, and the sight of her girlfriend standing before her dressed only in a tee shirt, which barely covered the sheer briefs she wore, was exactly the tonic she needed for her disjointed evening. Holly took a moment to drink in the view, letting her gaze slowly drift down the length of Sadie's body and back up again. She met Sadie's teasing grin with one of her own, shook off her jacket, and stepped into the room.

"Hey, babe," Sadie murmured, reaching for her. Holly went willingly. They stood in the middle of the room, holding each other tight. Just holding, breathing each other in.

"Can we talk about what happens next?" Sadie's voice was quiet, muffled slightly where her face was pressed into Holly's hair.

"Yes," Holly said, relieved that Sadie had got straight to the point, especially when everything that had happened with her parents was still so fresh in her mind. She pulled away and motioned to the bed.

Once they were seated, she snaked an arm around Sadie's waist and pulled her close.

"I know you know there's been something on my mind these past few days."

Sadie nodded, kissing Holly tenderly on the forehead. "Yeah, and I get that you probably didn't want to burden me with it, with everything else that's going on. At least, that's Mum's theory."

Holly smiled. "You talked to your mum about me?"

"Yeah." Sadie chuckled. "Kind of weird, getting relationship advice from my mum."

Holly giggled and kissed Sadie. "Well, she was right. I didn't want to burden you, or confuse you, with all of *my* confusion."

"And now?"

"Now, I'm still confused." She smiled wryly. "But I know I need to tell you. To share. If we're going to have a future, then keeping stuff from each other isn't a great start, is it?"

Sadie shook her head. "Tell me."

"God, Sadie, I have so much to think about." She sighed. "I just need some time. Ugh, I know that's the worst cliché in the book."

"What do you need to think about?"

"You…me…everything has turned my ordered little world upside down in a very short space of time." She looked up at Sadie. "I feel like I've been on a rollercoaster that's a bit out of control, ever since you got here. And—" she held up her hand as Sadie attempted to interrupt her, "—don't get me wrong, meeting you has been amazing, and I love you, I really do. But meeting you and falling in love with you, and all the dramas we've had to go through, it's all emphasised just how...directionless I am lately. I told you I had no idea what to do about a job or career, or even where to live. None of that has been resolved by meeting you. In fact, it's just added to the whole confusing pot of everything."

She sighed, and pushed her hands through her hair. "I have no idea what I'm doing right now. And that is just not me. That doesn't mean I don't want this, what we have. I just don't know how to fit it into everything else. And..." She trailed off and took a couple of deep breaths. "I had such an argument with my parents tonight. Well, not an argument. More like I tried to explain what was happening to me, and how I wanted to see about making a future with you, and, well, they were less than impressed."

"Because it's me, or because I'm a woman?"

"Both, I think, in equal measures. It was hard to tell. Things got...emotional."

Sadie stared at her. "So, are you saying that they could talk you out of this?"

"No, that's not it. But, you know, we have only known each other two weeks. And I know we are both pretty sure that this should continue, but I'm just thinking I might need us to take it a little slower. Give me some...space."

Holly dropped her gaze to her hands, which were clenched into tight fists in her lap. Sadie reached across to caress them.

"Babe, that's okay." She slipped one finger under Holly's chin and lifted her head until they were eye to eye. "I will happily give you space. But please, promise me that you'll talk to me. You've kept a lot of this to yourself this week, and like you said, we should share this sort of stuff with each other. Don't shut me out."

Holly grimaced. "I won't. I didn't tell you any of this before, because I was trying to protect you. You've got so much going on, you don't need me add—"

Sadie cut her off by kissing her. When she drew her lips away, she gave Holly a wry grin.

"Nicole would be hysterical at this, but babe, please believe me when I tell you I want to know what's going on with you. I want us to share. I want us to be there for each other. I'm…I'm kind of new at this relationship stuff, but with you it's okay. I trust you."

Holly kissed her quickly and smiled as they moved apart again. "Okay, I'll try. Just please, believe me when I tell you I love you. That part I *am* sure of."

Sadie nodded and smiled.

"What?" Holly asked, bemused.

"Well," Sadie began, scratching at the back of her head. "I'm kind of finding this a bit ironic. I mean, you were the one who came after me, not really taking no for an answer, and now you're the one wanting to slow things down."

Holly's cheeks tinged with a faint blush. "I know. I'm sorry," she whispered.

"It's okay," Sadie murmured, leaning over to nuzzle her neck. "It's just such new territory for me, being the one who's pushing for it to be more serious, more committed. It's kind of weird, but okay, all at the same time."

Holly laughed and pulled Sadie against her. "I will try not to take too long to figure this all out, I promise. I'll probably miss you so much this week, I'll be desperate to get a flight booked."

Sadie rubbed her thumb across Holly's bottom lip. "Just say the word, whenever you're ready. Okay?"

Sadie's thumb on her lip was seriously distracting. Having unburdened herself of her thoughts, and having been met by such love and positivity from Sadie, Holly was suddenly aware of their closeness, and the intimacy of the room.

Her mouth sought Sadie's and she kissed her fiercely. Her arousal was instant and rapidly swept through her entire body like a raging lava flow. Sadie moaned as Holly's tongue explored her mouth. In the next moment, Sadie's hands were in her hair, gripping almost painfully. The obvious need in that action started something burning in Holly, so deep and so exquisite. She let it run loose throughout her aching body. She ran her hands up Sadie's arms until she gripped both her wrists. Pulling them down and trapping them behind Sadie, she let her tongue travel the length of Sadie's neck down to her collarbone, using her nose to nudge aside the loose neck of the tee shirt so that she could lick and nip across Sadie's chest. Sadie tried to wriggle free of Holly's hold, but she simply tightened her grip. The need to just…possess Sadie was the most intense feeling she'd ever known.

"Babe, wh—?"

"Shush. Just…let me," Holly whispered. She raised her eyes briefly to meet Sadie's, and whatever was displayed on her face stilled Sadie's struggle. Sadie's eyes darkened and her lips parted, her tongue slipping out to wet them. Holly groaned and lunged in for another deep kiss that had her clit throbbing instantly and powerfully. Pushing gently, she manoeuvred Sadie to lie back on the bed. Holly carefully removed what few clothes Sadie wore, letting her fingers and tongue roam where they pleased on the deliciously warm skin that was revealed. She leaned over Sadie, her hands placed either side of her shoulders, and stared at her firm breasts, the nipples already rock-hard. Sadie was breathing heavily, and when Holly raised her gaze, she could see the need painted on Sadie's face. Her own body temperature reached incendiary levels.

"Please…" Sadie begged, lifting her body slightly, pushing her breasts nearer to Holly's mouth. She reached out for Holly, who grabbed her wrists again and pushed her arms above her head, pinning her down. "Please, Holly…" Sadie's voice was a tortured groan ripped from her throat.

There was a roaring in Holly's ears. She'd never had anyone beg before. Never had anyone want her so badly. What she and Sadie did to each other, the desire they created within each other, was the most incredible connection she'd ever shared with another human being.

She placed her knee between Sadie's legs, pressing forward to spread them wide. In the next moment, she pushed her thigh, encased in the rough denim of her jeans, against Sadie's centre. She wrapped her lips around a firm nipple. Sadie's gasp ricocheted around the room as Holly tugged hard on the peak. Rocking her thigh into Sadie, feeling a damp patch forming on her jeans and not caring, she licked and sucked each nipple in turn. Sadie's moans were strained and only increased the throbbing between Holly's own legs. The turmoil of earlier in the evening was well and truly forgotten. All that she felt, all that she was, was desire and need and arousal that scorched her veins and every millimetre of her skin.

Sadie was pushing herself against Holly's thigh, her whispered words begging Holly for a closer contact, a firmer rhythm. Holly was only too happy to oblige. She didn't want to tease, didn't want to make Sadie wait. She wanted to hear her, feel her, share with her the passion that enveloped both of them in the moment. Still holding Sadie's pinned wrists in one hand, still sucking on the engorged nipple between her lips, she ran her free hand down Sadie's body. When she reached the damp, crisp hair at the apex of her thighs, she didn't hesitate. She let her middle finger slide through Sadie's wetness, rubbing a few gentle circles over her clit before pushing into the slick heat inside her. Sadie arched off the bed and cried out. Holly's blood boiled. She added a second finger, thrusting as deep as she could, pulling back out and then plunging straight back in. She could feel Sadie rapidly tightening around her, and knew it wouldn't take long.

"Kiss me." The words were wrenched from Sadie's throat, sounding almost pained. Holly moved swiftly, tearing her mouth away from the soft breast and hard nipple that she had been feasting on to devour Sadie's mouth instead. She matched the rhythm of her fingers inside Sadie with the thrusts of her tongue in her mouth, and moments later, Sadie's convulsions started, her hips jerking off the bed as her orgasm claimed her. Holly rode it out with her, kissing her, keeping her fingers buried deep inside her, while the aftershocks sent tremors through Sadie's body.

"Oh, fuck," breathed Sadie after a couple of minutes, once her breathing had slowed and her chest had ceased its heaving. "Holly..."

Holly laid herself over Sadie's naked body and let go her wrists. As Sadie wrapped her arms around her, Holly kissed her softly, across her mouth, her cheeks, her eyes. When Sadie suddenly pushed her onto her back and began pulling roughly at her clothes, she submitted without a single thought of resisting. And when, minutes later, Sadie plunged two fingers inside her while her tongue bathed her clit, Holly gave herself, wholly and fully, to every sensation her beautiful lover could elicit from her ravenous body.

CHAPTER 24

Sadie didn't want to move. The heat from Holly's body tight against hers was almost too much, but if she let go, Holly would wake and the day—and their goodbye—would begin. She opened her eyes fully and could tell from the brightness edging the blinds at the window that it was well past dawn. She didn't have a set time to get on the road, but equally, she didn't want to be riding late into the night. She sighed. Her bladder was insisting she move. Crap. She tried to ease away as slowly and as carefully as she could, but mumbling from the curvy woman enclosed in her arms told her Holly was waking.

"It's okay," Sadie whispered, "I'm just going to the bathroom."

Holly grunted, and Sadie giggled, extricating herself from Holly's arms.

After using the bathroom, Sadie padded back to the bed to find Holly wide awake and watching her every move. Holly's gaze was intense, and Sadie didn't need to ask what she was thinking. Soundlessly, reading each other instinctively, they brought their bodies together one last time. Fierce kisses and urgent, knowledgeable hands and tongues rapidly elicited powerful orgasms for them both. Afterwards, they lay sweating and panting, enclosed in each other's arms again.

Sadie kissed Holly's forehead where it rested just below her chin.

Holly sighed. "I guess we'd better get up and get you out of here?"

"Yep, I guess so."

When Elsie answered the door, Sadie could instantly tell from her drawn expression that something was wrong.

"What's happened, Gran?" she asked, before she'd even stepped over the threshold.

Elsie waved a hand in the air between them. "Don't worry, she's okay now."

"But?"

"She had a bad night. I'm not sure what happened, exactly. She had a severe headache, had to wake me up to get her some of her strongest painkillers."

They reached the kitchen, and Elsie sat down. Sadie remained standing, itching for her gran to finish telling the story.

"She didn't really settle after that, kept saying it was hurting so much. I stayed with her, and eventually, she did get some sleep."

Sadie noted the dark smudges under her grandmother's eyes.

"Where is she now?" Sadie asked.

"Still in bed, but she is awake. You'll have to say your goodbye there, I'm afraid. We called the doctor first thing, and she said Christine should just rest up today. She'll visit later."

"God." Sadie exhaled sharply. "Now I don't want to leave."

Elsie smiled wanly. "We knew you'd say that. Go on through and see her."

Her mother was propped up against the pillows in the bed, a thick cardigan wrapped around her upper body, the doona covering her legs.

"Hey, Mum," Sadie said softly as she stepped into the bedroom.

"Hi, darling." Her mum's voice was stronger than she would have anticipated, and some of Sadie's tension drained away.

"Gran said you had a rough night."

Christine shrugged. "A particularly nasty headache, that's all. I'm just a bit tired now."

Sadie sat down on the edge of the bed and took one of her mum's hands in her own. It was cool and felt extraordinarily light and fragile, like a bird's wing. She swallowed back her anxiety and pasted a smile on her face.

"I'm wondering if I should call Marie and see if I could stay a bit longer. Now that he's out of the house, I could—"

"No, darling." Christine held up her free hand. "There's no need for that. I'm okay. You've got a job to get back to." She patted Sadie's hand. "We've arranged for you to come back in two weeks, haven't we? That time will fly, trust me."

Sadie sighed. "I know, it's just…" The fear eating at her gut was almost paralysing.

"Hey," Christine said softly, squeezing Sadie's hand. "I know. But you cannot put your life on hold for this. For me. We don't know how long this is going to take. And I would feel very guilty if I kept you away from all the other things in your life that are just as important to you."

"I guess," Sadie whispered.

"Your gran will look after me, don't worry."

Sadie raised her gaze upwards, and exhaled slowly. When she brought her gaze back down again, her mother was smiling at her.

"Okay," Sadie said reluctantly. "You win."

Christine smiled. "How's Holly?"

"She's…okay. We talked last night, about the future. She's a little…confused about some things, about her life. Not about me, or us," Sadie hastened to add as she saw her mother's face fold into a frown.

"You had me worried for a moment."

"Yeah, well, she had *me* worried for a while. But I think I understand what's happening for her now. She's used to having everything all mapped out, totally under her control. And now it isn't, and it's thrown her. We'll be all right, though, I think." She paused, thinking back to Holly in her arms that morning. "No, I'm sure we will."

"Good, because she's lovely, and I think you two are wonderful together."

"Aw, thanks, Mum," Sadie said, blushing. Christine laughed and gently patted Sadie's heated cheek.

"Got time for a coffee?" Elsie asked as she appeared in the doorway.

"Ah, I'd better not, Gran. I should get on the road. I heard there's rain on the way later, towards Albury, and I don't want to get stuck out in that."

"Fair enough," Elsie said. "You say goodbye to your mum, and I'll see you in a minute."

Sadie swallowed and turned back to her mother. "I hate this," she whispered but reached for her anyway, gently pulling her into a hug.

Christine wrapped her arms around her, pulling her close and kissing the side of her head.

"I know, sweetheart. But I'll see you soon, yes?" She kissed Sadie again and rocked her gently. "I love you, my darling daughter. And I am so, *so* glad you came back. This has meant the world to me. Thank you."

She pulled back, and Sadie saw the wet streaks on her face. Sadie swiped at her own tears as she managed to push the words, "I love you too, Mum," out past her sobs.

They came back for another close hug, crying and laughing at the same time. It was a while before her mum released her and wiped at Sadie's damp face with the sleeve of her cardigan.

"Go on now. Get on your way before that storm comes in."

"I will. I'll call you tonight, okay?"

"You'd better!" Christine smiled and stared at her for a moment. "My beautiful daughter."

Sadie blushed, and before her tears could take hold again, pivoted on her heels and walked off in search of her grandmother.

CHAPTER 25

Sadie pushed open the front door and laughed when she heard a squeal from the kitchen.

"You're back!" Nicole's beaming face greeted her from the kitchen doorway.

Sadie dumped the panniers on the floor beside her, kicked the front door shut, and strode quickly down the hallway into the waiting arms of her friend. They'd always been huggers, and after two weeks apart, they giggled as they enfolded each other in tight arms. Nicole, being that much shorter than Sadie, burrowed her head under Sadie's chin and laughed loudly when Sadie had to spit tufts of curly hair out of her mouth.

"What are you doing here?" Sadie mumbled into her hair.

"I thought coming back to an empty house might be a bit much. Plus, I knew you'd need food and stuff. So I took a punt on when you'd get back and let myself in about an hour ago."

Sadie squeezed her. "You're the best. Thanks." Nicole's thoughtfulness never ceased to amaze her.

Nicole giggled. "It's true! Glad you worked that out. So, good to be back?" she asked, lifting her head to grin at Sadie.

Sadie smiled, but her heart fluttered. "Yes, of course."

Nicole cocked her head. "You sure about that? You don't seem that thrilled. Oh, wait, you're missing your girlie, aren't you?" She smirked, and Sadie slapped her ass, laughing when Nicole glared at her.

"Yes, I am missing Holly. But you know, I'm kind of missing Mum too."

Nicole nodded and extricated herself from Sadie's arms. "I get that. That's cool."

Sadie smiled. "I need a beer—got any?"

"See, this is why I am your bestie. I knew that's what you'd need after riding all day, so it just so happens I hit the bottle shop yesterday and got you all stocked up." She grabbed Sadie's hand and pulled her into the kitchen.

"Sit your ass down, and I'll get us some drinks. Tash is on her way, too, so we can have a proper catch up."

"Cool." Sadie grinned as she watched Nicole skip over to the fridge. Easing herself down onto one of the couches, she sighed in contentment as she stretched her legs out. She kicked off her boots and leaned forward to shrug out of her jacket. As she sat back, a bottle of beer appeared over her shoulder, and she grabbed it gratefully from Nicole's outstretched hand.

"Awesome, thanks. You're the best," she said, tipping her bottle in Nicole's direction before downing a long, cold gulp.

"I know," Nicole said, taking her own big swallow of beer.

They sat talking quietly, sipping their beers, until Tash arrived about twenty minutes later. She popped open her own beer, snuggled down next to Nicole, and within minutes, the pair of them were subjecting Sadie to what she could only describe as an interrogation about her two weeks away. They ordered pizza and devoured that along with more beer. It was only when Sadie started yawning, at around nine o'clock, that Tash and Nicole sheepishly acknowledged they ought to leave her in peace. Sadie grinned sleepily as she saw them out of the house. That reunion, from them in particular, had been just what she needed to come home to.

Alone in the house, she felt an ache she couldn't quite describe. She missed Holly; she knew that much, and she would call her soon for a goodnight chat. She missed her grandmother, obviously; the house was way too quiet without Elsie in it.

But she missed her mother too, and with a strength that astonished her.

"Hey, boss! Great to have you back," Nathan called as she stepped into the Bike Rack the next morning. She looked around. The cafe looked good, nothing out of place, everything clean and tidy. She smiled as she took in the familiar surroundings. It was good to be back.

She made her way down to her office. Trixie was in there, hunched over the computer, furiously tapping away on the keyboard.

"Hey," Sadie said as she walked in.

Trixie popped her head up and grinned. "You're back. Cool. How was the trip?"

"All good," Sadie replied, knowing she'd never elaborate on what happened back home there in her workplace. She wasn't that close with any of the staff that she felt the need to share.

"How's things?" Sadie asked, motioning Trixie to stay where she was in the chair, while she perched on the edge of the desk.

"All good. No dramas. Whatever you said to Nathan before you went away worked like a charm. He's worked his ass off." Trixie grinned when Sadie laughed.

"Good, glad to hear it. Wanna hand over to me now, while it's quiet out front?"

"Sure, let's do it."

The day passed quickly. Sadie shook her head in disbelief when she glanced at the clock and saw it was creeping up on four o'clock. Nathan had just finished mopping the floor, and Sadie was wiping down counters. Their last customer was just finishing a cappuccino, and Sadie suddenly realised how tired she was. It had been a long few days—two days riding and then straight back into the flow of work. No run for her. Instead, she'd head straight home and get into a long call with her mum and gran. She smiled to herself. It still seemed surreal that she could plan for that—a long chat with her mother. She shook her head. Crazy times.

"I miss you," Sadie whispered as Holly answered her call. It was Thursday night, five days since they'd last seen each other, and Sadie was struggling. She'd never felt like this about any woman before, and part of her was still bemused as to how it had happened. She heard Holly's quick intake of breath and smiled. "Miss me too?"

"Oh, God, like you wouldn't believe," Holly replied, her voice also soft. "I know I said I needed time and space and all that crap, but God, this is torture."

Sadie chuckled. "Then book a flight. Come and see me."

"Soon, I promise."

And there it was again. Holly's hesitation. Her reluctance to commit to a visit. For all her words about missing Sadie, she still hadn't done anything that suggested she was serious about coming to Sydney. It was starting to worry Sadie, and she didn't know how to broach it without sounding like she was nagging.

"Spoken to your mum today?" Holly's question broke the silence that had suddenly inserted itself between them.

"Yeah, at lunchtime. She says she's okay. Gran said it too, so I have to believe them." She exhaled loudly. "It's hard, not being there."

"I know, babe. Would it be okay if I popped in to see your mum this weekend? Do you think it would help you if I saw her and reported back to you?"

Sadie felt a warm glow start somewhere deep in her chest at Holly's words. "Oh, Holly, that would be so good. Sure you don't mind?"

"God no, I'd love to see Christine and Elsie again. And if it would help put your mind at ease..."

"It really would. Thanks." She lowered her voice to a seductive tone. "I'll think of some way to make it up to you." She chuckled as she heard Holly groan.

"Oh, God, so not fair. You know exactly how I'd like you to make it up to me."

"Uh-huh. Would it involve me kissing you? And touching you? Licking you?"

"Stop! Really, *really* not fair." Holly's exasperation was evident and only made Sadie laugh more. *Time to play.*

"We could do something about that, you know. Right now. If you want," she said, keeping her tone low.

Holly gasped. "You mean...phone sex?"

Sadie had tried this only once before, but it hadn't been a success—her girlfriend at the time just collapsed in giggles at the prospect. Something told her that wouldn't happen with Holly.

She lowered her voice to a whisper. "Oh, yeah. You're in bed, right?"

"Y-yes."

"Wearing anything?"

"Tee shirt…and…undies." Holly was already having trouble stringing words together, and that turned Sadie on even more.

"Close your eyes." She waited a moment, listening to Holly's breathing. "Imagine me kissing you, right now. I've got one hand tangled up in your hair, the other stroking your neck."

Holly whimpered.

"You like that?"

"Oh, yeah."

"Now imagine your hand is mine. Stroke yourself, from your neck down over your chest to your belly. Nice and slow."

"Uh-huh…"

"Slip your fingers under your tee shirt and up to your breasts. You're not wearing a bra, are you?"

"N-no." Holly's voice was strained.

"Mm, good." Sadie swallowed, images of how Holly would look whilst touching herself invading her mind. "Okay, keep that hand moving, over to your breast, and press your nipple into your palm."

"Oh, God…" Holly's breathing was already ragged, and Sadie's clit was responding to both the sound and the scene she was describing for both of them. She could see in her mind's eye exactly how Holly's hand would look caressing her own breast, how her back would arch into the touch. And at the same time, she could feel how soft that breast would be, filling her hand, the nipple drilling into her palm. She moved her fingers down to the waistband of her track pants.

"Are your nipples hard for me, Holly?"

"Yes," came the throaty response, swiftly followed by a shuddering intake of air.

"Are you getting wet for me, Holly?"

"Fuck…yes." Holly's voice was tight with arousal.

Sadie groaned and slid her hand down inside her sweatpants, inside her underwear. "God, you make me so wet, too, babe," she murmured as her fingers found wetness and heat. "Move your hand now. Move it down, babe, inside your undies. Touch yourself for me."

Holly moaned, low and long, and Sadie's clit pulsed beneath her fingertips.

"Sadie…" Holly's voice was a tortured whisper, and it sent shivers down Sadie's spine.

"Make yourself come, babe. I want to hear you." Sadie's fingers were working their magic between her own legs, Holly's sounds only adding to the exquisite sensations they were eliciting. She listened keenly as Holly's breaths turned into gasps.

"Oh, babe, I want you," Holly panted. "Want you so much, I—"

She cried out as her orgasm hit, and Sadie increased the pace of her own fingers to rapidly follow Holly over the edge, little dots of colour spinning on the back of her eyelids as she came.

"Oh, wow," Holly murmured. "Oh my God. I've never… God, that was fantastic."

Sadie giggled. "Yeah, it sounded pretty good from where I was."

She heard Holly sigh. "Wish you were here," Holly said quietly.

"Me too." Sadie hesitated, before saying, "Book a flight. Please?"

There was a moment of silence. Then, "I will. I'll talk to Mum tomorrow about getting some time off."

Sadie closed her eyes in relief. "Thank you. I love you."

"Mm, I love you too. Don't doubt that, please."

"Okay. It's just…"

"What?"

Sadie huffed out a breath. "Sorry, I don't mean to bring the mood down."

"Tell me."

"I'm just struggling with your struggle, if you see what I mean. I…I just want to see you, that's all."

"I know," Holly said softly. "I'll get my head sorted, I promise. And I will talk to Mum tomorrow, okay?"

"Okay."

Holly struggled through work on Friday, her attention elsewhere. Memories of that incredible phone encounter the night before kept intruding. Not that she minded that much, given how delicious the whole experience had been. God, Sadie talking her through that had been one of the sexiest things she'd ever experienced. She got a little rush of heat throughout her body every time she thought about it. And then, of course, thinking about Sadie brought her mind back to wondering just what it was that was holding her back. Why couldn't she shake off this doubt about making the move to Sydney?

She reached the end of her shift, handed over to Matthew, and wandered home. She'd had no chance to talk to her mother about taking some time off to go and visit Sadie, and it was niggling at her that maybe, subconsciously, she was stalling again. Sadie would start having even more doubts about them if she wasn't careful.

It was cold, and she bundled herself up in her jacket and gloves. Her walk home passed by in a blur, her mind refusing to settle on any one thought, leaving her feeling muzzy-headed by the time she turned into their street. When she reached the house, she found her father outside, tinkering with the engine of their car in the fading daylight.

"Hey, Dad, everything okay?"

"Hi," he said, looking up and smiling warmly. He waved in the direction of the car. "Just routine checks, nothing wrong."

Holly nodded and started to walk towards the front door.

"Holly." Her dad's voice called her back. Something in his tone put her on guard.

"Yes?" She turned to face him, masking her face against the worry that was suddenly eating at her guts. His face, however, exuded warmth and affection, and she relaxed a little.

"I know we don't talk much, but I was wondering if we could have a little chat. Now, if you have time?" He seemed nervous, his hands fidgeting at the rag they held.

She cocked her head. Her father wanted to chat? How bizarre. Anxiety was quickly replaced by bemusement. "Sure, Dad. How about I get changed and meet you in the kitchen. Want a coffee?"

He smiled. "That would be lovely, thanks."

She nodded and went into the house, her mind struggling to deal with this new development in their relationship. Her father had always left any emotional interaction with Holly to her mother. He wasn't cold, just simply not a man who expressed emotions that obviously.

Her father appeared just as she was stirring milk into their coffees, and she handed him one of the mugs as he sat down at the table.

"Thanks, sweetheart," he said, taking a sip. "Now, sit."

His voice was firm and brooked no argument. Intrigued, she sat.

"So, ever since Sadie left town, you've been, well, not yourself." He looked at her, his face colouring slightly, but his gaze unwavering.

Holly swallowed, completely at a loss as to where this conversation was going. "Uh, no. I haven't. I miss her," she finished quietly, and was pleasantly surprised to see him smile in response.

"You, um, you really love this girl, don't you?" His voice wobbled slightly, and her heart melted. Her normally stoic father was trying his best to get to grips with this new version of his daughter, and she loved him even more for it.

"I do, Dad. It's okay, we don't—"

He raised a hand. "Hear me out, please?"

She closed her mouth and nodded. What on earth?

"I know your mother was upset the other night, and maybe she said some things in the heat of the moment. Things that might have hurt you or confused you."

Holly stayed silent but dipped her head once in acknowledgement.

He sighed. "It's funny how things change when you become a parent. Things you forget. Like how it is to be young and in love and wanting to be with that person all the time." He smiled. "Your mother and I… When we met, we were really young. Eighteen. And for me, it was love at first sight."

She watched as her father blushed crimson. He cleared his throat before continuing.

"Both our parents forbid us from seeing each other. Did you know that?"

She shook her head in amazement. "No, neither of you ever told me that."

He chuckled. "It all comes back to haunt you in the end. I was supposed to go off to university in Sydney, had it all mapped out. My parents were furious that I'd give that all up for her. And hers, well, let's just say they had much higher expectations for their daughter than a bloke like me. I changed my area of study so I could stay local, we both got jobs, and we got engaged as soon as we could." He glanced away, and then back again. "I don't begin to understand you having the feelings you do for a…a woman." He fiddled with his mug. "But, neither I nor your mother have any right to tell you what you can and can't do. Not at your age. If you want to be with…her, if that's what genuinely makes you happy, then do it. Don't listen to us. We didn't listen to our parents, we fought them every step of the way to be together. And we've never regretted it." His gaze bore into hers. "You should only have to regret the things you don't do, not the things you actually do."

She knew tears were falling down her own cheeks, but was astounded to see his eyes moisten too. He coughed and looked away. Without hesitating, Holly stood and walked round the table to pull him into a tentative hug. He'd never been one for hugs, or any overt display of affection, so she wasn't sure how he'd respond. When he lifted his arms to gently pull her closer, a sob escaped her throat, and she didn't make any effort to stop the flood of tears it unleashed.

When her mother came home around seven that evening, Holly was waiting for her in the kitchen, her father alongside her. He squeezed Holly's hand once in encouragement when her mother's eyebrows rose.

"Mum, I need to talk to you," Holly said, pleased when her voice came out as determined as she was feeling.

Her mother sat, and Holly could see her hands shaking as she placed them on the table in front of her.

Here goes nothing.

"I'm going to move to Sydney. I'm going to give my relationship with Sadie a real go, and at the same time see if I can kickstart my marketing career in the city there." She waited, watching her mother's expression. It moved from overt shock—her eyes popping wide and her mouth falling slightly open—to a look of barely controlled anger. Her mouth tightened into a grim line, and her hands moved to grip the edge of the table.

"I really don't think—" she began, her voice clipped.

Holly held up her hand. "I know you are only saying everything you've said recently because you love me and want what you think is best for me. But I'm old enough to make my own decisions. And my decision is to give this a go. I'd rather do it with your blessing, but I'll do it anyway, whether you give that or not." She hadn't meant that last sentence to come out as harsh as it did, but she'd had enough. Enough of her own fear and indecision, and enough of the anger she'd had to face from her mother this past week.

She watched as her mother's eyes flicked to her father's, and she saw her mother's face fall slightly at whatever they found there. Judy turned her gaze back to Holly, and breathed deeply for a couple of moments.

"Fine. If that's what you want. We'll be here when—" she stopped at the sound of a small cough coming from her husband, "*if* it all goes wrong." Her face softened slightly. "There's always a place for you here, never forget that."

It wasn't a ringing endorsement, but it was a start.

Holly swallowed. "I won't. Thanks, Mum."

CHAPTER 26

Sadie grinned, looking around the bar of the Park Hotel. It was packed. Friday night and it seemed as if the entire twenty-something population of Manly had come out for a drink. She grinned even wider as Nicole burst out of the crowd with three beers wrapped in the fingers of her left hand. They all moved backwards into the small space they'd snagged near the doors to the garden.

"Cheers!" Nic tapped each of their bottles with her own, and they took a long drink.

"So, how's your first week back been?" Tash leaned forward slightly to direct the question at Sadie; the noise in the bar was already at a level that made subtle conversation impossible.

"Good," Sadie said. "I miss Mum, and Gran, but talking to them every day has been good."

"And Holly?"

Sadie blushed. "Yeah, I miss her too. A lot."

Nic nudged her arm, and Sadie laughed.

"It's so sweet," Tash said, and she smiled when Sadie slapped her playfully in the bicep.

"I'm not sweet. Ugh."

Tash and Nicole giggled. The conversation switched to work, and they regaled each other with stories of awful customers or colleagues for a while.

After getting the next round in, Sadie asked, "Hey, any news on living together? What have you decided?"

Nicole dipped her head, and Tash laughed.

"This one—" Tash pointed at Nic with her chin, "—has finally agreed to move in with me as a trial. We'll give it a go for a few months and then see how we feel."

Sadie smiled and patted Nicole's arm. "That's really good news. I'm pleased for you. Really."

Nicole raised her head and blew Sadie a kiss. "Thanks, Sades."

Sadie sipped some more of her beer, leaning back against the cool glass of the garden doors to soothe her overheated body. It was starting to get stifling in the bar, and she wondered about stepping out into the garden, even for just ten minutes. As she pressed back against the frame of the door, she became aware of her phone digging into her thigh from the pocket on the leg of her cargo pants. She pulled it out, intending to merely slot it into the pocket of her shirt. As she did so, the display lit up to show a list of missed calls. Two were from Holly, but there were five from her grandmother.

Her blood froze in her veins, and her heart rate shot up. Thrusting her beer into Nicole's hand and ignoring the look of shocked surprise on her friend's face, she pushed open the door behind her and stepped out into the cooler air of the garden.

She took a few paces away from the door, until the noise from the bar dulled to a low hum, then flipped through the display to see if her gran had left her any messages. There was one text, timed a few minutes after the last of the calls, about twenty minutes previously.

Call me as soon as you get this

Her gran answered after only two rings.

"Oh, Sadie, thank God!" Elsie sounded frantic, and Sadie's heart clutched in her chest.

"Gran, what is it?"

"It's…it's your mum, love. She had a seizure."

Sadie's stomach churned. She'd read about this when she'd finally plucked up courage to research brain tumours. This was not a good development. "Where is she? How is she?"

"Oh, Sadie." Elsie's voice wobbled, and Sadie heard her gulping in air. "She's in the hospital. It's not good. Can you get here?"

"Shit, Gran, I'll try. Is it…is it that bad?" She shut her eyes against the pain that swept through her soul.

There was a pause. "Sadie, it…it is." She let out a sob. "Get here, okay?"

The car rental desk at Melbourne Airport was devoid of customers, and within twenty minutes of leaving the plane, she was buckling up her seat belt and putting the car in gear. She was tired; the early start to get on a standby flight was already catching up with her, but adrenaline was also pumping through her veins, keeping her forging ahead on what she needed to do.

She took a moment to check her phone and saw that Holly had responded to the brief text message she'd sent her late last night.

I'm worried, what's going on?

Sadie sighed. She didn't have time to get into it with Holly, but she needed to tell her something.

Mum in hospital. Not good. Just arrived Melb. On way to see her. Will call later

The reply came back seconds later.

Oh God, so sorry. Call when you can. Love you xx

Shoving the phone in the pocket of her pants, she pulled out of the car park and headed for the freeway.

Although it was tempting to break any and all speed limits en route to Ballarat, Sadie played it sensibly. Getting delayed by a cop eager to dish out a ticket would only keep her away from her mother for longer. She kept it right on the limit the whole way, thankful that the road wasn't particularly busy. Parking up at the hospital was more difficult, but after swinging the car up to the top level she found a spot. She pulled out her phone and called her grandmother.

"Are you here?"

"Yes, Gran. Where do I go?"

Elsie gave her directions to the room, and within five minutes, Sadie was walking through the door to pull her gran into a long hug. Elsie was trembling, and Sadie noted the dark circles under her red-rimmed eyes. After letting go of her and easing her into a chair, Sadie stood by her mother's bedside, gazing down on her unconscious form. Sadie's heart was thumping hard in her chest. She reached for her mother's hand and held it tightly.

"I'm here, Mum," she said softly. There was no reaction, of course, but she kept hold of her hand, rubbing her thumb over the cool skin.

She heard a sound from behind her and looked round. Izzy was sitting on a chair in the corner of the room. Sadie had been so focused on her mother, she hadn't realised Izzy was there.

"Hey," Izzy said quietly.

Sadie nodded. She didn't know what to say to her sister. And right there and then, all she wanted to deal with was the condition of her—their—mother.

She turned away from Izzy and looked instead at her gran.

"So, what have the doctors said?"

Elsie passed a weary-looking hand over her face and let it drop to her lap. "It's…it's unlikely she'll regain consciousness."

Sadie closed her eyes as a pain like nothing she'd ever felt before seared through her. Her throat closed up, and she had to work hard not to let out a cry of anguish. They'd only just got started again. How could life be so fucking cruel?

"How…long?" she asked, eventually.

Elsie shook her head, and she heard a whimper of distress from Izzy behind her. "They don't know. But, probably…" Elsie shuddered and wrapped her thin arms around her own body, rocking slightly in her seat. "Probably this weekend," she finished in a whisper.

Izzy let out a sob into the quiet room, and it sounded overly loud and intrusive. Only just biting back her own grief, which threatened to overwhelm her in that moment, Sadie turned to Izzy.

"Did you manage to see her this week?"

Izzy nodded, her eyes hidden in pools of tears.

"Good," Sadie said quietly. "I'm glad. When you started avoiding her while I was around, I…I worried that me coming back had ruined what you had with her." It probably wasn't the time or the place, but she needed to say it.

"It wasn't you," Izzy choked out. "I was the stupid one who let that happen." She looked at their mother and then back at Sadie. "I'm just glad I did spend time with her this week. We sorted it out."

"That's…that's really good to hear." And it was. It gave her a huge sense of relief to know that the amazing progress she'd made with her mother hadn't damaged anything else.

Sadie perched on the bed, still holding her mother's hand, and the three of them sat in silence for a while, the only sounds in the room the beeps from the various monitors her mum was hooked up to.

"How long can we stay here?" Sadie asked, looking quickly at both of them.

Izzy shrugged. "As long as we need. Given the circumstances…"

Sadie nodded and swallowed. She didn't want to cry. There'd be time enough for that later. Right then, she just wanted to be there, having whatever connection she could with her mum before she was gone.

She heard the scraping of a chair behind her, and looked up again. Izzy was motioning to their grandmother, who nodded.

"We're just going to get some coffee," Izzy said. "Want one?"

"That'd be great, thanks. Latte, no sugar."

"Okay. Come on, Gran, I'll buy you one of those choccie muffins."

Their grandmother smiled wanly and took Izzy's hand as she led her out of the room.

Sadie didn't know if Izzy had deliberately left her alone with their mother, but she was grateful for the opportunity nonetheless.

She shuffled more fully onto the bed and leaned over her mother.

"Hey, Mum. I don't know if you can hear me. I'd like to think you can, somehow."

She paused, wondering if this was ridiculous. The chances of her mum hearing and acknowledging what she had to say were remote, to say the least. But she knew she needed to do it. This was goodbye, so soon after they'd only said hello again. She had to say what was in her heart, had to believe her mum would hear it, somehow, and take it with her.

"I am so glad you and I made our peace, Mum. Knowing you again, even for just this short amount of time, has been so good. I can't…I can't believe I have to let you go now. It's so unfair." She blinked rapidly, as tears began tracking down her face. "But I'm trying to be thankful for what time we did have. It was special. And it's changed my life, I think. So, thank you, Mum. I won't forget you. You'll always be with me." Her voice cracked. "Keep looking out for me, okay? Wherever you are? I love you, Mum." She gave up on words then, her lungs heaving with sobs, and she carefully laid her head down on her mother's chest and wept.

"Hey." Holly's voice on the other end of the line was subdued, but it was still a balm to Sadie's soul. "How are you?"

Sadie sighed. "It's…hard. She's unconscious. They say she won't last the weekend."

"Oh, God, babe. I'm so, so sorry."

"Thanks," Sadie whispered. "I don't have long to talk. I want to be back in the room with her. But I just…wanted to hear your voice."

"I'm here, Sadie, whenever you need me, okay? I'm here."

"I know. Thank you. I'll call you again later."

"Any time. And if you want me there, just say and I'll be there. Okay?"

They said their goodbyes, and Sadie jogged back to her mother's room. Every time she left the room, she feared the worst. But each time she returned, her mum was still there, still breathing.

"No change," Elsie said softly, as Sadie re-entered the room. "How was Holly?"

Sadie shrugged. "Fine. Worried. Upset."

Elsie nodded. Izzy reappeared a moment later.

"I just called Dad. I thought he could do with an update, given that it's a few hours since he was here."

Sadie nodded. "Does he want to visit again?" She didn't want to leave her mother's bedside, but she'd have to if he came.

"Strangely, no," Izzy said. "He's upset, but I guess maybe he doesn't want to see her like this anymore? The last time they spoke was Tuesday, when I was there for tea. He came to the house to get some stuff. He seemed…shocked. Like he couldn't believe it was happening. But things were okay between them, I guess. Gran?"

Elsie nodded. "It was the best I've seen them together since this all started. I think perhaps that's when he said his goodbyes, in his own way."

"Well, I can't lie," Sadie said. "That makes it a hell of a lot easier for me."

Izzy smiled, and the sight brought a gentle pleasure to Sadie's bruised heart. "Easier for all of us, I reckon," Izzy said with a wry grin.

The hours passed. They took turns going for food and drinks and comfort breaks. It was unspoken, but none of them wanted to leave the room for any length of time. They dozed in chairs, despite desperately trying to stay awake, their tired bodies thwarting them. Doctors or nurses paid regular visits and always reported the same thing: no change. Darkness fell.

It was nearly eight thirty when the silence in the room took on a different timbre. Afterwards, Sadie couldn't say who had realised it first. But within moments of each other, all three of them came into an awareness of what had changed.

Christine's breathing had stopped.

The three of them rushed to the bed. Izzy slapped her hands over her mouth in a vain attempt to hold back her sobs. Sadie grabbed her mother's chilled hand and felt Elsie clutch at her arm. It was Elsie who started crying first, but it didn't take long for Sadie and Izzy's sobs to join hers. When the nurse and doctor arrived to call it, the three women were clung to each other in a tangle of arms, holding each other tight, joined in grief.

"Any more news?"

Holly turned to look at her mother, who had just walked into the lounge room. Holly was sprawled on the couch; the TV was on, but she had no idea what program was playing. She'd only put it on to have some kind of background noise to stop her going crazy with worry.

"No, nothing since she called me at four."

Her mother perched on the arm of the couch. "Have you eaten?"

Holly nodded. "Don't worry, I'm looking after myself."

"It's my job to worry," her mother said with a small smile. She opened her mouth as if to speak, then closed it again.

"What?" Holly asked.

"I…I wanted to say, no matter what I said recently about Sadie and… everything, I am genuinely sorry this is happening. I know from what you said they were just starting to rebuild their relationship. This is an awful way for it to end."

Holly sighed. "It is. Thanks, Mum."

Judy leaned over to squeeze Holly's forearm before she stood. "I'm pouring myself a glass of wine, would you like one?"

"Please. That'd be good."

Her mother left the room, and Holly turned her disinterested attention back to the TV screen. Oh yeah, some kind of cop show. She'd thought solving a crime would keep her mind busy. Yeah, that hadn't happened.

She jumped as her phone rang. Sadie's name appeared in the caller display.

"Hi, babe."

"She's…she's gone," Sadie whispered.

Holly's insides churned at the agony apparent in those words. "Oh, God, babe. Oh, God, I'm so sorry."

She listened to Sadie cry for a few minutes, having no idea what to say or do to calm her grieving girlfriend.

"Sorry," Sadie mumbled.

"You don't have to say sorry, babe. I just wish I was there with you so I could hold you."

"I'd like that. Could you…meet me at the house? Would it be weird for you to stay there?"

"God, not at all! Are you going there right now?"

"In about fifteen minutes. I'm taking Gran home with me. Izzy's going back to her place. She just wants to be alone right now."

Mentally storing away the fact that Izzy and Sadie seemed to be on speaking terms again, Holly said, "Then I will aim to get to the house in about half an hour, okay?"

"Sounds good."

"Do you need me to bring anything? Have you eaten?"

"No, not hungry. But don't worry, there's stuff at the house. We'll figure it out later."

"All right, I'll see you there. And I'll hold you all night, okay?"

"Please…" The word was tortured and cut loose the hold Holly had maintained on her own emotions up to that point. As they ended the call, her tears fell. She cried not just for Sadie but for all of them. She was curled up on the couch, sobbing, her arms wrapped around herself, when her mother returned with their wine.

"Holly! What's happened?"

She choked out the words around her sobs. "Christine died. Sadie just called."

Judy's hand flew to her mouth, and her eyes instantly moistened. "Oh no, that's awful. Poor Christine. And poor Sadie." She knelt beside the couch and pulled Holly into a warm hug. "I'm so sorry to hear that."

"It's so unfair!"

"I know, sweetheart. I know."

Holly let her mother hold her until her sobs had diminished.

"Thanks, Mum." She pulled back and sat up, wiping her eyes on the sleeves of her hoodie. "I'm going to see her. I'm meeting her at the family house in about half an hour. I won't be home tonight."

Judy nodded. "Of course you need to go. Do you want a lift?"

Holly blinked in shock. "Y-you'd do that for me?"

Her mother smiled and flushed slightly. "I'm trying, Holly. I-I know I've not been the most supportive mother this past week or so, but I'm trying now, okay?"

"Mum…" She ran out of words and instead hugged her mother to her again. "Thank you," she whispered.

"Right," Judy said, clearing her throat. "Let's put this wine away and get you ready to go, okay?"

Sadie answered the door, and Holly reached for her instantly. She looked bereft and lost, and all Holly wanted to do was take all that pain away. Knowing she couldn't do so was killing her. So she did the next best thing and simply pulled Sadie into her arms and held her as close as she could. She rubbed circles on Sadie's back as she cried against Holly's neck.

"Oh, babe," Holly murmured.

After a few minutes Sadie straightened. "I'm so glad you're here. Come in, it's cold out here on the step." She managed a small, wry smile, and Holly followed her through the open doorway into the house. As Sadie shut and locked the door behind them, Holly removed her boots and coat.

"Come on through," Sadie said, grasping her hand and urging her gently towards the kitchen.

Elsie was sat at the table, a tissue pressed against her face. She looked forlorn, and it broke Holly's heart. Without saying a word, she stepped across the room and bent down to wrap her arms around her.

"I'm so sorry about Christine," she said against Elsie's hair.

"Thanks, love," Elsie managed before more sobs racked her thin body. Holly held her, aware of Sadie moving around the kitchen behind her. Moments later, glasses of wine were placed on the table, and Sadie pulled out a chair for Holly. She eased back from Elsie enough to sit down, then tugged Elsie's arm towards her to hold it tight. All three of them reached for their glasses.

"I don't know if it will help," Sadie said, motioning to the wine the glasses contained. "But I know Mum would have reached for the bottle, if she was here."

Elsie smiled at that, and Holly raised her glass. "To Christine," she said quietly. Elsie and Sadie tapped their glasses against hers, and they all took a gulp.

Haltingly, over the time it took to drink their glasses of wine, Sadie and Elsie told Holly about the day. It brought more tears for both, but they made it clear they wanted Holly to know that Christine had passed peacefully. And that in her death had come some kind of reconciliation between Sadie and her sister.

"It's early days," Sadie said. "But we'll see how we go."

"I'm glad," Holly said. "And Christine would be so pleased too."

"That she would," Elsie chimed in.

Holly convinced them to let her make them something light to eat. From what she found in the fridge, she rustled up a feta-and-spinach omelette with some salad. Pleased when both plates came back empty, she shooed the pair of them out to the lounge room while she cleaned up. Sadie dropped a sweet kiss on her cheek as she left the room, her fingers twining with Holly's for a moment as she did so.

"So glad you're here," she repeated, her eyes moist.

"Me too."

When she joined them in the lounge room, Elsie was dozing on the couch, and Sadie was blindly watching the TV with the sound turned down.

"I think we should get her to bed," Holly whispered, pointing at Elsie.

Sadie jumped; she'd clearly been miles away and not even aware that Elsie was sleeping.

"Yeah, right. Okay, I'll do it." She stood and walked over to her grandmother, nudging her gently until her eyes crept open.

"Hey, Gran, I think you should get to bed, yeah?"

Elsie simply nodded and allowed Sadie to pull her up to a standing position.

"I've got it from here, love." Elsie smiled weakly. "Thank you for looking after me. Both of you." She smiled at Holly. "I'll see you in the morning."

"'Night, Elsie."

When she'd left the room, Sadie reached for Holly and flopped the pair of them down onto the couch. She pulled Holly close and snuggled in against her, her nose burrowing into the sensitive spot just below Holly's ear, her arms sliding around Holly's waist.

"God, you feel good," Sadie murmured against Holly's neck. "Seems like forever since I got to hold you like this."

"Only a week, but it feels like a lot longer, I agree."

"Thanks for being here. I need this."

"I know. I'm so glad I can do this for you." Holly twisted slightly so that she could snake an arm behind Sadie and pull her even closer. "Whatever you need from me the next few days, you've got it, okay?"

"Uh-huh." Sadie's voice was muffled and sounded sleepy. Holly gazed down at her, and saw her eyelids flutter closed. Her breathing was already deepening.

"Babe, let's go to bed. You're exhausted," Holly said.

"Mm."

Holly giggled, in spite of the circumstances. "Come on, sleepy, up we get." She pulled her arm out from behind Sadie and loosened Sadie's hold on her. "Come *on*."

Sadie grumbled but gave in, pushing herself upright and accepting Holly's hand to help her stand.

"Which room are we in?" Holly asked as they wove down the hallway, an arm around each other's waist.

"I guess my old one. I hadn't really thought about it. God, I don't even know if there's a bed in there—I haven't set foot in that room since I came back."

"Well, let's take a look."

The door to the room was shut. Sadie opened it and reached for the light. A plain, sparsely furnished room awaited them. There was a double bed, one small bedside table, and a bookcase. Nothing personal adorned the shelves, and a painting of a bucolic landscape was the only decoration.

"I don't know if it's better that it looks nothing like my room or not," Sadie said quietly.

"Probably better? No memories to deal with on top of everything else?"

Sadie shrugged. "Yeah, you're probably right." She stepped into the room. "Bathroom's just there, let me check there's towels and stuff."

They took turns using the facilities, then quietly undressed in front of each other. Although Sadie's gaze almost involuntarily swept over Holly's naked body, Holly knew there was nothing sexual in it. This was definitely not the time for that. She stepped forward when Sadie motioned her into the bed, and quickly slid under the doona, opening her arms for Sadie to come into once she was lying on her back.

Sadie pressed close, and Holly sighed. "Feels good."

"Yeah," Sadie murmured, and Holly could tell she was already drifting.

She wriggled a bit until Sadie was comfortably tucked under her chin. Making sure both arms were securely locked around her girlfriend's body, she whispered, "Goodnight," and kissed the top of Sadie's head. Sadie muttered something in response, twitched, then settled. Holly closed her eyes and breathed in the incredibly satisfying feeling of having Sadie back in her arms again.

CHAPTER 27

"Hi." Izzy looked unsure of herself, hovering on the doorstep.

Sadie smiled and stepped aside to let her in. "Good to see you, Izzy." She'd promised her gran she'd make an effort to keep up the momentum of whatever had shifted between her and her sister in that hospital room. Seeing Izzy visibly relax at her greeting warmed her.

"Gran's in the kitchen, making coffee."

"Cool." Izzy smiled at Sadie as she shrugged out of her coat and murmured her thanks when Sadie took it from her to hang it up.

"How was work?" Sadie asked over her shoulder as they walked down the hallway.

"Okay. Difficult at first. Everyone had heard and wanted to offer their condolences. It's nice, but it just makes me cry."

Sadie turned to look at her. "Yeah, I guess that must be hard. My boss has called but only to leave a voicemail. I'd probably struggle to talk to her directly too."

Izzy nodded, and they stared at each other for a moment.

"Sadie?"

"Yeah?"

"Can we fix this? Us?"

Sadie smiled. "Yeah, I reckon. I'd like to try, anyway."

"Me too." Izzy's smile was wide, even though her eyes still carried the sadness of her grief for their mother.

They walked into the kitchen together, and Elsie stood to welcome Izzy with a small hug.

"Coffee's made," she said, gesturing to the pot in the centre of the table. "Sit."

They both obeyed, and the three of them sat in silence for a while as they sipped their drinks.

It was Izzy who braved the subject they were all supposed to be discussing. "So, have either of you read her instructions?"

Sadie glanced at Elsie. "Yeah, we read them last night. How about you?"

Izzy nodded. "Yeah, same. Seemed fairly straightforward, didn't it?"

"Yep. Guess we just have to get on with it now." Sadie hunched her shoulders, then forced herself to relax. It had to be done. Their mother had left detailed but relatively simple instructions for her funeral, and they'd been pleasantly surprised to discover she'd been organised enough to leave it all paid for in advance. All they had to do was make all the necessary calls to set everything in motion.

Izzy took a deep breath. "Then I guess we better had. I'll do the funeral home and the caterers if you'll do the RSL Club and the florist?"

"Deal."

"Dad's doing the papers for the announcement, and all the invites—it's all their friends, so it makes sense that he does that."

"That's…that's good of him," Sadie said, begrudgingly acknowledging his input.

Izzy cleared her throat, clearly not sure what to say. She looked away and reached for her phone.

"So, it's on Friday, and I'd really like you there with me, if you can?" Sadie lifted her head to gaze into Holly's eyes. "It's at two in the afternoon. Would your mum be okay about you taking that time off? I think she and your dad are invited to it anyway."

"Hey, of course I'll be there," Holly whispered. "And I can either travel with you or them, whichever you prefer."

"With me would be wonderful, if you don't mind."

"Why would I mind?" Holly leaned over to kiss Sadie, and Sadie let herself get lost in those soft lips for a few moments. They'd not really kissed at all since she'd been back. God, was that only three days ago? It felt like a lifetime. There had been plenty of hugs and snuggling. She wrapped their bodies tighter under the doona. But anything else had seemed…wrong, somehow, and it hadn't surprised her that much that her libido had gone dormant since Saturday.

Her days had been spent quietly, staying home with her grandmother, starting to make plans for clearing the house ready for it to be sold—her father had contacted the lawyer to say he didn't want to live there anymore—and crying. Often. Her grief came at her in haphazard yet tumultuous waves. Sometimes it would drown her, leaving her sobbing for what seemed like hours. At other times she could go on with normal life as if she'd almost forgotten about it. She'd spent each evening with Holly, and each night Holly shared her bed, her presence alone enough to soothe her.

Holly pulled back and stroked her fingers through Sadie's hair. "I want to be here for you. Supporting you. You don't ever have to ask if it's okay."

"Okay," Sadie said, inching her way back under Holly's chin. Something about this position was so comforting. So safe. She'd found herself resorting to it many times over the past three days. Holly didn't seem to mind, her arms squeezing Sadie closer, throwing one leg over Sadie's hip to pull their lower halves together. Sadie was immediately aware of the heat between Holly's legs, pressing gently up against her thigh, and her libido chose that moment to awaken, startling her with its insistent, and instant, need. She moaned softly.

"You okay, babe?" Holly's voice held concern, and Sadie groaned inwardly. How could she explain that, out of the blue, all she wanted was to feel that wet heat enclosing her fingers? To lose herself in the mindless excitement of Holly thrusting her hips up against her body? That, despite her grief, she wanted an episode of passion so raw she would feel nothing but alive?

She raised her head and gazed at Holly, not sure how to find the words. When Holly bent to kiss her, ravenously, she was startled, but a moment later immersed herself in it, meeting Holly's tongue with a fervour that wrenched a groan from both their throats.

"I know you need this," Holly said against her mouth, her breathing ragged. "It's written all over your face. Take it. Take me."

Sadie growled and pushed Holly onto her back. She stared down at her, at her flushed face and neck, at her nipples hardening moment by moment.

"I don't know why now. But I do. I need you. This."

Holly merely nodded and pulled Sadie down to her again, her lips warm and soft against Sadie's mouth. Sadie pressed against her, pushing between Holly's legs and beginning a steady, pumping rhythm with her hips. Holly gasped, and her hands reached for Sadie's ass, bringing them even closer. The heat between them was intense, perspiration already forming on their chests, their bellies. Sadie kept her mouth hovering over Holly's, not quite kissing, but mingling their breaths, their cries.

"I can't..." Holly gasped, clutching at Sadie. "Need...more."

Shifting slightly, Sadie quickly pushed her hand between them and ran her fingers through the delicious wetness she found between Holly's legs. Oh, God, this was exactly what she needed. Holly moaned as Sadie ran a single finger back to Holly's clit and rubbed a slow series of circles against it. Holly's hips bucked, and her head pushed back against the pillow.

"Yes...faster," Holly moaned, and Sadie obliged. She could feel Holly's clit swelling under her touch. She dipped her head and wrapped her lips around one of Holly's nipples, flicking her tongue against it in time with the movements of her finger on Holly's clit. Holly came with a strangled cry and clung to Sadie as aftershocks jerked through her body. Sadie was close herself and couldn't wait for Holly to recover fully.

"Please," she whispered. "Inside me. Now."

Holly didn't hesitate. Chest still heaving from her own pleasure, she slid her hand between them and slowly pushed two fingers inside Sadie.

"Oh, God, *yes*." It was perfect. Just...perfect. She rocked herself against Holly's hand, forcing those fingers deeper inside herself. When Holly twisted her hand slightly so that the heel of her palm came to rest on Sadie's clit, white light flashed across the backs of her eyelids. She came moments later, the flush of it spreading to every nerve ending in her body as if she'd been electrocuted.

She collapsed across Holly's body, panting heavily. Holly's fingers wound themselves into her hair, and she murmured soft, indecipherable words into the air between them. Sadie's eyes slipped closed, and her breathing calmed.

"Love you," she murmured, her head heavy with sleep. "So much."

"Morning, love." Elsie stood as Sadie walked into the kitchen on Friday morning. They stared at each other for a moment. Elsie's face held an expression Sadie was sure mirrored her own—disbelief that this day had come, a huge reluctance to get started with it, but an acknowledgement that somehow they had to get through it.

Sadie made herself a coffee and forced herself to eat a couple of slices of toast. She couldn't stomach more, but the sensible half of her brain knew she'd need it to survive the morning. Her phone chirped as she finished the last mouthful, and she held it up to see a message from Nicole.

Thinking of you today. Call me later, if you want xx

They'd spoken the night before, but only briefly. Sadie had been too upset to talk much about it. The eve of the funeral had seen another wave of grief sweep over her. Having kept her head above it for the time it took to arrange the day, once all that was done, it was as if a block had been lifted and her emotions came flooding back. Holly had held her close all night, as Sadie frequently woke from fevered dreams. Holly left early to do a morning shift at the hotel and would be back at the house by one.

Sadie cleaned up the kitchen and helped Elsie tidy the lounge room. Whilst the wake was at the RSL Club that her parents had frequented over the years, Izzy at least would be coming home with them afterwards, and possibly a few others. They wanted the place to look presentable for whoever showed up.

They each headed off to their rooms to shower and dress, and met up again an hour or so later in the kitchen. Elsie looked striking in her black suit with a deep blue blouse underneath, her platinum-grey hair shining. Sadie had only bought her own suit the day before, a task she had dreaded and which had upset her as much as she had anticipated. Her suit was also black, and she wore a jade-green blouse under the fitted jacket.

"You look lovely," Elsie said wistfully.

"Thanks, Gran. I'd rather I didn't, if you see what I mean."

Elsie nodded, and gave her a quick one-armed hug. "Come on, Holly will be here soon. Let's get a quick lunch put together."

They made up a plate of veggies and dips, knowing they'd only want to pick at something while they waited. Holly arrived just after one, looking stunning in a black skirt suit and turquoise-blue top. She was wearing heels that brought her nearly up to Sadie's height, and a part of Sadie's brain registered just how sexy that was, despite the circumstances.

"Hi, babe," Holly whispered, leaning in for a gentle kiss. "You okay?"

Sadie nodded. "You look stunning," she whispered back. "Is it inappropriate to say that?"

"It's okay." Holly smiled, albeit sheepishly. "It's not the best of times, but thank you."

Sadie kissed her again and held her close.

"Hello, love. You okay?" Elsie greeted Holly warmly as she walked into the hallway and found them in each other's arms. Once again, nothing seemed to faze her gran, and Sadie felt a rush of pride.

"I am, Elsie, thank you. How are you?"

"Wishing today was over already, quite frankly." Elsie's voice was gruff.

Sadie winced, but she sympathised with her gran's position.

"I think we all do, Elsie," Holly murmured, but to Sadie's relief she didn't sound insulted, just understanding. Once again, Sadie was flooded with gratitude at the incredible sensitivity her girlfriend possessed.

The journey out to the funeral centre didn't take long. When they pulled up, she could see her father and Izzy climbing out of a car. Among them, she, Izzy, and Elsie had all agreed that it would be best if Sadie stayed away from her father. Izzy had offered to accompany him for the day, whilst Sadie, Holly, and Elsie would stay glued together. When their father's back was turned, Izzy risked a small wave at Sadie and their grandmother, then focused on her part in the day's proceedings, placing a hand on her father's arm and directing him into the building.

Sadie's group waited a few moments before following, then made their way to the room where the service was being held. It was packed; her mother had been a popular member of Ballarat society, and many people had wanted to be there to say their goodbyes. Sadie's eyes blurred as she followed her grandmother to the front of the room, and she gripped Holly's hand tightly. They sat in the row to the left; Izzy and their father were at front right. Whilst it might have been normal for a family to sit together, the funeral director had been sympathetically understanding to their situation, and the arrangements had been easily accommodated.

The civil celebrant stepped forward in front of the casket, which Sadie could barely look at, and a hush fell over the room.

Sadie closed her eyes and braced herself. The warmth of Holly's hand in hers, which she hadn't let go of since they'd arrived, soothed her and anchored her in place.

The service wasn't overly long, something else her mother had been adamant about in the plans she'd left for all of them. But it was moving and emotional, and Sadie was a wreck by the time it came to an end. Holly had wrapped her arms around her halfway through and held her close, occasionally kissing the side of her head, or her ear or cheek, whenever Sadie's sobs threatened to overwhelm her. The strength Holly's love was imparting was the only brightness in an otherwise awful day.

Sadie, Izzy, Elsie, and their father formed a receiving line at the end of the service, with Sadie and her father as far apart from each other as possible. She seethed silently as he soaked up the attention from all the well-wishers, playing the grieving husband as if an Oscar depended on it. He hadn't looked at her once during the service or afterwards, but she was fine about that. She knew the damage between them was irreparable.

Finally, they escaped the stream of condolences and made their way back to the car. Elsie was in a bad way, sobs making her entire body shudder, and Sadie stopped her before they climbed into the car.

"Gran, if you just want us to go home, we can. You don't have to go to the wake."

Her grandmother wiped at her eyes once more. "No, it's fine. I want to go. There's some people I'd like to spend time with." She gently stroked Sadie's cheek, a touch that made Sadie's throat tighten against another sob of her own. "I was always going to be like this today. Don't worry, I'll manage."

"Okay, if you're sure."

"And what about you?" Holly asked as she opened the car door. "Are you okay to do this?"

Sadie nodded. "I feel as if I should. To honour Mum."

Holly gazed at her for a moment, then nodded. "Okay, but I'm not leaving your side all day. Just so you know." The wink she gave Sadie was gentle and playful, and it brought out the first smile Sadie had managed since the day began.

"Oh, God, it feels *so* good to get out of those shoes!"

Sadie chuckled as Holly groaned and sank back into the couch, rubbing her feet. She was amazed she could even remember how to laugh after the agony of the day. At least the wake had passed by quickly, nothing more than a blur of people all offering their sympathies. Some of the people she vaguely recognised from her childhood. Most of them she didn't. She'd been aware of a few fingers pointing, elbows nudging as people stared. But each time, she'd focused instead on Holly's warm hand in hers, and memories of how she and her mum had been together these past few weeks. That was all that mattered, not the petty gossip mongering of people who probably didn't even know her mother that well, never mind their family history.

She'd also managed to completely avoid her father, with no small thanks to Izzy who'd run interference all afternoon. She smiled. She and her sister hadn't spoken much at all during the day, but she was actually looking forward to her arrival at the house any moment. If nothing else, she needed to express her gratitude for what Izzy had done. But she hoped there'd be a chance for more between them, a chance to work out how to rebuild *their* relationship, much in the way she'd done with their mother. She was also pleased that no one else had invited themselves to the house. It would just be the four of them.

"When Izzy gets here, do you want some time with her alone?" Holly's arms pulled Sadie tight against her curves, and for just the briefest of moments, Sadie's mind went blissfully blank as her body reacted to the soft lushness of her girlfriend.

"If you don't mind, yes. I want to talk to her, see if we can find a way forward. She was so good today, keeping him away from me."

"Yeah, she was amazing. Not that I think he wanted to be near you anyway, but she made sure that your paths didn't cross at all."

Sadie kissed Holly, lingering for a minute. "And you were amazing too," she said quietly when she pulled back. "Thank you so much for all the love and support you gave me today. I know there's no way I'd have got through it all if you hadn't been there."

Holly smiled, and Sadie watched her eyes fill with tears. "It was my pleasure," Holly whispered. "I love you, I want to be there for you."

Sadie was about to respond when the doorbell rang.

"I'll get it," Elsie called from the hallway.

Somewhat reluctantly, Sadie untangled herself from Holly's arms and stood up. "How about we find some wine, and me and Izzy can talk in the kitchen while you and Gran get comfy in here?"

"Great idea." Holly stood and walked off in the direction of the kitchen. Sadie watched her go, her hips subtly swinging, the skirt clinging to her so deliciously it made Sadie's mouth water. She mentally admonished her libido and made her way out to the front of the house, where Izzy was removing her coat and shoes.

"Thank God I can get out of these shoes," she wailed as she hurriedly kicked them off.

Sadie laughed lightly. "Yep, Holly just said the same thing. So glad I never bother with heels."

Izzy smirked. "With your height, you don't need to. Those of us more vertically challenged will take all the help we can get."

Elsie laughed as she hung Izzy's coat up, and the sound warmed Sadie's heart. Watching her gran struggle through the day had torn at her; it was great to see her relax just a little bit.

"Holly's just getting us some wine." She turned to Izzy. "I thought maybe you and me could talk in the kitchen, while Gran and Holly chill out in the lounge room?"

Izzy smiled. "Sounds like a good plan."

Elsie patted both their arms and smiled at them. "I'll see you girls in a little while," she said.

Sadie and Izzy walked down the hallway, passing Holly as she left the kitchen with two glasses of wine in her hands. Sadie nuzzled her nose for a moment as they crossed paths, which made Holly smile. Izzy cleared her throat from behind Sadie, who turned to face her sister. Izzy was blushing.

"Public display of affection too much for you, sis?" Sadie asked, trying to keep the sarcasm out of her tone, but it was there. She heard Holly hiss in a breath.

Izzy held up her hands in a placating gesture, her glance flicking between Sadie and Holly. "I'm…I'm just not used to it. But that's my problem, and I'll work on it, okay?" Her conciliatory tone calmed Sadie in an instant, and she felt a little guilty for sniping at her sister.

"Okay," she said quietly. "Sorry for the dig."

"It's okay. Hey, how about that glass of wine?"

Sadie caught Holly's eye and smiled as Holly winked at her. She watched Holly head for the lounge room, before tearing her gaze away and following her sister into the kitchen.

Holly had already poured them a glass each and left them on the table. They raised their glasses to their mother once more, then sat chatting for a while about the funeral and its aftermath.

"I didn't know even a quarter of the people in that room," Sadie said, chuckling. "All of them offering me their condolences, and I'm looking at them thinking, 'Who the fuck are you?'"

Izzy snorted out a giggle. "Yeah, me too."

"Really?"

"Oh, yeah, I had nothing to do with that side of their life either. I knew a bit of Dad's family, and a couple of Mum's closest friends, but that was it."

"Hey, listen, thanks so much for being the buffer between me and him. It made the day so much easier for me."

Izzy waved off her thanks. "It was easy. It's not like I'm his number one fan either, but at least he's never treated me like he has you. Besides, he was too busy lapping up the attention as the grieving husband to worry about where you were." She looked down at her wine with a disgusted expression on her face.

"Yeah, I saw that. It was revolting."

"Oh, yeah. Couldn't help himself, I guess. Always the fucking politician." Izzy paused and sipped her wine. "I wonder how much I'll see of him now, actually. I only really saw them together. It would never have occurred to me to see him on his own the way I did with Mum."

"Does that bother you?"

"No, actually, it doesn't," she said with a rueful laugh as she shook her head. "And I've only just realised that."

Sadie hesitated, then plunged in. "And what about us, Iz? Did you mean what you said earlier this week about us fixing this?" She waved a hand between them.

"Yes, I did." Her sister's tone was firm.

Sadie nodded and smiled. "Then once we've got the house sorted out and all that crap, how about you come to Sydney for a few days? I'll show you my life, and you can spend some time with Gran."

"I'd really like that," Izzy said, her bottom lip trembling, as she stared intently at Sadie. "I know I've struggled with your sexuality, but I am working on that. I want to know my big sister again. I want to be part of your life. And I miss Gran so much."

"Then let's get you booked on a flight soon, yeah?"

"Definitely." Izzy's smile lit up the room.

CHAPTER 28

"Do you really have to go?" Sadie whined as Holly attempted—for the third time—to extricate herself from Sadie's embrace.

Holly giggled and planted a sloppy kiss on Sadie's forehead. "Yes, I do. You know that. I've got to go to work. With the funeral, we couldn't get reorganised enough to give me any time off today too."

Sadie exhaled loudly and loosened her hold. "Okay, okay. Off you go."

Holly pulled back, and Sadie flinched at the cool air that shot into the bed as Holly lifted the doona off her body. As soon as Holly had departed the bed, Sadie grabbed the doona back with two hands and yanked it up to her neck.

Holly stood by the bed, laughing down at her. "Sook," she said. "Look, I'll come back here after work, yes? You've got a heavy day ahead. So, we'll make some tea, or have a drink. Whatever. Relax for a bit."

Sadie lifted her face away from the warmth of the doona. "You know what, how about we go out for tea tonight, just you and me? Izzy can spend the evening with Gran. I think they'd like that. And I'm feeling a bit claustrophobic, spending all our time in this house."

Holly smiled. "Sure, babe. Whatever you want. How about a great Japanese place I know, not too far from where we live?"

"Sounds good. I love Asian food."

"Cool, I'll call them later and book a table. I'll text you the address and what time."

"Perfect."

Sadie watched as a delectably naked Holly strolled off to the en suite. They'd simply held each other the night before, both of them too tired and too emotional to make love. It had been wonderful, though. Being held close to that warm, beautiful body all night had given Sadie more satisfaction than she would have imagined only a few months ago. The transformation she'd undergone since meeting Holly was incredible. But she knew that some of it was also down to what had transpired with her mother. She silently sent a thank-you out to the universe for that too.

"You okay?" Holly was back in the room, towelling herself dry, the flick of the cream cotton revealing tantalising glimpses of the body beneath.

"I'm fine. Just…thinking."

"Are you going back to sleep?"

Sadie stretched her arms over her head and arched her back, revelling in the small pops along the length of her spine. "No, I think I'll get up. I'm hungry, actually. Maybe I'll make a big breakfast for Gran, Izzy, and me, if they're up for it."

"Sounds good. I'm jealous." Holly smirked and dropped her towel on the end of bed. "Time for a little make-out session before I go?"

"I thought you were in a hurry?" Sadie asked, even as she swept the doona to one side and reached for Holly's hand.

"I was," Holly murmured, "but you just look adorably sexy right now, and I need to take advantage of that."

Sadie chuckled, and then forgot about everything except the feel of Holly's skin on hers and Holly's mouth plundering her own.

"How much of this are we giving to charity?" Sadie called from her position in the kitchen.

"All of it," Elsie replied from out in the hallway. She was emptying the cupboard where the sheets and towels were stored. "Your father said he doesn't want any of it. He just wants the books, everything in the garage, and the photo albums."

"All right. Then we're going to need a lot more boxes. We've already filled ten and there's still heaps to pack up."

Sadie sat back on her heels, giving herself a breather. She wasn't upset by what they were doing, probably because everything in this house was so remote from her. She had no memories tied to these things, just whatever memories she cared to hold on to from events that had taken place, both recent and in the past. And whilst those kept hitting her at random moments, she was coping. Just.

"Why don't I call the charity and see if they've got crates or something we could use. They're benefiting, after all."

"Yeah," Izzy said, turning to face her from her spot kneeling on the floor in front of one of the cupboards on the other side of the room. "That would help."

They'd been at it for two hours. Izzy had stayed over, sleeping on the sofa. She could have slept in their parents' room, but the idea had freaked her out a little. Sadie didn't blame her.

They could have left the clearance a few more days, but it made sense to make use of Izzy's free time at the weekend to do it sooner rather than later. There'd been some tears, of course, but all three of them had supported each other and hugged it out where necessary. It was slow going, but it would take as long as it took. Not having to factor their father into the equation helped hugely.

"Let's take a break," Sadie said. "I'll put the kettle on and call the charity. We'll see where that leaves us for the rest of the day."

They stopped at about four. The charity had sent a bloke with a truck to take away what they'd packed so far and to leave them some stronger and bigger boxes for the next day. They sat at the kitchen table, hands wrapped around hot mugs of tea.

"That heat feels lovely on my old bones," Elsie said.

"Feels good on my young ones too," Izzy chipped in, and they all chuckled.

"Hey, I meant to tell you earlier. I'm heading out for tea with Holly tonight. You two have the place to yourselves." Sadie smiled across the table at her sister and grandmother.

"Lovely," Izzy said, squeezing Elsie's hand. "Shall we get takeaway?"

"Sounds good to me." Elsie grinned. "Pizza. I haven't had pizza in ages."

"Perfect. Where are you guys going?" Izzy asked.

"Some Japanese place Holly knows."

"Cool."

"Actually, I should check my phone and see what time she wants to meet me. I want another shower before I head out. I feel really dirty."

"Oh, yeah, that's a great idea. I'm dirty *and* aching. A shower would be bliss." Izzy sighed.

Sadie retrieved her phone and read the message Holly had sent her.

Table booked for seven. If you've changed your mind it's okay, just let me know. Don't know how hard today has been for you xx

She texted back to confirm—now more than ever she wanted a break from the house, a different atmosphere. Some place not filled with memories and emotions. Sighing as those emotions threatened to break through the veneer she'd placed over them during the day, she headed for the shower.

Holly smoothed down her pants and flicked open one more button on her shirt. Then did it up again as her mind admonished her libido for thinking it was in any way appropriate to show that much cleavage. *The funeral was only yesterday, have some sensitivity.* The trouble was, since the funeral had happened, all Holly could think about was the future, and their future in particular. With everything that had taken place this week, she'd had no opportunity to sit down with Sadie and talk about moving to Sydney. *Tonight, I hope that chance will come.* If Sadie still needed to share her emotions about her mum's death, then Holly would be there to hear it. She couldn't push Sadie. But equally, she couldn't let Sadie go on thinking she wasn't committed to the idea of a future together. She grabbed her bag and left her room. Her mother appeared from the kitchen.

"You off?"

"Yeah. Out to dinner with Sadie. Going to that Japanese place near the post office."

"Nice. We haven't been there for a while. How is Sadie?"

Holly had seen her parents at the funeral, but only to say a quick hello.

"She's okay, actually. She and her sister took some big steps forward to reconciling yesterday, after the funeral. It's given her a lift."

"That's good to hear."

"I'll probably stay with her again tonight, okay?"

"Sure. Have a nice evening."

Holly smiled and tried to tamp down the sense of shock at her mother's calm words. That she hadn't freaked out about Holly staying out again was testament to the progress they'd made this week. *Long may it continue.*

Sadie was waiting for her outside the restaurant when Holly approached, and she couldn't help the beaming smile that spread across her face at the sight of her gorgeous lover.

"Hey, you," Holly said, nuzzling her nose against Sadie's neck, sliding her arms around her waist as she did so.

"Mm, hello to you too," Sadie murmured. Sadie's arms enfolded her, and they stayed like that for some moments.

"Hungry?" Holly asked eventually.

"Yeah, I am actually."

"Good, then let's go in."

They were seated quickly and sipped at glasses of water while they perused the menu.

"Wow, it all sounds so good." Sadie's eyes were wide, and Holly laughed.

"Yeah, I've been here a few times with my parents, and we've never had a bad meal. Choose whatever you like, it's all good."

Decisions made, they placed their order with the waiter and sat back gazing at each other.

"You look gorgeous tonight," Sadie said quietly.

"Thank you. So do you." Holly cocked her head. "You don't look as tired as I thought you might."

Sadie shook her head. "I slept amazingly well last night, considering. Exhaustion, probably."

"Probably. I wasn't aware of you waking at all, so I hoped it had been a good sleep. How was today?"

Sadie talked her through what they'd achieved at the house, until their meals arrived and all conversation ceased while they ate. They giggled as they ate morsels off each other's forks.

"So cheesy," Holly said, after she'd sampled a piece of Sadie's curry dish.

"I know, but I don't care," Sadie replied, winking.

"Sadie?" A man's voice came from behind Holly, and she turned swiftly to see who it was. Not recognising the man and woman standing right behind her, she turned back to look at Sadie. She seemed equally bemused.

"Yes? I'm sorry, do I know you?"

"Oh, sorry, you probably don't remember us. We used to live next door to you when you were a kid. We knew your parents quite well." He glanced at the woman beside him. "We just wanted to say how sorry we are about your mum. Such a dreadful shock."

Holly watched as the Sadie who had been joking and winking only moments before, and who had been cheerily smiling all through the evening, crumpled in front of her.

"Th-thank you," Sadie mumbled, and her eyes glistened. "I really appreciate that."

"Well, we just wanted to say it," the woman offered. "Sorry to interrupt your meal."

Sadie waved a hand in the air between them. "No worries."

"We'll leave you to it," the man said, and they gave Sadie sympathetic smiles before turning and leaving.

Holly looked back at Sadie. "Are you okay?"

Sadie sighed and put down her fork. "Seem to have lost my appetite." She held Holly's gaze. "I forgot," she said quietly. "For a few minutes there I'd forgotten what happened. It was just you and me, and this amazing food. How could I forget?" She sounded distraught.

Holly reached across the table and took her hand, squeezing it tightly.

"It's natural. My granddad died a few years ago, and I know what you mean. Almost like when I did something normal it seemed like nothing had changed."

Sadie nodded slowly. "Yeah, that sounds about right." She wiped at her eyes. "I know normal life has to carry on, but I don't want to forget her."

"You won't." Holly squeezed her hand again. "You know you won't. And at the same time, she wouldn't want you to stop your normal life, would she?"

"No," Sadie said. "You're right, she wouldn't." She paused, her fingers rubbing gently through Holly's where their hands were linked. "So, is now a good time to ask if you've got a flight booked yet to come and see me? Talking of normal life and all that."

There was an edge to Sadie's tone that unnerved Holly. It was almost accusatory, as if she expected the worst.

"Well, no, I haven't, but—"

Sadie pulled her hand back. "And how did I know *that* was going to be the answer?"

Before Holly could speak, Sadie roughly pushed her chair back and stood. Her eyes were blazing with anger.

"Sadie, wait, hear me—"

"No!" Sadie's voice was loud, and it turned the heads of a couple of other patrons in the restaurant. "You've made it pretty obvious you can't commit. Let's just stop pretending, shall we?" While she was talking, she pulled a fifty dollar note from her wallet and threw it on the table. In the next instant, she had grabbed her jacket and was marching off through the restaurant to the front door.

"Sadie! Wait!" Holly called after her, disbelief and anger vying for top spot in the front of her mind. What the hell just happened? Urgently beckoning the waiter over, she asked for the bill and made up the difference from her wallet to add to the fifty Sadie had thrown down. Struggling to get her coat on as she weaved around tables, she finally managed it and yanked open the door to the street. Quickly walking up the footpath, she swung her head left and right, desperately searching for a sign of Sadie, but she was nowhere to be seen.

Holly could feel her blood start to boil. Damn her! Why didn't she give Holly a chance to explain? Sadie and her fucking insecurities. She wanted to scream. She glanced around again. Well, there was only one place Sadie was likely to have gone, so Holly turned left and headed down Mair Street, searching for a cab. If Sadie thought she'd seen the last of Holly O'Brien, she was very, *very* wrong.

"You're back early," Izzy called as Sadie marched down the hallway and past the kitchen. She averted her gaze, not wanting to connect with either her gran or Izzy. The smell of the pizza they'd ordered turned Sadie's stomach.

She stomped into her room, closing the door forcefully behind her.

Damn Holly and her unwillingness to take this—them—seriously. Just what the hell was her problem? One minute she said all the right things, the next she was giving Sadie the brush-off. And this week, of all weeks. Jesus. It was bad enough having to deal with her grief over her mum, never mind finding out that the love of her life didn't feel the same way. What did Holly want? Just something casual, where they'd see each other every few weeks for some—she had to admit—incredible sex? Is that all they were?

She flopped down on the bed and kicked off her boots, taking childish satisfaction in the loud clunking sounds they made as they hit the floor.

No, the last thing she was prepared to do, with everything she felt, was have Holly treat them as casual. Sadie's love ran too deep for that. If Holly couldn't make a more serious commitment to them, then, as much as it hurt, Sadie would have to walk away. She shuddered at the thought. She had been so sure Holly felt it as deeply as she did. What was her problem?

Of course, running out of the restaurant hadn't exactly given Holly a chance to explain. She remembered Holly's shocked expression as she'd stood up from the table. Her attempts to talk to Sadie. She groaned and clenched handfuls of doona.

Oh, God, she'd done it again. Run off. Overreacted.

Her cheeks flushed with embarrassment. Why did she keep doing this? When was she going to learn that running away from difficult situations wasn't the answer?

She huffed out a breath. She needed to talk to her. Let her explain what was going on. See if they could work it out together. Because they had to. They were just too good together not to try.

Holly's cab dropped her at the end of the driveway, and she quickly paid the driver before climbing out. As the cab drove off, she stood for a minute or two, sucking in deep lungfuls of cold air. She needed to calm down just a little before she walked in there. Yes, she had to get her point across, and yes, being forceful would help that. But she didn't need to go in there ripping Sadie's head off.

Finally ready, she walked up the driveway and rang the bell.

Izzy answered, half a slice of pizza in one hand. Her mouth dropped open as she took in who was on the doorstep.

"Holly?"

"Is she home?" Holly's words were clipped, bordering on rude, she knew, but there was no time to waste.

Izzy nodded. "Came in about ten minutes ago looking like thunder. Stomped off to her room. Just like the old days." She started to smile but stopped when she saw the look Holly was giving her. She cocked her head. "Everything okay?"

"No," Holly said, "but it soon will be. I hope. Can I come in?"

"Shit, of course," Izzy said, quickly stepping to one side. "Sorry."

Holly looked down the hallway as she slipped off her coat. Elsie was in the kitchen doorway, concern etched all over her face.

"It's okay, Elsie. Just a big misunderstanding that I hope to put right in the next few minutes." She walked down to greet the older woman, giving her a quick hug. "Can I ask you something?"

"Of course, love."

"Were you serious when you offered me a place to stay in Sydney? If that's what Sadie wants too?"

"Wow," Izzy whispered behind her.

Elsie grinned, her eyes glinting. "Oh, yes. Most definitely."

"Good." Holly squared her shoulders. "Just wanted to check."

She turned and walked towards Sadie's room. The door was shut, but she didn't knock.

Sadie's eyes snapped open as her bedroom door was flung open. Standing in the muted light from the single lamp she'd switched on was Holly. A very angry-looking Holly.

"What the—?" Sadie began as she struggled to get herself upright.

Holly slammed the door closed, shaking the picture on the wall.

"You need to listen to me, Sadie. Don't interrupt me. Just listen."

Sadie glared at her. "How about you—"

Holly took only three strides to reach the edge of the bed, where she promptly pressed her hand over Sadie's mouth.

"Shut up, and listen."

Sadie's eyes widened as she stared at Holly. This version of Holly was a little scary and—oh God—more than a little hot. She nodded, and Holly slowly removed her hand.

"I love you, Sadie Williams." Holly's voice was strident, her eyes blazing. "I plan on loving you for as long as you'll have me. If you'd have given me even five minutes in the restaurant, I would have told you that the reason I haven't booked a flight to visit you is because I have made a much bigger decision about my future, and it needs some discussion between us." She took a deep breath, and sat down on the bed beside Sadie. "I want to move to Sydney. I want to make a life there. With you."

Sadie's heart was hammering under her ribs, and there was a rushing sound filling her ears. Her body flashed hot and cold all over. She grabbed at Holly's hand, needing something to anchor her, because she feared she was about to float up to the ceiling with pure, unadulterated joy.

"You can speak now," Holly whispered sheepishly.

Sadie cleared her throat; it was closed up, tears threatening to drown her again. "I don't... Are you serious?"

Holly nodded, her face changing to an expression that seemed part love and part fear. Did she doubt how Sadie felt about her?

"Completely." Holly's voice was firm, despite the worry in her eyes. "And we don't have to do this next bit yet, if it's too much, but Elsie suggested I could move in with you two. She figured you and I would do that eventually, so why waste money renting when I could be there with you from the start? But, you know, if that's too much to start with, or—"

Sadie cut her off with a kiss. She devoured Holly, pulling her close, feeling the softness of Holly melt into her arms.

Holly gasped into her mouth as they came up for air. "Oh...wow. God, was that a yes?"

Sadie laughed, throwing her head back at the delight that consumed her and threatened to combust her. "Oh, hell, that is *definitely* a yes. Are you crazy? Of course it's a yes! You and me. Together. Every day and every night. Holly, that's... God, it's all I want." She pulled Holly to her again and wiped gently at the tears that were gushing down Holly's cheeks. "I love you, Holly. So much.

And I can't wait to start our life together, whatever that involves. As long as we're together, that's all I want."

Holly kissed her softly. "Then that's what you'll get. Promise."

Sadie smiled but then flinched as Holly's expression turned sour again.

"But you have to promise me something too," Holly said.

"Wh-what?"

"Any time anything gets a little tricky with us, stop bloody running away! It's not the answer. And it drives me crazy every time you do it." Holly sighed. "I know where it comes from. I do. But you are a different person now, living a different life. And you have to be stronger about facing up to things. I hope I don't give you any reason to doubt us, or that we have too many arguments about stuff, but if that does happen please, *please* promise me you'll just talk it out with me?"

Sadie flushed and ducked her head. Holly had every right to demand this of her, she knew that. "I will. I do promise you that. I feel like a complete idiot for falling into my old habits again. If it's any consolation, I had just about figured that out before you came crashing through the door."

Now it was Holly's turn to blush. "Yeah, um, sorry about that."

Sadie chuckled.

"You just made me so mad, Sadie!"

Sadie laughed louder. "Yeah, I can have that effect on people. You'd better get used to it."

She grinned as Holly smirked and leaned in for a kiss.

"I plan to," Holly murmured as her lips nibbled at Sadie's mouth.

Sadie ran her fingers slowly and softly down Holly's face, stroking her cheeks, her jaw, her neck. She saw Holly's eyes darken, her pupils dilating, and she smiled even deeper.

"Stay the night?" she murmured.

"Just try and stop me," Holly whispered.

Sadie moaned, deep and low in her chest, and reached for the buttons on Holly's shirt. As she peeled the soft material away from Holly's shoulders and drank in the sight of her firm breasts cupped by black lace, she shuddered. Holly's breathing hitched, and her hands reached for Sadie's hips, gently tugging. Holly lay back, and Sadie moved on top of her, her lips never leaving

Holly's skin, her heart pounding out a crazy rhythm that should have scared her but didn't. She was swamped with emotion and didn't know whether to laugh or cry.

One look into Holly's eyes settled her; reflected back at her was the bliss she felt in that moment too. Of it just being them, together, excited about what life would bring them in the coming weeks, months, and years. She laughed, unable to contain it, and Holly seemed to understand and joined in her laughter, raining kisses on Sadie's face, which only made Sadie laugh more.

Sadie shivered as pleasure, both physical and emotional, swept through her body in a hot wave.

So this was what it felt like to be completely happy.

She could live with that.

About A.L. Brooks

A.L. Brooks currently resides in London, although over the years she has lived in places as far afield as Aberdeen and Australia. She works 9–5 in corporate financial systems and spends many a lunchtime in the gym attempting to achieve some semblance of those firm abs she likes to write about so much. And then promptly negates all that with a couple of glasses of red wine and half a slab of dark chocolate in the evenings. When not writing she likes doing a bit of Latin dancing, cooking, travelling both at home and abroad, reading lots of other writers' lesfic, and listening to mellow jazz.

CONNECT WITH A.L. BROOKS:

Website: www.albrookswriter.com
Facebook: www.facebook.com/albrookswriter
E-mail: albrookswriter@gmail.com

Other Books from Ylva Publishing

www.ylva-publishing.com

The Club

A.L. Brooks

ISBN: 978-3-95533-654-7
Length: 227 pages (72,200 words)

Welcome to The Club—leave your inhibitions and your everyday cares at the door, and indulge yourself in an evening of anonymous, no-strings, woman-on-woman action. For many visitors to The Club, this is exactly what they are looking for, and what they get. For others, however, the emotions run high, and one night of sex changes their lives in ways they couldn't have imagined.

Drawn Together

JD Glass

ISBN: 978-3-95533-789-6
Length: 244 pages (80,000 words)

Zoe Glenn Edwards, graphic novelist, is determinedly single and happily married to her work. Dion Richards, author, is trapped in a hostile sham marriage and only happy when she's working. Both creatives are well-known in their respective fields. When they inevitably collaborate on a new project, what happens when two "unavailables" discover they're unmistakably Drawn Together?

Flinging It

G Benson

ISBN: 978-3-95533-682-0
Length: 376 pages (113,000 words)

Midwife Frazer and social worker Cora have always grated on each other's nerves, but they have to work together to start up a programme for at-risk parents. Soon, the unexpected happens: they tumble into an affair. However, Cora is married to their boss, and both know it needs to end. But what they have might turn out to be much more than just a little distraction.

Fragile

Eve Francis

ISBN: 978-3-95533-482-6
Length: 300 pages (103,000 words)

College graduate Carly Rogers is forced to live back at home with her mother and sister until she finds a real job. Life isn't shaping up as expected, but meeting Ashley begins to change that. After many late night talks and the start of a book club, the two women begin a romance. When a past medical condition threatens Ashley, Carly wonders if their future together will always be this fragile.

Coming from Ylva Publishing

www.ylva-publishing.com

Hold My Hand

AC Oswald

When Bethany and Savannah split up, Bethany is heartbroken. But a year later they meet again and their feelings are as strong as ever. So why did Savannah leave her?

Bethany is devastated by the answer and realises she will lose Savannah again—to cancer.

In a world where time is fleeting but love lasts forever, Savannah and Bethany can only hold each other and live their dreams.

Under Parr

(Norfolk Coast Investigation Story—Book #2)

Andrea Bramhall

December 5th, 2013 left its mark on the North Norfolk Coast in more ways than one. A mysterious WWII bunker under Brancaster golf course holds a gruesome secret. A skeleton, deep inside the bunker.

Can DS Kate Brannon unravel who the victim is and how they died—almost 70 years later?

Dark Horse

ISBN: 978-3-95533-785-8

Also available as e-book.

Published by Ylva Publishing, legal entity of Ylva Verlag, e.Kfr.

Ylva Verlag, e.Kfr.
Owner: Astrid Ohletz
Am Kirschgarten 2
65830 Kriftel
Germany

www.ylva-publishing.com

First edition: 2017

Credits
Edited by Gill McKnight & CK King
Proofread by JoSelle Vanderhooft
Cover Design by Adam Lloyd
Cover Photo by © Alanpoulson | Dreamstime.com
Vector Design by Freepik.com